JORGE ZEPEDA PATTERSON

MILENA

—or—

The Most Beautiful
Femur in the World

Translated from the Spanish
by Adrian Nathan West

RESTLESS BOOKS
BROOKLYN, NEW YORK

First published as *Milena, o el fémur más bello del mundo*
by Editorial Planeta, Barcelona, 2014

First Restless Books paperback edition May 2017

ISBN: 9781632061256
Library of Congress Control Number: 2016940779

Cover design by Jason Booher
Set in Garibaldi by Tetragon, London

Printed in the United States of America

1 3 5 7 9 8 6 4 2

Restless Books, Inc.
232 3rd Street, Suite A111
Brooklyn, NY 11215

www.restlessbooks.com
publisher@restlessbooks.com

Esta publicación fue realizada con el estímulo del
Programa de Apoyo a la Traducción (PROTRAD)
dependiente de instituciones culturales mexicanas.

This publication was realized with the assistance of
the Programa de Apoyo a la Traducción (PROTRAD),
dependent on Mexican cultural institutions.

MILENA

—or—

*The Most Beautiful
Femur in the World*

To Clara, Sergio, and Camila

1

Milena

HE WASN'T THE FIRST MAN to die in Milena's arms, but he was the first to do so from natural causes. The ones she'd murdered had left no trace, no remorse in her soul. But the death of her lover plunged her into desolation.

Sex had always ended up imposing itself in Rosendo Franco's life. The day he died was no different. Under the lash of the Viagra flooding through them, his coronary arteries found themselves in a troubling dilemma: either pump the blood necessary to keep up his ferocious rhythm as he penetrated Milena or take care of his other organs. Faithful to Rosendo's past, they opted for the former.

An image rose up in the mind of the owner of the newspaper *El Mundo*. The contraction in his chest thrust his hips forward, letting him penetrate deeper. He said to himself that at last he was going to come, that he would reach that point that had been eluding him for the past ten minutes, as he feverishly mounted his lover's white hips. Rosendo had always believed his last thought would be about the newspaper that had been the object of his dreams and worries; in recent years, whenever he thought of death, he would feel a burst of frustration, imagining his great life's work left orphaned. And yet now, his brief death throes were devoted to squeezing out a drop of semen to say goodbye to his last love.

It took Milena a few seconds to realize the sounds the man was emitting weren't moans of pleasure. Her lover clutched her by the waist as his death rattles heaved against her reddened back like waning waves on a stretch of shoreline. The old man pressed his forehead into the nape of the woman's neck. From the corner of her eye, Milena saw her hair shifting softly, propelled by the dying man's lethargic breath, then the curl was still and silence reigned in the room.

She stayed a long time without moving, save for the copious tears that slid down her face and died on the carpet below. She cried for him, but above all for herself. She told herself she'd rather die than go back to the hell Rosendo had rescued her from. Even worse, she knew that this time the vengeance would be ruthless. She saw herself three years back, stripped naked in front of those two enormous dogs eager to tear her to pieces.

She didn't understand why they'd started threatening her again these past few weeks after leaving her in peace for months. Now, without the old man's protection, she'd end up a sack of flesh and bones rotting in some ravine, and it wouldn't matter that men had once paid twelve hundred bucks for the pleasure of dipping their wick inside her. She imagined her body being discovered later, and the surprise of the coroners as they examined the graceful femurs of her long legs. The image pulled her from her trance and made her move at last. She sat up halfway to look at the corpse's face, clean a trail of saliva from his chin, and cover him with a sheet. She glanced at the blister pack of Viagra on the nightstand and decided to hide it in a last act of loyalty toward the proud old lion.

She walked to the bathroom, driven by her heightened senses, with a survivor's febrile clarity. Her mind was on the contents of the suitcase she would have to pack before she caught a plane, though the only thing that mattered was the black book hidden in the bedroom closet. Not only was it her final vengeance against those who had exploited her, but the secrets it contained also guaranteed her survival.

She never made it to the airport, her name wasn't Milena, nor was she Russian, as everyone believed. And she didn't notice the drop of semen that fell on the floor tile.

2

The Blues

IF HE'D BEEN ABLE to sit up in his coffin, Rosendo Franco would have been more than impressed with his drawing power. The funeral home had transferred the less illustrious dead to other branches in order to dedicate every available room to hosting the two thousand attendees at the viewing for the owner of *El Mundo*. Even Alonso Prida, the country's president, had stayed there twenty minutes, with the better part of his cabinet in tow. Prida no longer had the majestic, imperial demeanor that had characterized him during his first year in office; too many unexpected scrape-ups, too few expectations fulfilled in what was supposed to have been a spectacular return for the PRI. Still, the presence of the Mexican leader charged the atmosphere with tension, and after his departure, the majority of those present relaxed and started to drink.

Two hours before, at five in the afternoon, Cristóbal Murillo, Franco's private secretary, decided coffee was an undignified beverage for the honored visitors who had come to take their leave of his employer, and ordered the funeral home to serve glasses of the finest red and white wine. In the main hall, set aside for the VIPs he had chosen, he had champagne and hors d'oeuvres passed around.

"Death has its zip codes, too," Amelia said to herself when she saw how the funeral home had been parceled out into little reservations, their inhabitants distinguishable not only by the cut of their apparel, but also by their ethnic traits. She wasn't close to Rosendo Franco's family, she had barely even known him, but her position as leader of the main party on the left made her attendance at the funeral obligatory. Once more, Amelia rued the presence of the three escorts who had accompanied her for the past two years and were now bursting like battering rams through the densely packed crowd to make way for her. Her wavy head of hair, her eyes framed by her enormous lashes, and her olive skin were the unmistakable traits of a figure as known as she was respected in the country's public life, thanks to her long years of activism in the defense of women and children abused by men in power. A Mother Teresa of Calcutta with the daunting beauty of a young María Félix, as a journalist had once described her.

As she crossed through the succession of rooms, she noticed it was only in the second one, the one with the most humble guests, that cries of mourning could be heard. There were the printing-press workers and secretaries, bemoaning the death of the proprietor, whom they'd revered for so many years.

When she reached the main hall, Amelia noticed two camps. Some thirty family members and a few close friends of the deceased surrounded the coffin like a commando unit, ready to guard that final bastion from the thick hordes of politicians elbowing their way into the room. Occasionally, a governor or minister would pull away from the rest of the functionaries and creep over slyly to offer a brief word of condolence to the widow and her daughter before going back to his colleagues to say goodbye and heading toward the exit.

A few seconds passed before Amelia could make out Tomás, a columnist for *El Mundo*, leaning under a broad window on one side of the room. The mere sight of the disheveled figure, the tousled hair

13

and the glassy eyes of her old friend, calmed her down, as it had so many times before. There was something in Tomás's presence that soothed her warlike spirit.

"You managed to make it through the seven chambers of purgatory," he said, greeting her with a fleeting kiss on the lips.

"Judging by those in attendance, I'd say this is more like hell," she responded, looking over the guests packed into the room.

For a moment, the two of them stared at the bands of politicians, and little by little their eyes converged on Cristóbal Murillo, the lone ambassador arbitrating between the two groups in the room. He came and went, now addressing a newly arrived secretary, now consulting with the businessman's widow. He passed from one side to the other, confident of his usefulness to all present. He was servile when necessary and imperious when he could be. Tomás had never seen him so cocksure and expansive. Murillo even seemed to have added an inch or two to his short stature in the past few hours. After three decades of parroting his boss, he was acting like the heir to the throne. And he definitely looked the part: with the help of a number of plastic surgeries, he'd achieved a passable likeness to the newspaper owner's visage. Not for nothing had people started calling him Déjà Vu behind his back.

"So, since you're on the inside, what do you know? What's going to happen to the newspaper without Franco?" Amelia asked Tomás. "Don't tell me that clown will be taking over management!"

He shrugged and arched his brows, and instinctively the two of them looked at Claudia, Franco's only daughter, who stood with her mother at the foot of the coffin, one arm draped over her shoulder. From afar, the heiress gave no sign of grief beyond the pallor of her countenance, set off by her elegant black dress. It occurred to Tomás that her head of indomitable red hair was ill-suited to any funerary apparel. Though her shoulder was touching Doña Edith's, her wan gaze, lost in the mosaics on the floor, showed that her mind was far away. He imagined his ex-lover was absorbed in some family scene from her childhood.

A waiter with canapés of salami and ham blocked their view of the Franco family, and Jaime's figure rose up behind him.

"I hope they didn't keep that in the same fridge as the bodies," he declared.

Neither gave any sign of what they felt on finding themselves there with their childhood friend, but they still hadn't forgiven Jaime for his behavior during the Pamela Dosantos case. The famous actress's murder had shaken the country the year before; Tomás had been involved as a journalist and Jaime as a security specialist. Inseparable during their childhood and adolescence, the three friends formed part of a quartet known as the Blues, named after the color of the paintings Jaime's father brought back from France, and they had been insepa-rable during their childhood and adolescence. The crisis provoked by the killing of Dosantos, lover of the secretary of the interior, had ended with mixed results: threats against Tomás had been averted, he and Amelia had struck up a relationship three decades after breaking off their adolescent forays, and Jaime became a key factor in the case's resolution, but with methods his colleagues had found reprehensible.

Despite his casual tone, Jaime had to force himself to address Tomás and Amelia. During their teenage and university years, the two young men had vied for their friend's affections, both with scant success, given her attraction to more mature men. But now, at forty-three years of age, Jaime found his deep-rooted obsession with his first love stirred up by the new relationship between the journalist and the politician. He asked himself, as he had before, whether his aversion to marriage and stable relationships was related to the foiling of his desperate passion for Amelia in his youth. Seeing her now next to his old friend was no consolation. For the umpteenth time he made a mental comparison of himself and Tomás: he listed their physical attributes and professional achievements, and again, he found it inexplicable that Amelia would choose his friend. On one side, there was Jaime Lemus, ex-director of the intelligence services and owner of the county's foremost security firm. Powerful, self-assured. Tanned, lean, and muscular body, sculpted features, hard, but harmonious. In sum, an attractive and desirable figure. His elegant demeanor and his five-foot, ten-inch frame contrasted with that of Tomás, a good four inches shorter, not fat exactly, but soft and harmless, with graying hair, a ready smile, and a warm gaze. In short, the face of a man who radiated benevolence.

"What time did you get here?" Tomás asked in a neutral tone. He didn't want to be gruff, but he had no desire to greet Jaime with open arms.

Amelia, on the other hand, stiffened immediately and ignored his extended hand. Jaime clenched his jaw and tried to regain his composure.

"A little while ago. It wasn't so bad hearing stories about Rosendo Franco. He was a real personality."

"Like what?" Tomás asked.

"One of his friends refused to sell him some land on the edge of the city, where Franco wanted to build the new printing press," Jaime told them. "No matter how much he insisted, the guy held out, waiting on a better price. One day, Franco found out his friend was a fanatical reader of the horoscope in *El Mundo*; the first thing he did every morning was read it to know what lay in store for him. So Franco called the guy in charge of the section and told him what to print for Sagittarius the rest of the week. Then he invited his friend to lunch that Friday, the day when the stars would offer all those blessed by the sun in Sagittarius a unique real-estate opportunity. That day Don Rosendo got the land."

Tomás and Jaime laughed, but muted themselves, remembering where they were. Despite herself, Amelia smiled slightly; the force of habit from so many years together began to overcome the resentment she felt toward her old friend.

"I think I know a better one," Tomás said. "Two or three years ago, the main movie-theater chain decided to stop announcing their lineup in the paper, saying people were using the internet and their phones to find out the film schedules. The expense of the newspaper seemed superfluous to them. Franco didn't bat an eye, though he stood to lose a good deal of money. He just ordered the entertainment pages to print a page with the film schedules, but with the hours wrong: instead of at seven p.m., it would say the film started at eight. The box office turned into a complaint center: at every screening, there would be five or six people furious that they'd shown up an hour late. The next week, the theaters started publishing their ads again."

As they laughed, Amelia looked at Jaime and Tomás and couldn't help but be filled with nostalgia: she saw herself thirty years before, surrounded by her friends in a corner of the playground at school, where the Blues were a closed-off group, rejected but also envied by the rest of their classmates. She remembered Jaime and his blustering defense of his karate lessons, which absorbed him in his teenage years, and the feigned disdain from Tomás, who looked down on any athletic pastime, obsessed with his books but also anxious over his own lagging muscular development.

Fortunately for Amelia, who preferred to avoid Jaime, the arrival of the omnipresent Murillo kept her from having to interact further with him, even if he was right beside her.

"Some setup here, right? Impressive, no?" Franco's private secretary said, his eyes roving the room. "And tomorrow, the first section is ninety-six pages with all the letters of condolence we're running," he added with enthusiasm, while tugging at his shirtsleeves to show off his diamond cufflinks.

His audience met his comment with impassive expressions.

"The boss would have been proud," he murmured in a low voice, full of false humility.

"I'm sure the boss would have rather been in the offices of his newspaper today than in a casket," Amelia replied.

A fleeting look of rage crossed the little man's face before a servile expression replaced it. Jaime watched him with his head tipped slightly to one side, like an anthropologist observing an extravagant ritual. Murillo looked at Amelia askance, with a prideful, defiant expression.

"Well, there's no doubt about it," he said. "He died like a king, right on top of a beautiful and very young little lady. That was my boss!"

Tomás observed the man's sexagenarian wife weeping at the side of the coffin.

"Very young?" he asked. "Who?"

"A Russian, top of the line, a lover of his. He was almost half a century older than her, but he kept her happy. You know what Tigre Azcárraga used to say: 'Power takes off ten years, money another ten, and charm ten more.' And so he swore he was only ten years older than Adriana Abascal." The private secretary cackled, and no one else joined.

"You knew her? How do you know he died in her arms?" Jaime pried.

"Well, that's the hypothesis the police are working from, after examining the body. And I met the blonde the first time I went to look at the apartment. I was the one who rented it, on Don Rosendo's instructions. A hell of a woman!" Murillo said with a lascivious mien.

"What was her name?" Jaime asked.

"I don't know, I can't remember."

"And you're sure she was Russian?" Tomás asked.

Again, the two friends seemed to be competing.

"Don Tomás, Señorita Claudia has been asking if you might come over a moment so she can discuss something with you," Murillo added, seeming like he wanted to get away as quickly as he could.

The journalist was unable to hide his satisfaction, and his eyes turned back to the redheaded woman still standing beside the casket.

"Let's go over together and give our condolences to the family. I still have more to do today," Amelia said.

Tomás nodded, though he felt an uncomfortable tingling on the back of his neck. Amelia knew nothing of the affair he'd had with Claudia five years back, although her intuition bordered on witchcraft, or at least that's how it seemed to him.

As they walked toward the coffin, the bodyguards set in motion, barely two yards from Amelia, but she motioned for them to stay where they were. It seemed like bad taste, offering your sympathies flanked by those guard dogs. The three Blues filed past the deceased newspaper baron's wife, daughter, and other close relatives. Tomás noticed the deep circles under Claudia's eyes. With her father's passing, enormous responsibility had fallen onto her shoulders all at once. Her mother never meddled in her husband's business dealings and had no entrepreneurial acumen. Rosendo Franco's sole living brother was a drunk, and Claudia's two uncles on her mother's side were deadbeats. The only member of the Franco family she could trust was her cousin Andrés, the renowned Mexican tennis player, but he hadn't been in the country for years. The journalist asked himself what role Claudia's husband might play in all this, but the distance he'd kept during the funeral suggested some sort of tension in their marriage. The idea pleased him vaguely.

Tomás drew out his greeting to the widow and cut short his condolences to the daughter, aware as he was of Amelia's presence. In any case, Amelia was distracted. She had no knack for commiseration: there was nothing she could say that didn't come out as a cliché. She imagined the interchange of phrases repeated dozens of times in the course of the viewing must be as unpleasant for the widow as it was for her. There was something artificial in these viewings that made Amelia uncomfortable: she thought the living should be able to bury their dead in privacy and mourn in the familiar spaces they had shared with the deceased. Social conventions obliged the grieving to put their suffering on display in front of strangers who mimicked a pain they weren't feeling. She asked herself how many of the sobs she heard around her were the result of the recent death and how many the product of the self-pity that tended to spring up at these events. The body in the coffin was a mere catalyst for tears that had nothing to do with it.

Amelia said goodbye to the remaining guests, kissing her fingers and then opening them in a kind of blessing of the masses. She still had to face a long and delicate conversation with Andrés Manuel López Obrador, the historical leader of the left, who'd split off from the PRD months ago; she wanted to explore the possibility of some kind of coalition with him against the present government. It wouldn't be easy: "Every organization composed of three Trotskyites has four factions," she recalled despairingly. Still, she had to try.

Jaime looked around the room trying to find Cristóbal Murillo. The Russian had awakened his curiosity and he sensed that, if Amelia were no longer there to intimidate him, Franco's talkative assistant would happily open up. Any kind of enigma was an irresistible challenge to Jaime, especially in cases with a member of the elite involved.

Tomás stayed beside Claudia, waiting for a group of politicians to wrap up their expressions of continued devotion to the family. Even when they didn't know her, the women would hug the widow and console her with an affection and feeling borne, he supposed, of female solidarity. A tribal atavism: women comforting women, widows taking care of widows. The men's approach, on the other hand, showed a protective sentiment more projected than real: "Anything you need, Doña Edith"; "Don't you worry, Don Rosendo had many friends"; "We'll be here for anything the family needs"; "Just say the word"—phrases that evaporated in the air faster than the aroma of the men's costly colognes. As soon as they'd turned their backs, these supposed protectors would search the room for somebody to latch onto and talk about their business dealings and things they needed done.

At last, a breach in the parade of mourners allowed Claudia to pull Tomás into a small office not far from the coffin.

"You don't know how sorry I am . . . " he began to say when a finger placed over his lips stopped him.

Claudia laid her head on Tomás's chest with her arms hanging at her sides. He embraced her carefully, assailed by sensations: tenderness in the face of female vulnerability, commiseration with her grief, discomfort at her husband's proximity. But more than anything, an immediate, unexpected erotic impulse that soon erased any other consideration.

She pulled away before she could notice his agitated breathing.

"I want to ask you two favors," she said. Her tone was intimate, closer to the kind shared by a couple who have spent their entire life together than by two lovers bound by four days of shared passion five years past. "Alfonso Palomar, the current managing editor—I don't trust him to run the paper, not to mention that weirdo Murillo. But I won't be in any shape to go to *El Mundo* for the next few days. And it's not like I know that much about the business anyway. I'm not sure what I'm going to do, but what I do know is there's no way I'll let those conmen take charge. What if you do it?"

The request took him by surprise, and he only responded after a long pause.

"You're right, Claudia, letting either of those two be in charge would be like handing the Catholic Church over to Luther. The problem is, I'm not the answer. I'm a columnist, not an editor. It's been fifteen years since I've been in the field, and I've never led a section or a supplement, let alone a whole paper. If you want, I'll help you find the right person for the job."

"My father had an office in the editing room that he never used," she said, ignoring Tomás's objection. "I'll send a letter to management telling them that you'll be representing the publisher's interests in the upcoming days. Palomar will leave the newspaper tomorrow. You'll have to authorize the cover and the first section before they go to the typesetters. Any check over fifty thousand pesos will require your approval. We'll celebrate your nomination as general director on Monday."

Tomás examined her and tried to detect some sign of mental unbalance in her gaze but didn't find one. Her words sounded certain, as if she'd thought the matter over for hours.

"I never wanted to be my father's successor, and that's why I never trained for it. I loved him so much, I was always trying to find something to grab hold of to avoid thinking about his death. It's ridiculous, as if I was betting on his immortality. After I met you on that trip to New York, I realized that if the time came, you were the only one I could trust, and knowing that has been a relief. You might not have experience, but I have faith in your honesty and intentions. It's true we were only together a few days, Tomás, but haven't you ever met someone, and even after you lose them, you feel like you're still together?"

Tomás couldn't speak, but his eyes were moist. So much time missing her, years assuming their affair had been a fleeting diversion in the life of a rich girl. Four days when she had slipped into his bedroom, behind the backs of the rest of the troupe accompanying her father on his tour through the hallowed temples of American journalism.

"And the second favor?" he asked.

Her eyes settled on Tomás, scrutinizing him, like a poker player wavering before betting all her chips.

"This morning, Cristóbal Murillo gave me a sealed envelope. Apparently, my father asked him to do so in the case of his unforeseen death. What was in the envelope led me to a safe in a bank vault where there was a package with money and two letters. One talked about someone named Milena, asking me to protect and help her. The other one looked like a note dashed off under pressure to alert me to a grave danger."

"Milena?" Tomás asked, rooting around in his mind for that name.

"Despite what has been said publicly, my father died in his lover's arms in an apartment he went to several nights a week. The initial police reports leave little room for doubt as to the circumstances of his death. He was deeply in love with a girl, judging by the emails I found on his office computer," she said, and then added, "After seeing the strange messages he left me in the lockbox, I looked through his mail; the old man wasn't too crafty with his passwords."

"And who is Milena?"

"I never believed my father could feel so passionately. He always showed complete control of his feelings. He was a consummate manipulator, as we all know," she said to herself with an intensity Tomás perceived as something akin to tenderness.

"What do the letters say? Who is Milena?"

"It's confusing, but I know she was up against death threats and my father was protecting her. In the messages they exchanged, he tried over and over to calm her down. In the first letter, he asks me to make an effort to try and understand and sympathize with her, and to watch out for her future. But the second one is very strange."

Claudia took out the letter, covered in a few bare scribbles, and read.

"*Protect Milena. But take the black book away from her and destroy it. It could ruin the family.*"

"And where is the girl? Do you know anything about her?"

"Nothing, she vanished."

They remained standing in silence beside the desk in the makeshift office in the funeral home. For lack of something better, he hugged her. He was starting to understand the position her father's request had left her in. Taking charge of the newspaper was a formidable task, though she knew it was something that would have to be done sooner or later. But the responsibility of safeguarding her family's integrity against this mysterious, elusive threat was an unforeseen challenge perhaps beyond her powers.

"Did your father ever refer to the black book? Does he mention it in any of his emails?"

"Never. Just in that letter. I don't even know where to begin."

"Maybe you need to comb through that apartment she disappeared from. I doubt she left anything of value behind, especially not the black book your father was worried about, but at the least we can get the most obvious starting point out of the way. Let me do it, I'll handle that," Tomás said, not knowing how or when he could carry this promise through.

"Please, do it fast. I don't know what this danger could be."

Tomás pondered in silence and asked himself if Rosendo Franco was afraid the Russian would blackmail him somehow, if she had some compromising video or details about some dirty dealings. There had to be more than a few the old man had been wrapped up in.

"So how do you feel about that, about protecting . . . her?" Protecting *your father's lover*, Tomás thought.

"Does it seem sick to you? I thought so myself. In a certain way, it's an act of disloyalty toward my mother. But this is what he wanted. You have to see the intensity in their exchanges. Like it was their last days on earth and they were pouring what was left of their lives into them."

In fact, that was the case, Tomás thought, at least for Rosendo Franco. And from what Claudia was telling him, the same could be true for Milena, if the threats she had received were real.

"If you look at it that way, this may be the best homage you could give your father."

"Besides, there's the other warning. It seems urgent, hasty. There's no doubt we should find her and get hold of the notebook."

The journalist nodded.

"Yeah, but why me?"

"First, because I don't know what kind of dangers this girl is up against, and it would be better not to attract attention. We can't run the risk of the black book falling into the hands of the police or anyone else, not without knowing what it contains. Second, very few people, not even Milena herself, will understand the nature of my intentions. And, above all, my father told me about what you and your friends did in the Pamela Dosantos case—the files you uncovered and the help you got from some insanely talented young hacker. You're the only person I can trust for an investigation like this. Or am I wrong?"

Despite her categorical tone, Claudia's words sounded to Tomás like a determined little girl rattling off all the reasons Santa Claus has for preferring to enter through the chimney. Nonetheless, her proposal was seductive, irresistible.

As he felt himself giving in, Tomás asked himself how much of her talent for manipulation Claudia had inherited from Rosendo Franco. The suspicion grew when she took a ring of keys from her pocket with a tag from an apartment in the Anzures development: Rosendo Franco's love nest, presumably. But the kiss planted on the corner of his lips made him temporarily forget the commitments he'd taken on.

When he left the funeral home, Tomás failed to notice that Amelia's SUV and her bodyguards' vehicle were still parked in the lot.

Amelia had received a call from the office of Andrés Manuel López Obrador rescheduling their meeting. Her first impulse was to go to the office, but then she decided to call her secretary, Alicia, to pass on instructions about her most pressing obligations.

Jaime rapped his knuckles against her window.

"It's lucky I found you still here. Do you have a few minutes?"

He tried to open the door, and the guards ran to Amelia's aid, but she waved them off. Jaime asked the driver to leave them alone, and, despite herself, Amelia agreed.

"Get in," she said drily. "But I have to be at a meeting soon."

Years had passed since she'd been alone with Jaime, and it wasn't a feeling she enjoyed. But she couldn't shut the door in the face of someone she'd considered a brother for so long.

Now that he was finally face to face with her, Jaime didn't know where to begin. Amelia's previous demeanor had wounded him, and when he saw she was still around, he decided to confront her, despite his usual habit of carefully planning anything of special significance.

"I know you don't care for my methods, Amelia, but believe me, there are times when nothing else works in this rotten world we live in. In the end, we're on the same side."

"And what's that have to do with anything? Has death got you turning reflective?" she asked, pointing to the funeral home. She regretted the harshness of her words, but she felt Jaime had betrayed her with his conduct those past few months. The manipulative man he'd become, so full of secrets, was light years away from the boy she'd grown up with.

"What's that have to do with anything? You practically ignored me inside. I don't deserve that kind of scorn. If only you knew what you've always meant to me."

She sat there quiet, surprised by the unusual emotional intensity of Jaime's tone.

"Beside my bed, I have a matching set of designer earrings and a bracelet from Egypt that you would have liked," he said. "Twenty years ago, I was going to give them to you, at that party we threw at my house to celebrate me getting back from my master's program in Washington, remember?"

Amelia agreed faintly, her mind drifting back to women in frilly dresses and men in tuxedo jackets, tents set up in a garden and a half-dozen officious waiters.

"I was in love with you, Amelia. And I'm sure we would have ended up together if he hadn't gotten in the middle of things. That afternoon, I was going to give you the jewelry. For hours I waited for the right moment, and when I saw you disappear, I thought I could finally catch you alone. That image of how I found you in my father's library has haunted me ever since. It took me a long time to forgive you, but here I am. Him, on the other hand, I never saw him again, I never said a word to him. He knew I loved you, but he didn't care, he didn't care about destroying his son if he could have his little fling."

Amelia listened in silence. He must have repeated the story a thousand times in his tormented mind, she thought. She had been aware of Jaime's feelings, but she never imagined the depths of his passion.

"I'm sorry, Jaime, but you took everything wrong," she said after a few seconds. "Your father and I had a real, intense relationship. I won't go into details, but it was important for both of us and lasted a long time."

"I've never let go of that jewelry," he answered, as if he hadn't heard her. "I used to look at it every couple of nights to recall my father's betrayal. Now, I do it as a way to resurrect my hopes. I needed you to know that."

He got out of the car before she could say anything, and she watched him disappear around a corner of the funeral home.

3

Milena

HER NAME WAS ALKA and she was Croatian, though after three days locked up in a dark closet without a bite to eat, she began to feel like a nameless animal with no country of origin. The nakedness, hardly helped by the old blanket thrown in the back of the space where they'd confined her, made the feelings of loss and anonymity grow. The first day, she pounded the wood for hours, more indignant and angry than afraid, waiting for a shadow to cross the light under the door and set her free. The second day, she was filled with self-pity and sorrow and collapsed, depressed, on the floor of the hovel. But on the third, every other consideration vanished before the desperate urge to drink and eat. The fear of being raped was nothing now compared to the need to bring some nourishment to her lips. On the fourth day, she started gnawing on a wooden hanger, the only thing she could find in that dark-black hole. That day, they took her out.

Alka spent the first sixteen years of her life in Jastrebarsko, an ancient town half an hour from Zagreb, with six thousand people rotting alive in houses and another thirty thousand in its ramshackle cemetery. She lived just three blocks from the graveyard and every path led her past the decrepit tombs, many of them in various states of collapse. During her childhood, her playmates had used femurs and tibias as makeshift swords: first to play D'Artagnan, then Darth Vader. When she reached adolescence, and her long, sculpted legs became the object of sudden admiration in the village, Alka promised herself that her femur wouldn't end up as an ersatz foil in the hands of some wannabe fencer.

The day she escaped was the happiest in her life. It wasn't the first time she'd ridden a train, but it was the first time she'd done so with no thought of turning back. She was leaving behind a future boxing produce in a plant, in an insipid marriage with one of the few young men who hadn't left for Zagreb or another European country.

Alka spent the train ride to the capital with her friend Sonjia absorbed in the landscape slipping past, devoured by the frame of the car's window. But her soul was not weighted down by remorse or nostalgia. In the window, she was contemplating the reflection of her big blue eyes and the contours of a face that had still not lost its adolescent plumpness. Her only thought was that leaving behind her old life had been much simpler than she'd thought.

Fifteen days before, Sonjia had told her she was going to Berlin; a Zagreb businessman was going to open a new branch of his successful Balkan restaurant there, and he needed waitresses who would give it a touch of authenticity. Alka felt it was destiny calling. She could stumble along in German thanks to her grandfather, the village watchmaker and an unconditional Germanophile. (Alka's mother suspected her father-in-law's parents had been collaborators during the Nazi occupation, though it was never discussed.) For a few days, Alka pressed her friend to invite her to Germany without making any progress. Sonjia's boyfriend, a Hungarian living in Zagreb, wasn't convinced they needed another waitress, despite the fluent German she professed to speak. Only when she sent a full-body photo with the dress she wore out to the dance clubs did he decide to take her on, saying that with that face, she could even become hostess, which paid much better than serving tables.

The adventure ended almost as soon as it had begun. In the station in Zagreb, they met Sonjia's boyfriend, Forkó, prematurely bald, stubby, with kindly features. Alka found his flattery a little excessive, and the way he eyed her up and down gave her the creeps. Still, the electrifying euphoria kept her from dwelling on anything that might cloud her recently acquired freedom. After a late breakfast, they hit the road in his car, a blue Peugeot with comfortable seats and the aroma of newness, something the girls took as a foretaste of the bonanza awaiting them.

They were supposed to cover the four-hundred-mile drive between there and Prague in a single day, then sleep at a friend's place before heading on to Berlin. In fact, they drove only forty. Hardly had they passed Durmanec, still far from the border, when Forkó told them he had to get something from an acquaintance's house. They pulled off the highway and passed over a through road before exiting onto a country lane that led to an old house, run-down and solitary. When he got out of the car, he invited the girls to come in and stretch their legs, have a glass of water, and use the bathroom if they cared to.

Three men received them with hugs and congratulations and spoke to Forkó in a language that sounded like Greek. The oldest one, a corpulent character of around fifty, took an envelope of cash from the back pocket of his pants and passed it to the Hungarian; Forkó counted the bills, thanked him, and walked out the door he'd come in through without giving the girls a second glance. Sonjia called to him and tried to follow his steps, but a punch to the ear knocked her to the floor. The three men laughed and looked down at her.

Alka was paralyzed. In that instant, she knew she would never make it to Berlin and wouldn't be a waitress in a Croatian restaurant.

In spite of herself, she looked over the three men's faces, aiming for some kind of visual contact that might provoke their solidarity or pity. The capacity of her big, expressive eyes to incite empathy had been her greatest defense throughout her life. But the attempt was fruitless: three crocodiles would have inspired more hope than the indifferent and obtuse faces looking back at her.

She was much prettier than Sonjia and the three examined her with curiosity; there was more greed than lust in their eyes. The oldest approached her and squeezed one of her breasts; with the other hand, he cupped her buttocks. There was no prurience in his actions, just scrutiny, like a baker feeling the dough before he throws it in the oven. Without thinking, Alka slapped him, more from fear than anger. He smiled and hit her in the stomach. She fell forward, gripped by pain; she felt her lungs give out and thought she was fainting. She balled up on the floor, trying to catch her breath, while the jabs of pain radiated through her body. She felt hands pulling at the zipper on her back and others tearing at her panties. Indifferent to the desperate efforts she was making to suck air into her lungs, one of them yanked her into a sitting position by her hair and then tugged her dress off in one go. They had stripped her bare in a matter of seconds. She fell to the floor again while the three men walked around her trying to evaluate her body from all angles. She heard laughter and what she thought was hands slapping against one another.

She assumed they would want to rape her now and told herself she'd bite and scratch, even if it cost her life. One of them grabbed her hair again, stood her up, and pushed her toward a door in the back of the room; another opened what looked like a small closet, and when she looked back at them, the one holding her by the hair shoved her so hard she smacked against the back wall. Then the door closed and she sank into the darkness. Two days later, they threw a plastic water bottle inside; by the fourth day, when they let her out, she'd nearly eaten the entire wooden hanger.

They pulled her out roughly, showering her with insults, and led her back into the main room. The leader was no longer there, but his two henchmen were. One of them tried to tear off her damp towel, and she resisted, knowing it was the last bit of dignity available to her: a little rag was all that stood between her and the animal kingdom. Her resistance made the man furious, and he tore it away and struck her hard on the left temple. It wasn't as tough a blow as she'd received days before, but in her weakened state, it took its toll: she fell on her knees to the floor, and stayed there prostrate for a long time, like a Muslim at the hour of prayer.

When she finally looked up, one of the men came over with a plate with a half-eaten hamburger. He let her take a bite before offering her a sip of water. Then they undid their flies and motioned what they expected of her. Only afterward did they gave her the rest of the hamburger.

She never saw Sonjia again. She didn't dare ask about her and, not knowing her captors' language, couldn't have. They took her to the outskirts of Teplice, on Czech territory, a few miles from the German frontier, to what seemed like a cheap hotel on the road linking Prague and Dresden. She spent thirty-six hours shut up and sedated, watched constantly over by one of the Greeks, in a windowless room where men passed through to look at her. Finally, a Spaniard bought her for thirty thousand euros.

Alka spent her seventeenth birthday in a car with two other girls heading toward Marbella. Though she spent the entire trip under the influence of the powerful sedatives they'd forced on her, she managed to learn her first word in Spanish: *vacas*, cows. That was the word the two men driving the car used to describe the three women, whom they had wrongly assumed were *eslovacas*, Slovakians. Nevertheless, the nickname stuck. Darva was Milk Cow, for her enormous breasts; Kristina was Spotted Cow, because of the freckles all over her body; and Alka was the Lean Cow, for her long legs and elegant torso. The owner of the brothel they arrived at gave her the working name "Milena." She accepted it with resignation, and never said her real name again in the years that followed. In the end, she thought that Alka had died and was buried in a cemetery in Jastrebarsko.

Me, I don't like to go with hookers. It's a hell of a lot of money week after week, and after seeing some of them I wonder if I've caught some kind of infection. The thing is just that the ones who don't charge are even worse. I'm tired of spending money like a jerkoff. You invite chicks for dinner in a restaurant or you pay outrageous bar tabs and then they don't want to fuck you on the first date. Some don't even offer it to you the second time, which means your money's gone down a black hole. Then there are the ones who let you cop a feel on the second or third date but won't even think of stripping down. By that time you've spent a fortune and you've got a major case of blue balls. The worst are the ones who make you pony up for a weekend at the beach in Cuernavaca before they'll fork over the whole enchilada, as the gringos say. And then, to top it off, they're a dead lay, that's the word my friend the Galician uses. By this time you look at your bank balance and you realize you could have been balls-deep for weeks in a centerfold-quality piece of ass, fucking like a king with all you've invested.

And as far as diseases go, the professionals get themselves checked out, and they're cleaner than a lot of these born-again virgins that you have to carry off to the sack with kid gloves before you find out they're crawling with more germs than a handrail in a subway car.

And as far as oral goes, they drive a hard bargain—I mean that literally. With civilians you need to fuck a good three or four times before they understand that you're not putting your hand on the back of their head to smooth out a cowlick. But what can you do about it? They're all afraid you'll think they're sluts if they do a solo on the skin flute. Like you're a douchebag and you can't tell how much flight time they've logged as soon as they grab onto the stick.

Anal? Forget about it. That's almost like exchanging rings. A band with a rock on it for the privilege of slipping it up in their sphincter. For fuck's sake, who made women so complicated?

With a hooker, on the other hand, it's different. There's no stress and no doubt, no dinners out and no unnecessary expenses. You arrange the price and the service and that's that. Guaranteed happiness.

I don't like hookers, but I guess I like the other ones even less.

F.D., EX-TECHNICAL DIRECTOR
OF THE MEXICAN NATIONAL SOCCER TEAM

4

Amelia and Tomás

SATURDAY, NOVEMBER 8, 11:00 A.M.

TOMÁS CHOSE TO CHECK OUT the penthouse Rosendo Franco and his lover shared in the Anzures development, more out of curiosity to see the love nest of the Mexican press baron than out hope of finding the little black book that was keeping Claudia awake at night. And in fact he didn't find it. The couches and chairs were hacked and gutted, the bathroom fixtures torn from the walls, and the walls broken open with sledgehammers. The violence of it all overwhelmed him. These weren't just the ravages of a very thorough search, he thought, but of raging, savage fury. He looked over the scarcely discernible bedrooms and then ran down to the street, his heart pounding.

The night before, he'd thought Claudia's fears about the black book were exaggerated. Now he wasn't so sure. He decided to call her to meet and bring her up to date on what he had found, but she didn't answer the phone. He imagined she was sleeping after the frenzy of the past two days. He dialed Amelia's number, and twenty minutes later they were walking through the park near her house.

"I didn't know you and Claudia were so close," Amelia said when he finished telling her about the conversation he'd had with the heiress and his visit to the wrecked apartment.

"We're not. I feel like the one-eyed man in the kingdom of the blind that is the editorial offices of *El Mundo*. Five years ago, we took a trip to New York together with other executives from the newspaper, and I think I was the only one to save myself from her contempt for all the lapdogs her father brought along with him."

"Being the one-eyed man among the blind isn't much of a qualification for heading up a newspaper, is it?"

Amelia sensed something was missing from Tomás's tale, but she couldn't figure out exactly what it was that sat ill with her. It was hard for her to understand that the newspaper owner's daughter would entrust a responsibility of that magnitude to a columnist she barely knew. And even stranger was the fact that she should ask his help to find a vanished woman and her compromising little booklet. Tomás was a good political analyst, but his talents as a detective could hardly be called top-notch.

The journalist didn't answer. He squeezed her arm and indicated with his eyes a curious scene in front of them in the park. A woman was pretending to concentrate on her telephone screen while she looked askance at a gray bulldog at the end of an elegant leash defecating profusely in the middle of the sidewalk; she must have known that the city ordinances required owners pick up after their dogs, but was too prim to actually do it.

"I read somewhere that if an alien landed in one of our parks on a Sunday, it would think that the supreme beings on this planet were dogs, and that the humans were a race of slaves dedicated to serving their masters. How else do you explain that one species agrees to pick up the other's excrement with its hands?"

Amelia nodded and half-smiled, more because of Tomás's attitude than his comment. She had already gotten used to the way her partner would introduce these digressions and sarcastic phrases into crucial moments of the conversation. At first, she'd found it exasperating and a little bit manic, but with time she came to view it tenderly; she saw it was his way of protecting himself. She came to assume these little twists and turns were intended not to distract from the subject, but rather to buy time to broach it properly, and in passing they gave her a sense of what he was sensitive about.

The invitation to take charge of the paper attracts him and makes him anxious at the same time, she said to herself.

"There's one thing I agree with Claudia about," she said. "There's no one there at that office she can lean on. Some of them are morons, and a lot of them are rotten to the core. But can't she poach a good professional from somewhere else?"

"They don't grow on trees. It would have to be the deputy director of one of the other papers. But it's not like the press is a breeding ground for talent these days. The best journalists and editors have left for other areas, they're taking on personal projects. The economic crisis in the dailies and the cutbacks have led to this awful cannibalism in the media world, and the mediocre ones are the only ones to survive it."

"And how do you feel being faced with that possibility? Maybe the dailies are going downhill, but *El Mundo* could still have a big impact. In a country where the courts play into the hands of the powerful, a good press is our last refuge for a fair hearing."

"I've been turning it over in my head since last night. It excites me to think about what *El Mundo* could become with a more professional, independent editorial line, but I have to ask myself if I'm capable of heading up a project on that scale."

Amelia stopped, turned to stand in front of him, took his head in her hands and kissed him. Then, she looked around to be sure there weren't any photographers lurking nearby—something he couldn't stand but she couldn't avoid either. Her relationship with Tomás wasn't a secret, but she didn't care for her private moments being splashed around all over social media. It was embarrassing enough that her two bodyguards were the constant witnesses to her intimate life.

"I don't have the least doubt about that," she said affectionately.

He thanked the gesture and grabbed her around the waist. The woman with the bulldog looked at them with a smile that could have conveyed complicity or ironic disapproval. Tomás turned his eyes away and contemplated the offering the dog had left on the cement: its owner tugged at the leash, turned around, and went on her way.

"Maybe you could bring reinforcements, stay there through the transition while Claudia learns to place her trust in some director you train for her," she added.

"Maybe," he said, and furrowed his brow, trying to imagine some respectable candidate from among his colleagues.

Now it was she who pulled at his shirt to turn his attention toward what was happening on a bench in Río de Janeiro Park, where their walk had taken them: a teenager was kissing the muzzle of a little Yorkshire terrier she had in a basket.

"Well, that will certainly confuse your aliens about the relationship between the two species, no?"

Tomás laughed. He enjoyed those diversions and moments of relief the urban landscape offered while they conversed, walking through the Colonía Roma near Amelia's house. He had taken such a liking to their weekend walks that he'd come to think theirs was a peripatetic affair. Not that they had stopped having sex for that year they'd been seeing each other as lovers, but those first weeks they were together, an intense, animal passion had consumed them, a product, perhaps, of the long wait. They had known each other since they were six, and they had flirted with the idea of an affair when they were twenty-three, but its time didn't come until they were in their forties. In the past few months, the intensity had waned into a mature relationship, and even if they still chased each other around the kitchen table from time to time, Tomás felt that these outings were when he loved her most. And that was true despite the two unnerving guards escorting them from ten feet away.

"And what do you think of Claudia's other request, finding out where that Milena ended up and getting hold of the fated black book? The thing about the penthouse sounds nasty. What's your gut tell you?" he inquired.

"First, tell me what you know about her and what the hell her role in Franco's life was."

"Everything's all mixed up. Rosendo Franco died in his bed, more or less as the newspaper printed it, but his bed was no longer the one he shared with his wife in Las Lomas; it was this penthouse in the Anzures development, where he practically lived with his lover. It seems that for the past few months he'd been spending most of his nights with her. From what Claudia could figure out, Milena is around twenty-five years old, from Eastern Europe, and Franco rescued her from prostitution."

"He was a noted womanizer, but I didn't know he was a whorehouse connoisseur as well."

"I don't think he went to brothels, but when political bigwigs get together, they often hire high-class prostitutes to close the deal, like a little dessert course after their meetings."

"And beyond the fact that he died in Milena's bed, why is the daughter so interested? You believe this thing about the black book?"

"It seems Rosendo was crazy for the girl. Claudia told me her father always had lovers, but that never stopped him from going home regularly to sleep, and he never abandoned his wife the way he had this time."

"All these men in denial about aging turn weird when their testosterone levels start dropping. Age makes them soft. They use women up and cast them aside their whole lives, and then they turn into old-timers with chicken hearts weeping out these adolescent love songs."

Tomás was surprised by the bitterness of Amelia's words. He told himself the old wound from her relationship with Carlos Lemus, twenty-four years her senior, was still far from healing.

"The most worrisome thing is that the girl's life could be in danger, if she's even still alive. In Rosendo's emails, he promises to keep her safe from whatever threats she seemed to be facing. Claudia says there is something he repeats obsessively: 'As long as I'm alive, no one will touch a hair on your head.'"

"It could be something the old man said to make himself necessary to her. Maybe he exaggerated the risk she was in to guarantee her dependence or submission, who knows," Amelia said.

"Everything's a maybe, but if Franco did make moves to get her out of the world of prostitution, it could be the threats were real. He had a great deal of power, politically speaking, but the mafias that deal with cross-border trafficking are hardly a bunch of schoolgirls. Whatever it is, Claudia's afraid for the life of this Milena, and she's got it into her head to fulfill this promise to her father to protect her and to safeguard the reputation of the Franco family by getting back that little black book. A weird way of showing loyalty to the old man, I suppose."

"That, and curiosity to know Rosendo Franco's only love, apart from his wife. A morbid attraction, no?" she said.

"Could be," he responded. "I get the sense that reading her father's emails gave Claudia a very different impression of her father figure from the one she believed in before. In recent years, they weren't very close; maybe it's a way to close the distance."

"The girl could really be in danger. Is there anything else we know about her?"

"She vanished, but it's not like the police are looking for her. Franco died from a heart attack, so there's no need to investigate any further. I don't know if Claudia will want to report the damages to the apartment. I don't even know if she's found out about them yet."

"Jaime could probably help," Amelia said in a doubtful tone.

She decided not to share with Tomás Jaime's strange declaration of love from the night before. The two friends' relationship was tense enough already.

"Probably," he conceded, looking her in the eyes. They both knew their friend's talents, but they were equally aware that calling on him was making a pact with the devil. What they didn't know was that Jaime Lemus was already on Milena's trail.

5

Jaime

HER NAME WASN'T MILENA ASIMOV and she didn't come from Slovakia. The file Jaime had in front of him was only a few pages long, but it had all the essential information. A copy of her passport proved that Alka Moritz had been born twenty-six years ago in a village called Jastrebarsko in Croatia. She was six feet tall, had blue eyes, blonde hair, a thin nose, and an angular, well-proportioned face. There was something ethereally delicate in her features, the face of a benign fairy, even if there was nothing subtle or slight about the rest of her body. The photos his staff had been able to get off some porn page showed her protuberant breasts and buttocks, probably from surgeries ordered by the pimps who farmed her out.

For any prostitution ring, Milena would be a prize of immeasurable value, Jaime thought to himself. Her presence in Mexico was already a mystery. Latin America tends to be a recycling bin for prostitutes from ex-communist countries, who are in high demand in Western Europe and the United States; only after their best years are over do their owners bring them into secondary markets. That wasn't the case with Milena: the copy of her immigration card in front of him proved she had shown up in Mexico from Madrid ten months ago. Everything indicated she was at the peak of her beauty and sex appeal. Something about this girl's story didn't add up. This was exactly the kind of challenge that fascinated Jaime.

His interest grew when he found out Tomás would be taking over the newspaper the following Monday. That, and the fact that Claudia had a private meeting with his friend right there in the funeral home. He remembered when he had run into Tomás at Claudia's wedding a few years back: all he could remember was Tomás's mood, wavering between nostalgia and abjection. Like a cast-off boyfriend, Jaime concluded, and that set his bloodhound instincts in motion.

Jaime Lemus had become one of the most important security consultants in Latin America. His business, Lemlock, received contracts from local governments, multinational corporations, and municipalities to set up closed-circuit camera systems, digital-information protection, police-force training, and everything related to cyber-intelligence. For years, he was the real or *de facto* head of the Mexican intelligence services, and when he withdrew to the private sphere he took the best specialists and technicians with him. He also had the trust of the FBI and DEA, often passing them information that even the Mexican government wasn't in a position to share, because of legal restrictions or because they didn't have it in the first place. His business was responsible for, among other things, the network of cameras watching over the streets of a dozen Latin American cities, including Buenos Aires and Mexico City. Four countries in the region, among them Cuba, had used Lemlock's services to develop monitoring systems for tapping into telephone calls and social-network activity. Jaime benefited from all of it. His real passion wasn't for growing his company's revenues, which were already big enough, but for rooting around in the information his work gave him free access to. Lemlock's hackers, its sophisticated technology, and Jaime's role as a consultant gave him a privileged relationship with the intelligence services of numerous countries and enormous weight with the Mexican political class, which both feared and needed him.

He was interested in the changes that *El Mundo* would go through after Rosendo Franco's death for two reasons. First, the paper's website had the highest traffic for any news site in all of Mexico, and the most followers on Twitter and Facebook of any of the media companies. Its influence was significant not only in Mexico, but also among the Latino population in the United States. Lemus knew how terrified even the Mexican president, Alonso Prida, was of a negative hashtag. Jaime had honed the art of optimizing content placement on the Net to control the rise and fall of politicians in public opinion; now, he wanted influence on *El Mundo*'s page.

Then, of course, there was his love for Amelia. Despite what had happened the day before in the parking lot, Jaime was keeping his hopes alive. He knew Tomás and Amelia had started seeing each other two months back, but he was gambling that the journalist's flakiness would sabotage things, and he was more than ready to guarantee the breakup came sooner rather than later. In the attachment he had sensed between Claudia and Tomás, he glimpsed something that might be the perfect fuse: he just needed to get closer to the Blues one more time and prepare to strike.

6

Tomás and Claudia

MONDAY, NOVEMBER 10, 11:45 A.M.

A TEEMING OFFICE has something sinister about it, Tomás thought as he surveyed the editorial headquarters of *El Mundo*. It doesn't matter how easygoing the team members are; all of them divest themselves of their status in the outside world and succumb to routine, becoming cogs in a wheel, each subject to the mores and rituals dictated by the office's singular culture. The ritual of the morning coffee; the way to greet the influential secretary; the jokes every Monday at the expense of the soccer fanatic; the exchange of glances in the presence of the arrogant deputy director. Tomás Arizmendi had never been part of an office; he spent his first years as a reporter on the street, and the last fifteen years, as a columnist, he'd barely set foot in the editing room. But today he would be named director of the entire floor, that miniature universe that unfolded in the eight thousand square feet between the elevators and the photo archives forty desks away. Even so, Tomás remained fixated in part on how and when he would tell Claudia that the apartment her father stayed in with his lover had been destroyed.

Five minutes before noon, she appeared in the doorway of Tomás's temporary office. She closed the door behind her and stood alone with Tomás. Outside, almost two hundred employees waited.

"You ready, Director?" she asked.

"I'm really nervous."

"I'm shitting myself, I'm so scared," Claudia confessed.

They both laughed. Just then, Tomás understood how easy it would be to fall in love with her, and how hard things would be if he did.

"I sent you the text of what I'm planning to say out there, then they'll do a quick summary of your words and mine, throw in a few pictures, and it'll be up on the Net right away. Tomorrow, we'll put a photo under the cutoff line."

"The cutoff line?"

"On the lower half of the first page. A respectable placement, but without hogging the spotlight."

"Perfect, do it," she said. "Today we're going to grab a bite together, you and me, knock back a couple of tequilas, and see what we're going to do to get all this up and running. We'll meet at three at El Puerto Chico, how's that sound?"

Three hours later, Tomás walked the eight blocks to the Spanish restaurant. Claudia was already waiting for him at a table, leaning against the wall under an enormous painting of the Cantabrian coast. From afar, her red hair blended in with the base of the painting, like a bonfire on the verge of spreading out over the meadows crowning the cliff that overlooked the waters of the Atlantic.

"The salted fish in this place is the stuff of legends, boss."

"Don't be an asshole," she said. "Talk to me that way again and you'll be the shortest-lived director in the history of Mexican journalism."

Tomás was going to answer her when a server set down their shots or tequila and he remembered what the deceased minister of the interior, Augusto Salazar, had told him about hidden microphones and waiters the government kept on their payroll at the main spots in the city where politicians wined and dined.

Once they were alone, Tomás felt under the table for a microphone. He found two gobs of chewing gum but no surveillance equipment.

He felt ridiculous and asked himself if you could even locate such devices with your fingertips.

They toasted to the memory of Rosendo Franco and the newspaper's future.

"I was moved by what you said, Tomás, and more importantly, I think you moved the editors and reporters, too," Claudia said. "You really think good journalism can save *El Mundo*?"

"We'll never know if we don't fight for it, don't you think? Anyway, it's better to die for a good cause than live for a bad one."

"I'd be thankful to you if we didn't die for either reason. More than six hundred people work at the paper."

"Daily papers are dying the world over, Claudia. Sooner or later, print is going to be confined to a small group of readers. But I'm still convinced that society needs someone to handle the news, the reporting, the opinion columns, and the only people who can do that are the experts, professionals working in a well-trained, organically organized newsroom."

"If it's not on paper, it will be on the internet, I guess, but right now, when everything gets given away for free there's still no way of making online news profitable." She paused as the waiter brought over the sardines and tuna-stuffed peppers they had ordered. "From what I've read, analysts don't only seem to think the press is on its last legs, but also that there isn't even a business model capable of bankrolling a newsroom of full-time journalists. You can't sell information anymore. That means none of these platforms has a future."

"Okay, I see: you're an expert on the subject now. Maybe there's more of your father in you than you think. What you're saying is true, but I prefer to think the overwhelming abundance of information has made professional curators indispensable, people who can sort out the wheat from the chaff. Right now, we might get a tweet that tells us Mick Jagger is dead," Tomás said, knocking on wood as he did so, "but until we see it on the *New York Times* website or somewhere similar, we're not going to believe it. Never has the community needed credible editors and journalists as much as now."

"But how do you foot the bill for that kind of journalism?"

"Obviously they're not willing to pay for the kind of puff pieces and gossip *El Mundo* has been cranking out to try and keep up with 'what people want to read'—gossip about Lady Gaga or political intrigues you can find anywhere. *El Mundo* has got to become a brand that says credibility and respect. Its features need a quality and depth you can't find anywhere else."

"I agree, but the journalism you're talking about costs even more. Give a young reporter a thousand bucks a month and he can publish three stories a day; a good investigative reporter costs two or three times as much and can only publish one or two a week. At the end of the day, the outcome could still be that the newspaper shuts down, but with even more debt."

The restaurant employee took away what was left of the first course and put a large tray of salted fish and green salad in the center of the table.

"Have you found out anything about Milena?" Claudia asked.

"I'm meeting with Jaime Lemus tomorrow to talk about that. He can help us."

"He's the one who was with you at the funeral yesterday, right? The guy who worked in the CISEN?"

"In the CISEN and lots of other places. An expert in security and intelligence."

"And the other two, what's their story?"

"Mario Crespo is a university professor, but right now he's at a seminary in Puerto Rico. The other is Amelia Navarro, everybody knows her."

"That woman is something else," she said. "She's nothing like the traditional politicians."

"She's really more of an activist, with a gender and human rights agenda. She ended up in the party almost by accident. Deep down she's not with the PRD. She'll resign in the next few months."

"And you trust this friend of yours, Jaime?"

He reflected a few moments. To describe who Jaime was and what he did was no simple matter. He decided to tell the truth.

"Jaime gets the job done, but sometimes the price is high. For him, nothing is off-limits if he feels the ends justify it."

"So how does that make him different from any politician?"

"Touché," Tomás said. "When I was railing against the political background of the Pamela Dosantos assassination in my columns a year back, the world came crashing down on me. Lots of people would have liked to see me dead to keep me from publishing the state secrets she had piled up in the course of her affairs with the elite. Some people even tried to make that happen. I'm alive thanks to Jaime."

"Well, I like him so far," she said, and lay one of her hands on top of his for a second.

"Right, but in the process, terrible things happened. The mission got out of hand, someone made a mistake, we think, and some tough guys under his command cut off the fingers of Mario's son Vidal and shot his friend Luis Corcuera in the leg. All this because they got caught up in the investigation of Pamela's assassination. They managed to reattach the fingers, though you can see Vidal's hand is still stiff. Luis limps when he walks, and he holds a nasty grudge against Jaime. It's too bad, because together they'd make a hell of a team."

"I'm sorry. Were the people responsible punished, at least?"

"The guy who did it is dead."

"Better," she said.

"That's not all, though. Another of Vidal's friends got killed, along with almost his entire family. Only the kid's sister, Marina Alcántara, survived. You might remember the case. The father was a well-known accountant."

"I remember a nasty picture from one of the afternoon papers. So people who worked for Jaime were responsible for that, too?"

"Not directly. It was the drug cartels, but my impression is that they were looking for him."

"Did it all get resolved in the end?"

Tomás wavered briefly before answering: "Yeah."

"Then go to him. He'll help us find Milena."

Turning toward the server, who had just returned, she ordered a macchiato for each of them, no dessert.

Now Tomás saw why the information about the penthouse couldn't be kept back any longer. He hadn't wanted to distract from his nomination as director or their saucy chitchat those past few hours. But he figured the awful description of all that had happened last year had set the scene, and now he could tell her what had happened in the place where her father died.

A crease, invisible up to now, emerged between her brows as she listened to the news.

"There must have been something to my father's fears about the danger his family might be in, Tomás. We have to find that girl."

7

Milena

2005–2006

THOSE FIRST DAYS, she welcomed each client with a tinge of optimism. There was no way the men could be indifferent to her situation, she told herself. Her next lover would be her key to escape. She looked them in the eyes the way old sailors look at maps, invoking the experience of the voyage in a single glance. But that was when she still believed in human beings, or at least in their desire to atone for their sins. The look they gave her back could be covetous, contemptuous, timid, ashamed, very occasionally compassionate, but never supportive or receptive.

Just in from Marbella, barely seventeen years old, she lost her virginity to an Arabian sheik, the winner of an auction. With time, she found that rich Arabs looked at sex the way the French looked at food: they preferred talking about the experience to the experience itself. The man who deflowered her spoke his mother tongue in long stretches while uncovering various parts of her body, like a gourmand declaiming his relish with each new bite of stew, but the final onslaught consisted of barely a half-dozen thrusts and a couple of exhausted sighs. The man collapsed beside her and forgot her for awhile, then seemed to remember something, lurched up in bed, and pushed her aside brusquely. A smile crossed his lips as he saw the trail of blood on the sheet, and the smile didn't vanish while he walked to a dresser and took a box out of the top drawer. He took out an anklet and slipped it over Milena's foot.

More than that night, she remembered the next day: the sharp, abrupt ache she'd felt at the sheik's hands was nothing compared to what they subjected her to twelve hours later. The four men who ran the prison-house she'd ended up in gathered up around her bed in the morning, and did all they'd been kept from doing until her virginity had been sold off. For the next twenty-four hours, she lay there crippled by pain and shock. She never saw the anklet again.

Two days later, the parade of customers started, all of them wealthy, many of them foreign. In the early years, they only assigned her one person a night, and always a regular. Not that they were looking out for her, but she brought in a fortune, and the people who paid it had specific requests. Usually they'd take her to a suite somewhere, and often she'd have to spend the night. Few were inclined to pay a thousand or two thousand euros for a half-hour of company.

From girlhood, Milena had been good with languages. She spoke Serbian and Croatian, a bit of German, and passable English. Over the years, she would master the last, along with Spanish and Russian, would polish her German, and would pick up enough French, Italian, and Arabic to make herself understood—all this given the diverse makeup of her clientele. Early on, she tried to explain to each customer how she'd been kidnapped, the outrages she'd suffered, and her desperation to escape. The men's responses wavered between discomfort and open irritation. They hadn't paid that kind of cash to listen to someone's problems. At best, her begging led to a mirthless shrug, as when someone refuses a coin to a beggar, pretending to have no money in their pockets.

Before a week had passed, a client told her captors the girl's accusations and her world turned upside down. They burned the soles of her feet with cigarettes and shut her up for three days with no clothing, food, or drink in a dark, stinking cell, like the first time. When they took her out, they shoved her head under the water in a bathtub. Then they moved her to a rundown brothel in an old part of town, and for a week, she had to do eight to ten men a night for forty euros a session. The man in charge was told to give her the drunkest, most repugnant customers, though they insisted she always use a condom.

After that lesson, Milena stopped looking to her clients for help. Only once in a while, when someone took the initiative to ask who she was and where she was from, would she dare hint she might like to change her situation. No one took the trouble to try and free her: the most sensitive ones were also the ones most easily intimidated by the guard who showed up and left with her on every "date."

Even those timid feints ceased six months after her first punishment. Natasha Vela (one of the three Natashas who lived in the house: she'd been born as Valeria, but the clients went nuts for those Russian-sounding names) managed to flee with a customer who'd fallen for her. It didn't take twenty-four hours for her captors to get her back. She was holed up with her john in a hostel in Marbella's center, thinking they wouldn't be noticed if they just stayed clear of the places the well-heeled tourists frequented. The pimps beat up the guy, the Dutch owner of a small printing press, and told him he'd be dead if they saw him again or he breathed a word to the police. They found pictures of his wife and family among his papers, and that made things easier. They took him to the airport and put him on a plane to London. Natasha they dragged back home and decided to make an example of her for the others, beating her to death with sticks in front of the rest of the girls.

8

Amelia

IF I'D BEEN BORN in the nineteenth century, I'd have been burned at the stake, Amelia said to herself. She had gotten up with a grim premonition. All through the morning, she thought over recent events and discussions, with the sense that something didn't fit, and felt her soul shifting microscopically from her body, like a slightly off-center portrait. Nothing in Tomás's words or mood revealed a change of attitude during the weekend they spent together. On Sunday, they had breakfast in bed, read the newspapers and supplements, took a walk through the city's historic center, and ate chiles rellenos in the Café de Tacuba.

But she perceived a diffuse and hard-to-grasp lightness in Tomás's presence. At night, afflicted with insomnia, she would attribute her lover's distraction to his new responsibilities and the worries overwhelming him; the morning after would mark the start of his first full week as director of *El Mundo*. With that, she managed to get a bit of sleep, but when she woke up, she looked at the man lying at her side and saw that a part of him wasn't there. In the shower, she couldn't figure out the sudden appearance of Claudia in Tomás's life. No one turns a newspaper over to an outsider, or puts their family secrets in the hands of a person they haven't seen in so many years.

Seven hours later, in her office, she still couldn't shake off the feeling of abandonment. She went to the bathroom, washed her face, and decided to push her thoughts aside. She had an hour free before her work lunch with the revenue secretary, Héctor Villalobos, and she decided to spend it studying the prospective budget coming up for a vote in the Chamber of Deputies. After two years as president, Alonso Prida was having trouble fulfilling his campaign promises. After a glamorous return to power, the PRI only held onto a precarious minority in the chambers, and they'd lost public opinion months ago. The lunch would be a tug-of-war: the minister wanted to negotiate the PRD's votes with Amelia to get unanimous support for his budget proposal for the following year.

She had barely started jotting the first few notes in a thick document covered with numbers when Alicia interrupted her over the intercom.

"Vidal is calling for you, he says it's an emergency and he wants to talk to you in person. He's five minutes away. Will you see him?" Alicia was the only secretary to a member of the political elite who didn't call her boss *sir* or *ma'am*.

"You don't know what it's about?"

"Remember how you were looking for outside assistance to analyze the budget? Vidal heard about it and I think that's what he's interested in."

"Vidal? What does he know about that stuff?"

"I think he's coming with someone," Alicia said, and Amelia could see her secretary knew more than she was saying. But she was like that, a Samaritan, always helping out with other people's problems. And her assistant also knew how much she cared about Vidal.

She had to stop perusing the voluminous documents in front of her, but it didn't matter, it had been more than four months since she last saw Vidal. He was the son of Mario, one of the four Blues, and she considered him her nephew. She knew the boy was excited about the job he had with his friend Luis Corcuera. They'd managed to set up lucrative contracts with a number of American businesses. She also knew he was in love.

"Hey, you remember Rina, no?" he said, pointing to the young woman who came in on his arm. Her name was actually Marina, but since she'd come back to Mexico, she'd insisted on being called by her childhood nickname.

Amelia glanced at the girl. It was easy to tell poor Vidal was in trouble, or would be soon. Rina must have been his same age, or maybe a little younger, but she was several stories above him on their society's unwritten but merciless hierarchy. A striking woman with a strange presence, she was tall and pale, with jet-black hair that made her blue eyes stand out. She wore tight, tasteful jeans, high heels, a black blouse, and a blazer that added an elegant touch. Her aplomb marked the strongest contrast with Vidal's nervousness and timidity.

"Vidal, so nice to see you! I missed you. It's been a long time since you've visited." Amelia exaggerated the warmth of her greeting in an effort to compensate for the young man's shortcomings, and he blushed, flattered by this attention from the PRD president in his beloved's presence.

"You'll have to forgive me, Amelia. I've been busy with Luis developing software for some firms in the United States."

"Rina? Are you Marina Alcántara?"

Amelia didn't know the sole survivor of the massacre of the Alcántara family, but she had seen her in photos not long before. And yet the woman in front of her bore little resemblance to the image of the student that she remembered. She imagined being orphaned and living alone in another country for a year had obliged her to skip a few stages on her way to adulthood.

"Thanks for having us, Señora Navarro. It's an honor. I know all about the work you do for women."

"Please, if you're one of Vidal's friends, then you're practically part of the family," Amelia responded, taking her nephew's arm. He turned to look at his companion, unable to repress a proud smile.

"Rina's back in Mexico City after finishing her studies in the US. Jaime tells us the danger's past."

The girl interrupted.

"I'm looking for work, Amelia. My relatives managed to get me some interviews in banking and finance, but what really interests me is the public sector. Making rich people richer doesn't appeal to me."

"What exactly did you study?" Amelia responded, and looked back without meaning to at the thick file on her desk.

"My master's is in political science and public finance, and before that, I studied administration at the ITAM."

Amelia stared back at the girl, this time with more interest. She had noted something strange about her eyes earlier, and now she saw what it was: they were placed very close together. That, and her angular nose, gave her the vague air of a character from Almodóvar. It didn't surprise her that Vidal was so taken with her.

"Well, maybe I have something for you here until something better comes along," she said, looking again at the budget project. "A temporary position, and the pay isn't much."

"Money's no problem," Rina responded.

Amelia figured the girl had inherited her father's assets, which were likely considerable.

"Then we can start whenever you're ready," Amelia said. "In a few days, they'll set the government's budget for the coming year, and I don't have time to analyze some of the areas that interest me."

"I'm happy to. But doesn't the party have trained economists working on the documents?"

"Of course, but they all have their agendas. What I'm most worried about is making sure certain line items for social programs don't end up getting cut. I need good analysis in that area, comparisons with other countries, the minimum investment standards necessary for a project to be viable."

"If it's urgent, I can start right now," Rina answered. "Since I've been back, my family hasn't left me alone. They think they need to protect me like I was still fifteen."

"I'll make you a proposition. I'm going to lunch, where I'll be talking over these very subjects. In the meantime, I'll put you in the meeting room next door, you can look the document over, and when I return, we'll talk it over and I'll tell you what worried me. If you like, I can bring you something to eat. Sound good?"

"You're very kind," Rina said, and for the first time, the girl's expression gave away her youth.

Amelia called Alicia and asked her to take Rina to the meeting room and give her whatever she needed.

"How is Luis? What's he been doing all this time?" she asked Vidal once they were alone. When Vidal had brought up his friend, an idea began to germinate in Amelia's mind. She remembered the revelations the brilliant hacker had dug up in the case of Pamela Dosantos's murder.

"He went to live in Barcelona with his father a few months after all that happened, but we stayed in touch while he was there. Last week, he came back and went to Guadalajara a few days, and now he's in Mexico City because his old man is insisting he go see the doctor who first operated on his leg. But he's going back to Spain in two weeks or so."

"I'd like to have a coffee with him. Would you ask him if we could meet?"

"I'll check with him right now," Vidal said, and tapped out a message on his cell-phone screen.

She looked at her nephew and told herself what a waste it was that the four Blues had only produced two offspring, especially given that both of them, Vidal and Jimena, Tomás's daughter, were so charming. She stroked the boy's hair and gave him a kiss on the cheek goodbye.

"You'll let me know, right?"

"Wait, Amelia. What do you think of Rina?"

"Well, I just met her. You can see she's got her head on straight despite what happened. It must have been awful. I suppose now she should take it easy and not push anything," she said cautiously. In reality, the advice was for Vidal: she didn't want to see the boy's heart broken, and to all appearances he was chasing a dream that wasn't likely to come true.

Vidal's phone buzzed and interrupted whatever he was about to say.

"It's Luis. He says he can do tonight, he wants to know where to meet."

"If he doesn't mind, tell him to come to my office when he likes, I'll be working late on that godforsaken file."

Two hours afterward, Amelia found Rina in the meeting room just as she'd left her. She hadn't even taken off her jacket, and the coffee beside her was untouched. It reminded Amelia of how Tomás slept: when he got out of bed, nothing but a couple wrinkles in the pillow showed that anyone had spent the night there. But the profuse pencil markings on many of the pages showed that Rina had moved little but worked a great deal.

"Hey. Did Vidal leave?"

"I threw him out so I could get some work done."

"So what did you find out?"

"I focused exclusively on the budgets in the social sector. Expenses for the upcoming year grow 6.5 percent, which isn't bad. That's more than in other sectors, but when you break it down, you see it's highly politicized. It's concentrated on programs that generate quick successes and votes, but it does nothing for people in extreme poverty or the indigenous population—those groups that barely vote. I did my thesis on that."

"I'm going to take care of a couple of urgent matters in my office and then I'll come see you and you can show me everything you've found. What you're telling me is a godsend when it comes to shining a light on those bastards."

Rina nodded without looking up from the papers. Amelia left, but before closing the door, she looked at the girl, who had already forgotten her. She liked how she got absorbed in her work, homing in with those eyes that were so close together. She seemed reliable and devoted, but what Amelia liked the most about her was that, without being disrespectful, she treated her like an equal, irrespective of her position.

She spoke with the party chief from Quintana Roo, who brought some names of the candidates for the election the following summer. The PRI had wrested control of Cancun from them two years ago, and Amelia wanted to get it back. But the candidates he proposed seemed the same or even worse than those from the opposition. She cut the visit short and promised herself she would find time to search out someone honest and respected.

After writing some emails and sketching out a speech to give at a ceremonial function the next day, Amelia went back to see Rina. It was late, but the girl didn't seem to notice. She had papers scattered across the table, some barely visible in the faint light from the wall lamp.

"Rina! How can you see? You're all in the shadows."

"You're right, I'm going cross-eyed."

"So, what did you find?" she asked, switching on the overhead lights.

"I need more time, but I can already tell they're eliminating programs without having to say so: the budgets assigned to some of them are so lean that it turns them into empty shells. Everything to do with the handicapped, for example."

"I imagined that. Sons of bitches. We'll have to make a list of the programs affected," Amelia said. She saw how much work that would imply and added: "Take it slow, we're not going to fix everything in a day. Go get some rest for now and tomorrow we'll keep going, okay?"

"I don't mind," the girl said, and lowered her voice. "I don't have anywhere to go."

"What? Where are you staying?"

"Sorry, I put that wrong. They've turned the apartment I bought over to me, but I haven't moved in yet. They just finished the kitchen, it's super nice, though," Rina said. "I'm still with my aunt and uncle, but I can't stand the sappy way they look at me anymore. For them I'm the *tragic orphan*."

"Tell me something, Rina. Did you maybe come back to Mexico too soon?" Amelia asked, as gently as she could.

"I finished the studies I left the country for. New York isn't my home, and I'm not going to turn into a globetrotter to escape what I went through. I need this: a job I like, meeting people, having my own place. Getting away from everyone who looks at me like my soul's been broken."

Amelia was surprised by the young girl's poise.

"I understand, you can count on me," she replied, coming forward and laying a hand on the girl's forearm. "Or, better yet, I'm going to count on you, because you're going to save me from the wolves trying to take me down."

Alicia interrupted to announce the arrival of Luis Corcuera. Amelia told her to bring him in.

Luis had changed a lot since the one time Amelia had seen him, in a hospital bed eleven months before. The boy who limped into the room looked much more mature than his twenty-five years. She supposed that for him, as for Rina, tragedy had sped life up. He was wearing jeans and a blue button-down, name-brand boots, and a thin black leather jacket. Despite his elegant dress, his five-o'clock shadow and his buzz cut gave him a slightly delinquent air, but the long eyelashes surrounding his brown eyes removed any hint of hostility from his face.

"Luis, come in, thanks for stopping by," Amelia said.

"It's a pleasure. I'm happy to meet you. I've heard a lot about you from Vidal. Well, from Vidal and from the press," he responded.

Amelia waited for the two young people to greet each other, and after a disconcerting pause, the girl spoke.

"So you're the famous Luis," she said, and for the first time, a broad smile transformed her face. Besides showing off her immaculate set of teeth, it pulled her eyes aside, giving her features a fascinating harmony.

Luis seemed to notice the irresistible, strange beauty.

"And you must be the beautiful Rina," he said with a laugh.

They looked at each other briefly, and Amelia felt like a stranger in her own meeting room.

"Sorry I didn't introduce you two! I assumed you'd met, since you're both friends of Vidal's . . . "

"We've never met, but I feel like I already know her; she's all Vidal ever talks about," he said, walking around the table and looking at the graphs scattered on its surface.

Rina didn't take her eyes off him.

Puzzled, Amelia interrupted.

"If I can have you for a few minutes, Luis, I need to consult with you about something," she said, and pulled him toward the door of her office. "Excuse us, Rina, we'll pick back up afterward."

The young people said goodbye, smiling at each other.

Once they were in her office, she told him Milena's story and about the need to find her.

"I don't want you to get involved, not even a little. I just want you to tell us where to look. Tomorrow I have a meeting with the chief of police and I want to give him a few clues. They have a cyberintelligence unit. They're probably not even close to your level, but you can put them on the right road to start looking, right?"

Amelia saw Luis light up. The mere mention of a mystery to be solved made his pupils dilate and his nostrils flare, and he drew his lips tight. Luis lived to resolve conundrums and enigmas, as Amelia knew. Amelia told herself she had perhaps been mistaken to presume their conversation could stay a simple consultation. In fact, she didn't even have a meeting with her friend, the chief of police yet, though she figured she'd see him in the coming days.

Luis grabbed a pencil and paper from the desk and drew a series of concentric circles. Amelia followed his tracings, trying to make some sense of them, and then realized once he spoke that it was nothing but a tic while he worked out his thoughts.

"First of all, ask for Milena's real name, her legal status, when she's entered and left the country. We need to figure out her phone number, her credit card, her emails, her Facebook, Twitter, and Skype if she has them. If we get one, we can figure out the rest."

"And how do we find out where she's holed up?"

"The easiest way is through her cell phone, because with that, we can localize her immediately. If she makes a credit-card purchase, she's no more than an hour away from the store. Email will give you access to her network of friends and family, who will get back in touch with her sooner or later. Skype is useful because lots of people who live in another country use it to communicate with people back home, plus people think it's secure."

"Perfect. Thanks a million, Luis, this has been very useful. You want to leave me your phone number and email?"

"If you don't mind, I'd rather you get in touch with me through Vidal. Working with this stuff can make you a little paranoid."

"I hear you, it's the same for us in politics. I have ways of making calls that can't be traced."

Luis just stood there with a stoic expression, looking her in the eyes.

What is the deal with this generation? Amelia said to herself. *Where do they get this nerve?*

Amelia signaled for them to leave and they returned to the meeting room, where the girl still hovered over the files. Her gaze fixated on Luis and followed him again as he walked through the room.

"Let's wrap it up for today, Rina. You want me to drop you off anywhere? I'm going to Colonía Roma."

"No, thanks a lot, I have a car."

"I don't," Luis said. "Will you give me a ride?" he asked Rina.

"My driver will be happy to take you wherever you'd like," Amelia interrupted, but neither of them seemed to hear her.

Amelia shut off the light, went down with the two others to the street, and thought sadly of Vidal.

9

Milena

SHE TRIED TO LOOK AT something else, something besides her long, emaciated face, while they dyed her hair black in a neighborhood salon. The woman insisted on spinning the chair around and making her look at herself in the mirror, as if she was torturing her instead of squeezing tubes of dye into her hair. And it was a kind of torment, seeing her face like that: the deep rings under her eyes and her skin, drawn after four days without sleeping, shut up in a hotel. Beyond asking for what she wanted, she said nothing to the employee, worried she would give away her accent. She felt exposed when she left her hovel, as if at any moment a group of thugs might burst into the place. Twice, she'd turned her head abruptly, thinking she'd seen a silhouette in the window facing the street. Both times, a trail of dye ran down her face.

She never made it to the airport to buy her ticket and flee the country. She had her passport and twelve thousand dollars in her pocket, but, remembering the Turk's threats, she thought it was better to hide out. The Thursday before, after fleeing the apartment she shared with Rosendo Franco, she made it halfway to the airport before telling the taxi driver to turn off toward the nearest Holiday Inn. She remembered that the prostitution rings stayed away from that company, and she couldn't run into one of her former bosses or one of their goons. Let alone someone from the Russian mafia.

She knew the immigration agents on the traffickers' payroll would report on her. She ran the risk that they would be there waiting for her wherever her plane landed, if she even managed to get onboard. She'd seen the power of those international organizations, and she knew their long arms could reach her anywhere.

And then there was Leon. Her brother was eighteen now, and the traffickers had always kept their eyes on him. For the more than nine years that Milena had been in their hands, they would show her photos of the boy and her parents and warn her Leon would be pimped out and her parents killed if she ever tried to flee. "Your job pays for your brother's freedom," they told her.

But down to its very last cell, her body refused to go back to the life she'd once lived. Only Franco's affection and maneuvering had made it possible for her to escape the difficulties of the years when she'd been forced into prostitution. Thanks to the old man, she'd come to know lost freedoms and get a sense of what life on the outside could offer. Her earlier existence was even more repulsive from outside than from within the layers of resignation she'd built around herself when she lived it.

The Turk would come for her. She knew it: his henchman had warned her time and again in recent weeks, even when Franco was protecting her. The newspaper owner took her without paying for her, and that went against the only code the traffickers respected.

For four days on the lam, she'd been paralyzed by fear. Room service with drawn curtains allowed her to stay at the hotel indefinitely. She dozed off but never felt rested. There were times when she felt the urge to call her family and tell them the danger they were in, but she worried that doing so, whether from the room or from her cell phone, which she kept shut off the whole time, might give away her location. She wasn't brave enough to go outside and use a public phone. Anyway, what would she say to a family she hadn't talked to in years? Where would she tell them to run?

Now, as she watched them dye her hair, she began to regret her choice. The dark color made her face look severe, and she wasn't like that. After twenty-six years as a blonde, she could barely recognize herself in that hard, determined visage staring back at her from the mirror. Not because her face had been gentle before: the years of abuse and neglect had left her looking stony, with a vacuous gaze. But before, it was a gaze of defeat, of sheer surrender. The brunette Melina possessed a determination and fierce rancor she thought she'd lost long ago, in the closet of an abandoned farmhouse on the outskirts of the German border. Little by little, she reconciled the sight before her with her renewed spirit. She decided she'd never go back to prostitution, and that she would never let them take her alive, not before she'd made the facts in the black book public. She had left it hidden in the hotel, and she felt vulnerable without it. She motioned to the employee to give her the bill. Nonetheless, when she saw the computer on the receptionist's desk, she couldn't resist the temptation to say a last goodbye to Rosario Franco.

10

The Blues

"HELLO, MR. DIRECTOR," Jaime said to Tomás as he arrived at his and Amelia's table.

The journalist examined his friend's face, looking for some trace of sarcasm, but his expression seemed sincere.

"Thanks. You can buy the first couple of rounds."

"And Amelia," he added, "my apologies for greeting the Fourth Estate first. There are hierarchies now, you know. Besides, I'm not really sure where the opposition stands in the hit parade in this country." He gave her a light kiss on the cheek.

Jaime's casual manner could have led her to think the scene in the funeral-home parking lot had been a dream. Despite the long years of friendship, she concluded, she would never manage to understand him. But she decided to bridge the distance that had grown between them those past months. Hating him would mean rejecting a part of her own biography.

"That was some funeral. I don't remember anything like that since Camilo Mouriño died, and he was secretary of the interior and Felipe Calderón's right-hand man."

"Yeah, they buried him like he was a national hero," Jaime responded.

"The number of guests at a funeral hasn't got much to do with the virtues of the deceased," Amelia said. "Lots of people show up just to make sure the person's really dead. They bury big shots so respectfully, people who own the people who surround them. Family members cry their eyes out for nasty people like they owed them something. The daughter who was abused by the father; the children that begged for his attention. The father goes soft in his old age and they confuse that with love, forgetting how terribly he humiliated them, how he strong-armed everyone in his professional life, how he meddled in his children's marriages. Dictators and satraps, people responsible for the worst crimes, they leave the world with elegies and honors."

Amelia's severity was genuine, but there was something in it as well of the discomfort she felt on finding herself between her current boyfriend and Jaime, who had suddenly become a pretender to the throne.

"Which brings us to what I wanted to talk to you all about," Tomás interrupted. "Our national hero's beloved is nowhere to be seen." He explained to Jaime what he already told Amelia: about the wrecked apartment, the threats.

"I ought to confess," Jaime said, "Melina intrigued me from the first time I heard of her at the funeral, so I asked a couple of my people to take a look around." In reality, an entire division of Lemlock had been at work those past few days putting together a file on her.

He took a tablet from his blazer and looked over some notes. The three Blues were in a private room in Rosetta, a restaurant on Calle Colima in Colonía Roma. Jaime had assured them the place was discreet and they needn't worry there, but every time a waiter came over, Tomás felt nervous.

"Milena isn't Russian," Jaime said, moving his finger across the tablet. "Her name's Alka Moritz and she was born in Jastrebarsko, Croatia, on August 23, 1988. She has a Mexican work visa as a model and public-relations agent. She hasn't left the country yet, or at least there's no record of her doing so. She has an American Express tied to Rosendo Franco's account. No charges in the past few days. There's no cell in her name, either. Most likely Rosendo gave her one of his. We'll have to look in the newspaper's files and see which phones are assigned to the owner. She entered the country ten months ago, but it's like a black hole swallowed her up until June of this year. That's when she started traveling with Franco and spending money on his credit card. Before that, there's no record of her comings and goings or any sign of her existence apart from the date she entered the country. We can't find anything about her past in the international databases, either."

"What does that mean?" Tomás asked.

"It means she was kidnapped. In the sex trade, there are lots of different ways of doing things. The worst is how the Russians work, and it's spread all over Europe. They buy women and literally treat them like slaves. They don't even pretend there's any kind of salary or commissions to work off some exorbitant debt; they just use the women until disease or drugs finish them off. They live in the same place they're whored out from, locked up with no days off, unless they get sick or hurt and need to recover. And when they go out to turn tricks, an enforcer follows them straight to the front door of the hotel."

"I find it hard to believe they can't escape, even kidnapping victims sometimes manage to get away. There's not some customer they can ask for help?" Tomás inquired.

"These women are terrorized and many of them are forced to become drug addicts. All are threatened with revenge against their families. The harassment and torture start from the beginning and leave them defenseless. I'd guess an attractive prostitute like Milena could pull in three hundred thousand a year for her minders, if not more. The Russians don't work with a long-term perspective in mind:

they wring the girls out to the max because they know the supply of Romanians, Slovaks, Africans, and Latin Americans is inexhaustible."

"If they're Russians, they must be pretty well-known here in Mexico. It shouldn't be difficult to find them, right?" the journalist said.

"We say Russian when we talk about the method. But this approach has extended to numerous other people who have followed suit: Greeks, Turks, and Lebanese around the Mediterranean; Ukrainians, Hungarians, and Russians in North America, and all of them in Europe. In general, the mafias from the ex-Soviet countries are the ones in control of finding the girls and selling them wholesale, but once they go up for auction, the victims can end up anywhere in the world. Milena came to Mexico from Spain. I've already asked a friend from Interpol to get me the details of her time there."

"Pimps and human traffickers are closer than ever now," Amelia said. "Before, the guys used to come to an arrangement with the local police and women from the region; now they form part of a long chain offering Venezuelans or Romanians, they make deals with immigration agents, with the Federal Police, and even with the narcos who extort them. The Russians and those from similar countries are at the top, because they were the first to start moving people internationally. With globalization, organized-crime networks have entered the global marketplace."

During her time in Congress, Amelia had been president of the Committee Against Human Trafficking, and prostitution remained a focus of her professional activity.

"In Mexico, it's even more complicated because the drug cartels have got their hands in it," she continued. "At first, it was just extorting the brothels, massage parlors, and table-dance joints, but now they're more interested in direct exploitation. Pound for pound, moving women brings in more cash than drugs: they're much easier to transport and you can sell the same product over and over to numerous clients instead of just once. In Mexico, the Russians and the narcos work together. The Zetas, for example, protect the brothels and the dives where the girls work all over the Gulf of Mexico, including in Cancun, where most of the money comes in. The European and Asian mafias have used the narcos' contacts in immigration and among the coyotes to move girls into Mexico, and even the US."

"Listen," Tomás interrupted, "if narcos are going to be mixed up in this, we need to take a good long look at what we're doing. Last time, Vidal ended up with his fingers cut off and Luis with a bullet in his leg."

Amelia felt the urge to tell him that it had been Jaime's henchmen who got to Vidal and Luis, not the narcos.

"It's just a matter of finding Milena to make sure the girl is okay," Amelia said. "That shouldn't be too difficult or too risky. Don't you think?"

Jaime and Tomás listened to her talk and both thought back to their high-school days thirty-five years before, when they'd first come to be known as the Blues. Amelia developed early. Her progressive parents, both psychologists, encouraged their only daughter to question authority and always treated her as an adult. The Blues coalesced around her, united in their struggle for lost causes and their striving for the plight of the defenseless. They were outsiders among their classmates, but also a quartet fighting for justice. They defended students humiliated by their peers and waged war on arbitrary and inept instructors. Hearing Amelia stand up on Milena's behalf, they recalled the dozens of times she'd dragged them out of inaction. In the end, all of them had wound up feeling somehow responsible for the evils of the world.

"Evidently, Rosendo Franco got her out of working as a hooker," Jaime said. "He must have taken her by force, if she went on getting threats, even after she got with the old man. The mafia thinks it still has a right to her, and even more so now that her protector has died."

Tomás explained the black book to Jaime and watched his pupils dilate.

"We have to find that book," Jaime said, almost to himself. Amelia noticed how her friend's chest swelled with nervous breaths.

"Don't rush into anything," Tomás said. "I promised Claudia no one would see the contents of the book before her."

"Rosendo Franco's keeping secrets?" Jaime said with a smile.

"We don't know, but I'm definitely keeping my promise."

"First we need to find the girl," Amelia interrupted. She was uncomfortable with the way her boyfriend had declared his loyalty to Claudia. "Assuming Milena is in hiding and the people chasing after her haven't caught her."

"Agreed," Jaime said. "So we need to find her before they do."

11

Luis and Rina

TUESDAY, NOVEMBER 11, 10:30 A.M.

HOW CAN YOU LOVE a person you don't know? Rina asked herself while she watched Luis pick up his laptop and carry it over to the window to try and improve his 4G connection. He lifted it over his head, as if the signal would come to rest there like a butterfly over the bewitching surface. His naked torso and his long, athletic frame made waves of tenderness and longing rise within her. Maybe it wasn't love she felt, Rina reconsidered, but the intense aftershocks of joy that emanated from her grateful body.

"Does moving it around like that do any good?" she asked.

"No, I look like an imbecile, right?"

"Yes."

"Do you always say what you think?" he asked, amused. He held the computer away from his body, but now he was focused on his friend. Since the time they met, barely fifteen hours ago, she had remarked that he walked like a penguin, and that he had huge ears and too much hair on his ass.

"Yes, especially if I feel like I can trust the person."

"And you're not worried about offending me?"

"Nothing I say to you will make you stop wanting me," Rina said.

Luis looked at her, still wrapped in the sheets.

"I think you're right."

The night before, they hadn't found a good reason to stop talking, or to stop caressing each other later on. In the morning, she called Amelia's office to say that she would start the new job the day afterward. They slept, what little they did, in his room at the Hotel del Paseo de la Reforma; now she wanted to go with him to the doctor, where they would examine his leg. They never made it to the appointment, though, because they found Milena first.

The night before, they'd said the girl was the thing fate had used to bring them together. Neither of them drank much: he didn't like the idea of outside stimuli stirring his brain, and she'd drunk a bottle of wine a day for six months after her family's murder before getting scared and going almost cold turkey for the six months afterward. Still, they toasted a few times in Milena's honor with beers from the minibar.

Rina didn't know anything about Luis. For the moment, the feeling of satisfaction and relaxation after the sex was enough. She hadn't felt that for a long time. Despite the usual self-consciousness about her body, she walked naked through the room as if they'd just celebrated their silver anniversary, and every time she lay down over his chest, it was like returning to her true home. Rina had felt alone and beaten down those first weeks in a foreign country, and it seemed her life had no meaning with her family gone. Now, she came to see the success or failure of her relationship with Luis would be linked to the fate of that woman who had brought them together.

He, on the other hand, needed no further motivation than the mystery of her disappearance. He stretched out for his laptop and set it down over his naked belly.

Twenty minutes later, he was reading out the emails Rosendo Franco and Milena had exchanged. Rina was moved by the intimacy of their dialogue, by the old man's love cut short, by the dark, sordid abyss that loomed over the young foreigner. Franco didn't hide his docile, unconditional devotion. Nor did she disguise the drunken bliss of every moment she shared with her protector. For her, each one was borrowed time before her inevitable death. Rina and Luis noted she never said she was in love with her benefactor. Franco had called her Lika, normally preceded by the words *my dearest*. She always signed off with *Thanks, Rosendo*, even when her affection was clearly something more than mere gratitude.

Rina and Luis grew worried as they read the increasingly frequent threats Melina received and passed on to Rosendo. They could feel her grief and worry, even as she lived in her powerful benefactor's shadow.

"She must be terrified now," Rina said, stirred.

"There's no activity in her email account after Franco's death. Most likely she opened it just to communicate with him. I'm going to set up an alert. If she or anyone else logs in, we'll know," Luis said, and shut off the light. They went on talking in whispers until sleep overcame them.

In the morning, they made love again, had breakfast in the room, and then showered together, at Rina's insistence. She was convinced you didn't know anyone thoroughly until the water coursed over your heads, pressed your hair down to your cranium, and washed your mask off your face. All Luis was thinking was he should extend his stay in Mexico to keep from having to leave her too soon.

Rina was trying on one of Luis's shirts when the alert sounded, and the laptop showed someone had accessed Rina's account. He pressed a few keys and a new window opened on the screen. The cursor flickered.

"They're reading old messages," he said while he opened another window. "I have the IP where they're logged in."

"Is it in Mexico?"

He didn't answer right away. Instead, he kept typing.

"A salon in the city center. I don't know if it's her."

"Why don't we find out? We're just ten minutes or so from Zócalo."

Luis hesitated, remembering his wounded leg.

"She doesn't know who we are, and neither do the people looking for her. We'll just go see if it's Milena or not," Rina said.

"Are we taking your car?" he asked.

"A taxi will be faster. Don't close your laptop."

Twelve minutes later, they got out in Calle Isabel la Católica, fifty feet from the salon. They each glanced at the laptop screen to make sure the window with Milena's email remained open.

"They're still reading it, right?" she asked, while Luis paid the taxi driver.

Rina didn't wait or slow down when he called for her to stop. She entered the salon and saw Milena right away, absorbed in the screen of the desktop in the small salon's reception area. Rina knew what she looked like from when Luis had shown her images from old advertisements that her minders had posted. Now her eyes were red and her hair freshly dyed black. She must have asked to use the computer on her way out, Rina thought, imagining she wouldn't be tracked on a semi-public computer.

She turned to the hairdresser furthest from the desk and asked if they did leg waxing. "We use the best quality wax, no knockoffs," the employee, a dark-skinned girl with impossibly blonde hair, told her. Rina said that she would call the next day to set up an appointment and walked out. She took care to make sure Milena didn't see her face, but she was still glued to the screen.

"It's her, but she's not blonde anymore. She's still reading Franco's emails," Rina said when she met back up with her companion.

"Well, I hope she wraps up quick, because if I can find her, other people can, too."

"So now what do we do?"

Before Luis could answer, they saw Milena walking out. Unsteady and baffled-looking, she stood still for a moment, feeling the world in disarray. She wore big, dark glasses, but the sun still blazed ruthlessly over her face, as if to punish her for getting rid of her golden hair. When she started to walk, the two young people followed her.

She was dressed in raggedy jeans, an oversized sweatshirt, and flat-soled tennis shoes, but she was still taller than either of them. Her baggy clothes couldn't hide her shapely body, and men turned around as she passed by. Milena was the kind of woman who would have trouble blending in, regardless of how she dressed or made herself up, Luis thought.

They crossed two blocks before she disappeared into the Holiday Inn on Calle Cinco de Mayo, a few steps from the Zócalo in the historic center. Luis hesitated, then entered the hotel, followed closely by Rina. Milena was nowhere to be seen, but he saw the elevator go up and stop at the fourth floor. The lobby was almost empty: just two elderly women, Germans by the looks of it, were there, arguing over a map of the area about which route to take. There were no porters in sight.

Luis took Rina's arm, went to reception, and asked for a room on the fourth floor. The employee looked at the couple suspiciously, perhaps because they had no baggage, but the American Express Platinum overcame any doubts. Luis asked for two keycards, and they got into the elevator and went up to their room.

Rina paused behind Luis on their floor, seeing that two doors, 411 and 418, had the DO NOT DISTURB sign hanging out. She imagined one must belong to Milena. She entered their room and found Luis bickering on the phone with the front desk because the Wi-Fi password they'd given him didn't work. He returned to reception, telling Rina not to leave.

In the lobby, he saw the porter was back at his post and decided to ask him about the internet connection. He was a thin man of around forty who wore his uniform with an elegance suited to a finer hotel. Three guys cut him off, and Luis stopped a few feet away. He thought he saw one, a man in a gray suit, pass the porter a hundred-dollar bill. He turned around, sat in an armchair in the lobby ten feet from the men, and leaned over his computer keyboard. He managed to make out some words. The men seemed to be thanking him for giving up the blonde's location. The porter said the woman never left the hotel, they exchanged a few more words, something about the room, before the porter turned to the reception desk. Luis walked away and called Rina's cell phone.

"They're coming for Milena, take her to our room. If you don't find her in sixty seconds, go back. Promise? And one more thing: call her Lika, the way Franco did, and tell her Claudia sent you. Hurry!"

Luis stood waiting next to the elevators, typing away on his laptop as if firing off an urgent email. The three men joined him. While they watched the elevator descend, one of them pointed toward the emergency stairwell. Luis figured they would take Milena down that way if she put up any resistance.

When the elevator arrived, Luis got in with them and pressed the button for the second floor in a last attempt to slow the thugs down. A sidelong glance at the guy in front of him left little room for doubt as to his job: three gold rings, four tattooed knuckles, a bracelet with real or fake diamonds. When the elevator opened on the second floor, Luis walked out into the hallway, waited until the two metal doors had nearly slid closed behind him, and turned around, hitting the button again.

"Sorry, I'm on the third," he said, feigning an embarrassed smile as he got back in and pressed three.

"You idiot, we don't have time for this," the man with the gold rings said.

The guy in the gray suit put his hand over the other's bare, muscular arm.

Luis nodded, looking down, and walked out as soon as the doors reopened. Once in the hallway, he cursed himself. He'd bought a few seconds, but now he couldn't go back up. Rina would have to face what was about to happen alone.

As soon as she'd gotten the call, she went out, though it took her a few seconds to find the keycard, which Luis had left in front of the TV. She went to 411 first, because it was furthest away, and her philosophy was that everything was always harder than it seemed. She tapped on the door, so the maid, who had vanished into one of the rooms she was cleaning, wouldn't hear. After trying again, she went to 418. Milena opened on the third attempt, expecting room service.

"Lika, I'm Rina, I'm a friend of Claudia Franco, I'm here for you. You need to leave right now, there are men coming to take you away."

Milena looked at her a moment, and then, without a word, she turned around, grabbed her bag, and went out. As they turned down the hall toward Rina and Luis's room, they heard the chime of the elevator doors.

Once they were inside, Rina heard her heart pounding and felt the adrenaline course through her veins. The feeling fascinated her. She sat on the bed and put a finger over her lips.

Rina's phone buzzed, and a WhatsApp from Luis appeared on the screen.

Did you do it?

Yes, I'm in the hotel room with her.

Ours?

Yes. Where are you?

In the lobby. I can't come up because they saw me. Cut off the ringer on your cell. Go into the bathroom and don't answer if they knock on the door. They don't know our room is occupied.

What do we do now?

Nothing. Wait and hope. I'll tell you when they're gone.

Luis wanted to call Amelia, but he put little faith in institutional solutions: he didn't like the thought of the head of the PRD calling her friend, the city's chief of police, and having the thing end in a shootout at the hotel. Or even worse, for her to turn to Jaime Lemus, the asshole responsible for his limp. The bad guys had beaten him to finding Milena because they had already been tracking her for five days. The concierges were the link between the tourist or business traveler and the drug dealers and human traffickers.

Rina and Milena looked one another over from opposite sides of the bed. Milena asked herself what kind of a mousetrap she'd wound up in. Rina gestured toward Milena's hair and then made a slicing motion across her neck. They both smiled: the cut was deplorable. Rina put a finger over her lips again and motioned with the other hand for Milena to follow her to the bathroom, as Luis had said, before closing the door silently. She wet a towel and tried to clean one of Milena's blackened eyebrows and a smudge on her forehead.

When Rina had wiped away the traces of dye from Milena's face as best she could, the two of them looked into the mirror. The effect surprised them: now that the Croatian's hair was black, there was a strange similarity between them. Both had long, straight hair, slender faces, prominent cheekbones, and blue eyes. Milena's features were more harmonious, Rina's more individual. But anyone who saw them in the street would say they were family, Rina thought.

A message from Luis interrupted their exchange of glances.

They just left, but one of them stayed behind in the lobby.
OK. Let us know.

She told Milena what he'd said, and for the first time, she heard the girl speak.

"So who are you and why are you helping me?"

Her voice was rough, with just the slightest note of an accent in her fluent Spanish.

Rina realized how difficult answering that question would be. She didn't know Claudia personally, and she had barely ever seen Tomás. To talk about the Blues and their relationship with Amelia, or what role Luis played in all that, would have taken ages, and it didn't seem true even to her. She decided on something simpler.

"Claudia wants to meet you and help you."

"Why?"

"I don't know. But I think you could use a bit of help, no?"

Two more messages from Luis appeared.

Get whatever's necessary from Milena's room, but don't bring a suitcase.
And tell me when you're ready to come down.

Luis watched the third guy, who had stayed behind and was drinking a beer at a small bar table with a view of the hotel's main entrance. They must have thought Milena was out and left him there to wait for her return, because he didn't take his eyes off the street. Luis stepped out onto the sidewalk again to make sure the man in the gray suit and the other with the gold rings weren't waiting in a car, but they seemed to have disappeared.

After the lookout's second beer, Luis guessed it wouldn't be long before he would need to go to the bathroom. He sent another message.

Go down the service stairway and wait behind the door. I'll let you know when you can come out.

A few minutes later, the man got up as expected and looked around for the bathroom. He vanished into a room by the reception desk bearing the clear image of a tobacco pipe.

Luis rushed to the emergency door, opened it, and the three of them crossed the lobby. Even Luis was surprised to see Milena had copied Rina's outfit—jeans, jacket, and boots—and combed her hair the same. The concierge watched them until a ringing phone caught his attention.

They got to the sidewalk and hurried down Calle Cinco de Mayo. They'd barely gone thirty feet when a taxi stopped for them. Before Luis could say a word to the driver, Rina cut in: "Take us to Río Balsas 37, in Colonia Cuauhtémoc."

12

Tomás and Amelia

TUESDAY, NOVEMBER 11, 5:00 P.M.

"TOMÁS, WE FOUND THE GIRL you were after," Amelia said. She had called his cell, guessing the newspaper's lines would be tapped.

"Really? Is she somewhere safe?"

"Yeah, but I think we should talk about it in person. Is today shaping up to be a late one?"

"Yesterday I left at midnight, and today's looking similar. But I have to know what you've found out."

"What time is your Page One meeting over? Can I drop in around six?"

"I'll wait for you here. Hey—don't I even get a kiss?"

"Here's two. One of them's decent."

Tomás looked at his watch. It was almost five, and his secretary reminded him it was time for the Page One meeting with his editors. He told himself he'd have to get Milena out of his mind and focus on putting together a good layout for the next morning.

The section coordinators started taking their seats, each with the latest version of their news budget. He was aware of his lack of experience and the adversity of Herminio Guerra, the deputy director, who felt more qualified and criticized his decisions behind his back.

The editing at *El Mundo* obeyed an immense collection of habits, codes, and values that Tomás didn't completely understand. He broke the rules when he asked for the heads of Sports and Culture to show up to the Page One meeting. Normally, the deputy director presented important news from those sections to the group, but Tomás insisted the editors themselves be present. He thought the paper's approach was too political and wanted to give their topics more weight.

Today, he tried to keep up the provocation: if his position at the paper was going to be temporary, at least he would make sure it was worthwhile. He waited for everyone to be seated and made a show of counting heads.

"Thirteen to two," he said. "Even Prida's cabinet has a better gender balance than our editorial staff."

Those gathered looked at each other, then turned their attention to the only two women present: the Culture editor and the deputy director of graphic design, who was only there because her boss was on vacation.

No one seemed to care for the comment, least of all the women, who laughed nervously as if to plead forgiveness from their colleagues. It struck Tomás that the misogyny there ran far deeper than he'd believed.

"Today we've got an obvious choice for a headline, the kind you don't even think about," Guerra said. "The revenue secretary gave his answer to the government. His declaration could go right across the front page: 'You have to know numbers to govern.' That's a hell of an exchange."

Tomás ignored him and told them to run down the day's news. He said the name of a section and the person in charge laid out the two or three most important stories of the day. The director took notes on his pad. Finally, with a click of the pen, he issued his verdict.

"We're going with 'FIFA intercedes in soccer in Mexico,' and underneath, 'Morelia and León have one month to sell their second teams before being expelled.' And lower down, 'PRI budget punishes poor.' Put in a graph and a little table. The centerpiece will be the end of the truce in Ukraine, we'll put in the photo of the militiaman aiming the mortar."

"Sir," Guerra said, "the revenue secretary's statement is the first head-on confrontation between the two ministers. They're the main candidates to succeed Prida. It's four years from now, but the battle for the candidacy starts now, and we can't afford to miss out."

"Agreed. Put that in third," he told the graphic designer. "A photo of the two officials facing off, like a boxing match, with their previous declarations, but under the fold. I want the FIFA thing to really stick out."

"That's a mistake," Guerra said.

A frozen silence overtook the room. Even the Deputy Director himself was surprised at his audacity.

"I prize disagreement, Herminio," Tomás said. "They tell me it's not common in these parts. Some other time, I'll take your perspective into consideration, but not now. Journalists have turned into underlings of the political class, a mirror of government officials, and as a consequence, we've started making the news for them. People are right to quit reading. These little dustups among politicians matter mostly to the politicians themselves. From this day forward, we're going to prioritize the topics that most affect the lives of our present and future readers. Now then, let's get to work," Tomás concluded, standing up.

He returned to his desk, and his hands quivered as he picked up his cold cup of coffee. He had never been the imperious type: that wasn't part of his personality. But the role of director had so much power, and he would have to wield it somehow.

Emiliano Reyna, editor and deputy director of opinion, tapped on the glass door. Tomás waved him in and he entered.

"You won that round, Director. You really shook them up," he said, "but I warn you: Guerra won't just stand there with his arms crossed."

Reyna was the only friend Tomás had at the newspaper. He was still grateful to him for risking publishing the column calling out the former secretary of the interior a year back. Of all the vices a person can contract in a newsroom, cynicism is the most frequent, but for some strange, fortunate reason Reyna had remained immune.

"Well, I'm more amused than I had imagined, my dear Emiliano. At least it makes the sleepless nights worth it," the director said. "We'll have to start thinking of a replacement in case the bastard steps too far out of line."

"I'd recommend you tread carefully. He's got control over half the section chiefs and the majority of the reporters on the important beats. He's the one who put them where they are."

"Then we'll have to move the pieces around, little by little," Tomás said. "Do me a favor, write me up a confidential report of the editors and reporters who got there because of their loyalty to Guerra and not their qualifications. We'll start with them. I'd like to can someone now to set a precedent, but I need to be able to do it without losing face in front of the editors. There's always one person the rest of the team thinks is an incompetent bootlicker . . . Don't get me wrong. This isn't a sleazy power struggle between one side and the other; it's about a conception of journalism. The paper won't move forward as long as what leads is the kind of strident message people like Guerra go in for: journalism filled with declarations, political rows, demagoguery. We need young people and women in directorial positions, a fresh focus, and a lot more guts."

His explanation was cut short by a woman gesturing behind the glass door: from outside, the graphic designer was showing him a mockup with the cover editor in tow. Tomás waved them in.

"I have a proof for you, sir. Don Herminio already approved a proposal for the headlines."

"'FIFA intercedes in soccer in Mexico,' 'PRI's budget punishes poor,'" Tomás read. "Exactly what we shouldn't do. From now on, we're running headlines the way people talk, not in telegraph language."

"*El Mundo* has always gone with a punchy style, sir, it's more dynamic and more attractive for readers," she said in a muffled voice.

"It's contrived and absurd, people don't even tweet that way. Change it to 'FIFA prohibits ownership of more than one team' and 'The PRI's budget punishes the poor.' I'd prefer to go with a smaller typeface for the headline than have it written in Sitting 'Bull language. Unless another Berlin Wall goes down, I want to stay away from that type of thing."

When the two young people walked out, Reyna and Tomás broke into laughter.

"I see you're having fun here," Reyna said. "I hope you give me a push, too. I've been wanting to make changes to the editorial pages. They're stuffed with Don Rosendo's old hobbyhorses and politicians rehashing the same old clichés."

"Plus, politicians don't even write their own texts. They're unbelievably boring," Tomás said.

"Give me a week and I'll get you a proposal to change it up. Te tinca?"

"Te tinca?"

"Does that work for you. It's a Chilean phrase, my wife's from there."

"As long as you don't put it in an editorial . . . We're not trying to go too slangy," the director answered. He was surprised that Emilio was married; he had always thought he was gay. Newsrooms are like that, or maybe every place where people work under pressure: the members live with their backs turned and interpret every gesture or shift in tone of their coworkers without knowing a thing about their private lives.

When he was by himself, Tomás spent a few minutes going over the letters piled up in the tray on his desk. Most of it was company mail. He called his secretary into his office to tell him about the invitations that had come in by phone and email. Miriam Mayorga had been Rosendo Franco's secretary and was now, for a few days, his assistant.

"They called from Los Pinos," she said. "The president wants to invite Doña Claudia and you to lunch whenever time permits. He knows she is in mourning. Three cabinet members and two governors would like to meet with you, too, all of them separately."

He noted down the invitations to talk over with Claudia and then told Miriam to be sure Amelia's car and her escorts were allowed into the parking deck. She didn't show up until a quarter past six. Tomás was sweating with impatience.

"Conjugal visit," Amelia said as she entered. "Since you're not going to fuck in my office anymore, your lover's going to the mountain."

Tomás laughed. Months had passed since they'd given up their ardent encounters on her sofa or office desk. Their carnal fits had grown into the pleasant, if predictable, regularity of weekend reunions at her home.

"Let's just say that the environment of the Party of the Democratic Revolution isn't exactly an aphrodisiac. I prefer your bed. And it won't be easy here unless sharing your affection turns you on," he said, kissing her and pointing at the security camera that scanned the director's office.

"Who spies on journalists?"

"I guess Franco was a little paranoid. Come on, let's go to the balcony, this is my chance to get in a smoke."

They walked out onto the minuscule space that served as the editors' smoking deck and the November cold struck them in the face. Amelia had to press her body against Tomás, but she still preferred the balcony's chill to the teeming fishbowl of the newspaper's offices. A solitary reporter in shirtsleeves huddled against the darkness of the horizon but stubbed out his cigarette and stepped away once he made out the new arrivals' identities.

"Don't ask me how, but Luis Corcuera found Milena. She was holed up in a Holiday Inn downtown."

"Luis? What the fuck is he doing mixed up in this? Wasn't he in Barcelona?"

"Long story. I saw him by chance yesterday and asked him for advice. Vidal just told me Luis and Rina had her hidden somewhere safe. He didn't want to say anything else over the phone."

"You didn't see her?"

"The curiosity was killing me, but she must already be confused with the two kids showing up there and she might get spooked if a bunch of other people she didn't know started parading through. The only person she knows anything about is Claudia. She should be the first to speak with her."

"You're right. Where can they meet?"

"Talk to Vidal. He'll take them and Milena."

"Perfect. I'll work it out with Claudia."

Her eyes followed his thin cigar as it fell to the floor and he stomped it out with the tip of his shoe. Amelia noticed a small ember still burning despite the pressure from his shoe, but Tomás was no longer looking down. The sight of it made her feel fragile. She swore she would never let her lover toss her aside like that.

As if aware of her sudden glum mood, Tomás hugged her and buried his face in her hair.

"I don't know how I'm going to manage all this," he said.

She stroked the back of his head and pulled him into her neck, but stopped. A mere wink, and all she wanted was to comfort him and strengthen his self-confidence. A second before it was she who needed solace. Amelia's image as an *all-powerful woman* was a disadvantage when it came to emotional exchange, she thought. From childhood, she had been the leader of the four Blues, thanks to her sharp tongue. Her fellow students and teachers all feared her withering nicknames and sarcastic comments. As an activist, she had been unstoppable in pursuit of her causes, and in Congress, her oratory and unquestionable ethics made her a rival who inspired respect. But recently, she felt more and more ill at ease with the role of Iron Lady of the Left she'd been saddled with by friends and foes alike, starting with her own partner. Tomás thought she was so strong that her insecurities as leader of the PRD had no room in their midnight conversations.

"What do you lose by trying?" Amelia responded. "As long as you look at it as a way station, it's just a learning experience. The important thing is for you to feel good about the changes you can make, and if they don't let you make them, then quit. You won't have lost anything."

"Deep down, I'm not afraid of how difficult the job is; I'm afraid of getting trapped. They court me like I'm a celebrity. What if I end up liking it?"

"Well, the fact that you know the risk is there is already a good sign. The real danger with this type of job is thinking they're sucking up to you personally and not to your position, that it's because you're special. Whoever takes it like that is fucked."

Tomás saw she was speaking from her own experience as leader of the PRD. But it was easier for Amelia, she hated the political class. It was impossible she'd ever be tempted by power in any of its manifestations.

"Well, almost all the good ones who make it this far lose their sense of direction. They get coddled, and their job turns into making sure their privileges don't run out."

"You should have more confidence in your own virtues, my love. You're better than you know, and if you need proof, I'm here to remind you of it."

"See why I love you? You're the alter ego with the best ass I know." Amelia laughed.

"Give me a kiss before you go back to pestering politicians," she said.

The president of the PRD, of course, was among the politicians he'd have to pester. Each had considered *El Mundo*'s potential conflict of interest, and both consoled themselves thinking it wouldn't last long. In six months, she would be giving up her post, and he didn't think he would make it too far as director.

Tomás kissed her back, but when he was finished, what most excited him was the thought of letting Claudia know they had already found her father's lover.

THEM II

I had never been with a hooker before I met Sofía at a convention. She said she was an economist. Later she confessed she was really an economistress. *In the mornings, she assisted the director of a consulting firm, and in the evenings, she sold her body in the bar of an executive hotel.*

I liked her from word one. She had a particular way of looking at you, warm and intense, like you were the only guy there in a room packed full of people. Maybe that's why I got hooked on prostitution, almost without realizing it. By the time she told me what she charged, price was an afterthought.

It was only after the night was over that I realized I'd been turned. I had always criticized friends who went to whorehouses. Paying for sex struck me as denigrating for the man and awful for the woman. But there was nothing awful about Sofía. A few weeks later, she called me to ask if I had plans for the weekend. That Saturday, we went out for dinner. Did she really like my company, or did she just see me as another client? I couldn't say, so I took two hundred euros in cash with me, just in case.

We ended up in my apartment, where we had sex and watched TV until midnight. I was in heaven: I was the best lover in the world. I had managed to get a pro to do it with me for pleasure on her night off. And the feeling didn't vanish completely when I heard what she said before she left: Leave a little present for me in my purse, please?

I kept seeing her for six months, until she told me someone from work— from her day job, not her night job—had asked her to marry him. By then I was addicted. I tried to replace her with lovers, but there was no substitute—too much emotional involvement, too much complaining. Some women got uppity the first time I smacked them on the ass; others would let me bite them, but then they'd call off the next date. I never had the chance to use the handcuffs again, or the whip with the metal tips.

Now I stick with professionals. I pay for their pain and everybody's happy. The only problem is it keeps getting costlier and more risky for me to come. To use my knives, I've had to go to some nasty, dangerous, down-and-out places. The last time they made me pay eight hundred euros for a drugged-out whore who barely reacted. How I miss Sofía.

I.G.B. MUNICIPAL TREASURER,
MARBELLA

13

Jaime

JAIME LOOKED AT THE TRANSCRIPT of the calls between Amelia and Tomás on his desk. Once again, Luis had gotten the drop on his intelligence team. The specialists at Lemlock had also detected Milena's email login from the salon in the city center, but the kid was closer and had got there before they did. His men had scoured video cameras overseeing traffic in the area, but the ones posted on the corners closest to the salon hadn't captured any blondes with Milena's features.

Jaime calmed down, thinking it wouldn't be long before he figured out where Rosendo Franco's lover was being kept. His team was tracing the phones of all the Blues and their acquaintances in real time, but he had missed his shot at showing Claudia and Tomás he was capable of taking care of security issues that might arise for *El Mundo*. Luis was becoming an unexpected bother, and Jaime had to do something about it. For now, he'd need to find a way to cut into communications between the young man and Vidal, and he wasn't sure what method Luis used to keep in touch with his friend.

He thought of Vidal and a wave of warmth ran through his body. That kid was the closest thing to a son he'd ever have. Something about his basic goodness and his eternal desire to please reminded Jaime of himself when he was a teenager, spending day after day mastering new techniques and abilities, trying to get his father to admire him.

That was before he'd destroyed Jaime's life. Despite the positions he'd held in Mexican state security, Jaime still felt he had many steps to go before he'd make it out of his father's shadow. Carlos Lemus had been the country's attorney general and the head of its most important law office. Everyone knew that a suit against one of Lemus's clients was doomed to fail. Even worse, Carlos Lemus himself knew it, and he lived to show it.

But Jaime thought he would surpass him one of these days. The opportunity to bring *El Mundo* into his sphere of influence was an unmistakable sign.

Thinking about Lemlock reminded him of the importance of bringing Vidal into the business. In case he fell, the kid could carry on with the project. He had no heirs, and though he was healthy for forty-three, he knew he was running a high-risk operation. The year before, he had barely sidestepped the Sinaloa Cartel's execution order.

He liked Vidal's smarts and his good intentions; the fact that he was savvy with computers made him the perfect person to consolidate Jaime's cybersurveillance operations. Not yet twenty-two, he was still naïve and immature, but Jaime hadn't been much different at that age, and anyway, the confidential information that filtered through the office would do away with the boy's illusions. There was no rush; he had all the time in the world to get him ready. It was more important to do it right than to do it quickly.

For now, Vidal had done him a favor without knowing it. The iPhone 5S he'd given him months back, to be able to contact him in case of danger, had now helped him figure out where they had Milena hidden.

His team had managed to identify the gang that had exploited her: a Romanian with the nickname of Bonso seemed to be in charge, but Jaime knew that in the prostitution world there was overlap between groups in charge of different aspects of the business: transport, production and sale of pornography, supplying women for table dances, escort services and brothels.

The information from the call logs showed that the Romanian and four other women had come in on the same flight as Milena, from Marbella to Madrid and on to Mexico. One of the foreigners had renewed her papers two months before to get into a clinic where they treated the early symptoms of AIDS. Patricia Mendiola, one of his investigators, interviewed the girl that same morning. She went by Danica, but her passport identified her as Barbara Petrescu, and she was only twenty-eight years old, though she looked forty in the photo in her file at the clinic. It took a lot of patience and a "donation" of a thousand dollars to convince her to let them drive her to Lemlock's offices to tell her and Milena's story. Jaime called Patricia and told her how to run the interrogation. He would watch on the monitors.

The woman they guided into the room looked terminally ill. Dark bags under her eyes, her haggard face, her partly bald scalp, and her hunched posture gave little doubt about the gravity of her infection. Her broken voice was the very sound of desolation.

"When we showed up in Mexico, they stuck us in a house close to the Colonía Irrigación," Danica said in an unmistakable gypsy accent.

"Who gathered you up? The same people who put you to work?" Patricia asked.

"The Turk, a real bad guy," the prostitute responded with a tremor.

"And what's the Turk's name?"

"I don't know, but there's nothing Turkish about him. I think he's Algerian or something. I had a Turkish boyfriend once and he didn't look anything like that fucker."

"Who's the Turk's boss?"

"Who else? Bonso, the midget."

"What's that guy's name? Where's he from?"

"He's Romanian, like me," Danica said. "But I don't know his name, everybody calls him Bonso. That's why they put this *B* on us." She stood up, turned around, and lifted her skirt to show a tattoo on the upper-right-hand part of her backside. "They mark us so everyone knows we're their livestock. The Turk says it's for our own good, so the doctors don't have to struggle when they give us an injection. It never hurts if they aim for the spot just under the B." She laughed, revealing that she was missing two of her upper front teeth.

"Did you know Milena? Was she in the same house?"

"I told you before. We got to the country together, but they always gave her special treatment. I don't know why. I mean, she was the prettiest one."

"Special treatment? Like what?"

"It's not like they were nicer to her, but they always kept an eye on her . . . The fucking circus when she disappeared, you should have seen it."

"What do you mean, when she disappeared?"

"It was a thing for me because that was one of the last parties I got to go to. Before I got sick, you know?"

"So what happened at the party, Danica?" Patricia asked. She had given up the neutral tone she had maintained throughout the interview and was now addressing Danica warmly.

"It was in March or April, close to Holy Week. There were six or seven guys there who had been partying since earlier. We didn't show up till around midnight. From the beginning, this big, tough-looking old guy was glued to Milena, he wouldn't leave her alone. Then we heard he'd started asking for her every week, and I don't remember too well when, but like two months later, she didn't come back from her date with him."

"She didn't come back? What happened?"

"The guard who had taken her came back, but she wasn't with him. The old guy's escorts said she wasn't going to work as a whore anymore and they should leave her alone. You should have seen the shitstorm after that."

"Bonso and the Turk didn't go try and get her back?"

"First, they beat the shit out of Brigite, Milena's roommate, for not warning them she was about to fly the coop. They had to pull the Turk off her because she was half-dead. And when Bonso showed up, he started kicking her, too. Real bad stuff."

"They didn't go look for Milena?"

"It was really weird. Like they were scared that she had left them. I don't get why they were freaking out so much over one whore. Well, it turns out the old guy's the owner of a newspaper and he's someone with a lot of pull, because the next day this big-shot from the anti-human-trafficking office shows up, this guy we used to service from time to time. He talked to Bonso and told him not to stir up any shit."

"And they obeyed him?"

"They were bummed out. I never saw Bonso like that. The other day I ran into Sonia, the Venezuelan chick, during a checkup—I think she got the bug, too—and she said that like a month ago these dudes came through and tore up the room Milena had stayed in. Apparently they didn't find anything, because Sonia says they grilled her to see if she'd left anything behind or if she'd seen any notebooks."

"Notebooks? That belonged to Milena?"

"Yeah, right, she was always writing shit in these little pads. But it looks like she didn't leave any of that, just some clothes and books the guys took with them."

"And Brigite? You think she'd know anything?"

"If she knew something, she took it to the grave with her. The guys that tore up the apartment took her away and Sonia says she never came back. She says later she saw a photo of a half-rotten body in a tabloid and it had the same mole by its bellybutton as Brigitte. Go ask her. Sonia's got a big mouth."

"When did you leave the house? Have you found out anything else?"

"It was like six months ago they found my problem during a checkup. Once that happens, you're no use to them."

"And they let you go?"

"Fuck that. I worked my way out. For two weeks I worked my ass off for the sadists. The shit those sons-of-bitches did to me . . . " She lifted her sweatshirt to show the scars and burns on her belly.

Patricia shook her head, and the girl covered back up.

Jaime turned down the volume and started thinking. Why would Bonso start threatening Milena when the newspaper owner was protecting her and the inspector knew about him? He was taking a risk the economic consequences of losing a single prostitute didn't justify. Franco was a guy who could sit at the same table as the attorney general, even the president. He could have put an end to the whole gang, or gotten the Romanian kicked out of the country at the very least. What did Milena represent to make the pimp take such a risk? There was something explosive in that woman's past, or in her notebook.

He called his crew to get them tracking Claudia right away; that night, Vidal would drive her to where they had hidden the Croatian. They'd have to be careful with Claudia's security detail, the one that used to take care of her father. Tomás and Amelia's attempts to hide Milena from him were childish and futile, but they still offended him. He didn't have their trust yet, but he would. He swiped his finger across his screen, tracing the red dot that followed Vidal's movements.

14

Claudia and Milena

THIS KIND OF DECADENCE required money, time, and taste, Claudia decided after sinking into a sofa. The apartment, really half of a duplex, had a cluttered vintage look: red velvet, folding screens with oriental patterns, antique wood furniture and armchairs covered in fabric with arabesque prints, tufted carpets in disarray, thrown over one another as in a fabric store. The owner of the place, a certain Marina Alcántara, who went by the name of Rina, had an unclassifiable face, a slightly strident voice, and moved her torso in time with her head, as if her neck and spine were welded together. Her large hands and feet accentuated the impression of slowness her languid movements produced. The boy who accompanied her, undoubtedly her lover, to judge by the rapturous way those strange eyes of hers followed him around the room, looked normal, if normal meant handsome, five-foot-eleven with perfect teeth. Like a twenty-two-year-old Ben Affleck. They made an attractive, sophisticated couple that fit the setting perfectly.

"Sorry I can't offer you anything," Rina said. "They just put in my kitchen and I don't have a single glass or anything in the pantry yet."

"Don't worry," Claudia said. "But let me send one of my men out for groceries for you. The basics. Do you need anything in particular?"

"I have no idea what she'd want," the hostess said, pointing to the bedroom where Milena had gone. "Anyway, Vidal already went to the convenience store for some drinks and stuff for sandwiches. Tomorrow I'll stock the kitchen properly."

Luis explained how they found the Croatian and slipped past the three men chasing her. Claudia liked his orderly mind, the precise way he chose his words, and the almost cinematic wealth of details in his description.

"Why did you take such unnecessary risks? You didn't even know her, did you?" she said when Luis had finished his story.

The two young people tried to explain the admiration they felt for Amelia and Tomás and the solidarity they felt for a person in danger, but Claudia was convinced that behind those reasons, what mattered most was the excitement of solving a mystery, the allure of adventure, and the wish to break the monotony of two lives in which so much was already taken care of.

When Milena walked out, she forgot everything. The Croatian recognized her immediately, sat down beside her, and embraced her. Claudia had expected any other reaction, and yet she hugged the girl back, moved. She guessed that being Franco's daughter meant she was now the closest person to that girl on the continent. As the embrace lingered on, Claudia felt less and less comfortable. Sunk down in the couch and by far the shorter of the two, she found her head pressed against Milena's breasts. The firm implants reminded her of Milena's work and the sexual tie that had brought her and Claudia's father together.

Luis and Rina watched. He was embarrassed, she relished it. Eventually, they left them alone and walked out to the street, saying they would wait for Vidal to return. The bodyguard took the hint and went for a smoke.

"First, tell me how he died," Claudia finally said, her eyes focused on Milena's bare feet.

"He died on top of me."

Claudia suppressed a wave of nausea as she imagined her father agonizing on top of those huge fake breasts. She stood up to suck in a breath and turned her back to Milena. A sordid image crept into her mind: a naked old body on top of a girl who could be his granddaughter.

"Don't judge him," Milena said. "What we had was beautiful."

"With an almost fifty-year age difference between you? And an economic arrangement to boot?"

"You don't understand anything."

The two women fell silent. Claudia had a knot in her throat. She felt she had said something callous, and yet she didn't feel like taking her words back. She regretted agreeing to meet Milena. Had she looked for her to express grievances she'd barely guessed at until now? Was she indignant because her father hadn't died in his family home, surrounded by those close to him, instead of in the arms of an unknown woman whose only link to the Franco family was a young, ready, and willing vagina? Then she remembered her father's order to get back Milena's notebook to eliminate whatever danger the family might be in. She decided to calm down and try to slowly gain the girl's confidence.

When she turned around to face her, she saw Milena had started to cry in silence, without making the least effort to wipe off the thick tears draining down her slender face. Then she spoke.

"All I wanted was for the kids not to play war with my bones. I got out of Jastrebarsko when I was sixteen . . . "

15

Milena

2006–2010

AS THE DAYS SLIPPED BY, the men ceased to be eyes offering her hope and became a succession of lustful mouths and dicks. After she saw Natasha Vela's fate, Milena gave up any thought of going back to her life from before. Now every day's purpose was to do what she had to, keep pulling in the highest fees, and stay out of the underworld of those sleazy brothels she'd been thrown into for her week of punishment. Milena blotted out every corner of her existence, and the life she'd led as Alka Moritz was left behind in an impenetrable and growing fog. Even her memories of Croatia were painful. Desperation inoculated her against any outbreak of nostalgia.

The house routine was like iron. The girls who lived there— between twelve and twenty of them, depending on the season—were treated as high-priced goods. Once a week, they went to the salon for a trim, a touch-up, and a mani-pedi. Every morning, one of their overseers led them through the exercises in a workout video, and a cook made sure their diets didn't have too many carbs. "A pig stuffing himself on acorns doesn't eat better than this," the Turk used to tell them.

Occasionally, they'd have to do a line of coke so that they wouldn't turn it down at a party or with some especially generous client, but the handlers also made sure the girls didn't get hooked on anything.

In other brothels, the pimps would get the girls addicted and use that to control them, but that wasn't the case for the elite girls who were enslaved. Surveillance was such that there was no need to drug the girls up to control them, plus doing so could harm the merchandise.

They never saw their clients at the house. Usually they'd go to hotels or apartments, and sometimes their customers had a special suite in some trusted hotel.

In reality, the girls had a lot of free time inside the confines of the large house where they resided. They worked seven days a week, depending on demand, and during the day, lots of them would talk or watch television. They weren't allowed cell phones or computers. The first year, Milena grew close to several of the girls, but she decided to keep her distance once she found out one of them was in tight with their captors. They moved the girls around anyway, and that made it hard to form close friendships. The mafia that had bought Milena ran brothels all over the Mediterranean, and the girls were transported from place to place, depending on where tourism was heaviest. That meant they could offer new merchandise to their clients in Istanbul, the Greek islands, Rome, Venice, and Marseille. Milena was one of the girls who stayed in Marbella longest, because three or four regular customers, high rollers, took a liking to her. She got used to losing friends as they shifted the prostitutes around, and even she had to spend a few summers in Ibiza.

Soon, she began taking refuge in reading. She had been an excellent student in school and had always had a fascination with words. In the last year of high school, in an attempt to attract the attention of the handsome professor who came once on a visit from Zagreb, she even wrote reviews of some of the books they were required to read. At first, she devoured the cheap novels thrown out by the tourists she serviced at night. She read everything without a second thought. But, little by little, she acquired a taste for good prose, for more intelligent, elaborate plots, and when she saw a book on a client's nightstand, she wouldn't hold back her questions. That led to her getting recommendations that better suited her preferences. The first time she asked her captors for a book, they laughed at her pretentiousness, but when the stylist who visited once a week brought along the titles she requested, they didn't stop her. They got used to seeing Milena stretched out in an armchair, absorbed in her reading. They even ended up encouraging her passion, because it made their jobs easier: she gave them fewer problems than her nervous, noisy colleagues.

The hundreds of men who passed between Milena's legs left less of a mark than the pages that turned before her eyes. The sordid black and white of her brutal existence lost substance alongside the rich array of colors left in her mind by the stories she'd read.

At some point, she started writing tales about her clients. Looking at their clothes, she tried to guess what they did and where they were from. She deduced their temperament and personality from the way they initiated sex or took off their clothes. She didn't care if the biographies she pinned on those bodies were true or false; she just wanted them to be consistent, plausible. The way they left money on the table told her whether the guy was cheap or reckless, timid or stern when it came to business. His reaction as he was caressed betrayed his mental health, or lack thereof; his postcoital behavior gave away more than any psychological exam.

She filled whole notebooks, and lost them repeatedly in the periodic searches that happened when she went out to service a client. She didn't worry too much about her notes' disappearances; they weren't there to be kept or read by anyone else. They were just a way of forgetting her fate, and sometimes of exorcising the abuse she'd suffered at the hands of some particularly cruel or violent individual.

She always wrote in Croatian to keep the meaning secret, but her conjugation and syntax ended up following Spanish grammar. Once, one of her captors asked a cook from Zagreb to read a few pages of one of Milena's notebooks he had taken, and the man replied that it was a barely comprehensible mishmash. They went on taking them from her, but they didn't go to any special trouble to make her stop writing them.

Her luck got worse as time began to erase those Lolita-like features that turned the customers on. By the time she turned twenty, some of her regular suitors had moved on to younger bodies. Inexorably, her gaze grew hard, professional, ill-suited to satisfying the requirements of men who showed up looking for adolescents or women who looked like them.

At first, Milena was happy for the change. More and more, it disgusted her to dress up in schoolgirl skirts, braid her hair, or fake silly smiles intended to look innocent. But her entry into adulthood brought disadvantages: with the loss of her earlier clientele, her market value declined and along with it, some of her privileges. On busy weekends she had to do more than one client a night, and even worse, they decided to remodel her physique.

Her almost flat chest, which had earlier been a plus, was a handicap in adult prostitution. To take care of it, they sent her to a clinic that brought her bust up to a round 34C, and even though her ass had always looked good, they pumped it up until they turned her into a blonde with a *mulata*'s figure. Now, Milena was again the clients' favorite in Marbella's sex industry: her exuberant, hypersexual body contrasted with her elegant, aristocratic face, reminding people of Greta Garbo.

Even so, her triumphant return and the recovery of a few privileges didn't console her. In fact, it made her even angrier. She had survived for four years thanks to the conviction that the friction of flesh and the fluid exchanges she was forced into each night didn't affect her body, let alone disturb her soul. To take care of the first, when she got back home, she would always take a long bath. For the second, she stifled her emotions with the stories she threaded together while the men rammed her between her thighs. But the surgical disfigurement of her figure destroyed that unblemished physical purity she had managed to fool herself into believing she felt. On the horizon of her flesh, where all had once been vertical, she couldn't recognize those new protuberances as her own. For weeks, she couldn't look at herself in the mirror. She couldn't bear the look of the slut staring back at her.

For the first time, something like hatred began to overtake her spirit. Up to now, she had felt numb, as if this life wasn't hers and somehow, at any moment, destiny, which had turned her into a victim, would give her back her liberty. Forkó, Bonso, and the Turk would be left behind, like a hazy, dark, and terrible dream. But the transformation of her body made her descent indelible. Now, she knew she would bear its scars, buried inside her flesh until the day of her death.

The hate burning in her breast, hard as the silicone implants that had just been put inside her, turned more on her clients than on her masters. She was aware that the pimp and the gorillas who watched over her were like her and the other girls, pieces in a well-oiled machine devoted to servicing those men who came every night to smear her with their viscous liquids. The next day, each of them went on with his normal life, beyond the boundary of that hell they financed, thinking they had integrity and that paying a stack of euros got them off the hook for any wrongdoing.

She promised herself that one day, she would take revenge. The next August 23, the day when she turned twenty-two, she decided to run away.

16

Claudia, Milena, and Tomás

TUESDAY, NOVEMBER 11, 11:30 P.M.

THE HIGH-PITCHED RING of the doorbell made the two women jump. When she got up to open the door, Claudia noticed her body had gone numb from sitting so still and listening for so long. Her jaws were clenched and sore, and her hips had grown tenser and tenser as the narrative went on, as if her own body were withdrawing from the aggressions Milena described.

Tomás came in, followed by Vidal, Luis, and Rina.

"Hey," the new arrival said, "you must be Milena. I'm Tomás, I'm a friend of Claudia's, and the director of Don Rosendo's newspaper, for now. You already know everyone else, right?"

She nodded and shook Tomás's hand timidly. Men in general, but especially men that age, had never brought her anything good.

"It's a little late for all of us," Tomás said, excusing himself and turning to Claudia. "We need to take some decisions about your safety. Can I speak to you for a moment?"

They walked to the kitchen.

"A few minutes ago, they informed me some men broke into your father's house in Las Lomas. They held down the staff and turned his office inside out. It's not clear what they were looking for, but they left the place a wreck."

"Thank God my mother is at my place, she wanted to spend these days with me," Claudia said. "Did they hurt anyone?"

"No, they shut the gardener and two maids in a closet. They're fine. The authorities posted a unit in front of the main door."

She took a few seconds to calm down. Their eyes converged on Milena, and they asked themselves once more what this woman was hiding. She looked back at them suspiciously from the other end of the room. The secrets she and Claudia whispered in the kitchen had dispelled the feeling of complicity that had grown between the two of them over the past two hours. The Croatian's features hardened.

Claudia tried to push aside the news she'd just heard and walked over to Milena, took the girl's hand, and led her back to the sofa she had gotten up from.

"Are the people after you the same ones who held you prisoner before my father met you?" she asked softly.

"Yes."

"How far do you think they would go to find you? Will they give up if they can't do it soon?"

"I don't think so. According to their code, I committed the worst crime possible, and now I'm condemned to death. They won't rest until they find me. Remember what I told you about Natasha Vela? That's what will happen to me if the Russians catch me. Or something worse." In fact, Milena had no idea what would happen if the Russians caught her, but she didn't expect anything better than what happened to Natasha.

"It seems like they're looking for something, because they ransacked the apartment where you lived in Colonía Azures and now they've done the same to my father's office. Do you know what it could be?"

Milena buried her head between her knees. Slowly, terror gave way to confusion. Did they want her, or just the notebook? What was the point of destroying the places she had been?

"I won't let them hurt you," Claudia said, and laid her hand over Milena's. "Do you trust me?"

Milena didn't answer. She just squeezed Claudia's hand. That was enough for Claudia to get up and walk back to the other end of the room, where everyone else was waiting. She told them what Milena had told her.

"She can stay here in the apartment," Rina proposed. "I'll say she's a cousin who's come to visit."

"A cousin with an Eastern European accent?" Tomás asked. In fact, the Croatian's Spanish was quite good, save for a slight rasping sound when she pronounced her *r*'s.

"Look, I'll say she's here from Montreal. Luis says we look like relatives, right? Besides, no one ever comes over. An interior decorator friend was fixing up the apartment for me and she just turned it over."

"It's not a bad idea," Luis said. "As far as these mafiosos know, there's nothing tying Rina with Milena. There's no way for them to trace her here. It could be just for a few days, till you get her out of the country or find a permanent hiding place for her."

"Or while we neutralize those sons of bitches," Tomás affirmed.

"Of course," Claudia added, excited. "If my father kept them in line, I don't see why we can't do the same."

"For now, we need to let her rest," Rina said.

"I don't want her to be by herself, otherwise she might get scared again and bolt," Tomás hinted, looking at Claudia suspiciously. Her optimism seemed misplaced to him after those goons had broken into her father's house.

"We can stay here," Rina said.

Luis nodded while Vidal looked down. Tomás realized his nephew hadn't opened his mouth since his arrival.

Claudia told Milena what they'd decided and assured her she would come back the next day, maybe to have lunch together in the apartment. The Croatian nodded. She just wanted to be alone.

Tomás got into Claudia's car, but first he asked the driver the newspaper had assigned to him to drop Vidal at his home. Vidal accepted the offer in silence. On the way to Campos Elíseos in Polanco, where Claudia lived in a top-floor apartment with her husband, they talked over the situation briefly. The bad guys were interested in more than getting the prostitute back.

"Any news about the goddamned notebook?"

"Nothing yet, we're still getting to know each other. But I think I'm going in the right direction. It's just a matter of getting her to trust me. It's clear we're all she has, at least in Mexico. But how do we guarantee her safety? We don't even know who's after her. What was she talking about when she said the thing about the Russians?"

Tomás described the phone call he'd gotten from Jaime Lemus on his way to Rina's apartment. Lemlock had information about the identity of the mafioso chasing after Milena, a guy named Bonso, of Romanian origin. Everything indicated he was working for the Russian mafia, which dominated human trafficking. He proposed the three of them meet early the next day to catch up and work out a strategy to protect the Croatian and get hold of the black book.

Claudia told him she wanted to spend some time with her mother in the morning. She had to find a way to convince her to leave the country after what had happened at her house. She would ask her to go relax a few days at the apartment the family had in Miami. They made plans to meet the next day at ten thirty in the offices of the newspaper. When they got to her home, they waited in the car until Tomás's chauffeur returned from dropping off Vidal, and talked over the most important issues at the newspaper: the invitation to lunch at Los Pinos, the deputy director's moves against him, the need to find an honest and capable general manager to take charge of administration. Chatting about those problems at the newspaper was a relief after the previous hours in the shadows of the world of mafiosos and pimps.

Before he stepped out of the car, Claudia put a hand on his thigh and said, with a hint of affection, almost in his ear, so the chauffeur wouldn't hear: "Thanks for everything." Tomás waved her off, but the pressure of her hand lingered a few moments.

17

Vidal

HE DIDN'T HEAR THE QUESTION Silvano Fortunato, Tomás's chauffeur, had asked him, even though he was in the passenger's seat next to him. Vidal still couldn't process what Luis and Rina had said to him moments before on the sidewalk.

"Where will the young gentleman be heading?" the driver asked again.

"Oh, sorry. La Condesa, by the Glorieta de Popocatépetl," he answered, emerging from his reverie. "You know where that is?"

"Piece of cake, kid. Buckle up, this thing's a rocket, I'll have you there in no time."

For God's sake, I've got Cantinflas behind the fucking wheel, Vidal said to himself, and tried to ignore the man, who went on rattling off clichés and corny jokes while they sped through the cold and almost-empty streets.

Vidal wanted to cry, to hit someone, to smoke pot for days on end, or get in a truck and flee the city: anything but be shut up there on his way home, driven around like a kid by this flap-jawed chauffeur.

"At Paseo de la Reforma, we'll take a little detour, my young friend. It's the safest thing, given the crime these days. The streetlights scare off the weirdos, and that way I'll get you home safe as a turtle in its shell," the driver said. His passenger continued to ignore him.

When they reached the house, he left the man with a laconic *goodnight*. But that couldn't keep Don Silvano from one more of his surreal commentaries.

"Goodnight, kid, and get home safe. Stay in the shadows," the man said, even though he'd dropped him off ten feet from the door and it was impossible to walk beneath anything but darkness with the moon barely shining.

When he entered his room, Vidal remembered that he had finished all his weed. He decided tequila would be as good as marijuana. He got a bottle downstairs and returned to his room, where he looked at his phone. Maybe he was waiting to see a last-minute message from Rina trying to make up, or at least one from Luis asking for some kind of forgiveness. But what he found, as he downed the first swig of alcohol, was an email from Jaime: "We need to chat. I want to show you some things at Lemlock. Can you come tomorrow? I'll get in touch early and we'll set something up. This stays between us for now. Take care."

The second drink of tequila sent a wave of affection for Jaime surging through his body. He was the only one in his circle of friends who treated him like an adult. His parents, Tomás, and Amelia still saw him as a little boy, and Luis and Rina had stabbed him in the back.

Everyone knew there was something special between him and Rina. They hadn't seen each other much, because they'd both studied outside the country, but they had written constantly after the Alcántara family's tragedy. He was the friend she had turned to in her worst moments. More than once, she had said that he was her soul mate, that they were kindred spirits. When she came back to Mexico, Vidal took it for granted that their friendship would evolve into something more. Just a week before, she had asked him what he thought of the apartment she was moving into: he remembered her nervousness as she looked at his face while they passed through each room, trying to read his reaction. Vidal took this as a clear sign that she was imagining a life for them together in that space that she was showing off so proudly. Now he saw that what he had believed would be his love nest was actually the graveyard for all his dreams.

When Luis called to say he and Rina had found Milena that morning, he had the feeling something didn't add up. The day before, they hadn't even known each other. He went to his friend's apartment filled with dark premonitions, but he never imagined the confession he would hear: worse, it wasn't even a confession, but an expression of gratitude for introducing them to each other. Luis hugged him, and Rina gave him a sisterly kiss on the cheek. He would have liked to explode and throw their betrayal in their faces. The twenty-four hours of love they'd experienced, whatever pleasures they might have shared were a pathetic fling compared to the eleven months he'd spent idolizing Rina, the depths she and he had plunged to together, the emotional summits they'd scaled, each one pulling the other when times became tough. It wasn't right that Luis got to keep her: he probably didn't even know her family nickname, let alone her hatred for everything that began with the number nine, the meticulous way she spread dressing on every leaf of lettuce, her aversion to penguins, or her inclination to pick at the wax in her ears when something got on her nerves.

He wanted to pound Luis with his fists and reject Rina's hug, to turn around and never see either of them again. But instead, he accepted their thanks, feigned a happiness he didn't feel, tried to smile, and sank into silence.

For years, he'd questioned his father's emotional subordination to his three friends, always worrying about other people's needs, never about what he was missing. Mario mapped his life out according to other people's whims, and his son swore he would never follow in his footsteps. But now he was surprised to find he'd inherited that tendency, and was left holding the bag while Luis and Rina were in love. He was the hapless go-between for an affair that tore at his insides.

He told himself his passive acceptance was an intelligent strategy: that the union of those two would end sooner or later, because he was the one who truly loved Rina.

But then he remembered the intense exchange of glances between his two friends: the way their bodies engaged in an invisible choreography, like planets subject to a gravitational force that only existed for them. A solar system with two stars—them—and one satellite—himself.

Not much later, it occurred to him that his inability to react had nothing to do with strategy, but was mere cowardice: his fear of renouncing Rina once and for all, the need for affection that made him satisfy others' expectations, his emotional dependency on those he admired.

How did other people travel through life without screeching to a halt when they saw the trampled flowers? In that hug between Rina and Luis, was there some little crack where a drop of remorse might squeeze through for the pain they'd inflicted on their closest friend? Or was the selfishness of their love just blind, and did every other feeling ricochet off of it?

After the third glass of tequila, Vidal had worked up a number of resolutions. He would stay close to his friends, but he would never lose his dignity again. He would thicken his skin. He would stop being the unconditional support taken for granted.

And then he remembered Jaime's message and knew the path he needed to take. Maybe he had always known it, even when the repulsion his uncle provoked in Luis had pushed it out of his mind. Now Luis himself had dynamited any obstacle. He wasn't doomed to be Mario if he could be Jaime instead. He opened his email again on his phone and typed out a response.

18

Claudia, Tomás, and Jaime

WEDNESDAY, NOVEMBER 12, 10:30 A.M.

CLAUDIA ASKED HERSELF how the two men in front of her could possibly be close friends. Apart from their age, Jaime and Tomás couldn't be more different. The Italian suit and the made-to-measure shirt with the monogrammed "JL" contrasted sharply with Tomás's wrinkled tie and calamitous blazer, which had clearly managed to elude the dry cleaner's. Lemus's assertive tone, peremptory and articulate, was the opposite of the reflective dodging and parrying that characterized the journalist's conversation. Jaime's hard stare was the antithesis of his friend's watery, mocking eyes.

And yet Claudia recalled the description given that very morning by Miriam Mayorga, her father's former secretary, now beholden to Tomás, to describe the firm and decisive style the new director of *El Mundo* employed when he had taken the reins: "He's got just the right amount of asshole in him," his assistant had said. Maybe deep down, the two friends had more in common than it seemed.

They were in a small meeting room to one side of the enormous office where Rosendo Franco had worked when he was alive. Claudia refused to take over her father's desk. It was still colonized by his mementos: a golf trophy, a photo with President Clinton, another with María Félix, a replica of his yacht, a miniature printing press, a portrait of his famous nephew from when he won the Australian Open. Under a lamp, two glasses cases lay side by side, like somber coffins waiting for their occupants in some provincial funeral home. Claudia preferred to work at the six-person table alongside it, which she had made into her own desk.

In front of her and Tomás, Jaime unfolded a map showing the mafias tied to prostitution in Europe and the Americas. He explained that the Kosovars were experts in moving human cargo and stolen goods, and the Romanians and Greeks ran brothels up and down the Mediterranean. But the Russians and Ukrainians were the elite among these groups, with the Slovaks, Georgians, Serbs, and Romanians as their usual men on the ground.

In Mexico, the phenomenon was more mixed. Colombians and Argentines controlled the traffic of South American women that fed the table-dance circuits and the high-dollar escort services, but the European mafias had set up their own groups to watch over the small number of women from their countries working in Mexico and, more importantly, to get them into the US. Young women from the Balkans, Romania, and Bulgaria got duped into these schemes with the hopes of being brought across the border illegally and finding their American dream. Even then, the intermediaries sometimes wound up pimping them out in Mexico on a temporary or permanent basis.

That appeared to be the case with Bonso, a Romanian who said he was Italian, had ties to businesses in the Canary Islands and Andalusia, and did a little bit of everything in the sex trade. He had three or four high-end brothels that supplied escort services and men's clubs for elite clientele. He also worked as a broker on behalf of other European mafias trafficking women to Cancun and the US through Mexico.

"So this Bonso—is that his last name?" Tomás asked.

"According to his passport, his name's Neulo Radu, but he seems to have gone by Bonso his whole life; it's on every piece of evidence we've found on him."

The truth was, he'd gotten that name forty years back when he showed up in Milan fresh out of adolescence looking to make his fortune. A friend started calling him Bonsai for his short stature, and he was happy to adopt the name, thinking it had something to do with samurais. Eventually, he realized he'd made a mistake and ended up changing it to Bonso.

"Is it really possible this guy's so powerful?" Claudia interrupted.

"On their own, these groups don't have much muscle. Just enough to rule over the girls. But they have extensive ties with politicians and leaders, especially in the case of a guy like Bonso, who provides hookers to the biggest fish in the country: from narco cartels to governors and generals, board members of the biggest companies and, as we know, owners of mass-media outlets."

Jaime regretted that last phrase, but Claudia didn't even blink. Tomás made a gesture of disapproval, but continued to press the point.

"So you think it would be possible to have a word with this Bonso?"

"Talk, yeah, I could arrange a meeting," Jaime said confidently. He in fact had no idea how he might approach the Romanian. "But I'm not sure it's a good idea for us."

"Why?" Claudia asked.

"Because even if he's a creep from the gutter, I'm sure he's a world-class negotiator. When he gets the idea that there's a girl who interests you, the price is going to go up. And unfortunately, price can mean a lot of things: influence trafficking, maybe even favorable coverage in *El Mundo*."

"What?" Claudia exclaimed. "He's not going to want us to publish a full-color photo of his daughter's debutante ball, is he? Or is he?" she added sarcastically.

"No, but they're brokers who exchange favors: sympathetic coverage of a general or for a failing casino, a crime that shows up on page thirty-eight instead of page twelve in *Breaking News*. It could be constant blackmail in exchange for Milena."

Breaking News was a tabloid owned by *El Mundo* with a daily circulation of more than two hundred thousand, and it was the reference point for police reporting in Mexico City.

"That's a price we can't accept," Tomás cut in.

"Exactly," Jaime agreed. "That's why we have to come up with the right strategy to confront this fucker before we decide to sit down and talk with him."

"Wouldn't it be easiest to get her out of the country, send her back to where she's from?" the owner of the newspaper asked.

"Sending her back to her village could be counterproductive. I'm not saying this is Milena's case, but sometimes the parents themselves, or an uncle or a father-in-law, are the people responsible for selling them to traffickers."

"No, that's not what happened with Milena," Claudia affirmed. "She told me she ran away from home at sixteen, tricked by someone who told her they'd get her a restaurant job in Berlin."

"Sometimes," Jaime continued, "they threaten the victim with retaliation against the family if they ever try and flee."

"I'm going to see her today," Claudia said. "I'll ask her and try to get more info about Bonso and company."

"I'll wait for some additional reports from my team," Jaime said, "then we'll have the elements we need to work up a strategy."

They agreed to meet back up as soon as they had any news. Jaime left, pleased with the turn events had taken. Everything indicated he was well on his way to becoming Claudia's security consultant.

When they were alone, Claudia and Tomás discussed the most-urgent topics at the newspaper. They picked three candidates to interview for the post of general manager and accepted one of the times the president had offered to have lunch at Los Pinos: the following Monday.

As he left her office and headed toward his own, it struck Tomás that their dialogue had been less one of boss and employee or publisher and editor. They seemed more like a harmonious married couple working together to organize a dinner party for the following weekend.

On the way to his desk, Tomás remembered that he hadn't talked to Amelia since the afternoon before. In general, they only met on the weekends, at her house, and then only when the head of the PRD allowed it. They tried to eat together once a week and the rest of the time, they exchanged WhatsApp messages to wish each other good morning or goodnight or air out their worries or their sudden fits of desire, always in code to avoid some scandal caused by the very-predictable spies who intercepted their phone messages and emails. Tomás typed a quick "I miss you" and didn't think of Amelia or Claudia again for hours.

THEM III

I've spent my life with ladies of the night. Whoever talks down on them doesn't know them.

My true home is in those hours between two and five in the morning, when the drunk tells you you're his brother and the old whore shows you a gentleness you never got from the girl you always longed for. There are men and women whose soul is in the whorehouse. It's not the drinking or the sex; it's not the dim lights or the trashy music. Those just set the scene, the ecosystem where our species flourishes. No one in this family browbeats you for singing out of tune or stumbling.

There are people who live for soccer or golf, to make the priest happy or please their father: bland men and women who follow their routines to a T, like a prisoner shining the bars of his cell.

All I'm saying is there's more spontaneity in a rundown dive than in those sanitized lives, controlled by the clock on the outside and cowardice on the inside.

We guys who like the bohemian life have it easy. Nothing keeps us from giving ourselves up to our passion three or four nights a week.

Bohemian women, on the other hand, have it harder: they get called whores. Those women's only sin is belonging to our species. Night animals, nocturnal flowers that only open their petals to the sound of an out-of-tune piano and the intermittent flicker of neon lights.

You'll say I'm romanticizing. Maybe. All those years of boleros and the entire repertoire of Agustín Lara weren't in vain.

But still, the most admirable females I have known are from that world where the sun doesn't shine. The most beloved names—Amarilda, Zéfira, and Zulma—were never real, just sobriquets, but the women who bore them were realer than any Patricia, Marta, or Susanita, those daytime monstrosities I tried to hook up with once or twice.

Amarilda was the moon: pale and brilliant, generous with her curves. Sarcasm on the tip of her tongue, lavish eyes, hand always ready for a caress. She could calm down a young rooster hot under the collar just as well as she could raise the spirits of a down-and-out townsman. She died years back, after a botched abortion.

What I always remember about Zéfira is her bottomless cleavage and how firm her breasts were back in the days before silicone. The best table companion when you felt like raising the roof. She had a liver of steel and a raspy voice. Gorgeous, unforgettable. Two years back, I saw her one morning selling herself on the street in Tepito. She'd gotten AIDS sometime before, and I preferred to keep my distance, but I was happy to know she was still alive.

Zulma could have been a psychiatrist. She didn't talk much, she didn't sing, and only a very few times did she get up to dance. But for some reason, she was the favorite of all the clients when they needed to pour their heart out. In her white dress with black dots, with her thin lips painted blood red, she'd take your hand and listen to you without blinking, as if you were in a bubble, or the confessional. She had an innate wisdom that let her know if what you needed was an innocent schoolgirl's caress or someone to grab hold of your cock. I heard some guy beat her to death not too long back.

Admirable women, those ladies of the night. Though now that I think of it, I can't figure out why they all ended up so bad.

C.S., LEADER OF THE RAILWAY UNION.
SENATOR OF THE REPUBLIC.

19

Jaime and Vidal

WEDNESDAY, NOVEMBER 12, 1:00 P.M.

VIDAL AND JAIME were in Jaime's Lemlock office, seated in front of an enormous plate of thick glass that served as a desk. From his keyboard, Jaime was manipulating images on the three matching screens embedded in the walls. He needed to confer with his team and uncover the reasons Milena's persecutors were hunting her so desperately. But he was the one who had invited Vidal to come to Lemlock, and he couldn't let him down now. Perhaps the young man's help could still be useful in the case that was taking up so much of his thoughts.

"Burn this into your mind," he said to him. "Human beings are never what they appear."

And to demonstrate it, he showed him the dirty laundry of various well-known figures. Jaime let him read Rosendo Franco's private correspondence, where he cried like a schoolboy, showed him evidence of Alcántara's gambling addiction, and most painful of all, the nasty comments, both spoken and written, that Manuel, his close friend, had made behind his back.

"Stand up straight," Jaime said. "Don't let it get to you. It's not nearly as bad as it seems. Every relationship that lasts and is worth a damn goes through this kind of betrayal. Even marriages. These are the little episodes we human beings have to make up for the vulnerability we feel when we get too close to someone, brief acts of insubordination that help us bear mutual dependence. What do you think would happen if the Blues fessed up to all we've done to each other over the course of three decades? My guess is, we couldn't look each other in the eyes."

"Maybe you're right," Vidal responded, still stung by the cruelty of Manuel's words. "So I should ignore it and just keep going like I never heard anything?"

"Of course not! You need to make sure it doesn't affect you, but don't ever ignore it. The weaknesses you sniff out among the people who surround you are a resource in your favor."

"With all due respect, I'm not interested in finding out Manuel's weaknesses or anybody else's to use against them."

"This isn't about good and bad or about using these things against people. In fact you might use it *for* them."

"How so?"

"As I said, human beings aren't what they appear, but they're also not what they think they are."

"And what does that have to do with Manuel?"

"It has to do with Manuel, and Luis, and Rina."

Vidal reacted the way Jaime supposed he would have if he heard his own lover's name. The boy looked him in the eyes the way the German Shepherd he'd had when he was a boy used to do: head slightly to one side, his entire being absorbed in examining his face, hanging on his next word as if it were a matter of life or death.

"Understanding people's motivations allows you to understand what they're capable and incapable of better than they do," Jaime continued. "Often we hurt the ones we love most because we share in their weakness or we put faith in the structures they set up for themselves to try and get a grip on the world, even if they are almost always rickety. We'd avoid a lot of suffering if we were brave enough to confess to someone that they're not cut out for something; the truth, told at the right time, is worth its weight in gold, even if someone hates you for speaking it. You don't know how many times I've rescued Amelia, and especially Tomás, from situations where their romantic ideals could have harmed them."

"And how does that apply to Rina?"

"Human beings act out of necessity, and Rina's no different. Understanding her needs will help you make her happy, if that's what you want."

Vidal turned red.

"I'll show you. Are you ready to learn?"

For the next two hours, Jaime showed Vidal the sophisticated system Lemlock had devised for intercepting calls and digital communications, the best of its kind in Latin America.

When Vidal left the office, he had already decided what he was going to do with his life, or so he thought. On the walk back home, he couldn't stop looking at the map and the two red dots—Luis and Rina—that were moving across the screen of his cell phone.

20

Milena

SHE DIDN'T KNOW WHY, but as soon as she saw him, she knew the man would be different from the many she'd known before. She would be sure months later, when she agreed to kill for the first time. Perhaps Agustín Vila-Rojas's entrance into her life was so unexpected and overwhelming because he was interested less in what lay between her legs than in what lay between her parietal bones.

She met him at a private party attended by all the girls in the house, though it actually seemed more like a wake: a judge had just issued another round of verdicts against the bureaucrats and businessmen in Marbella, heirs to the corruption scandals left behind by the ex-mayor Gil y Gil and his cronies.

An important hotelier wanted to liven the depressing ambience that had settled over the city, and invited a dozen members of the elite to a cocktail party on a giant yacht moored in Puerto Banús. The guests went more to show the others they had nothing to hide than from any desire to celebrate what was, to all lights, the collapse of the real-estate boom that had made them all millionaires.

Vila-Rojas was in attendance, but that was all he had in common with the tourism and construction magnates there.

Milena had a professional smile pasted on her face and was listening attentively to a builder from Málaga. That was probably what attracted Vila-Rojas's gaze: the rest of the women could barely cover up their lack of interest in those discussions of fines and jail sentences the press had been covering. Between the relief of still being free and the fear of being next on the list, the men weren't much up for sex, and if they still fondled the girls, it was more from inertia than excitement.

In reality, Milena was examining each of the men to try and bring to life the story she was hatching in her head. She tried to imagine the role each of them would play on a lifeboat in the hypothetical case that the boat sank on the high seas. The guy from Málaga, the most nervous of all, would definitely be the first to freak out and drink seawater; the host, a man with an insidious smile, would probably turn out to be the cannibal. A half-hour later, she'd decided Vila-Rojas, reflective and reticent, would turn out to be the leader, once they'd gotten over the initial quarrels.

Bored of the conversation, Agustín took Milena around the waist and dragged her onto the deck. She was grateful to escape the almost unbreathable air of the cabin, thick with the smoke of cigars.

Amid the damp aromas of evening and the muffled lapping of the waves against the yacht's hull, they talked.

"How did you end up here? A fake boyfriend swindled you and put you to work?"

"I wish. At least then, I would have had a short honeymoon. No, I wanted to work in a family restaurant in Berlin, checkered tablecloths and all that, and instead I ended up servicing men between the sheets in Marbella. Flat on my ass. Literally."

"Kidnapped?"

"At sixteen," she said without a hint of self-pity. "And you? How'd you get to where you are? Scamming your rich girlfriend?"

"I look like that much of a dirtbag?"

"No, but you stare at everyone else like you don't belong to their circle. Like a person who's never been here before and is afraid to end up back in the gutter he crawled out of."

"You're a tough cookie," he said, cackling. "But you're not on the wrong trail. I didn't come out of the gutter, but almost. I left home in Granada when I was sixteen, like you. First, I tried selling used cars in Seville, but without much success. I did better conning tourists and breaking old ladies' hearts. With the money, I paid for my studies at the university. Everything else, as they say, is history."

The man spoke without looking at her, in brief stretches interrupted by silences. He didn't mention his stints in the financial markets in London, Paris, and New York, where he became an expert in the shadowy movements of capital across the globe. When he emerged from his reverie, seeming to notice his companion again all at once, Agustín asked why she had been listening so closely to the guys inside earlier.

She told him the cast of characters for her lifeboat story, and at his insistence, described the roles each would play in her imaginary shipwreck. When she finished, Agustín was staring at her.

"Did you ever meet those guys before?"

"No."

"You deduced all that from what they've said and done since you arrived at the party?"

"Yeah."

"Impressive," he said, "I've been dealing with them for years and I wouldn't change a word from what you've just said. Except maybe my part. I'm not so sure I'd want to stay on the boat. I'd rather get away and try my luck in the water with the sharks."

"I think you're the biggest shark of all. You'd swallow them up before they even knew what hit them."

He laughed again.

"You make up other stories like this?" he said.

"Only when certain clients inspire them. So two or three times a week," she responded.

Milena told him what her stories were about and promised to read him some of them if they met again. He looked for her a week later and continued to do so once or twice a month, until the tragedy that their meetings unleashed separated them forever.

21

Claudia and Milena

WEDNESDAY, NOVEMBER 12, 3:00 P.M.

DURING THE DAY, Rina's singular apartment looked different. The dead light of the lamps, the red velvets, and the lush décor lost their luster as the light poured in from the broad window in the living room.

Milena loved it, it was so different from all the places she'd been before. When she said so, Rina assumed she was talking less about the decoration than the friendly feeling that had grown among the three of them as they tried, with mixed results, to make breakfast. Rina imagined how depressing it must have been in the brothels where Milena had spent the past few years. She told herself that as soon as this was over and Milena was really free, she would introduce her to another type of people.

"One day you'll meet Amelia, you'll like her. You might have already seen her in the paper or on the news, she's the leader of the PRD. But don't think she's like other politicians. I've started working for her, you know?"

Milena tried to remember some female politician, but couldn't. She never cared much for the news, and even less since she'd arrived in Mexico. She only paid attention when they said something about the south of Spain or the crisis in Ukraine, because she'd been placed with some of the Ukrainian girls in Marbella. On TV, they had talked about Croatia during the World Cup, but otherwise it was never mentioned.

"I'm sure I'll meet her soon," Milena said without much interest, and flipped the blackened omelet in the frying pan.

"She's the reason I'm here," Rina said.

"That's what I wanted to ask you. Why are you and Luis helping me? Why are you taking risks for me? I don't want you to think I'm ungrateful, but you don't look like journalists or police. Are you from some charity?"

"Of course not," Rina answered, though she found the idea funny. "The truth is, we're victims like you."

They threw the omelets in the trash, deciding to try scrambled eggs instead, and Rina told her about her parents and brother dying at the hands of narcotraffickers, the violence Luis had suffered trying to help Vidal, and what Tomás and Amelia had done to save them. It was hard for Milena to follow the twists and turns of the story, and it still didn't explain why she was with those two young people now. She figured it must somehow come back to Claudia, Rosendo Franco's daughter.

"So, Tomás works at Claudia's newspaper. Amelia is Tomás's girl-friend and you work for Amelia. Is that right?"

"It sounds complicated, doesn't it? But don't make more of it than it is. Just think that we're trying to do justice."

"And Luis?"

"Oh, Luis is a sweetie-pie, just look at him," Rina said, wiping the whipped eggs from their misbegotten omelet on his face.

Milena decided to go along with the Mexican girl's lighthearted tone. She'd only gotten half an answer to her questions, but it didn't matter. It had been a long time since she'd been able to enjoy the kind of easy, fun environment she had there with the two young people.

"Well, he may be a sweetie-pie, but he cooks for shit. Take his bacon out of the frying pan."

When Claudia arrived a few hours later, they laughed through the story of their disastrous attempt to cook a Spanish tortilla, which had taken up most of the morning. For different reasons, each of them was a novice in the kitchen, and the mishmash of egg and potato sitting smug and inedible on the kitchen counter showed it. The wretched state of the kitchen made it clear than cleaning wasn't one of their strong points, either.

But Spotify made up for their culinary frustrations. Luis and Rina spent hours on it, trying to fill in the gaps in the foreigner's knowledge of Spanish music. Milena especially liked Lila Downs and Aterciopelados, whose lyrics were as different as possible from those of the old boleros Rosendo Franco had introduced her to or the pop and ranchera that she heard at the whorehouse. She knew nothing about classical music or jazz, but thousands of hours surrounded by women from all over the world had left her with a vast, if chaotic, musical repertoire.

Milena searched for the music from the Balkans she had liked in her youth, shared her favorite rock songs from Spain and a few tracks of Flamenco, and translated a couple of slow and brooding fados she'd learned from a Portuguese coworker. By the time Claudia showed up, they were belting out "These Boots Are Made for Walking."

Milena's transformation was shocking, or so it seemed to Claudia, who had only seen her once, the night before. Maybe it had something to do with the light Luis and Rina seemed to give off, their calm, abundant passion, or the way Rina treated the Croatian, as if she was an old school friend or a favorite cousin she hadn't seen for ages. It was true, there was something sisterly in the way Rina brought the girl coffee even though she hadn't asked for it, or the way the Croatian now wore her hair the way the Mexican girl had the night before.

Impatience began eating away at Claudia. She felt pressed to get on with the conversation that had been interrupted, to finally get the issue of the black book out in the open, and to find out if her family's name was in danger, as her father had feared. But she sensed that behind the distance and the coldness Milena projected, there was a nervous little doe that would flee at any sudden movement.

They ate the pasta and salad Claudia had brought with her from Trattoria Giacovanni and tried to imitate the Croatian's Italian pronunciation as she said the names of the dishes, gesturing like a mafioso. Claudia realized that for years Milena had been nothing but a piece of merchandise, and unfortunately that also included the time she shared with Rosendo Franco. She had lived the past few hours like any twenty-something, not wanting to do more than laugh and decompress after a stressful day. Claudia almost regretted cutting that short, but she was in a rush to know the rest of the prostitute's story. Luis and Rina seemed to understand and left, this time with the excuse of an appointment with the orthopedist treating the boy's wound, one they had missed the day before.

When the two women were alone, they cleaned the kitchen to the Cuban sounds of Albita, which Milena seemed to appreciate. Then they took their coffees into the living room and the Croatian girl picked up the thread of her tale.

22

Tomás, Claudia, Jaime, and Amelia

WEDNESDAY, NOVEMBER 12, 4:32 P.M.

THE CALL CAME THROUGH on Tomás's cell phone minutes before the Page One meeting began. Emiliano's name popped up on the screen, and Tomás guessed the opinion editor was calling to explain his absence from the meeting.

"Tomás, this is Emilio, I've been kidnapped by some guys who want to negotiate with you," the journalist said in a rush.

"What? Who?" Tomás asked. And after a pause, followed by what sounded like struggling, he heard another voice.

"It's not a kidnapping. I told your friend before, this is a negotiation between gentlemen," said a man with a foreign accent that Tomás couldn't place. He told himself he should record the conversation, but he had never familiarized himself with the app for it he had installed on his phone some time back.

"So what do you want to negotiate about?"

"You have something that belongs to us."

"I don't know what you're talking about. Let our deputy director go or I'll have to get in touch with the attorney general," Tomás said in the most menacing tone he could muster.

"The girl's not worth nothing to you. Give her back and there won't be no problems," the man responded. From his accent and his grammar, he sounded to Tomás like a Spanish gypsy trying to pass for Mexican.

"You'll find out soon that in this country, kidnapping carries a hell of a penalty. If you don't let Emiliano go now, they'll come after you with all they've got."

"Easy, easy, there's no need to talk about kidnappings and punishments. We're just talking like the businessmen we are. And we'll go on talking with Señor Reyna as long as we need to until we manage to convince you. But don't worry, we like having him here, we're having coffee and cake, waiting to come to an agreement. *Strictly business*, eh?" he said, adding the last words in English.

"Don't be a dumbass, Bonso," Tomás blurted. "If Elimiano isn't back here in an hour, you'll have hell to pay. I'll make sure of it."

Hearing his own name made the man on the other end take a long pause before bellowing: "And you have until midnight to turn Milena in, you piece-of-shit reporter." His voice was hard and bitter, with none of the malicious, singsong cadence he had used moments before. Then he hung up.

The journalist asked himself if he really should have pissed the mafioso off. Maybe he should have stretched the conversation out to try and locate the call's origin. But there wasn't an FBI team in the offices monitoring the phones the way they did in the movies. That made him remember Jaime. It would be smart to consult with him before calling in the police. But he would call Claudia first.

She couldn't reach her phone in time, and only picked up after the third try.

"What's up?" she hissed, unable to conceal her irritation.

"Claudia, there's an emergency. Sorry, but you have to come immediately."

"Is it important, Tomás? I'm in the middle of a conversation. If it's an emergency at the newspaper, you take care of it, you know what you're doing better than I do, and I'll get back to you in a couple of hours, okay?"

"It's not just an emergency at the newspaper. It probably has to do with what you're in the middle of. Understand?"

"Yes and no. Everything is calm here."

"Here it's not. We're looking at a literal life-or-death decision."

"Don't scare me, Tomás. I'm on my way."

Claudia hung up, and the fear in her eyes when she looked at Milena, who had been following her phone call closely, told the girl the emergency was somehow related to her.

"I'm sorry, dear, something's up at the newspaper. I'll be back as soon as I can, but please, don't leave the house. This is my number, call me if something comes up or you need help. Don't hesitate," Claudia said, passing over her card.

"Did something happen?" she asked, looking the woman in the eyes.

"Nothing you need to worry about. Take this time to rest. Luis and Rina will be back making noise in no time," Claudia said. She said goodbye with a kiss on the cheek and called her escorts to bring the car around to the front of the duplex.

As soon as she was alone, Milena looked for a bag to pack her few belongings and the clothing Rina had offered her. More than a concrete escape plan, she wanted to shake off the edginess Claudia's sudden exit had caused. Just like so many other times when she'd felt this way, she decided to open a notebook and try and write the ending of one of her half-finished stories entitled "Them," but she couldn't concentrate. After a while, she put Nancy Sinatra back on and started dancing.

In the meantime, Claudia's escort raced through the two miles between her and the newspaper.

"We cannot hand over Milena," she said categorically when Tomás told her about Bonso's threat.

"We can't let them kill Emiliano," Tomás responded in the same tone. "He has a wife from Chile," he added, without knowing what difference the woman's nationality made, maybe just because it was the only information he had to humanize a family he otherwise knew nothing about.

"We need to call the police, the secretary of the interior, whoever's necessary. We have to find him."

"Once we get the authorities involved, shit's going to go off the rails," the journalist objected. "I already got hold of Jaime, he's headed this way. I say we talk to him before making a decision. I also invited Amelia; she knows a lot about these trafficking networks and the chief of police is her friend. In case we need to make an unofficial consultation, I mean."

Forty minutes later, the Blues and Claudia were sitting at the meeting table in the offices of *El Mundo*. Tomás repeated the details of the phone conversation with Bonso as faithfully as he could. The deeper he got into the story, the more obvious Jaime's impatience became. Finally, he exploded.

"That call let that son of a bitch know for sure that you have Milena, and you may have given away her location," he said, taking his cell phone from the pocket of his blazer.

"Absolutely not," Tomás protested. "I never agreed that we had her and I certainly didn't say where she was."

"When you called him by his name, Bonso knew you heard it from Milena. How else would you know his identity? And when you called Claudia right afterward, he could have traced her location. At the very least, he knows where she was a half-hour ago, even if that doesn't necessarily mean the two of them were together. But if I was in Bonso's shoes, that's where I'd start looking."

Jaime called one of his contacts and ordered them to send a unit out to protect a woman at risk of being kidnapped. He asked Claudia for Rina's street and apartment number, and passed the information on. Then he lowered his head and said something barely audible. Tomás heard the words "agent" and "the place."

When the conversation was over, Jaime grabbed Tomás's phone and fiddled with it until he managed to activate the app that recorded his conversations. Then he showed the journalist how to use it if the kidnappers called back. He looked through the recent calls and saw that the number was Emiliano Reyna's, as the journalist had already told them. They could trace where the call had come from, but undoubtedly they'd find the kidnappers had fled and the phone had been turned off.

"If you'll allow me to venture an opinion, I suggest we set up an informal consultation with authorities *we can trust*," Amelia said, making air quotes with her fingers. "Two people are in danger and it's not the time for us to start playing God. A respected journalist like that, someone who doesn't have a dog in this fight, and a girl who's already been a victim of these gangsters for years."

"What authorities *we can trust* are you referring to?" Jaime asked.

"The chief of police here in the capital isn't a bad guy. We could find out if he has information about the gang. It would be worthwhile to know if Bonso's the head or if there's someone else above him. The federal government has a unit dedicated to human trafficking, and this is the type of group they specialize in. I met the guy who's in charge of it once."

"It's not a bad idea, but we'd have to do it without revealing anything about Milena," Tomás said.

"Look," Jaime said. "The risks Bonso is taking are ridiculous. Nobody puts their neck out like this for a whore who's gone AWOL."

Claudia and Amelia shared a disapproving glance, both taken aback by the term he'd employed. Unmoved, Jaime continued.

"There's something we don't know about Milena and her relationship with her minders. Something we might not like. Regardless, it doesn't make sense to get the authorities involved, it might even turn out bad for the girl."

"Maybe," Amelia intervened, "but the time Bonso gave Tomás to respond doesn't leave us with much room to speculate. We have to decide right now what strategy we can take to negotiate with this guy. It's stupid to imagine that playing amateur detective is going to get Emiliano out of this in the next six hours. We need to figure out who can influence this animal or who calls the shots for the gang."

"Amelia's right," Tomás said, turning to Jaime. "All these networks are related and they all have ties to other mafias. If we find a go-between, maybe we can negotiate under better conditions, or at least different ones."

"True. But I doubt the authorities will be content with a mere consultation. And we can take it for granted that Bonso's got people on the force looking after him. These guys never work without them," Jaime objected.

"Fine. What do you propose, then? Do you have a solution or are you just trying to look interesting?" Claudia said, exasperated.

All at once, she had realized that as owner of the newspaper Emiliano worked for, she was the one most responsible for his protection. Until now, her mind had been on Milena and their recent meeting, but now she understood that the life of her opinion editor had to be her first priority.

The three friends looked at each other, surprised. She-wolf, Tomás thought. Amelia looked at her attentively, as though seeing her for the first time, which was true, in a sense: finally, the little rich girl was showing she was more than just a pretty face with Papa's money behind her. Jaime just smiled.

"Let's look at one thing at a time," Lemus said after a long sigh. "First we need to take care of Milena. My people should be at Rina's duplex any second. We need to get her out of there and take her to a safe house. I'll take care of that. We also need to find out if she has the notebook and what's in it that's generating so much interest."

Tomás asked himself how the hell Jaime knew it was a duplex if he'd just gotten the address.

"No one look at that notebook till I've been through it. That's the deal, okay?" Claudia interrupted, looking at Tomás.

The three looked at her with surprise.

"Second," Jaime continued as if he hadn't even heard her, "Amelia's right: we need to find out who Bonso's boss is, if he has one, or someone who has influence over him, and we can't do that without the authorities. But I can get hold of whatever they have in their records in less than an hour." Jaime already had the information in his files, but he wasn't going to mention that yet. "Third, these trafficking and prostitution networks can't function without police and politicians shielding them. Before we start talking to government employees, we need to figure out which office is protecting this group in particular. That could be the key for negotiating with this bastard."

"And how do we find his protector?" Claudia asked.

"Give me a few hours," Jaime responded. "I already know who I need to talk to."

"Now that I think of it, I've got someone who might know as well. Or, should I say, Amelia does," Tomás said, looking at her with a complicit smile.

Amelia looked back undecided for a few moments, and then her face lit up.

"Of course! Madame might know . . . "

Before she could go on, Jaime put up his hand and told them to be silent as he stood and raised his telephone to his ear.

"There have been shots fired at Rina's. They're reporting deaths, we don't know who."

23

Milena

HIS INSTRUCTIONS WERE to watch and wait, watch and wait. Watching was fine for him, waiting not so much. Julián Huerta had been working as a field detective for Lemlock for ten months, and his assignments fascinated him: rooting around in other people's lives, following them around without getting noticed, opening envelopes sent to others and closing them again without a trace, going into apartments and looking through hidden photos and medicine cabinets. Finding a hiding place—and everybody had one—gave him immense pleasure. Since he was a kid, he'd spied on his girl cousins and friends in the shower or their bedroom, through half-closed curtains or old keyholes; it wasn't just the furtive sight of prohibited flesh, but also sharing the intimacy a person believed was hers and hers alone.

But surveilling Marina Alcántara's apartment had lasted more than eight hours and was boring him to death. At nine in the morning, he relieved a colleague who had kept guard all night. Both their reports would be exactly the same: Milena, the tall girl with black hair who occasionally glanced out the window, hadn't left the house she'd been in since the night before. They had orders not to intervene, but they were also not to lose sight of the girl if she left. The redhead and her guards had left almost an hour before, and inside, the house looked calm. But for the past few minutes, he had seen the occasional movement through the window; the woman was doing dance steps or something. Through the lenses of Huerta's small, powerful binoculars he saw the outline of the tall, pretty foreigner appearing and disappearing between the slit in the curtains. He felt tempted. He would just go to the tiny backyard, he thought, peep through the window, and watch her at his leisure. When he tried to turn off the ringtones and alerts on his phone, he saw the battery had gone dead.

Huerta was silently opening the gate to the yard when the rash braking of a car made him turn. Two men got out of a gray sedan driven by a third. They looked like police, marshals, or something like that—every possibility he imagined was worse than the one before. But he didn't back down. He didn't have the build for physical confrontation, but he had always been able to rely on his mouth.

"Hey there, gentlemen," he said, as if he was lost. "You don't know where the Martínez Nieto family lives, do you?" he asked, pointing at the other half of the duplex.

That might have been enough to save him if another vehicle hadn't screeched to a halt just then. Two of his colleagues from Lemlock, but he wasn't sure whether that was good or bad news. It was very bad, as he discovered two seconds later.

His two colleagues got out with their guns in their hands. One of the cops tried to pull his own while he turned to face them and was shot down; the other jumped behind Huerta and fired at the new arrivals. A human shield held fast by his captor's arm, all Huerta could do was play spectator to his own death: in the foreground, the tattooed knuckles and a diamond-crusted bracelet were in his face; further off, the thug who drove the sedan took down one of Jaime's men. The shooting lasted no more than a minute.

When the gunfight was over, Milena peeked out the window. She ran out to the yard armed with a leftover board from the shelf that had just been set up in the kitchen and a large bag looped over her arm. Only two men were still alive: a dark-skinned guy with tattooed forearms, drowning in his own blood, and another in a suit and tie sitting on the ground, looking stunned at a hole in his abdomen, his back leaned against a truck. She recognized the first guy, one of the cops on Bonso's payroll. Without thinking twice, she hit him in the head with the board; it didn't do much damage, but it made her feel better. Then she glanced at the elegant man bleeding out in front of her, unsure whether she should thank him or strike him as well. She threw the plank down and walked off quickly.

Julián Huerta had fallen victim to the first bullets. He was face-down on the pavement, his eyes wide open as if he hadn't wanted to miss a single detail of the spectacle he'd witnessed.

24

Amelia

THE LONG TRIP to Madame Duclau's home, prolonged by the dense rush-hour traffic, gave Amelia time to deal with the most-pressing issues at the office, even if it was only over the phone. Irreconcilable divisions on the left and the government's growing authoritarianism stripped her of any enthusiasm she might have felt for her political duties. She would have preferred to use the institutional resources she had at hand to help resolve the crisis Tomás was facing with his new responsibilities. The kidnapping of the opinion editor put her partner at risk if hostilities escalated. If something ever happened to Tomás, she would never forgive herself for stepping back just to show due respect to his job. Under normal conditions, she'd already have mobilized the police squads at her beck and call, but they still didn't know the identity of Bonso's protectors. On that point, Jaime was right. And then, she didn't want to get mixed up in Claudia's business, either. She needed to avoid taking too big a role in anything that might be seen as a territorial dispute around Tomás. The thought made her sad.

She knew Tomás well enough to know he and Claudia weren't lovers yet. But they might be soon.

Amelia asked herself what she would do when that happened. She had been in a relationship with her childhood friend for a year now, and they had gotten used to the shared weekends, the daily emails and WhatsApp messages, and the trips together when their schedules permitted it. But more than the time, what Amelia appreciated was the emotional security Tomás had given her. They knew each other so well and had for so long that being together was never an effort. "Sleeping with you is being alone twice over," Fito those had complained in his song "When It Rains, It Pours." For her, those would have been words of praise. Being alone was something she'd always liked, and even if she had enjoyed living with some of her boyfriends in the past, it was a struggle to make room for them. With Tomás, it was the complete opposite: being with him was like being alone, but with someone else, and that was the best feeling of all. There was no effort, no tension: they shared what they had, and both had room for the penchants and phobias the other had accumulated over four decades of life.

Tomás's recent celebrity, first as columnist and now as director of *El Mundo*, made the relationship more manageable, despite her prominence on the national stage. Few men were capable of dealing with a girlfriend who got recognized everywhere she went, chatted up in restaurants, and waved at in the streets. She wasn't sure Tomás would have handled it so well a year before. But something had changed. He didn't have the same profile as a party leader, but he knew he was still as important as her in the circles that mattered.

Now everything was at risk. Amelia asked herself what she would do if Tomás and Claudia got together. She knew Tomás loved her, but she was also aware of his emotional insecurity and his tendency toward promiscuity. Claudia gave off the aroma of recently tilled, damp black earth, of savage nature bursting with life, and it would be hard for her lover to resist burying his hands in it and covering his body. Tomás wouldn't be able to resist the call of a woman as powerful as the redhead now was.

This conclusion jabbed at her entrails, like a fist squeezing the organs and viscera just past her bellybutton. She told herself she'd never been jealous and wasn't about to start at forty-three years of age. She'd rather give him up than sniff his lapels or prick up her ears every time he picked up the phone.

Arriving at Madame Marie Duclau's home cut her miserable reflections short. The old woman was waiting in the doorway, elegant and covered in jewels. She greeted her with four kisses, two on each cheek. It had been years since Amelia had seen her, but she seemed identical, in body and soul, to the person she had met long ago. The woman was at least a decade older than her mother, who had been her close friend, but nothing in her face or her graceful posture betrayed her seventy-plus years: a happy mix of good genes and better surgeries had left her in a chronological limbo that was difficult to pin down.

"Amelita, what a pleasure to see you."

"The pleasure's mine, Madame Marie."

"Remember: just Marie. Don't make me feel like a grandmother, I'm younger than your mother," her hostess lied with a smile. "And by the way, how is Dolores? And your father? What's his story?"

"Mama is happy, she's still living in Cuernavaca, almost retired, though she keeps up a few therapy sessions. My father went to Miami, the truth is I don't see him much. Far as I know, he's good."

"Yeah, all that's so sad. I never understood why Dolores lasted so long with that man. From the day I met him, I knew he was a faggot, and I told your mother as much. I guess the job gives you a sense for those things."

Amelia's brow furrowed, Marie Duclau didn't apologize. She never did anymore: privileges of age.

"The important thing is you're a grown woman now: as beautiful as your mother, but with more presence, more élan. That's what you need to survive in the jungle with the rich and powerful, believe you me!"

"Exactly, Marie, that's just what I wanted to talk to you about; maybe you can help me." Amelia told her all the details of Milena's case.

The only thing real about Madame Marie Duclau was the "Madame" part: she wasn't French, and the last name she'd picked up from a very brief marriage. For decades, she'd been the unofficial director of public relations for various governmental offices, though she didn't have a business per se; she worked as a private consultant for ministers, governors, and bigwigs in the public sector. She'd suggest changes in their image and wardrobe, she'd spruce up the consorts of newly ascendant functionaries or people running for office, she brought in specialists in oratory and diction, and she'd been English teacher to more than one guest at Los Pinos. Her services were appreciated because she guaranteed absolute discretion. Her job, she always said, was to do a cultural and social upgrade on the politicians who hired her. But her real money came from something far darker.

Madame Duclau understood very well that power and sex were necessarily linked. All the brand-new governors and ministers soon tired of the limitless resources and the indulgences and trifles they could permit themselves, being above the law; power only makes sense if it's exercised, and few uses of it were as tangible as getting access to women who were formerly unavailable.

The euphoria and the need for stimulus invariably led to their libidos running wild. Career politicians tended to work out that issue by hiring secretaries and consultants to accompany them on their rises to the top, but that wasn't the case with the young men who had arrived into power recently. The revolving door at the top during the twelve years the PAN ran the show had made way for a sudden wave of men between thirty and forty years of age who seemed to exude hormones with every decision they took. It was known that in the cabinet of Felipe Calderón, the former president, made up of young men who had been stuffed shirts in the public administration before then, extramarital hijinks became an obsession. Many of the guys ended their traditional marriages to their old girlfriends from university and hooked up with women fifteen or twenty years younger, some of them from the art world.

Madame had evolved a strategy to resolve these difficulties with a maximum of discretion and damage control. Thanks to her close contacts with the big escort services, places quiet as churches, if rather less pious, she was able to supply companions for any occasion. She had a keen instinct for finding the right lover for each leader, whether it was for a night or six years in office. The girls liked having a long-term contract and the politicians convinced themselves the women's expressions of affection were genuine, preferring to ignore that it had all been arranged behind their backs. And Madame Duclau charged exorbitant sums for her work as an image and event consultant.

Amelia told the old woman the reason for her visit and that the clock was ticking for Emiliano. After listening to the story, the hostess maintained a long silence, never taking her eyes off a silver bracelet she turned around and around on her cadaverously thin wrist; the coloring of her hands didn't hide her age. Amelia imagined Madame Duclau was debating whether to help her in the name of their old friendship or maintain her policy of discretion in business matters.

She and Amelia's mother had become friends two decades before, when Marie was looking for a psychologist who specialized in disorders of the libido. A governor with aspirations to become president was suffering from a serious case of sex addiction that led him to flirt with every beauty who crossed his path. A businessman and a congressman had taken offense to the man's harassment of their wife and daughter, and were ready to ruin the politician's promising career. He never made it to the presidency, but he managed to stay off the front pages of the gossip rags thanks to Dolores's therapy. From then on, Madame Marie conferred with the psychologist regularly, and later cultivated a personal relationship with her. Amelia never completely accepted the counterfeit Frenchwoman because she had a sense, from the beginning, of her real profession, but she ended up appreciating that peculiar friendship Marie and her mother shared. And Amelia herself had to recognize that more than once, she was happy to find Madame Duclau visiting her parents' house. She liked her casual cynicism and her impudent judgments on the human race. She also knew the woman discouraged the more savage and violent forms of prostitution of the kind Milena had fallen into.

"Of course I know who Bonso is," the hostess told her. "A real bad egg. He showed up at the beginning of the year with a group of blondes from Eastern Europe. Someone from immigration services keeps him under their wing. I'd be willing to bet it's Marcelo Galván, a lifelong area chief, corrupt, powerful, who helps out these trafficking rings."

Amelia repeated the name in her mind over and over to keep from forgetting it without taking her eyes off Marie. She didn't want to write it down and make Marie uncomfortable.

"I had to deal with Bonso for a director from Pemex who was obsessed with having a Natasha all to himself," her hostess continued. "I looked over the Romanian's portfolio and there were three or four that interested me and the guy was drooling, you know? They all want to get in my good graces."

"Do you think Milena could be one of them? If I bring you a photo, could you pick her out?"

"I don't know, I doubt it. That was a few months back and the photos are usually too touched-up," her host said, "but I do remember

155

one thing: when he found out I was looking to set up a Natasha in a long-term arrangement, he pulled out one of the photos. More from curiosity than any real interest, I insisted on that one and he got pissy and stubborn and said that one was out of commission. I don't like them trying to push me around, so I asked, was he hiding something, was the chick ill or dangerous. Then he started freaking out because in this business, you're doomed if word gets around among the high-level types that a girl represents any kind of risk. So he explains to me hesitantly that this girl has been reserved for a very big fish from the time she was in Europe, and he has instructions not to let anything happen to her and never to let her out of his sight. That's why she could only do nights and wasn't available for any long-term arrangement."

"He didn't tell you where in Europe, or who this big fish was?"

"No, honey. I just asked whether the girl was violent or a trouble-maker and if that was why he was being shy about her. He said she was the very opposite: all she ever did was read and write. 'A goddamned enlightened whore, that's what she is,' he said to me."

"That's her," Amelia said. "Her name's Milena."

Minutes later, she got in her car and called Jaime Lemus.

"It's Marcelo Galván. We'll meet back up at the newspaper."

Then she dialed Rina's number, but didn't get an answer. The girl had also disappeared after the shootout at her home. Vidal had told her Rina had been with Luis at the doctor's office when all the killing took place, and that was a relief, but she hadn't answered her phone since. Amelia trusted she had taken refuge with one of her relatives. Despite what Jaime had said, she decided she would investigate with the help of her own sources and see if that didn't clear things up.

25

Milena

SHE HAD WALKED ALL AFTERNOON without being able to take a decision, not because she was weighing various options, but because she felt she didn't have any. First she rambled without any set direction, trying to escape the scene she'd just witnessed. Then, when she realized she was headed into Paseo de la Reforma, where there would be people everywhere, she ducked into a side street. She ended up sitting in a Chinese café close to the wax museum in Colonía Juárez. The recollection of the man in the dark suit leaning against the truck and bleeding out tormented her: he had gone there to protect her from Bonso's thugs and now he might be dead. She asked herself how many bodies would have to pile up before she would be free, or before she was murdered as well.

When she saw the façade of the Wax Museum, she remembered the taut figures of the people inside and told herself that all of them had passed through moments as dramatic, or more, than those she was living through now. Rosendo Franco had taken her there once to walk through the narrow hallways smelling of naphthalene and lined with sculptures in exaggerated attire. "Look at them, all tranquil there, with the tragedies and deaths the bastards have behind them," he had said then. And with that memory, she was filled with envy for the dolls' beatific attitude. She'd like to be that way, like them, *all tranquil there.*

Discouragement hung around her neck like a millstone. Lead in her veins and cement in her joints, or maybe the soulless wax of the figures she had envied moments before. She told herself her life was pointless, with nothing to hope for and nothing to enjoy, a source of misfortune for those around her. Then she made a resolution: that night, she was going to die. That was the only way to keep her family safe. With regret, she remembered Rina, the only person, perhaps, who would lament her death, even if they barely knew each other. Or maybe that was it: Rina liked her because she didn't really know her. The idea weighed down on her chest. She consoled herself with the thought that her disappearance would save the two young people: if they had been home that afternoon, they might already be dead.

She saw herself captured by a security camera at the moment she threw herself in front of the metro, and she found the image calming. There was nothing dramatic, just her body vanishing from the scene. Before she threw herself on the tracks, she would carefully place a briefcase on the ground.

The image made Milena smile. She opened her bag and took out the thick hardbound notebook. It had been with her since her arrival in Mexico and she had managed to hold onto it thanks to the decoys she passed off to her jailors: sheaves of nonsense she pretended to conceal in false hiding places. But this notebook she had never given them. It would be her legacy and her penance. She imagined the book's cover: *Tales of the XY Chromosome*, or maybe just *Them*, signed by "Milena, the whore who writes." Or maybe it would never become a book, but she at least trusted that the press would spread some of her tales around to scandalize and ridicule her most celebrated clients. She imagined the bishop with the milky skin fleeing southern Spain, the one who always blessed her after begging her to spank his chubby ass. She remembered the corrupt senator whose dick was getting hard and shooting his load while he recited articles of the Constitution from memory. She thought of the fifty-odd entries in her notebook and told herself that at least her death wouldn't be in vain.

She had two boxes to check off before her date with the subway. She asked the waitress when the station closed and figured she could get everything done that night if she rushed. As so often in her life, she turned to writing, like a meeting point marked on a map, the place she returned to every time she got lost.

The television wedged into a corner in the café distracted her. Any mention of Ukraine inevitably called her attention after so many years spent with Russian and Ukrainian clients in Marbella. In the course of recent months, when she was living with Rosendo Franco, she had read the issues of *El Mundo* he brought to the apartment, had followed the crisis in Ukraine, and had often asked herself which of the two factions of Ukrainians controlling the market in Marbella would end up benefiting from the situation. She knew the leaders of both. Ukraine was coming apart in a political and military struggle that pitted the population of Russian origin and those who defended Ukrainian national values and were looking westward. Both had their representatives in Marbella.

The newscaster translated Putin's call to restore "the glorious past of Mother Russia" into Spanish. Red-faced, the Muscovite leader riled up the crowd, and they lifted their fists in the air. "We will not abandon the Russians now living in Ukraine," the Mexican journalist repeated, with indignation and irony. The words of the Kremlin chief resounded in Milena's mind. She remembered parties in Marbella where she'd heard similar slogans from other Russo-Ukrainians. Normally, it was just boastfulness brought on by alcohol. Amid the clinking of glasses, one group would say to the other that the Russian community in Marbella should play a more active role in supporting the motherland. But not everything was the result of drunken effusion: more than once, she had seen guys in from Moscow exchanging names and numbers and making plans to tighten links between Kremlin politicians and the Russian mafia on the Costa del Sol.

It was a long time since she'd thought about all that. Reflexively, she placed her fingertips on the lining of her black book, but she didn't dare remove what she had put there months before. At first, she had been convinced that Bonso was the one chasing her down, obsessed with putting her back to work in the brothels. But the destruction of the walls and furniture everywhere he passed through and the things she had just heard indicated another motive: the explosive information her book contained.

26

Jaime and Vidal

WEDNESDAY, NOVEMBER 12, 9:20 P.M.

LIKE ALL THE LEMLOCK EMPLOYEES, Patricia Mendiola was working against the clock. Two hours before, Jaime had handed out assignments and set a meeting to review the results at 9:20 in the evening. Throughout the afternoon, all of them had worked at a vertiginous rhythm, still shaken by the shootout that had taken the lives of two of their colleagues and left a third in a coma. She herself had recruited the kindhearted Julián Huerta, a harmless peeping tom, even if he had a creepy of looking at her legs when she crossed them in his presence.

She had worked for hours putting together a profile of Bonso's gang, but she didn't know the identity of whoever was protecting him, and that was what mattered to Jaime most. Ten minutes before, he had called her office elated to tell her it was Marcelo Galván, a government worker in the immigration services. He had been one of her prospects, but she wasn't sure enough to put him into the report. With his name, she could have sketched out a clearer profile.

Shortly afterward, Lemus himself got the meeting started with the coordinators of the different departments. Patricia was surprised to see Vidal, Jaime's nephew, there.

Ezequiel Carrasco, an ex-commandant in the Federal Security Directorate, gave an account of the operation their colleagues had died in. They ran into three active-duty cops, apparently on Bonso's payroll. The gunmen formed part of the brigade assigned to Mexico City International Airport.

The coordinator of overseas operations, Esteban Porter, an ex-director at Interpol, offered additional data about Milena's background. She was born Alka Moritz in 1988. His former colleagues traced her to Spain starting in 2005, when she was seventeen years old. Every trace of her vanished thereafter, until she showed up in Mexico this past January 23. Not much was known about her long stay on the Spanish coast, but he was hoping to get better info in the next twenty-four hours: following Jaime's instructions, Porter had offered a small fortune to informants connected to the Spanish police and security services to try and figure out what had made them take the girl from the Iberian peninsula.

Mauricio Romo, coordinator of the company's team of hackers, described the security network set up to try and find Milena. They'd hacked into the public network of security cameras in the Mexico City metropolitan area, which included the streets and plazas and the metro and other modes of public transport. They'd tapped the phones of everyone who had any relationship with the Croatian: the Blues, Rina, Claudia, and their closest friends and relatives. Through Facebook, they'd gotten the email addresses of Leon and various members of Milena's family; a translator from Spain was already working with them and would be ready in case the girl sent any messages to her family in her language.

Finally, Patricia spoke. She gave a profile of Bonso and his protector, Marcelo Galván. He was a man with ties to the old political class and second in command of immigration services. But even he seemed to be a mere underling. He was part of a huge trafficking ring that supplied numerous markets: sexual exploitation, labor for plantations in Central

America, processing services for Asians looking to immigrate to the United States. It had the backing of a diverse group of businessmen with close ties to governors and politicians: the businessmen funded their campaigns, and they shared in the benefits of human trafficking. Patricia didn't dismiss the possibility that Bonso himself had gotten the ear of some of these politicians after providing them with female.

Patricia told the group she had gotten hold of the address of a brothel the Romanian owned and had it under surveillance, but she doubted it was the only one.

Jaime made notes while his coworkers continued with their presentations. Then he asked for a few concrete details—the address of the immigration chief, the names of Milena's family members—and laid out the steps they would need to follow in each phase of the investigation. He asked Patricia and the hackers to concentrate for the time being on the figure from immigration: his routines, his family, bank accounts, properties, friends and enemies, bad habits, and quirks.

"Whatever you find out, I want it by eleven tonight."

He dismissed them and stayed behind with Vidal.

"The upcoming hours are decisive. We have to find Milena before Bonso, or else we'll never see her again. Either they'll kill her or they'll ship her off to another country. Emiliano's life depends on it, too. He'll stay alive as long as Bonso doesn't have what he wants."

"You don't have to tell me that, Jaime," Vidal said, offended.

"I'm telling you so you don't hesitate if the ball ends up in your court. It's always possible Milena will turn to Luis and Rina. They seem to be the only ones she trusts."

"Maybe you're right," the boy said.

"And if I am, you know your friends will be in mortal danger, right? You already saw what happened at Rina's place. Their life will be in your hands."

"What do you mean?"

"You have to keep on both of them so you'll be the first one to know if Milena manages to reach them. That will allow us to rescue her right away. Otherwise the two of them will try and hide her and they could well end up as Bonso's next victims. *Capisci?*"

"What do I do?"

"You're already tracking Rina and Luis via GPS on your cell phone. Find a reason to meet with them and don't let them out of your sight. Remember, it's for both their good."

Minutes later, a chauffeured company car was wheeling him down the Avenida Insurgentes. He couldn't pick up Rina's cell-phone signal, but a red dot gave evidence of Luis's trajectory a few miles ahead.

Vidal felt better now. It seemed to him he was part of something strong, able to make a difference in the lives of others, of his friends. Luis and Rina thought they were invulnerable, but they had no idea of the danger they were facing. He would rescue them and get them to safety, no matter how they'd hurt him the night before.

The scene of a thankful and indebted Rina that played out in his mind was interrupted when he saw that the red dot hadn't moved for the past few minutes. It was stationary somewhere in Colonía Juárez. That's where he headed.

27

Tomás and Claudia

WEDNESDAY, NOVEMBER 12, 9:50 P.M.

TOMÁS PACED BACK AND FORTH like a prisoner in his cell. Claudia followed him with her eyes; she was too tired even to get up. To her, the last twenty-four hours felt like a long stretch of days, even geologic eras. Beside her was Emiliano's file from human resources. After flipping through it, she'd consulted the opinion editor's Facebook page. They were the same age, and his hobbies and tastes made her think they could have been close. She felt the possibility of his death on her shoulders.

"Don't go, I don't want to stay here alone," Tomás had asked her when Amelia and Jaime left on their respective missions.

Tomás called Guerra, the deputy director, and told him to take over editing. No one else at the newspaper knew about Emiliano's kidnapping, not even his family. They had no idea how to ease their anxiety before eleven, when the group would meet again, an hour before Bonso threatened to execute his prisoner.

Tomás examined the available options over and over. He had the feeling that he was forgetting something.

Claudia got up from the sofa to make her third espresso of the night. Days before, she had set up a capsule machine next to her father's desk to avoid having to ask her secretary for a service she considered personal. Or at least, that was how Tomás saw it.

He felt bad for her. Barely a week ago, as far as he could tell, her biggest problem had been finding a way to make up with her husband, or maybe to put an end to a marriage without children and without hope. He contemplated her back, a little less rigid than usual. A wave of affection made him cross the three yards between them. He hugged her from behind, putting his hands on her biceps and his chin on her shoulder. He whispered in her ear.

"Relax. You're doing a good job."

She didn't respond, she couldn't have. It felt like a ping-pong ball was swelling in her throat, and her eyes moistened as quickly as an ice cube melts in a hand.

They stayed motionless for a moment and then she did something he found strange and unexpected, when he looked back on it later. She pushed her behind into his crotch. He wrapped his arms around her waist. He turned his head and rested his cheek on one of her shoulder blades. They held the position until she felt Tomás's erection and made a slight movement to accommodate him. He squeezed her tighter.

No buttons were fumbled with, no zippers pulled down. No hands stroked torsos or ran through hair; there were no moans or heightened breathing. She just wanted to keep from falling apart, and was thankful for the feeling of relief that Tomás's embrace gave her, the feeling of being held in one piece. In contrast, every cell and neuron in his body was concentrated in the swollen and compact tip of his member, and though she kept pressing harder and harder against his abdomen, intuition told him this wasn't a burst of passion they were experiencing.

The sound of his telephone interrupted their embrace. He pulled away and brought the receiver to his ear. She straightened up and added powdered creamer to her coffee.

"It was Jaime, he says he has the information we need. He's coming here and he wants to push the meeting ahead as much as we can. I'll call Amelia to see if she's talked to her French friend."

Tomás and Claudia spent the next forty minutes talking over issues at the newspaper, both of them peering into the screens: hers was a huge desktop, his was a tablet that was never far from his reach. At 10:35, the meeting started.

Jaime and Amelia told the others what they'd found out. Amelia said everything, Jaime kept a few things back. The director of Lemlock told them he'd been able to trace the call Bonso made from Emiliano's phone. Apparently they were on the road at the time, maybe in an armored car or a truck with tinted windows. From then on forward, the phone had been cut off or the battery taken out. Either way, it was impossible to localize.

After going over the information at their disposal, the four of them agreed that the most urgent thing was to get hold of the immigration director, Bonso's only known contact. Amelia doubted the Romanian would execute Emiliano when he said: after the shootout, he must have guessed that they didn't have Milena either. By his logic, she figured, Emiliano would still be useful as a trade for the Croatian in the event that Claudia and her friends found her first.

Though what Amelia said struck them as reasonable, the others didn't feel they could gamble with the deputy director of opinion's life with nothing to go on but a hunch. They decided they should talk with Marcelo Galván, Bonso's protector, before midnight.

"We need a bargaining chip, and if possible, a way to scare him. Otherwise he'll deny any relationship with Bonso. My team is looking for skeletons in his closet. I'll have a report at eleven. I hope we find something. With that, I can go straight to his house or wherever he is."

"I want to go, too. He should know *El Mundo* is prepared to air out any dirty laundry we can find and crucify him publicly," Tomás said.

Jaime suppressed the urge to tell Tomás no. He would have preferred approaching Galván with a couple of tough guys in tow, but he understood that for now, he was still an outsider.

"Where could Milena be?" Claudia said, almost to herself.

"Or better still: Who is she?" Amelia responded. "What did she do to make these guys go crazy chasing her down?" She was still ruminating over Madame Duclau's words: "a fucking enlightened whore."

I go see whores because I love my wife, and thanks to that, we've had four happy years of marriage. Don't think I'm going outside for what I don't get at home. No, sir. I'm lucky enough to be married to a fine-looking lady who's not at all shy when it comes to fulfilling her conjugal duties. In fact, most of the tramps I go to bed with would come out losing if they had to go head to head with my Anita. But what can you do, even a guy who eats filet mignon every day is going to want to go out for tacos once in a while.

The guy who says he prefers monogamy is either lying or something downstairs isn't working right. A healthy monogamous man is nothing more than a frustrated animal, say what he will about it. More than one friend has destroyed his family because he ended up in love, so to speak, with his secretary, when all he really needed was to get off. It's better to deal with your dick's necessities up front than wind up getting your heart involved like a damn jerkoff.

Me anyway, I'm happy. Thanks to my escapades, I've always been faithful to my wife. No lovers, no one-night stands. My thing is just a purifying, detoxifying fuck every two or three weeks with one of the pros I pick out at the bar. Sometimes an elegant foreigner, other times an exotic, dark-skinned chick. I even fucked a mulata before. Variety's the spice of life, as they say. And after my relaxing session, I'm more romantic with my wife than before.

Anyway, let's be real. Who doesn't like to get down and dirty sometimes? How are you going to ask the mother of your children to lick your asshole? Not that I like that, but you get what I'm saying.

To sum things up: if it weren't for whores, I would have cheated on my wife. The only bad thing is that for a while, I only fucked her with my underwear on. I mean, that was six months ago. Now it's not even that. But whatever, who cares, that's what the sluts are for. I don't think it really bothers my wife that we don't have sex anymore. I mean, women are different, right?

J.G., ASSET MANAGER
MEXICAN STOCK EXCHANGE

28

Milena, Luis, and Rina

WEDNESDAY, NOVEMBER 12, 11:15 P.M.

THE IMAGES OF THE WAR in Ukraine on the TV screen still hadn't left her mind. If what she was beginning to suspect was true, the implications were terrible. The people looking for the black book knew the information inside it was also in her brain. They'd have to get rid of her, too. The only way out was to end it all.

Should she wink at the camera before throwing herself on the tracks? What if the station's video system wasn't working? Or somebody on the platform took the notebook before the authorities confiscated it? Or her notes never made it to the newspaper? Maybe no one would find the information about the Russian mob hidden in the notebook, but she was sure they would at least find the stories from *Them*. She remembered the names of the characters who signed her stories. All of them public figures in Spain and Mexico and all had passed through her bed, blathering on with their repugnant justifications for using women.

Sitting in the café those past few hours, she had revised and translated the last two stories. Originally they were in her mother tongue, but she had started to rewrite them in Spanish since she arrived in Mexico. Now all she needed was an introduction, and her work was done. Her stories would be more than just reprisal against the men who had abused her, a final payback from beyond the grave: she also aspired to make them experience some of the pain and humiliation her family had been through. Her last hope was that the recording of her tragic end would turn into a viral video on the Net and arouse more interest in her writings.

That led her to think she needed to do something more than jump onto the tracks to make the filmed finale a breathtaking spectacle. Maybe she should take off her clothes on the platform before calling it quits. She rejected the idea, because showing off her body would inject a sexual element that betrayed the spirit of her notes. It would be better to look straight into the camera, point out the notebook in her hand, and leave it carefully on the platform before leaping in front of the train.

She looked at the cup of hot chocolate in front of her and thought there wasn't much about life she would miss. For the moment, her only tie to the human race was the weary-faced, round-bodied waitress working the night shift. No risk of her being exploited for sex, Milena thought sarcastically. She'd have probably had a better chance at happiness with a body like that, no? She thought about the life she would have led as a farm girl in the hills in her country, probably beaten and abused by some huge, filthy husband. She looked back at the woman with the round, brown face and was filled with tenderness.

She'd given up the idea of going back to Croatia a long time ago. That life was over: for the inhabitants of the village, she'd always be "the whore." Prostitution was the only job she knew, and she didn't have the energy to learn another one. Sadly, she realized that nobody would miss her, either. For her family, she had stopped existing long ago, for Vila-Rojas she was a shameful episode in the past, and for everyone else she knew, she was just merchandise, a piece of meat to be bought and sold. Alka had disappeared a long time ago, and everyone would get alone without Milena just fine. Even more, she herself would get along fine without Milena. Her and the rest of the universe.

"Milena! You scared us!"

Rina and Luis burst into the café. Their expression was genuinely happy. Unable to contain herself, the Mexican hugged her long and hard before sitting at the table.

Milena didn't know how to reconcile her thoughts of death with this display of affection and joy.

"How'd you find me?"

"The cell phone I gave you this afternoon before we said bye, remember? I told you to call us if you had any issues."

Confused, Milena looked in her bag and pulled out the Samsung she had forgotten as soon as she'd taken it from Luis's hand. She lifted it suspiciously, as though it were a dead rat.

"Don't worry, it's recycled," he said, and though she didn't quite understand what he was implying, she supposed it meant it wasn't dangerous.

She looked at the two of them and asked herself how they fit into the story she was making up minutes before. Rina looked at her, relieved. The young people's passion moved her, but the memory of the notebook in front of her convinced her that her plan was the right one.

"Please, forget me. You're in danger just being around me. Don't you know what happened at your house, Rina?"

"I saw an email from Vidal, he told me two people got killed and you had disappeared."

"Look, we can't be together. They found me because of you guys."

"Impossible," Luis said. "I'm using my alternative cell phone and Vidal's the only person I've used it with. It's untraceable."

"Let me go on my own. I'm broken, I'm no good for anything. You both have your whole lives ahead of you."

"How can you say that? We're the same age! Anyway, don't you remember, you've got to teach me to dance Flamenco!" In fact, Milena was three years older than Rina, but they might as well be twin sisters.

Milena looked at the notebook in front of her. Again, she saw the woman struggling to serve the tables, the one she'd considered her last link with humanity only seconds before. Discouragement and fatigue overtook her body when she thought of running on and on like a scared animal waiting for the irrevocable end. Once more, it struck the most reasonable thing was to bring her life to an end. One final act of dignity.

"Do it for me, Milena. Don't leave me alone," Rina said, taking her hand.

Milena was perplexed. Except for Rosendo Franco, who was now dead, no one had spoken to her that way for a long time. The feeling was as strange as it was disturbing. Could this girl she barely knew really feel something for her? Maybe deep down they weren't so different. Rina had lost her entire family, as she had explained to Milena in a rush, and even so, she still had her life ahead of her. Milena had a family, but felt she was at the end of her road.

"You can't stay in a place you don't belong," she finally said to herself.

"It will just be for a bit, until we get the situation under control," Luis interrupted. "Then you can go to your country, or wherever you want. Money's not a problem."

Milena considered Luis's words. How could she tell him the truth was she didn't belong anywhere?

"Well, we can't stay here, we're too exposed. I found a safe spot where we can hide out a few days. We'll keep talking there," Luis said, standing up, and Rina followed him, picking up Milena's purse. More from inertia than faith, the Croatian got up, too, looked at the waitress one last time, and exited the café.

29

Jaime and Tomás

ON THE WAY to Marcelo Galván Espíndola's house, Jaime received the spec sheet his team had put together about the immigration chief. Galván was the most senior employee in his post, and had been area director under four commissioners, so he must have been a reference point for the teams that came and went during the constant back-and-forth in the government that had characterized those years. He represented the power behind the scenes in that office, and it wasn't surprising that he had become a key player in the human-trafficking networks.

The report showed Galván had taken thorough advantage of his strategic post. He had a dozen properties, some in other countries, most in his wife's name, including a large cattle ranch in the north of Mexico. Lemlock had uncovered various bank accounts in his and his adult children's names, but they were still working on the record of deposits and withdrawals.

"It's not much to try to incriminate him or scare him, is it?" Tomás said.

"It's enough if we know how to work it. Leave it to me."

Jaime called Galván from outside his house. "The best thing is to bum-rush him so he doesn't have much time to think," he had told Tomás. It was enough for the former director of Mexico's intelligence services to say it was a delicate matter involving him, better discussed in confidence. He took them to the library of his residence: classical sculptures and colonial paintings, apparently authentic, accompanied their walk down the hall. Galván must have felt very safe not to restrain his ostentation: owning artworks belonging to the country's patrimony was a crime in and of itself.

"Jaime Lemus, Esquire, and Doctor Arizmendi. What can I offer you to drink?"

In reality, Jaime wasn't a lawyer and Tomás didn't have his doctorate, but in Mexican politics, titles were as indispensable as a coat of arms at the Victorian court. They both ignored his invitation.

"Marcelo, I'm sorry to say that one of your protégés is about to murder a deputy director at *El Mundo*. We have the threat on tape. The guy's obviously gone off the rails. If he pulls the trigger, the best you can hope for will be a scandal in the national and international press."

"A scandal, no doubt about it," the official replied cautiously.

"A scandal that will sweep up anyone connected to it. After that, the only thing left for Bonso and his protector to do will be to flee the country or end up in prison."

"Easy, boys," their host said, with no trace of fear. "Life always offers alternatives, particularly to public officials with impeccable records like your humble servant here."

Tomás had to respect Galván's aplomb. To judge by his reactions, they had a long conversation ahead of them. Impatience began to eat at him: the minutes between now and midnight seemed to be slipping between his fingers.

"Let's leave off with the formalities," Tomás interrupted, grabbing the man's robe at the wrist. "We know you're protecting Bonso. If my editor shows up dead, prison is the least of your worries."

"Now why the violence, Don Tomás? I don't know what you're talking about," Galván responded, agitated.

The way he looked at the hand on his wrist showed profound, genuine, and bitter indignation. Tomás hesitated a moment and let him go. The man looked carefully at his wrist and closed and opened his fist.

"The important thing here is that all of us can help each other. We've come as friends," Jaime said, trying to take control again. He thought it would be better to appeal to Galván's interests than to threaten him. "If this Bonso goes through with his threat, the wolves will come out, and they'll chew up everything in their way, regardless of whether they're right or wrong. You know that in these cases, a lot of people end up hurt unnecessarily."

"Lots of people," the man said, and nodded.

"Even people who didn't know him, people in positions of public service that might have brought them into contact with him. Gossips ready to turn these kinds of relationships into a scandal are never in short supply. Here, for example, because it's a Romanian, all the officials who deal with visas and permissions could be affected, even if their only involvement was doing their job."

"A Romanian?" Galván responded.

"A Romanian working in sex trafficking," Tomás said. "All fingers point to Bonso, and you're his protector. Now let's cut the bullshit."

Jaime sighed with resignation, understanding it was time to change strategies. Tomás's impatience made it impossible to play nice.

"Look, Galván, here's the deal: either somebody stops Bonso in the next couple hours or lots of shit is going to go down. *El Mundo* has documents related to your accounts in Canada and Indonesia, the little hotel in Costa Rica where you launder your money, and the six apartments in that tower in Miami in your family's name. That information could go public tomorrow morning. Your career would be over."

Galván went pale, but kept his calm. He paused, his eyes fixated on the tassels of his Persian carpet, then looked up.

"It's just money. Whoever tangles with Bonso on this will end up dead."

"Is it your life you're worried about? You should have told me before," Jaime said. He tapped a few numbers on his phone and walked back down the hallway to open the front door.

"Come in," he said, and an immense man in a black suit, almost as fat as he was tall, entered the house.

They called him Tony Soprano, though the Mexican was taller and heavier. Jaime looked at Tomás perplexed, Galván terrified. That was the usual reaction Tony Soprano got from people.

When his boss gave him the signal, he walked to the middle of the library, the boards creaking beneath his feet, and laid a roll of gray canvas on the desk. He pulled it open to reveal his instruments.

Before Tomás could put the consternation that was already on his face into words, Jaime took him by the arm and led him toward the door.

"It would be better for you to wait outside," he told his friend, and then, turning toward Galván, added in an apologetic tone, "These journalists are softies."

Tomás went out to the street, lit a cigar, and walked along the sidewalk, staying in sight of the chauffeur, who remained behind the wheel of the car that had brought them there. Two men observed him from a black truck fifty feet away. He preferred to think they were his friend's associates.

One part of him hoped the fat guy would tear into that vile functionary inside and get a pass for Emiliano regardless of the cost. But another part compelled him to go back inside and put a stop to what was about to happen. He decided to smoke his cigar and wait.

Ten minutes later, Jaime came out. The fat guy stayed in the house.

"Let's go, there's nothing for us to do here anymore. Go in my car," he said, and waved over the truck with his men inside.

"What? Did you kill him?" Tomás said as soon as he got in his seat.

"Don't be melodramatic. We just had to scare him. It wasn't easy getting him to talk, we had to apply a little pressure. He says he can't do anything about Bonso, that the thing with the Croatian girl is taboo and out of his league. But he fessed up: the gang's protector is Víctor Salgado."

"Salgado? The one who was head of federal prisons?"

"You have no idea, do you?" Jaime said with an ironic smile, and explained.

Salgado was a colonel in the army when the president's office called on him to take charge of the penal system. When he gave up the job, after eleven years, he was the biggest link between the corrupt police chiefs, the army, and organized crime.

"He's the guy the businessmen hire when they get tired of the kidnappings in their area, the consultant a governor calls on when everything else has failed," Jaime said, and Tomás thought he heard a tinge of respect in his tone. "He can bring peace to an area just by selling it to the highest bidder among the cartels. Then he'll turn all the resources of the criminals and the police against the loser. He's the gateway to the darkest part of Mexico. He knows which generals are on the cartels' payrolls, usually because he's the one who put them there."

"So, like you, but on the dark side."

Jaime acted as if he hadn't heard his friend's comment and continued.

"Galván doesn't know why Salgado's after the Croatian, but he's convinced Bonso's just following his orders. He begged me not to get him involved because his life would be in play. But I still made him call. I pushed him to tell Bonso not to kill the journalist because the heat would come down on all of them, but Bonso told him to get fucked."

"So everything's lost."

"Not everything," Jaime said with a smile. "Thanks to that call, I know where Bonso is and who his boss is."

"How does that help us? It's almost midnight. By the time we get there Emiliano's going to be dead."

"No, not at all. Emiliano will remain alive as long as Milena's not in Bonso's hands. Your editor's still worth something if we find the girl. That gives me the time I need to come up with a plan."

Tomás breathed a sigh of relief and stayed quiet a moment. Then he asked, "How's Galván?"

"Where should we drop you, Tomás?"

30

Milena

DECEMBER 2011

THE UNUSUALLY COLD MORNING in Marbella seemed like a promising augur for her escape. Though the atmosphere was dense with a marine humidity unknown in her village, the cool early day reminded her of the frozen winds that whipped between the gravestones in the cemetery she used to thread through on her way to school. The ill-fated teenager who took those walks now made her feel tender nostalgia.

She couldn't allow herself to get depressed, Milena thought. She had 2,200 euros in her bag—tips she hadn't turned in—and the goodwill of someone willing to get her to Madrid. There, she would go to the Croatian embassy and establish her identity somehow, even though she didn't have a passport. Then she would call her family to warn them of reprisal.

Amaury Vives was visiting Marbella with friends on a late vacation to celebrate the end of school. He was one of a half-dozen young graduates from the best business school in Spain who had decided to indulge themselves with two weeks of partying before diving into the professional life that awaited them. They weren't millionaires, but they belonged to that comfortable class for whom the unemployment numbers were just a bit of bad news. Some of them would join the family businesses when their "wild retreat" was over, to use the term they had chosen for their escapade to the Costa del Sol. Their plan included calling the best escort service available: "It's the closest thing to fucking a supermodel," one of them had said.

At twenty-four years old, Amaury had only slept with a professional once before, and he was inevitably timid once they were alone. They were in a bedroom in the mansion in the Nueva Andalucía subdivision that the boys had rented. The excitement and the vague discomfort he felt being with a hooker made him come almost immediately. After that, he was able to relax. Knowing his friends would be a long time with the girls they'd chosen, he spent the next hour chatting with Milena. Behind that beautiful blonde, he'd expected to find a semiliterate farm girl from Eastern Europe, but soon they were speaking to each other in fluent Spanish about the books they had read. That made him interested in Milena's story. At first, she responded to his questions vaguely, but his indignant reaction when he found out how she'd been recruited and what her living conditions were like made her decide to tell him the whole truth. When their talk was over, Amaury promised he would help her run away, and they spent the last bit of time pondering an escape route.

Four days later, they were ready to try. He let his friends return to Madrid on the day they'd planned and extended the booking at the house for another two days. At first, he wanted to get his friends involved, but Milena dissuaded him, fearing one of them would change his mind or, even worse, give them away.

The idea was simple but viable. Amaury rented a car the day before and requested Milena's services in advance. Since it was just one girl, and the house had already hosted a party with lots of them days before, the pimps sent a lone guard, who waited behind the wheel of his car. As soon as the Croatian entered the house, they went to the backyard, jumped the fence that bordered a small hill, and descended until they reached the street where Amaury had parked his rented Renault.

They had been together two hours before her overseer realized she was gone. Amaury had tried to negotiate a longer visit, but that was the usual limit for a single girl unless the client in question was rich and someone they trusted. Still, they assumed it was time enough.

That first hour, Amaury drove as fast as possible up the A7. For the first stretch after passing Marbella, Milena felt the euphoria of escape and the pleasure of observing the unfamiliar countryside. Though Amaury was speeding, infected by the Croatian's excitement, she insisted on having the windows down, drunk on a freedom that had come so cheap. U2 blasted through the car's speakers and her long blonde hair danced in the wind.

Her enthusiasm turned to anxiety when the first two hours were over. She imagined the scene at the abandoned house, the frustrated gestures of the apelike man, the inevitable phone call to Bonso, and the implacable search. She looked at Amaury and asked herself if it hadn't been irresponsible to put a healthy young man with such a promising future at risk. He didn't seem conscious of the danger he was in. Maybe he thought he was just doing his good deed for the day. But she knew an attempted runaway could cost them their lives. He might already have a warrant out for some fabricated offense thanks to the mafia's ties.

Amaury tried to calm her down, and those next three hours, they drove slower to keep from attracting attention. They made it to Madrid at 4:30 a.m., and in the chill of Madrid, so different from the climate of Andalusia, Milena thought she felt once more a promising sign of the life that awaited her when she returned to her country.

She planned to go to the embassy first thing in the morning. Amaury searched for the address on his phone and told her it wasn't far from the house he lived in, next door to his parents. Milena wasn't interested in staying there. She feared her captors had gotten hold of her friend's information and were waiting in his home. She didn't tell Amaury why she refused, to keep him from worrying too much. She just said she'd be more comfortable in a café on Calle Claudio Coello, close to the embassy. He thought it was pushing it to kill the four hours in an empty coffee shop, but he understood she wouldn't necessarily behave rationally after her long captivity. Symbolic as it was, the proximity of the embassy made her feel closer to home.

Melina's intuitions weren't wrong. Before they made it to Jaén, three hours after their departure, Bonso already had the name of the person who had first rented the residence in Marbella, a friend of Amaury's, the one with the biggest credit line. They called him in Madrid that same night, saying a pipe had burst and the neighbors were complaining. The friend said Amaury was the last one at the house and gave them his full name and number.

Bonso's web of contacts fanned out, watching airports and train stations, hotels and public places. When things like this occurred, the different gangs that trafficked in women collaborated to one another's benefit: no one needed someone like Milena breaking the system's rules. At seven in the morning, when the first rental car companies in Málaga opened, an employee found Amaury in their database and sent his address and the make and model of his rented car to one of the cops on the gang's payroll. By eight o'clock, two men were having coffee in a blue truck a hundred feet away from the Vives family home.

Just then, Milena was in the bathroom of the restaurant where they were having churros and chocolate, taking off the skimpy clothes she'd had on and donning a tracksuit Amaury had bought on her instructions the night before. Neither had considered how strange her high heels would look with the informal clothes she was now wearing. She assured him it didn't matter. She wasn't planning to stroll through Madrid those next few hours.

At nine, Amaury stopped the rental car in front of 78 Calle de Claudio Coello, a beautiful, majestic building of several floors. Milena looked around suspiciously, but no one seemed to pay attention to the Renault or its occupants. Amaury made fun of his friend's worries and invited her to dinner that night. She shook her head, nervous about the long goodbye, and promised to call that evening. She got out of the car. The five yards that lay between her and the guard watching over the entrance seemed endless, but she saw none of Bonso's men. In deliberately rudimentary Spanish, she told the guard she was a tourist who had lost her passport and needed to talk to an employee of the embassy.

Five minutes later, she was seated in front of the ambassador's secretary. They made her wait more than half an hour, but she wasn't in a rush. All her fears vanished when she saw the Croatian landscapes adorning the walls. She assumed that from a legal standpoint, she was already home, and that was the only thing that mattered. A while later, an official had to tap her on the shoulder to rouse her from the stupor she had fallen into. The words he uttered were music to her ears: the first words in her language she'd heard in years. Introducing himself as an assistant to the ambassador, the man led her into a small office. It took her more than an hour to tell her story.

The official listened attentively, at times interrupting the narration to clarify a date or confusing detail. Occasionally, he noted something down in a small journal he would take from his pocket and then put back. Finally, he asked her to wait in his office while he started the process of getting her a provisional passport. Establishing her identity as a Croatian citizen was the first step before they could offer her consular assistance. She insisted on calling her family to warn them of the danger they were in, but the man was firm about which priorities came first.

Forty minutes later, he returned with a report in his hand. He didn't open it. He'd talked with the police, he said, and had gotten in touch with the special unit in charge of human trafficking: a car would come for her in fifteen minutes and drive her to the station to take down a report. Milena was scared, and she said all that mattered to her was getting back to her country. She didn't want anything to do with Spanish authorities or the police. She urged him to call her family to let them know the danger they were in, but he stated that only the ambassador could authorize long-distance calls and refused to allow her use of his personal phone for a non-official call.

He told her that going to Zagreb on her own would do nothing. If what she said was true, these were European mafias active in several countries. She would be captured again, maybe even killed, along with her family, as a punishment for escaping. The only solution was to collaborate with the police so Bonso's gang could be taken down. He told her the embassy closed at five p.m. and she would have to leave the building anyway. It was best to go now, when the police could protect her. Then he assured her an employee from the embassy would get in touch later to give her an envelope with cash and the reservation details for a hotel room. That was standard procedure for nationals stranded without a passport or resources.

At 12:15, he said the detectives were waiting outside in their car. He walked her out himself, saying he would try and visit in a few hours and giving her a hug goodbye. Resigned, Milena got into the car where three people were waiting for her. As soon as it started moving, she looked at her companion in the back seat, and a chill ran up her spine: though she didn't have a clear idea of how a Spanish detective should look, it was almost definitely nothing like the man sitting beside her.

There was no need to drug her during the two hours they took to return to Marbella: she had broken down completely. Like a ragdoll, her head thrown back in her seat, she watched the clouds pass and asked herself if this would be the last time she saw the blue sky of southern Spain, the one thing she might miss from the life she'd spent there.

Bonso was waiting for her in the house Milena had lived in with fourteen other girls. She assumed the first thing would be a long interrogation about her escape. Then she saw there wouldn't be a prelude: they took her straight to what seemed to be a stage set for her punishment. The report by the embassy official must have made any examination unnecessary.

Bonso was accompanied by three thugs and two huge dogs on leashes. He was short, almost a midget, but still, the scene was terrifying. The gang had dogs trained to offer bestiality shows for tourists. For that, they usually used the women the clients didn't go for anymore. But the dogs were also a tool to terrorize the women. They might also be there to tear her apart. For the traffickers, nothing was worse than a runaway snitching to international authorities, because the girls knew all their methods and all their customers. The mafiosos would rather lose the investment a working girl like Milena represented than look weak in the eyes of the rest of the women and run the risk that more of them would try the same.

The presence of one of the women who had sex with the animals confirmed her worst fears. She must have been there to prepare the beasts, a Rottweiler and a German Shepherd. The long sheets of plastic stretched out on the floor of the room left no doubt that it would end in bloodshed. She saw the excitement of the bodyguards, who were used to all sorts of excesses.

Bonso made a gesture, and one of the men approached Milena and started taking off her clothes. She tried briefly to resist, but then thought that the sooner it was over, the better. Naked and trembling, she waited for the dogs to come over. Bonso got what he'd wanted: the girls' faces were filled with terror.

Thudding sounds at the front door froze the scene. One of the guards looked through the peephole and told his boss Torsi was there. Torsi was a key link between businessmen and the administration in Marbella and one of the city's biggest customers for high-class hookers. Bonso nodded and three men entered: Torsi, a six-foot, five-inch black assistant, and Vila-Rojas. Everyone was surprised to see him. He wasn't someone who liked to spend too much time in the port city's underworld, and he was careful with his image.

He saw Milena naked in the middle of the room, then the dogs and the plastic sheets, and looked at Bonso.

"What's going on here?"

"Nothing, just a little disciplinary discussion with one of the girls so she learns to obey the house rules. Isn't that right, dear?" Bonso said, turning to the Croatian.

She closed her eyes to show her assent.

"Is there somewhere we could talk?" Vila-Rojas asked.

Bonso pointed to his office door and started walking in that direction. Vila-Rojas followed, motioning for his companions to stay put. Twenty minutes later, both men emerged, and the visitors left the house without uttering a word. On his way out, Vila-Rojas shot a quick glance at Milena, who had covered herself with a sheet and was sitting among the other girls. Dogs, thugs, and hookers were in the same position they'd been left in.

"Everyone to your room," Bonso commanded. "You know now what will happen if you break any rules. And you," he said to Milena, full of hate and frustration, "you would have preferred punishment to what you've got coming to you."

Then he went back in his office, opened a false panel in the air conditioner embedded in the wall, took out a video camera, and made sure that his conversation with Vila-Rojas had been recorded, as all the sessions in his office were. He grabbed the envelope of cash Vila-Rojas had left on his desk and deposited it in his safe.

31

Claudia and Tomás

THURSDAY, NOVEMBER 13, 8:35 A.M.

HE DRANK HIS WATER in an obscene, almost animal-like way. Months ago, Claudia had changed out the clear glasses in the kitchen for thicker ones to keep from having to see her husband's gaping mouth. But she still found it indecent how he brought the glass up to his lips, as if they were burned.

When do you stop loving someone? At what moment do those little details that seemed curious and charming turn into irritating manias? When did her husband's absurd bedtime ritual become intolerable to her? When did the long silences between them stop being bubbles of intimacy and become interludes of hostility?

There was nothing alive between them anymore that could hold a man and a woman together. She knew that sooner or later they would have to face up to the failure of their marriage, but that wouldn't be now. There were too many uncertainties in the air after her father's death and her new responsibilities at the newspaper. For now, all she wanted was for her husband to go to work. Tomás would be there any minute to talk about his visit to Galván's the night before, and she hadn't even told her husband one of the deputy directors from *El Mundo* had been kidnapped.

Alejandro mentioned plans for the weekend, and she tried to ignore him, looking at the open copy of *El Mundo* on the table instead.

Any remark from her would drag things out. Still, he didn't seem to be in a rush. He painstakingly pulled the crust from a slice of supermarket bread, a quirk that she found better suited to a picky teenager than a professional executive. The butler announced Tomás's arrival, and Alejandro got up to receive him, but Claudia cut him short.

"Don't get up, I'll see him on the terrace. There's some delicate business we have to discuss. And don't wait up for me tonight. I'll probably be late."

Tomás greeted her with an almost-fraternal affection, as far as possible from the fantasies Claudia had experienced that morning in the shower. They sat down at a heavy wood table on a balcony looking down over the crowns of the trees in the Chapultepec Forest.

He told her about Víctor Salgado and brought her more or less up to date on the adversary they were up against.

"Another way to find Milena is to figure out what the hell Salgado's up to here," she mused. "He seems like too big a fish to take a personal interest in an immigrant prostitute, unless he was in love with her, too."

"I doubt it. If so, he would never have let her go with your father."

"I guess Emiliano's kidnapping was his doing, but it's hard for me to believe he's willing to go against us on this, knowing all we could come back at him with," she said. "But then, what can we unleash, really? By the way, when are we having lunch with the president?"

"Monday. For better or worse, I don't know whether this thing with Emiliano will be wrapped up in the next four days."

Both of them fell silent. The image of a grieving woman flashed through Claudia's mind—her head covered with a black kerchief, a victim of Pinochet's repression. That was her notion of what a Chilean widow looked like.

"I'm asking myself if my father ever found out Salgado was who he was up against. The emails with Milena don't mention him, they just talk about threats she was receiving, and he seemed to think he could neutralize them."

"Even Salgado wouldn't cross Don Rosendo, and that has to mean something. If we show that motherfucker that the power your father had is still intact, I'm sure we can negotiate from a better position."

Claudia nodded.

"Jaime says he can find a good go-between to deal with Salgado," Tomás continued.

"And you trust him? Jaime? We won't have to pay for it later?"

Tomás recalled it was the second time Claudia had asked him that question.

"I think we need to use every resource at our disposal, and if there's a price to pay, we'll worry about it later, no?"

Still, the question gave Tomás pause. Resorting to Jaime, there was nothing, or everything, to fear.

"Jaime should be at the newspaper by now. We agreed to meet at ten to decide what course of action to take. Amelia will drop in, too, even if it's only for a moment; she has a business meeting later."

Claudia noted Tomás's tone when he talked about Amelia's schedule, as if that morning they had shared their plans for the day. She didn't know if the black cloud that crossed her mind was jealousy or a touch of envy for that powerful and brilliant couple. And yet, sitting in the back seat of Tomás's car on their way to the newspaper, followed by her car with her escorts inside, Claudia felt again that something was pulling them together: the ease with which she used the word "we," the way she would softly touch his thigh to make a point, or how his hand grazed her hip when he greeted her. Were they the prelude to something that was bound to happen or mere gestures of camaraderie?

"Señorita Claudia, what a pleasure to see you!" said Silvano Fortunato as soon as they got in the car. "I never had the chance to offer my condolences. My sympathies for what happened to Don Rosendo, may God keep him in his heart. Please, give my regards to your dear mother."

"Thank you, I will. I'm happy to see you, too," she answered, reaching forward to touch the shoulder of Tomás's driver. For a few years, Fortunato had been assigned to Franco's home, and in her teenage years he had driven her to ballet classes.

"I don't know why the Reaper always takes the best ones first. Miss, you got every scorpion, snake, and cockroach you could imagine living like fucking kings over their neighbors and the bastards don't catch as much as a cold. In the meantime, we lost Pedro Infante, Manolete, and Kennedy. There's no justice in the world. That's why I'm almost always an atheist, God forgive me," the chauffeur said, quickly crossing himself.

"What do you mean, almost always, Don Silvano? Either you're an atheist or you're a believer," Tomás asked him, pleased to distract himself with something that wasn't the crisis of the past few hours.

"Probably you, being well read and a gentleman, find it easy to choose between apples and oranges, but the man on the street, he can't reach up to pick his fruit. There's neither apple nor orange in sight. All you can do is take what comes how it comes. And if it comes with a divine face, then God be praised, and if it comes from the earth, then to hell with Him."

"What does that mean, the man on the street never gets to pick? Sounds very comfortable, morally speaking, don't you think?"

"More than anything, a guy with hard luck is too busy trying to make a buck to go around plucking the petals off of daisies trying to decide what's what. Not making that buck, though, that would be a disaster. You snooze, you lose. Let it go, boss, let it go."

"I think you're a cynic, more than anything. I'm saying that respect-fully, Don Silvano."

"For a while I used to moonlight as a bouncer to make it to the end of the month. Standing around outside a bar. My orders were strict: 'Don't let in anyone who looks like you.' So I only let in light-skinned types with thin noses, people like you'd see in a commercial. I didn't find that especially right or dignified for a person like me, but it helped me put my son through prep school. So you see, I wasn't offered apples or oranges, there was nothing sweet about this. But whatever, I swallowed it. I follow the good soldier's philosophy: if there's food in front of you, eat it; if there's a bed, sleep in it; and if you pass by a bathroom, go ahead and take a piss, because you never know if you're going to find another one. Pardon my French, Señorita."

"You're acting all tough, but you're a sweetheart, everyone at the newspaper knows it," she said.

"Well, there's a time to pray and a time to tell God to fuck off, and I've lived through both. If and when we've been on speaking terms!"

"There's a time to work, too," Tomás said, relieved to see the news-paper building ahead of them and to escape another of the driver's philosophical tirades.

32

Milena, Rina, and Luis

THURSDAY, NOVEMBER 13, 10:30 A.M.

SHE HEARD THE CHIRPING of the birds and felt the darts of sunlight over her eyelids and asked herself if she was dead. Then she remembered that the night before Rina and Luis had frustrated her attempt to dive onto the metro tracks, and had driven her to the outskirts of the city, to a kind of cabin in the mountains. The intense aroma of bacon confirmed to her she was alive, and also that she was hungry.

Rina and Luis were making breakfast and making fun of one another's culinary abilities. The partially fried eggs and burnt toast were like manna from heaven to Milena, though she did leave one inedible strip of bacon untouched. Once more, the friendship between the other two embraced Milena as well, soothing her and making her feel a sense of belonging she hadn't known for a long time.

Luis said they were in a country house in the mountains between Toluca and Mexico City. It belonged to a friend of his father's who rarely used it. The night before, Luis had called to ask if he could stay, and had gotten the contact info for Hernán, the watchman who lived next door. They could stay as long as they wanted, and he said it was certain no one would find them. Milena knew that wasn't true: sooner or later, Bonso would locate her, and now he would definitely kill her. Again, she thought things would work out for the best: at least in Mexico there wouldn't be any dogs involved.

Luis tried to dispel her fears with his optimism.

"If we want to solve this problem once and for all, we have to find a way to get rid of Bonso," he said. "It can be done."

"Impossible. He has so many lives," Milena objected. "The three of us would only make him laugh." She could not stop trembling at what lay in store for them, however much she trusted Luis's ingenuity.

"It's not just the three of us: there are other people more powerful and more vicious than Bonso, and they're the people we need in our corner. But, to start with, I have to get online. I need to go somewhere with a connection."

"Get some groceries while you're out," Rina said. "If we are to survive here, it won't be thanks to your cooking." She looked at Milena. "Maybe you've got something up your sleeve; I've never had Croatian food before."

Milena tried to remember some of the braised dishes her mother used to make. She didn't think much of her own abilities, but she told herself anything would be better than her friends' shocking ineptitude. She told him some of the ingredients she'd need, and was surprised at how the thought of preparing those old recipes made her feel a burst of enthusiasm. She suddenly had the sense that life was looking for cracks to seep inside her again.

Luis went to a restaurant famous for grilled goat in La Marquesa, on the roadside a mile from the cabin. Their Wi-Fi was iffy, but he figured it would be enough to surf around as long as he didn't download any big files. He activated the software that let him navigate with IP addresses from the US and Canada and logged onto the Darknet to get familiar with the hardcore sites used by the human-trafficking networks. For most people, the web is a pristine, open universe: they don't know that beneath the surface lies a hidden, parallel dimension, a dark place where the pages don't allow their users to be traced. There is where the information about drugs, sex slaves, guns, and hardcore porn resides: places where you can hire a hit man or a hacker for illegal jobs. It took Luis a few hours in that universe to map out the sites that might serve his purposes.

After he left, the two girls spent the better part of the morning stretched out on the terrace. Don Hernán and his wife kept the place immaculate. The décor was cold, but there was lots of sun. Both of them laughed about how pale Milena's legs were: longer and shapelier than Milena's, Rina's legs were like a runner's.

The Mexican girl's way of talking made her feel good. She went from talking about her resolution to stop smoking before she turned thirty to her wish to live in a cabin on the beach with no possessions other than three bathing suits. She talked about how the little imperfections in Luis's body made him irresistible, and she argued for the need to decriminalize marijuana. It seemed frivolous, but it wasn't. Milena saw that Rina's ideas were the product of long reflection: she sincerely analyzed the pros and cons of each of her postulates in a language that was educated, sometimes exquisite. Or maybe it was that she talked in a way Milena had only seen in books. The Spanish she had heard up to now was the one spoken by pimps, clients, and prostitutes: colorful, coarse, and basic.

Milena was surprised Luis and Rina had just met.

"You seem like you've been together a long time. Are you thinking of getting married?"

"Getting married? No one gets married at twenty-three," she laughed. "He lives in Barcelona, he's just passing through Mexico."

Milena regretted her question. She felt provincial, like a redneck. She knew a lot about sex and novels, but not much else. For her part, Rina wished she hadn't spoken to Milena so frivolously.

"I think Luis is great, and we get along really well, but I don't even know if we're boyfriend and girlfriend. And why put a label on a relationship when he has a plane ticket for next week? The last thing I'm interested in right now is getting hooked, I've only just started feeling better."

Milena appreciated her confidences, less for the information itself than for how close she now felt to her. It reminded her of her teenage years, when she'd talk forever with her friends under the open sky and life seemed like a colorful prairie. She was used to women sharing secrets with each other in the prison-houses she'd passed through. That was their main pastime during the dead hours in that captive atmosphere. But there always seemed to be something false in those dialogues: enigmas, impossible plans, cynical and merciless revelations from women who pretended not to know, even if they had no choice, that life had already broken them.

What Rina told her spoke of a real world where people caught trains and planes, signed up for classes and then dropped out, went to a restaurant and got overwhelmed choosing their dishes, and suffered from the uncertainty of unrequited love. She would have liked to return the gesture with some juicy secret she had never shared, but everything that came to mind was dark, cruel, or repulsive.

She liked being with Rina for her approach to life: relaxed, but also serious. And yet the best thing about her new friend wasn't her words, but the gleam in her eyes and the animated way she gestured, swinging her arms like propellers. It was impossible not to get caught up in the enthusiasm her presence exuded. For a moment, she dared to think she could redeem her past, build a future. Then she remembered Vila-Rojas and a tingle in her lower abdomen told her otherwise. She decided to take a bath when the *B* tattooed on her buttock started throbbing insistently.

THEM V

Me, I'm jealous of whores, to tell the truth. Getting money to fuck is a sweet deal, right? But the thing is, they're a bunch of hypocrites and whiners. People go crazy trying to get sex and money, all you have to do is turn on the TV to see that's what drives all advertising. What's so bad about putting the two things together? Best of both worlds, right?

If I was young and looked like Richard Gere or Robert Redford—before the wrinkles, I mean—I wouldn't have hesitated to sell my body for a living. Of course, you have to make sacrifices; the customers wouldn't exactly be Julia Roberts, I reckon. But still, an hour sweating it out with a fat chick to make what some working stiff gets in a month wouldn't be too bad. And an orgasm is an orgasm. Or, as my godson says, for a good soldier, any hole is a trench.

But I don't have Brad Pitt's body and my teeth could be in better shape, so I'll never be able to make money off my physical attributes. Instead, I have to pay, and the price keeps going up, it seems to me: the halitosis, you know, it's getting worse and worse.

Now Rosario's the only one who will take my money. She says because of her sinusitis, her nose runs all the time and she can take care of me without noticing my problem. But I'm getting off-track.

What I'd like to say is, I'd be jumping for joy if I could make a living from sex like they do. They're ingrates, they don't appreciate the privilege life has given them.

I tell Rosario that when she comes to visit me, but she makes like she doesn't hear. She just looks at me, scratches her crotch, blows her nose, picks up the cash, and leaves the room. Pampered and ungrateful.

B.N. BISHOP OF ESTEPONA
SPAIN

33

Vidal and Luis

THURSDAY, NOVEMBER 13, 11:00 A.M.

THE SCREEN SHOWED a red dot moving threateningly toward a blue one. Surprised, then alarmed, Vidal saw the spot representing Luis on the map on his phone's screen was coming rapidly toward where he himself was located. How the hell could Luis have known he'd been tracking the three of them?

He had followed them at a safe distance, always in a chauffeured Lemlock car, all the way to the outskirts of Mexico City. When he was convinced his friends had stopped somewhere near the highway to spend the night, he and the driver reserved two rooms in a truckers' hotel close to La Marquesa. It was a rough night, his sleep interrupted by the impulse to glance back at the GPS and verify Luis's location on his phone, but nothing had happened between ten hours ago and now. The driver in the neighboring room had given no sign of being awake. He would have to deal with what was about to happen on his own.

Vidal prepared to explain to his friend what he was doing in the rundown café of a roadside hotel a mile away from where they'd spent the night. He thought of various circumstantial and improbable excuses. None of them seemed like they would work. Frustrated, he decided to tell the truth, and looked for the best way to frame it. "It's for your own safety," he heard himself saying. But that didn't sound convincing either. The strength Luis emanated and the insecurity

Vidal felt in his presence made the idea seem absurd. He would have to refer to how Lemlock's enormous resources could help Milena out, but he knew that for Luis, any mention of Jaime was sacrilege.

To Vidal's relief, the red dot stopped a fraction of an inch from the blue one representing his own location. He figured his friend was fewer than a hundred yards away, and when he looked outside, he saw Rina's car turning the corner. A few seconds later, he saw Luis enter the nicest-looking restaurant around. Neither of the girls was with him.

For now, he was off the hook, but he knew that soon enough he'd have to face Luis, who could use his GPS to detect Vidal, just as Vidal had done with Luis.

Anyway, he had no idea how far away the chase could take him. The night before, he'd called Olga, his mother, to explain his absence, saying he would spend the night with some friends. He did that often when a party threatened to stretch on into the morning. But his mother seemed to have a built-in polygraph, and could detect the inflections in his voice that showed he was lying. Vidal and his father always said a Gestapo interrogator would have been less suspicious than his mother when she sensed a crack in a family member's story. The day before had been no exception: Olga said goodbye to her child, making him promise to call her when he got home.

Vidal wondered whether his uncle hadn't overstepped by putting so much confidence in him. A few hours before, he thought he was doing the right thing, trying to compensate for Luis and Rina's imprudence. Everything indicated Rina had lost her head, and Vidal trusted she would recover her common sense as soon as she saw the sacrifice he was making by putting his own feelings aside to help them.

But Luis's unexpected appearance shattered his determination. Now he was burning with the desire to go to his friend and confess the truth, let him know what Jaime was up to, and rebuild the complicity that had always characterized their relationship. All it would take was walking a few steps, surprising Luis, and looking him in the face, and he was sure he'd be forgiven. He imagined the four of them in a mad dash on the back roads from one motel to the next, making Rina's car their second home. He even thought that if she and Luis insisted on staying together, he and Milena would have to hook up, if only because they couldn't rent so many rooms in all the different hotels they'd stay in. Maybe then, Rina's head would clear, and she'd realize she was losing her true love to the Croatian's embrace. Owning up to Vidal was the right path to take.

His smile disappeared when he felt his phone vibrate. It was Jaime. Vidal told him where he was, where Luis was, that he was certain Milena was nearby, and asked for instructions. When he hung up, a bitter taste in his mouth kept him from savoring Jaime's compliments.

A hundred yards away, Luis looked for pages related to Bonso. He found a half-dozen that might belong to his organization, but he was only sure of two. He clicked through similar ones to try and find some heavyweight rival he might pit against him, but the restaurant's Wi-Fi was too weak. By that time, he'd struck up a conversation with the sharp-eyed kid who brought him a sandwich and three coffees. Luis offered three hundred dollars to buy his cell phone; it was worth half that, but he had to offer five to get it. It didn't have GPS, but at least it offered a safe way to communicate with the rest of the world. He erased all the contacts and data, and turned his own phone off.

Afterward, he went to a small but well-stocked supermarket nearby, bought additional minutes for the phone and picked out the food Rina and Milena had asked for. After getting back in the car, he decided to ditch it: he drove twenty minutes toward Toluca until he reached the lot of a huge outlet mall on the outskirts of the city, where he figured Rina's car wouldn't be in danger parked for a few days, and walked over to a taxi stand. The taxi took him to La Marquesa and dropped him on the side of the road. He preferred to walk the last mile to the cabin to keep from giving away his location. He was happy with his work for the day: he had made some headway in his investigations into Bonso and had erased any tracks that would lead their pursuers to their location. Or so he thought.

34

Jaime, Claudia, Tomás, and Amelia

THURSDAY, NOVEMBER 13, 11:00 A.M.

AFTER VIDAL TOLD HIM Milena and the other two were likely in La Marquesa, Jaime didn't expect any new information from the meeting with his friends at El Mundo. But he also didn't want to let his growing influence over Claudia and Tomás slip. The meeting would have to solidify his position as consultant and go-to person for all the newspaper's security needs.

He was still thinking about how to get Milena out of Luis's hands and somewhere safe. For now, that was all he could do, because Bonso was still impossible to find: the number Galván had dialed to talk with him had gone dead. Perhaps he was smarter than they'd believed. Tracing him by phone was a dead end, but Jaime was confident Patricia would dig up all the brothels the gang ran. Sooner or later the boss would have to call or show his face at one of them.

Still, he was impatient. Víctor Salgado also had ample resources at his disposal. After the carnage outside Rina's house, his rivals had already picked up on the relationship between her and the Croatian and would be looking for her car everywhere. The system had probably picked up the vehicle's information on the highway to Toluca, and it was only a matter of time until Salgado and his men had it. All it would take was for one of the chiefs of police under his command to issue a warrant for the car, and then the wheels would start turning.

Amelia seemed to sense what he was thinking.

"I can't find Rina anywhere. She was supposed to show up at my office yesterday for work, but she didn't come. I sent my driver to her house early this morning, and there's no one there. Maybe the shootout frightened her, and she decided to hide out with one of her relatives. She also doesn't pick up at the number she left with my secretary. She must be with Milena, right? Have you heard from Vidal? Maybe he could tell us something."

Tomás had tried to get hold of Vidal to tell him to take care of Rina after what had happened at her home, but he didn't pick up his phone. Tomás assumed he was with Rina and Luis and let the matter go. The possibility that the four of them were together—absolutely logical now that Amelia mentioned it—had never occurred to him. He'd supposed Milena had run off scared and hidden out somewhere on her own, but that was impossible.

"It's best if we concentrate on the negotiations with Víctor Salgado," Jaime said. "That's even more important than finding Milena. Let's remember that as soon as we get Milena back, the clock starts ticking for Emiliano. The most urgent thing is to neutralize that threat."

"So what do you propose?" Claudia asked.

"I have the perfect go-between, he's going to try and set up a meeting tonight. When my contact found out it would be with the owner of *El Mundo*, he took it for granted that Salgado would be interested. You're the *new kid in town*," he finished in English, looking at her.

"Perfect. Tell us a time and place. Tomás and I will be there," the redhead answered as forthrightly as she could, though she still met eyes with Tomás, seeking his support.

"Do we need some kind of protection?" he asked.

"Not at all. Salgado's not hiding out and he doesn't have any warrants of any kind. The most likely thing is he'll see you in some restaurant. At worst, he'll say he doesn't know what we're talking about or he'll refuse any type of negotiation."

"That means we need to line up other alternatives, just in case," Amelia interrupted. "First, a plan to rescue Emiliano, if it comes down to it. I insist we bring in someone we can trust from the police, a higher-up, in case negotiations fail. Second, we need a definitive plan to keep Milena safe. When I was running the national network for the protection of battered women, we managed to get numerous women abused by men in power out of the country. They left with passports with fake names. Authorities from Sweden and Australia supported them. They were untraceable."

"Let's not jump the gun here," Jaime said, getting up and grabbing his coat to leave. "All this will be unnecessary if we work it out with Salgado. Let's talk at the end of the night and then evaluate where we're at."

A minute later, the meeting was over. Jaime rushed off to Lemlock, phone in hand, and Tomás went with Amelia into his office.

"Call me ungrateful," Amelia said, "but negotiating with Salgado on Jaime's terms doesn't exactly make me feel calm."

Tomás raised an eyebrow and looked toward the camera in his office.

"Get that out of here already," Amelia said, exasperated. "Do you have plans for dinner?"

"I've got to see Emiliano's wife. She called me early, when she got up and saw her husband hadn't made it home. I don't know what the hell to tell her."

"You have to tell her his situation. She has a right to know."

Tomás nodded curtly. Feeling for him, Amelia took his face in both hands and gave him a long kiss goodbye. Tomás was happy to receive it, but he couldn't stop asking himself if Claudia was looking at a monitor with the feed from his office.

35

Milena

JANUARY 2012

FOR THE WEEKS AFTER her failed escape, Milena sought refuge in old Russian novels. Anna Karenina and Raskolnikov became much more alive than Bonso and the faceless men who used her body at night. She ate without tasting and listened without hearing, obeyed her captors' orders, carried out the household routines mechanically and efficiently, but her heart was filled with the absolute certainty that only death would free her from her slavery. Once again, Vila-Rojas changed her life.

"You cost me a fortune," he told her weeks after the scene with the dogs, the first time they were alone together. "Now you're mine, precious."

"I'm not anyone's."

"I admire your poise, but you and I both know that's not true. Still, I can set you free."

Milena looked close at Vila-Rojas's face, trying to find a hint of humor in his tone or expression. But it was neutral, categorical. They were fully clothed, drinking whiskey in the living room of a large suite in one of his properties, the Hotel Bellamar, and as always, he didn't seem interested in her body, but in what she had to say.

"So what would I have to do for it?" she asked suspiciously.

"Work for me a few years. If you do it to my complete satisfaction, I'll give you a nice wad of cash and you can start over wherever you want."

"Is that why you stopped Bonso when he was going to punish me?"

"You got it."

"Why me?"

"You've got a rare ability to pick up on things other people don't see. You showed it to me the night I met you, at the party on the yacht. And your profession puts you in places where things get said. That could be useful to me."

"You want me to be your informant?"

"Much more than that. I'm not just interested in your eyes and ears. It's your access to their bodies that justifies the fortune I paid for you."

"I don't understand."

"You don't have to understand anything for now, just know that from now on your fate and mine are linked." For the first time since their conversation had begun, Vila-Rojas's words had some warmth to them.

Milena weighed the implications of what she'd heard and assumed it must be good news. Until then, only the pimps had decided her fortune.

"Unfortunately, there are two or three individuals who are putting our destiny in danger," he added.

"In danger? What do you mean?"

"That as long as those people are alive, I'm running serious risks, and you are, too, by extension. Unless you help me resolve the situation." Again, his tone was gentle. "For you, it would be simple to eliminate those obstacles, make them disappear from the map." He spoke as if they were talking about a minor inconvenience.

"You want me to become a hit man?" she asked incredulously. "What makes you think I would do a thing like that?"

Vila-Rojas didn't answer. He refilled his glass, this time with water, and sat back on the sofa.

"You don't have another option. All your alternatives have vanished. Look at you: if it wasn't for my intervention, there wouldn't even be a trace of you left in the stomachs of Bonso's dogs. And look, that's still a possibility; it's just off the table for now. It seems like a waste to me, given your faculties, but what can you do—those are the rules of the game, so I've been told."

"I don't think I have what it takes," she said.

She couldn't understand how the conversation had gotten to a point where she was talking about committing murder, and it hurt her to hear him talking about her as if she didn't matter. She liked to think it was just his way of negotiating. She was unable to believe Agustín didn't have feelings for her, even if his tough-guy exterior made them hard to recognize.

"You do, believe me. You're not the only one who knows how to size people up."

"But what about the risks? I'd be the first one they came to if I killed one of your enemies, and that would make people look at you, right?"

"Leave that to me. They won't find you out, and besides, no one but Bonso knows you're working under my command. And he owes me his life, too."

The image rose up in Milena's mind: a client she detested with his throat sliced open, bleeding to death in bed. She was less perturbed by the violence of the scene than the feeling of calm it produced in her. The idea wasn't completely disagreeable. She could reserve the right to limit her killing to human trash: she knew a dozen particularly cruel men whose premature deaths would leave the world a better place. It might not be a bad job, and if she was lucky, Vila-Rojas would keep up his end, and in two years, she'd be free.

"What do I have to do?" she asked.

She didn't dare admit that being useful to Vila-Rojas, working side by side on something so delicate, might allow the peculiar relationship of shared secrets they'd had till then to evolve into something deeper, more caring, more in line with the feelings he aroused in her. As if reading her thoughts, he went over to her, stroked her cheekbone with his hand, and kissed the other side of her face softly.

"You won't have to do anything. Just stay fit. And don't worry, we're not talking about beating anyone's head in. Our methods will be subtle. I'm more interested in your ability to read people and situations than in your athleticism. You belong to me now, but you'll go on working in Bonso's place. I've given instructions for your clientele to be restricted to wealthy businessmen and public figures. I'll make sure you're at all Marbella's upper-echelon parties."

"Who's going to tell me what to do when the time comes?"

"Once a week you'll have an appointment with Mr. Schrader, a retired, inoffensive German no one knows I have any connection to. You'll have a drink in the bar, then you'll go up to a room connected to this one. He doesn't know anything about our arrangement. He'll wait on the other side while you and I chat. On those occasions, you'll tell me who you've seen and what you've found out, and if it's necessary, I'll give you instructions on how to act. In the meanwhile, read those two books closely."

Vila-Rojas pointed to the nightstand beside the bed. Her eyes followed his arm, and she sat down and looked at two books with thick covers: one was a manual of toxicology and the other a textbook on infectious diseases.

She picked them up and examined them. Both were well-thumbed and had countless underlines, arrows, and brackets on the pages. It seemed that her reading days hadn't ended with *War and Peace*. It also seemed to be the first time in her life she'd ever had a purpose. The small revenge against her clients she'd found in her *Tales of the XY Chromosome* was about to grow exponentially.

36

Milena, Rina, and Luis

THURSDAY, NOVEMBER 13, 2:15 P.M.

FROM THE SOFA in the middle of the cabin where she was sitting, Rina watched Milena and wondered if she was missing her home country as she looked down at the dense forest through the window.

"Does that look like the countryside in Yastabarco?"

"Yastabarco?" Milena laughed. My village is called Jastrebarsko."

"Yeah, that. Is it similar?"

Milena looked back out the window and shook her head after a long pause.

"No. I don't even know if there are still woods there. When I was a child, they'd already logged the surrounding hills. They say it was because of the war, to avoid sneak attacks, but my grandfather said the people from the Fabrizio sawmill used that excuse to make themselves millionaires."

"Is Jastrebarsko pretty? Do you miss it?"

"I don't miss anything. If you start remembering, you'll never stop, and one day you'll wake up and hang yourself with your bedsheet. I'm just thankful not to have those sweaty men on top of me anymore."

Rina went on contemplating her: she imagined nauseating fat people, men with prickly hairs in their nostrils blowing hot air onto her lips, rancid sweat. Just thinking of letting a man like that put his dick into her body made her sick. Suddenly moved, she stood up and walked over to Milena on the other side of the room. She stopped beside her and stroked her hair with her fingertips. She took a tuft of it and rubbed it gently, as if evaluating the quality of a fine cloth. Rina wondered what its natural blonde tone must look like beneath the cheap black dye, and restrained the urge to cry.

"I'm going for a quick run, do you mind? If Luis shows up, don't start cooking. I want to learn a Croatian recipe."

In fact, she wasn't planning on running far. Her jeans and sneakers weren't the best thing for the mountain paths, but she felt the need for fresh air and some time away. Her new friend's misfortunes had reopened the deepest wounds from her own tragedy, and now she felt the panic coming back. She walked quickly along the dusty route they had taken the night before. The straw hat she found in the cabin and her broad, dark glasses could barely keep out the bright midday sun sifting over the path. Shortly before she reached a curve, she heard a car motor. She smiled in anticipation of Luis's arrival, and stopped to wait for her lime-green car to appear. Instead, there was a gray truck followed by a white one. Both pulled to a stop beside her.

"Milena?" a man in a black suit said from the passenger seat.

She nodded softly, paralyzed by confusion.

"Hop in. Claudia sent us," he added while another man got out of the back seat and opened the door politely. She didn't move. With their suits, manners, and earpieces, they didn't seem like two-bit triggermen. But all Rina could feel was panic. The image of her family in her living room covered in blood rose up with absolute clarity.

Woozy from the heat and the insistence of the man squeezing her arm, she settled into the cool seat he offered without uttering a word. She tried to say something, but the words got caught in her throat. The vehicles turned around and headed back the way they had come from.

Before turning onto the road, they saw a young man walking uphill with half a dozen plastic bags and what looked like a backpack on his back. The man in the passenger's seat gestured to his companion, who grabbed Rina by the nape of her neck and pushed her head down into her knees. When he was certain the boy was Luis, the driver called Patricia, who was in charge of the operation, and asked for instructions. The trucks slowed but didn't stop. Patricia said that it was the foreigner and not the other two who mattered, and they sped back up. When they reached the highway, they drove back to Mexico City as quickly as possible. On the way, one of the men tried to make conversation with the girl, but he couldn't get a word out of her. Rina had become aware of her captors' confusion: she supposed the glasses and hat had contributed to it, and decided to lead them on. Maybe that would help Milena and Luis reach safety in the meantime.

The sight of the trucks had unsettled Luis. The dust from the road and the tinted back windows had made it impossible to see the details of the occupants, but he managed to get a glimpse of one driver's earpiece. Fearing the worst, he hurried back to the cabin. There were only a few properties up there, so it was unlikely the trucks were coming from one of the other homes. He jogged for the last hundred yards, and when he saw the cabin, he left the bags and sprinted the rest of the way.

He shouted Rina's name as he entered. With the selfishness of a person in love, he hoped Milena's captors had let his girlfriend go. Milena met him with a beer in her hand.

"Where's Rina?" he asked, impatient and confused.

"She went out to run. You didn't see her? She took the same road we came up on."

"Dear God," he said, collapsing into one of the armchairs in the living room.

"What is it?"

"Did a white truck and a gray one come up here?"

"No one's been here since you left, just the maid to ask if we wanted tortillas a little while back."

Luis told her what he had seen and shared his fears with her.

"It's my fault," Milena lamented. "You should have left me last night. Today everything would be resolved and everyone could rest easy. Now Rina's life is in danger. Bonso will be ruthless when he realizes he's made a mistake." Milena did not cry, but her grave voice and tone made Luis's hair stand on end.

"I don't think it's Bonso; I saw one of them, and he didn't seem the type. But I'm still scared. They'll come back soon, when they figure out there's been a mistake. We need to leave. Get a backpack, I'll go for the bags of groceries and some bottles of water," he said, grabbing a pair of binoculars from the mantel.

"If they're coming back, let's stay here. When they come, we'll make the trade and Rina will be safe."

"That's not an option," he responded. "We don't know who they are. Come on, hurry, and grab a jacket or a blanket, whatever you find. I'll explain on the way."

Before they left, he scribbled a number and a few words on a piece of paper and left it on the table for Rina's captors. Minutes later, they plunged into the forest, following a barely marked path. Luis warned Milena to walk on the gravel and avoid the dirt where she might leave footprints. After four hundred yards, they came upon a sudden drop surrounded by boulders and he thought they could veer off without showing where they'd gone. They wound up on an outcropping and continued further down until they reached a small valley. Soon afterward, they climbed up again in the opposite direction from where they'd been. A half-hour later, they came to rest in a leaf-strewn clearing where the last rays of sunlight filtered through.

He would have liked to activate the GPS on his phone, but it was better to leave it off. It must have been what led the guys in the trucks to them. He turned on the cell phone he had bought with Milena's dollars from the waiter in La Marquesa and confirmed the captors hadn't left any messages. They didn't seem to have returned to the cabin. He turned the phone back off.

He looked at Milena, who had been silent throughout the walk. She was staring at some wild mushrooms, bent over without flexing her knees.

"Are they edible?" he asked. "Do you know anything about mushrooms? I have enough food in the backpack."

"I'm not looking at them because I'm hungry," she said, and dropped a piece of wild mushroom, disappointed.

She took the bottle of water he passed her and sat down beside him.

"Do you think they'll take long to get in touch with us?"

"I hope they do before nightfall. In these forests, the temperature can drop below freezing."

"And when the guys in the trucks call, what's your plan?"

"I don't know. Talk to them, figure out who they are, negotiate to get Rina free. But we can't stay there in the cabin with our hands tied. We've got to grab the bull by the horns," he said, and then laughed at the confusion on Milena's face. She had a surprisingly lopsided grasp of colloquialisms: one moment, she could rattle off a string of insults with the best of them, and next thing you know, she'd hear the most common phrase ever and be utterly lost.

"The important thing is to save Rina, even if we have to barter. Promise me you'll do it. I'm already lost, much more than you can imagine."

Luis was about to protest, to insist that her fatalism was absurd, but he held it in. There was something in Milena's words far grimmer than resignation, and there was something dead in her gaze. She seemed a person who hoped for nothing, who was going nowhere, who had already stopped being.

"What happened in Spain, Milena? Why are they pursuing you?"

She looked at him apathetically, filled her lungs, and started talking.

"I'd have preferred you never found out," she said, scraping at the dust with a thin stick. "Everything started when I met the Flamingos."

37

Jaime, Vidal, and Rina

THURSDAY, NOVEMBER 13, 6:15 P.M.

"TAKE HER TO THE MEETING ROOM, I'm going there now," Jaime said. Patricia had informed him that the truck carrying Milena was in the parking deck at Lemlock's offices.

It was a serious risk, he thought, putting his business into direct conflict with the mafias running prostitution. If that evening's meeting with Salgado turned out bad, he and Lemlock would face vengeance for hiding the Croatian. But that was the price he had to pay: a successful negotiation with the ex-director of prisons depended on the interview he would have soon with the prostitute.

When he stepped into the meeting room, he took one look at the girl and saw it wasn't Milena. With her glasses and hat off, there was no mistaking it. Rina looked at him fleetingly: with all that had happened, she still had the courage to face to him.

"If you had identified yourself, this wouldn't have happened," she said.

Jaime ignored the comment and turned to Patricia, who gave her account. Luis and Milena should still be at the cabin. He looked at the wall clock. There was no way to get the Croatian in time for their meeting with Salgado, the traffic at that hour would make it impossible. And that was without even considering the added complications Luis might bring. He decided not to waste time on them and to concentrate on the thorny meeting he had ahead of him.

"Rina, there are things about Milena you don't know," he told her. "You and Luis are in danger every second you spend with her. Her bosses are after her, and they don't care if they leave a trail of bodies in their wake. And right now, the life of a deputy director at *El Mundo* is hanging by a thread. My intention was to get Milena somewhere safe and separate you from her so you'd be safe, too."

"You could have told us, no?"

Again, Jaime ignored her comment.

"Can you call Luis? A truck is leaving right now to pick them up."

"We just tried," Patricia said. "It looks like his phone is off, or else he's not getting a signal. Anyhow, they're on their way and they have a written message from Rina to Luis. I'm hoping that convinces them."

"Good. Keep calling his cell and find Vidal to go with Rina. She can rest in my office," Jaime said to Patricia, and then, looking at the girl: "It's better if you spend the night here."

Minutes later, Vidal was back at Lemlock's offices, assuming his mission was over now that they had Milena. He was happy when he heard of the confusion, and even more when his friend rushed up and hugged him.

"I'm an idiot. But how could I know?"

"Don't be hard on yourself, you did what you thought best," he said. "Anyway, don't worry, Lemlock will take care of everything. I'm here to protect you."

She looked at him, perplexed.

"I'm not worried about me," she said anxiously. "I'm worried about Milena and Luis. The bad guys are after them right now."

"That's what I'm saying. Lemlock's resources are enormous!" he said with pride.

Even so, she wasn't convinced. She dug a finger into her ear.

Vidal didn't know what else to say, worried he would make his friend's mood worse. What would Jaime do in a situation like this? How could he make her feel secure under his wing? He imagined a mature, assertive version of himself, and Rina hanging from every word, swayed by his resolute movements. But all that occurred to him was to ask if she wanted something to drink, and she didn't even seem to hear him. She switched hands and picked at the other ear.

But two hours later, after eating something in the private room Jaime used when he slept at the office, Rina seemed more relaxed. Vidal's chatter seemed to put her to sleep and she ended up resting her head on her friend's shoulder. He sighed, thankful. Everything was back to normal now that Luis was out of the scene.

38

Claudia, Jaime, and Tomás

THURSDAY, NOVEMBER 13, 8:20 P.M.

SHE KNEW SHE HATED HIM the first time she laid eyes on him: Víctor Salgado reminded her of her father, but without the blood ties that made him bearable. Claudia greeted him with a curt nod to avoid any physical contact, and sat at the extreme opposite of the round table. They were in the private room in the restaurant San Angelín. Jaime was about to shake his hand, but he held back and did the same as Claudia. He and Tomás sat beside her in silence.

Salgado was a tall man, more fat than stocky. Everything about him exuded independence. He was drinking whiskey from a glass, making its ice cubes click rhythmically. To Claudia, there was something obscene in the movement, as though he were masturbating. He gave her a cheeky look and placed a thick Cuban cigar in his mouth, and two seconds later an assistant emerged from the terrace, match in hand, to light it. His body seemed to fill the room, as if everything in it belonged to him, including those present.

"There's no need for introductions, Don Víctor," Jaime said. "We can get straight to the point." But the host made a sign, interrupting him, and a waiter came in and took the new arrivals' order.

"True, there is no need for introductions," Salgado said once the waiter was gone. "But first, I would like to extend my sincerest condolences to Doña Claudia. I was friends with Rosendo before you were even born. Life pulled us apart with the years and yet I always cared for him, whether he knew it or not."

The revelation caught Claudia off guard. Salgado must have been near seventy, a little less than her father's age, so their knowing each other would make sense. But she didn't like the thought of Franco having ties to an ex-prison chief with such a nasty reputation. Something about his manners evoked an earlier time, one of black-and-white photographs, thick moustaches, and wide pants. An earlier time that hadn't been better.

"That will make things easier, I suppose," Jaime said. "If you'll allow me, Colonel, I'll speak with complete clarity. A pimp is now holding a deputy director from *El Mundo* captive to get back a woman who worked for him. For some reason, he's convinced we have her. As you may know, this woman was highly prized by your friend Don Rosendo, may he rest in peace. She has disappeared, and we're afraid for our friend's life. If Señor Emiliano Reyna comes to a tragic end, it would be a gratuitous and unnecessary scandal."

"Bonso doesn't seem to be aware of the consequences of what he's doing," Tomás interrupted. "Just for starters, next Monday Claudia and I will be dining in Los Pinos with the president. You can imagine the problems that could arise if we were to bring up the kidnapping with him, let alone the execution of an important figure at the newspaper. The Mexican government would go to no end to solve it."

Salgado looked at Tomás as though he barely registered his presence. Again, he stirred the ice in his drink. The man clicked his tongue with a condescending smile and explained.

"We're all part of the same food chain. The problem is, some of us don't recognize or don't want to know where we stand. It's been a long time since the presidents of this country, and others like them, have been on top, and they know it. Others don't: Rosendo Franco never found out, and until the end of his days, he still believed he was master of the universe."

"Well, if he wasn't, he did a damn good job pretending to be, because he always got whatever he wanted," Tomás said.

"He lived a full life thanks to my intervention. Otherwise he would have exited stage left, so to speak, after stealing the Croatian."

"It's hard for me to believe a prostitute has that much importance," Jaime said.

"It's a fact of biology that goes over my head, over yours, over Bonso's. Let me go back to the food chain. The real peak has to do with money and how it's handled. What do the president, the owner of an international consortium, and the head of a drug cartel have in common? All three of them need financial avenues they can channel their fortunes into, legal and illegal. The real masters of the universe aren't the heads of state or even the businessmen on the Forbes list; they're the movers and shakers of the big investment funds and the brokers operating on the elastic borders of legality. They're the ones who make Peru's GDP shoot through the roof because a mineral nets record prices, or allow Greece to breathe another six months in exchange for turning over their financial markets or some public–private business enterprise."

There was absolute silence at the table.

"Chapo Guzmán was the most powerful capo in Latin America and the most wanted man by the DEA and Interpol. But he was living hand-to-mouth before they caught him, he wasn't an executive director working nine to six to manage the commercial and financial logistics necessary for an international operation like the production and distribution of drugs. The people who really hold the power are the ones moving the Sinaloa cartel's billions of dollars through hundreds of investment accounts scattered throughout the world. An 'honest' president will leave office with fifteen or twenty million dollars in his possession; a less finicky one will do so with two or four hundred million. Bigger or smaller, it's a number that can't be tied to family members or put in a friend's name. It's been a long time since you could count on a trustworthy friend: loyalty's gone out of fashion. A millionaire from the Forbes list hides fortunes from the taxman in the course of his life. Beyond real-estate investments, you need professionals to launder your money."

"What does this have to do with Milena?" Claudia said.

"Well, it seems Milena turned into the apple of one of those masters of the universe's eye. I don't know the details, but at some point, they sent her to Mexico to get her out of the middle of some unforgivable mess. Someone high up either loves her or hates her a lot, because the instructions were very precise: keep her alive, never lose sight of her, and go on pimping her out. Not a month goes by that these people don't ask for information about her." And almost to himself, he added, "And in the past few weeks, it's been much more frequent than that."

"Much more frequent than that? What does that mean?"

"Nothing, I'm just trying to say that very important people are interested in Milena. People you can't say no to. The same ones who take the bankers' and politicians' dirty money. Their names aren't known to the public, yet no politician would refuse their requests. They are the true power. So no, I'm not going to lose everything I've earned in life. The president will hear your complaint, he'll call the attorney general, they'll move heaven and earth, and yes, maybe it will be bad for Bonso. But free Milena? Never. She'll end up in Costa Rica or Argentina in an arrangement not too different from the one she has in Mexico."

"It's hard for me to believe a secret bookkeeper could influence the decisions of the president or carry more weight than you, Don Víctor, with all your experience controlling security forces," Jaime said.

"If I was twenty years younger, I'd be running one of those financial outfits instead of this. You can do without us, but not without them. We're not talking about secret bookkeepers; these are absolutely legitimate brokers who manage billions of dollars. The financial circuits need them because they offer investment funds with the highest return rates on the market. When the money's laundered, they reinvest it in bonds, they speculate on currencies in the shady fringes where laws restrict most firms from operating. And everyone turns to them. They don't have faces, but if they set their mind to it, they can change Mexico's credit rating at Standard & Poor's. The president may or may not have his fortune in their hands, but he will never ignore a recommendation of that magnitude on the part of his own revenue secretary. Wouldn't you agree?"

"But he also wouldn't be indifferent to the outcry if the deputy director of the country's main newspaper was murdered," Claudia said.

Salgado eyed her up. Fifteen years before, he would have hit on her, and thirty years ago, he would have knocked her off her feet.

"You're certainly right about that, good-looking. In these matters, blood always comes with a price. Now that they're better informed, they have no reason to hold onto your deputy director. I'm sure he'll be set free in the next few hours. But make no mistake: the Croatian will have to go back or the bodies will keep piling up until she does. And from now on, they're on your conscience."

Salgado was arrogant, Jaime thought, but he was no fool. Setting Emiliano free would rob them of their opportunity to turn to the president during the lunch Claudia and Tomás had referred to. Not even they, with all their feigned ingenuousness, would dare ask the state to intervene in the case of a foreign hooker.

"Then tell me one thing, Don Víctor. Have you never been curious to meet Milena, to know her secret?" Jaime asked.

"I knew Milena, in the Biblical sense," he answered, making a gesture to excuse himself to Claudia. "Very beautiful. A little shy. I don't understand the passions she inspires. But as far as her secret, nothing. And I advise you all to follow my example: it would be the kiss of death for her and for whoever decided to snoop around. The order given has been to keep her alive. But that order ceases the moment she begins to talk about whatever happened in Spain."

As they left, Claudia commented that the man had seemed to her an intolerable braggart. Jaime thought that behind his self-reliance was an individual scared of change and of the possibility of becoming obsolete. Tomás just said he was a dangerous son of a bitch. The three of them agreed that before they went on protecting Milena, they had to find out about her past.

39

Milena and Luis

A LONG SILENCE REIGNED between Luis and Milena when she had finished the story of her life in Marbella. By then, they were surrounded by absolute darkness and bitter cold. She couldn't see Luis's face, and the intermittent forest sounds had a hypnotic effect. Luis was stunned by what she described, but she spoke as if she was speaking of things experienced by someone else.

Luis asked himself what would have happened to him if he'd been forced to commit such abominable acts for ten years after he turned sixteen. He doubted the girl could ever return from the darkness she'd been plunged into.

But Milena felt liberated: for the first time, she had let herself share with someone the terrible crimes she had committed, the burden of which she'd borne along for so long. She had the sense that Luis was capable of peering into the bottom of her soul without pushing her away.

"I'm really cold," she said, and before waiting for a response, she lay down over him and rested her head on his chest.

He wrapped an arm around her back and shifted against the stump he was leaning on, and she lowered her hand down his belly until she reached his groin. With satisfaction, she noted a growing bulge pressing against his jeans, but he took her wrist and brought it to his chest.

"Let's rest," he said.

His rejection confused her, then she felt humiliated and, finally, guilty. Provoking excitement and giving pleasure were her way of saying thanks, of getting close to a person of the opposite sex. Those were the only ways she knew to be close to men. She had been taught to see her beauty as her defining virtue, and that was what she wanted to offer to her protector and confidant. But she remembered Rina and was overcome by embarrassment and guilt.

Luis's reaction had little to do with fidelity and a great deal to do with the story he'd just heard. It was impossible not to relate the hand that crawled over his penis with the images that had taken shape in his mind as he listened to her words.

He took the phone out of his jacket, turned it on, and listened to a message. He memorized the number he was given, dialed it, and heard a man's voice.

"Hey, Luis, we're in the cabin. We have a written message from Rina."

"Then where is she?"

"In Mexico City, in a safe place. We can take you both to her. You're with Milena, right?"

"Who are you? What do you want?"

"We're with Claudia. It's urgent to protect you all."

"Tell Rina to call me on this phone at exactly nine-fifteen. Not a minute before or after."

Luis hung up and told Milena what he had heard. They stood up and decided, for their own reasons, to ignore what had just happened. It was better to remain silent, submerged in their own worries. Eight minutes later, he turned on the phone and heard Rina's voice immediately.

"I'm fine, Vidal's with me. They brought me to Jaime's offices, they say it's for my safety. They thought I was Milena."

"Are they holding you against your will?"

"No, nothing like that, I already called my uncle's house. I'm going by there tomorrow to get some clothes. And you? Are you coming?"

"I'm not sure. You're out of danger, but I'd rather think about it. I trust Jaime less than a dentist with rotten teeth," he said. "The way they took you was almost a kidnapping. The best thing would be to talk to Amelia. Ask her to call this phone at eleven."

"Do what you have to do, but take care. I'll tell Amelia to call you."

"I'm going to hang up before they trace my location. We'll be moving over the next few hours."

"You don't want to talk to Vidal?"

Luis hesitated a moment.

"No, we've already been on too long. I miss you. Take care. For me."

"You take care, too. For me."

The men in the cabin asked Patricia for instructions. She told them they hadn't been able to trace the call, but she ordered them to stay there in case Amelia managed to convince Luis and Milena to go back when they talked later.

For security, and because of the looming cold, Luis and Milena decided to start moving. By his calculations, the highway, which ran parallel to the toll road they and their pursuers had taken, should only be a mile or two away. He wanted to get close to be sure he'd have a cell-phone signal and an escape route toward the city. Even if the men in the cabin weren't a risk, he couldn't forget the threat of the traffickers, who were also looking for Milena.

In the hours since they had embraced, Milena still hadn't opened her mouth. When she reached the crest of a hill, three yards ahead of Luis, she stopped. Outlined against the light from the crescent moon, her curvy figure unleashed a wave of desire in him. He snuffed out the jolt of penitence growing between his legs and substituted it with commiseration for his friend. Milena would always be a sex object: for women, a menace evoking dirty sheets and abortions; for men, a hormonal urgency.

Luis summited the little hill, put his arm around her shoulders, and guided her down.

"You're not alone anymore, Lika. I won't let them hurt you."

Milena was thankful for the gesture and went along with him, but she knew her friend had no idea of the danger they were in. The real risk was that she would hurt him, even if involuntarily. As long as he stayed with her, he was condemned to death. The mafia would eliminate any possibility of their secrets getting out. Again, she told herself her death would solve everything. But something in the dangers he was facing and his willingness to help her touched her deeply. She felt the impulse to open up to him entirely, to show him everything in her little book, and above all, to share her doubts. Was the crisis in Ukraine what had brought this fury down on her, because of the dirt she had on the Russian mafia? Or was it just Bonso's impatience to have her back because of the pressure the prostitution rings were placing on him? Did they want to destroy the secrets she knew about the powerful clients who had passed through her bed? But she said nothing and showed him nothing.

"What were you doing today with the computer?" she asked.

Thankful for the opportunity, Luis now entered into a long account of his technical abilities, his status in the world of elite hackers, his ability to penetrate previously unbreachable databases without a trace, to find out anything and everything about an individual and turn his life into a living hell, if necessary.

"Is that what you're thinking of doing with Bonso? Turning his life into a living hell?" she asked.

"Something much worse."

40

Milena

2012

THE FLAMINGOS were a group of guys who took their pleasures seriously. And these weren't any ordinary pleasures. For more than ten years, they'd been getting together once a month, and their definition of fun had changed considerably since the early days.

They started seeing each other at the end of the nineties, when Vila-Rojas, a successful lawyer from Granada based in Marbella, united with three colleagues working in a similar field: laundering money on the Costa del Sol. One of them, Javi Rosado, had been a fellow student of his at the University of Seville; another, Jesús Nadal, he had worked with in his London days, when he worked in the legal department at Barclays; the third, Andrés Preciado, he had met on Wall Street. Over the succeeding months, two more joined their group, and through the years, the group grew to twelve. They were all Spaniards from the south, although none was from Marbella.

None of them had gotten a piece of the first tourist boom in the seventies and eighties. They came later, at the beginning of the nineties, at the time when Jesús Gil y Gil had a stranglehold on Marbella and institutionalized corruption drew mafia money like a magnet. The same thing happened in that touristy port town that had happened in Cancun, Punta del Este, and Miami: First, they were chosen as residences for the capos of various gangs thanks to the common denominator of easy pleasure and lax authorities. Later, the new residents—Russians, Arabs, and Europeans—took the opportunity to profit from explosive growth and an absence of regulation.

When money laundering became an industry of its own in the mid-nineties, people like Vila-Rojas and his friends were suddenly indispensable: lawyers, financiers with international experience, former accountants of multinational corporations. They did the work that the businessmen who'd come up around Marbella's picturesque mayor couldn't. The first generation consisted of old-school builders and real-estate speculators, who were able to multiply the value of a hectare by fifty thanks to their influence on public planning and ability to facilitate rezoning. But they lacked overseas contacts or the aptitude to manage the millions in secret cash that had started to flow into the Spanish coast. Vila-Rojas and others like him were the ideal mediators between traditional businessmen and the managers of illicit capital from other continents.

The Flamingos started as a group of friends, but as time went on, they began to see themselves as the puppet masters of life in the port. They barely saw each other apart from their monthly meetings, and they didn't work together, save for the occasional project in common. Even so, those get-togethers fostered closeness. It seemed to them it was only during their time together that they could revel in what they really were: the true bosses of the city. They kept a low profile in comparison to Jesús Gil and his raucous successors, who showed the typical garishness of the nouveaux riches. Only in their meetings, when they were in their element, did they confess their contempt for the hayseed local elite and give themselves over to pleasures and extravagances they avoided the rest of the month.

They started meeting at the Hotel Fuerte on the last Friday of the month. They got the name Flamingos from the general manager of the hotel restaurant when he saw the names Rojas and Rosado, Red and Pink in Spanish, on the reservation that the group made for the private dining room. Learning of the nickname, the members took a liking to it, remembering it was the same as that of a Vegas hotel where Frank Sinatra, Sammy Davis Jr., Dean Martin, and other members of the Rat Pack had hung out.

Their sessions usually started off with a midday lunch and finished at sunrise on Saturday, but after a hooker died from an overdose they decided to move their celebration somewhere private and began taking turns hosting their meetings. That was what caused their excesses to take off: each person competed to make *his party* the most spectacular and memorable. Weekend villas became scenes out of ancient Rome; yachts were overtaken by Amazonian pirates with voracious sexual appetites; there were exotic feasts and festivals of perverse videos.

When Agustín Vila-Rojas told Milena about the Flamingos, she didn't say that she already knew about their parties, but at least a half-dozen times, Bonso had been responsible for supplying the female consorts. She herself had taken part in one organized by a certain Rosas, who she now knew formed part of the brotherhood Vila-Rojas described. She didn't remember the man from Granada, and he didn't remember her.

Agustín explained that the party on the yacht where they had met a year before was the first one they had thrown after a long break, when the authorities had come out against money laundering and dismantled a good part of the networks they operated. Two members of the original group had fallen and several others feared for their freedom; another had disappeared. Agustín didn't know if he'd fled or been killed by criminals who wanted to be sure there was no trace of him left behind.

Operation White Whale, as the fight against money laundering on the Costa del Sol was known, ended up netting 250 million euros and apprehending fifty consultants, government workers, and businessmen. It didn't come close to eliminating the phenomenon during those years, but it was enough to make it more sophisticated. In a way, it benefited Vila-Rojas, because the arrests were a kind of purge: the survivors got more and better business. It was a mix of good luck and moderation that saved him. He had always been more cautious than ambitious; the investigators' files didn't even mention his name.

Despite everything, he and the remaining members of the Flamingos knew the bonanza of impunity was over. They put up walls around anything to do with the transfer and investment of capital, turned down any proposals that didn't come from their most trusted clients, and concentrated on a smaller number of jobs, to which they could devote their complete attention. The risk of jail wasn't related to the amount of money, but to how dirty the money was.

All in all, these new precautions didn't neutralize mistakes made in the past, and that was what kept Vila-Rojas up at night. He cleaned house and looked back over each of his files. In the end, he had a list of six guys he had dealt with before whose testimony could land him in prison. Three of them belonged to the Flamingos. "And that's where you come in, dear," he said to Milena.

41

Tomás and Amelia

FRIDAY, NOVEMBER 14, 1:10 A.M.

NEITHER OF THEM would go to bed. Tomás had arrived at Amelia's house a half-hour before, told her the outcome of the meeting with Víctor Salgado, and they took a shot together, "to lower the ailerons," as Tomás said. When he had knocked back his second tequila, she thought she'd never seen him drink so regularly. It was true Tomás had never taken on the kind of responsibility that now weighed on him. Whatever the case, his weakness for drink was worrisome. If he went on this way, she'd have to talk to him.

Is this what we've become, a couple that spies on each other and criticizes each other's excesses? Do I really want to be the watchdog keeping my lover from cutting loose? These thoughts depressed her and made her refill her wine glass to the top.

After a sip, she repeated the phone conversation she'd had with Luis two hours before, when he was somewhere out in the forest. She told the story of how Jaime had ended up with Rina instead of Milena and how Luis had run off with the Croatian to the mountains in La Marquesa. They criticized Lemlock's methods and Jaime's passion for intrigue. Amelia admired Luis and his crusade to defend Milena, regardless of the risk. If things fell apart, Tomás thought, the crusade wouldn't be particularly admirable anymore, and would instead look like a huge mistake: with enemies like Salgado and Bonso, the boy's temerity could end up getting people hurt.

Tomás's cell phone interrupted the parade of their worries. The screen showed it was Isabel, Emiliano's wife, and he imagined she was calling about him missing lunch. He would have liked to keep the deputy director's family in the dark about the kidnapping, trusting the negotiations with Salgado would work something out. He was afraid the woman could get mixed up in things, start a scandal, maybe get the authorities involved, and everything they'd tried so far could turn to dust. But what Isabel told him was that her husband had just come home and gone directly to the tub. He looked unharmed, but exhausted. All he wanted was to be left alone, to rest, and he said he would call the director in the morning.

Tomás hung up and hugged Amelia. The intensity he grabbed her neck with made her believe he was coming apart, and she felt him quiver a few times before he pulled away.

Tomás served himself another tequila and toasted to Emiliano.

"What will happen with Milena now?" she asked, once they had both drunk.

"I have no idea what will happen with Milena, and believe me, at this point, it's not my problem." Tomás knew they still hadn't found the black book Rosendo Franco had mentioned, but he didn't feel like ruining the solace the phone call had brought him. He also didn't want to encourage Amelia's inclinations; he felt she was addicted to lost causes.

"I understand the main thing is taken care of now, and I can't tell you how happy I am for Emiliano, but the girl is also a victim of circumstances, and we can't pass her off to those vultures."

"I'm not so sure she's a victim anymore. Milena's been part of these organized-crime rings for a long time; just think of the skeletons she's got in her closet. Anyway, I'm not motivated to let any of our people risk their lives in a matter that doesn't concern us."

Amelia couldn't believe what she was hearing. She would have seen the logic in those words coming from Jaime, who invariably hedged his bets, but not from Tomás, who was always prepared to tackle other people's problems, even if only symbolically.

"Milena didn't choose to be what she became, Tomás. She was your daughter's age when they took her."

He didn't like that comparison. The thought of Jimena in a brothel . . .

"Give it a fucking rest, Amelia. Can you not let me enjoy the fact that Emiliano's back in his home? Right now, they're pimping out girls Jimena's age in Thailand, in Madrid, here in Mexico City. Does that mean we need to leave now and go rescue them all?"

"I'm sorry I brought your daughter into this, it was in bad taste and I apologize, but Milena is a human being and fate brought her into our hands. You can't solve all the problems in the world, but you have to deal with the ones that wind up in your path."

"You haven't even met the goddamned Croatian, and I only saw her once. Besides, we don't know her past and everything suggests she did something much worse than just run away from her captors."

"We don't know what she did. What's obvious is she's a survivor and anything she's done she had to do, given the circumstances."

"Bonso or the Turk could say the same thing, no? They're products of their circumstances, too. We should look into the Romanian's childhood; he probably suffered from all kinds of abuse and misfortune. Does that mean those assholes need to be rescued, too?"

Amelia could see Tomás was having trouble saying his *r*'s and that the alcohol was making him take a harsher tone. She also saw that now wasn't the ideal moment for this, but she was on the hook, emotionally: she had made Rina and Luis's struggle to save Milena's life her own.

"Do what you like, but I'm not going to stand here while they kill her."

Tomás felt struck down again.

"What I'd like to do is rest, and it's obvious I won't be able to here." He tried to get up, but he grew dizzy and fell back on the sofa. "And I need to tell Claudia Emiliano's free, so she can sleep easy."

Tomás took his cell phone out and rang the owner of the newspaper. Amelia went to the kitchen for a glass of water. When she returned, she found Tomás asleep on the sofa, wrapped him in a blanket, and went to bed. Hours later, she felt his cold body arrive, hugging her tight, looking for warmth.

42

Jaime and Vidal

"**WITH EMILIANO REYNA BACK,** I want all eyes on Milena. The work crews should split up and tackle four lines of investigation. One will dig into Milena's past in Marbella, that's where the key to all this craziness lies. One will map out Bonso's gang: whorehouses, webpages, famous or influential clients, number of prostitutes, front businesses, etc. Another will try and get a grasp on Víctor Salgado. I want to know which politicians are on his side and how tight he is with the money launderers. The old guy was almost reverential when he brought them up. Last of all, I want a team tracking Milena and Luis's whereabouts."

Fifteen people were listening to Jaime in Lemlock's meeting room. Some were clearly suffering from lack of sleep: half had spent the night at the offices, but all hung on their boss's every word.

"Patricia will coordinate between the teams. I want one person from each reporting to her every six hours. Tomorrow we'll meet back up at nine."

When they dispersed, Jaime kept Patricia and Vidal back.

"What are you thinking of doing with Milena when we find her?" she asked once they were alone.

"It depends on what we discover about her time in Marbella. Milena could either be a major ace in the hole or a hot potato we need to get off our hands as quickly as possible. Everything suggests the pressure

239

from Spain has ramped up in recent weeks, and something provoked that. Right now, we're still in the dark."

"If we do find her, that doesn't mean we have to turn her in to Bonso, does it?" Vidal asked.

"We'll do what's best for everyone. With these things, you have to take your cue from your head and not your heart. We can't discard the possibility that turning Milena in might be the only way to save Luis or even Claudia. I hope you're aware of that. We won't know until we're certain who her protector is and why she was sent away. That's the only way we'll get a clear sense of what our options are and the risks each one involves."

Jaime gave Patricia additional instructions, and she left the room.

"Let me tell you another thing about Milena. Call this lesson number three for you. Misfortune doesn't make a person better, especially when it's this extreme. Every victim is dangerous; tragedy makes them desperate."

Vidal imagined Milena at sixteen, frightened and raped by her captors, but he simply nodded his head at what Jaime said.

"And me?" he asked "What should I do? Do I join one of the teams?"

"Your job is not to let Rina out of your sight. Sooner or later, Luis will get in touch with her, and you need to be there to find out what he says. He turned off his phone, so we can't trace him that way. Anyway, I think you and Rina have a lot to talk about."

"Yeah, I tried to get a sense of what's pushing her, as you said. I think she's disoriented. She's looking for something to give meaning to her life, but she doesn't know where to begin. She's scared of lots of things."

"Very good. You're going in the right direction. No one falls in love so fast unless there's some kind of pressing need there. It's not the person—your friend, in this case—but the longing for protection and purpose that's attracting her to Luis. For her, he represents safety and certainty."

Vidal fell silent. How could he offer Rina safety and certainty?

"You have a better chance than Luis at giving Rina what she's looking for," Jaime said. "Luis is always going to find his projects more important than people. You're not like that: I can assure you that if you had been in the same situation as Luis at the cabin, you wouldn't have run away with Milena. You would have gone back to Rina as soon as possible to try and protect her. Am I right?"

"Obviously. Just thinking that Bonso could have taken her away makes me sick."

"You have to convince Rina that you're her true ally."

"So I need to find out what Rina's real needs are? That's it? That's how you make a person happy?"

"No. There's a difference between needs and desires. There are women who get married to take care of their needs, but most of them are driven to it by their desires. I can assure you that Rina is the second type. Figure out what she wants, even if she doesn't know. When you do, she's yours. Try to get her excited about her projects with Amelia; she could become a key collaborator. That's a much more attractive path than playing second fiddle to Luis and his schemes. Over there, she'll be in the shadows. Here, she'll be a leader."

"And I'd be the one who opened that door for her," Vidal said.

"That's right, and she'll know she owes you for it. You have to be patient and delicate and get her to that point. Don't criticize what she has with Luis; it could be over next week, anyway. All you need to do is bring the conversation around to the important contribution she could make as one of Amelia's consultants."

"Rina will stay at home with her uncle these days and they look at me as part of the family. I can stay there the whole time, except nights. I'll take her to a bookstore café so she can buy the books she needs for her work with Amelia."

"Right, but don't forget your main job: finding Luis as soon as he gets in touch with you. Take a company car and also this," Jaime said, removing a stack of bills from his wallet. "Don't let her pay for anything."

When Vidal came back to see Rina, he was beaming with the confidence that comes from the keys to a powerful automobile and a few thousand pesos in hand. And more importantly, he had a plan to get his love back.

She was in the reception area ready to go, just waiting for him to return.

"I'm hungry as a wolf. Will you take me to breakfast?"

"I'd love to. Have you had *tortas de tamal*? It's carbs inside of more carbs, you won't be hungry for days."

"Cool. I'll call Amelia on the way. I left her hanging on the budget analysis. If she wants, I'll go on to her office afterward."

Rina said nothing more and gazed at the phone in her hand. Neither she nor Vidal noticed the car that was following them.

Me, I treat my whores great. They live like queens: they give me pleasure, I give them money. I mean, it's not fortunes we're talking about, but still, my wife would love to be able to afford the dresses I've seen on Romilia.

Like everything in life, prostitution's neither good nor bad on its own. I know men and women that work as domestics, and they get treated worse than whores. Juanita, the Ecuadorian girl who works for Juan Pedro, the guy with the hardware stores—she's a slave to her bosses. Every week my wife tells me something new and terrible they've put her through. Even that bony teenage son of theirs is fucking her behind closed doors, and I wouldn't be surprised if the father was, too. They'll end up knocking her up and then she'll be out on her ass. She'd have been better off as a hooker; at least she'd be getting paid for it.

I know brothels are creepy places and some women suffer like Job. But we didn't stop digging up minerals because of abuses in the mines, did we? They freed the blacks, but they didn't shut down the cotton plantations.

Now that I think about it, it's just a matter of regulation. Like on the plantations. If they introduced better working conditions, some oversight as far as sanitary conditions, and got rid of the bastard pimps exploiting the girls, it could be a legitimate business and everyone would be happy.

Just like if she was a dentist, Romilia could have her little office where she'd see her clients and she could set the hours and the prices. And that way, just like you choose a doctor when you're sick, you could choose the sex professional you liked best.

Of course, they'd need someone to supervise them, take care of them, protect them, arrange things with the inspectors. Now that I think about it, I could set Romilia up: I charge her a commission and then she can pay off the initial investment in installments. She'd have to work a full day, otherwise my little angel tends to get offtrack. Four clients a day, six days a week would be fine, and in eighteen months she'd recoup the investment and operating costs. And if I managed to get some of her friends in, the economy of scale would allow better margins.

That means the ideal service staff would consist of eight professionals, six on each shift and two to fill in when the chicks were on break or needed patching up.

I'd have a generous marketing plan (commissions among the hospitality workers and servers in the neighborhood, advertising on the web and in local newspapers) and a budget for recruiting new candidates, because the turnover's really high. Recruiting is highly specialized, so that means I'd have to outsource it. The easiest thing is to have a versatile inventory to address the various niche markets: mulatas, Northern Europeans, Africans, Latin Americans, and a couple of Spanish girls (maybe I could even bag the Ecuadorian for low-rent customers).

After making a few notes in Excel, I come up with the following numbers:

Income
  Six active workers per shift
  Twenty-four clients served per day minimum
  150 euros average per service
  3,600 euros per day
  108,000 euros per month operating at 100 percent
  54,000 euros per month operating at 50 percent

Personnel expenses
  Base monthly salary: 1,000 euros
  Commission per client served: 10 percent
  Cumulative monthly salary per employee: 2,440 with four clients per day; 1,720 with two clients per day.
  Estimated monthly payroll and commissions: 13,760 to 19,550 euros

Fixed costs

    Rent: 4,000

    Security (two guards): 3,000

    Equipment and supplies: 1,200

    Payment for inspectors and permissions: 5,000

    Medical and sanitary services: 1,500

    Accounting: 1,200

    Marketing: 5,000

    Miscellaneous operating expenses: 1,500

    Unforeseen expenses: 2,000

    Total expenses: 45,950 at 100% capacity, 39,760 at 50%

That makes an operating profit between 14,240 and 62,048 per month. In other words, an EBITDA ranging from 26 percent and 57 percent, depending on the number of clients served. The initial investment and then some could be recouped within six months. I could even be generous with my employees and offer them incentives: a bonus for employee of the month, a prize for whoever has the highest customer satisfaction.

    A solid business. The only bad thing is, even if I got laid for free, I never liked sleeping with people from the office. I'd still need my Romilia.

O.A. FINANCIAL DIRECTOR
OF HIGH-SPEED RAILWAYS

43

Luis and Milena

FRIDAY, NOVEMBER 14, 8:45 A.M.

LUIS AND MILENA couldn't get warm all night, but they still didn't embrace again, and barely spoke. It took them three hours to reach the road and a few more to reach the first few houses while they looked for a taxi. They went slowly, because Luis preferred to keep a certain distance from the road, away from where the vehicles passed; he knew that sooner or later their pursuers would take that same route to get back to Mexico City.

When day broke, they stopped and rested on some rocks with their faces turned to the sun, desperate for warmth. They still had food, but their water had run out some time before. Thirst made them get moving again. At the first shop they came across, they bought bottles of water and asked where there was a taxi stand. The cashier recommended they catch a bus and told them where to find one. They walked a few blocks to a strange outcropping of miserable shacks. It was just one more of the villages built by illegal investment on the foothills of the mountain range, far from the hand of God or the government.

Milena was surprised by the harshness of the poverty. Though it was cold, half the windows were just holes in makeshift walls of cardboard and brick. The streets were dust-covered grooves with nothing more to mark them off than the arbitrary arrangement of the houses on the hillside. An old woman and what looked like her grandson walked up the steep road carting buckets of water that seemed to tear at the shoulder joints of their filthy arms. Milena remembered a documentary about life in isolated African villages, scenes that she could imagine in indigenous zones but not on the outskirts of Mexico City, with its tall buildings and broad avenues.

A half-hour later, they squeezed into a local bus headed into the city. Milena said she was happy that at least for a day, the kids went to school or to some park far away from the misery of their hovels. Luis decided not to tell her that many of them would spend their days at some intersection downtown selling trinkets or begging for spare change.

Their stature and skin tone created a contrast with the rest of the passengers, and some of them stared. Luis hoped they'd pass for hikers. Standing up, compressed in the aisle, he was holding the backpack with his laptop between his and her bodies, like a young couple cradling their precious baby between their arms. And in a way, that's what it was: because that computer held the key for resolving Milena's dilemma, or at least Luis believed so. She liked that the other passengers took them for a couple in love, their only worry the potholes in the road that made them jump every few yards.

Two hours later, close to the enormous Tasqueña metro station, he checked into the kind of hotel where no one asks questions or shows ID. He paid for three nights in cash. Milena still had almost nine thousand dollars in her bag, but their attempts to remain anonymous worked out well for her economically, because they were obliged to eat in cheap restaurants and cantinas. Luis wanted to leave right away for an internet café and start his offensive against Bonso, but the sleepless night and the long walk had taken a lot out of both of them. They took turns cleaning up in a shower that stank of other bodies and climbed into the bed to sleep. He left his clothes on, because of the cold in the room, he said, and she put on a long T-shirt she fished out of her bag. They slept the whole morning, back to back.

At two in the afternoon, Luis woke up and observed his companion's relaxed face and deep breaths as she slept. There was something virginal in the image before him: a vestal figure in the moment before sacrifice. It was hard for him to reconcile Milena's face with the crimes he'd heard about the night before.

He went through his pockets looking for a scrap of paper to leave a note before he left the room. When he didn't find one, he opened the black book, the corner of which peeped out from Marina's bag, resting on a chair. He started to tear out a sheet.

"What are you doing?" he heard. The tone was hostile, distrustful.

Luis showed Milena the piece of paper he had pulled out and put the notebook back in the bag.

"I was going to leave you a note," he said. "I'm going to look for a public place with internet. Now that you're up, write down some of the names you told me yesterday. Rosado? Vila-Rojas? Do you remember the other Flamingos?"

Milena's withering gaze faded, and she got up and walked to the chair to flip through her notebook. Luis tried to avert his eyes from her body, looking at his backpack and going through the inside pockets to take out a pen.

While Milena wrote, Luis went to wash his face. Then he went over her notes and prepared to leave.

"I'm coming back around six. It would be best if you didn't leave the room. There's still fruit in the bags. When I come back, I'll take you to dinner. Sound good? On my way out, I'll tell the front desk not to clean the room."

"Do you think they ever do?" she said with a cheeky laugh while her eyes swept across it. She was happy now. The scene felt so domestic:

the husband leaving the house for a day at the office. Milena walked to the door and gave him a kiss on the cheek. "I'll wait for you here. When you come back, we'll have dinner and you can tell me about your progress. Will you bring me some newspapers? A book would be even better. I don't want to be shut up in here with just a TV," she said, looking at the junky set on the shelf. "If it even works," she added with a grin.

Luis passed by reception briefly, then out to the street. He had to talk to Rina as soon as possible.

44

Tomás

THEY ATE BREAKFAST like there was no tomorrow: mango, mandarin-orange juice, eggs in salsa verde, coffee with pastries. Tomás liked to get up late and make breakfast his main meal of the day. Amelia preferred to start the day with something more frugal, and only went along with his gluttony on those long, relaxed Saturday brunches when both of them read the paper and gave their running commentary. Even though it was a Friday, she decided to stay with him longer than usual and put off her work at the office, considering their argument over Milena the night before.

They didn't revisit the theme in the morning. Emilio's freedom still had Tomás elated, even if he was hungover. They compared the newspapers' front pages, decided President Prida needed to make changes in his cabinet after the years of attrition, and remarked that Jaime seemed more like his famous father by the day. Amelia had been left shaken up by a nightmare involving Claudia, but all her worries dissipated as they ran down the pros and cons of various ministers and their possible replacements.

Breakfast broke off abruptly when Isabel called Tomás to tell him Emiliano wasn't well. Tomás promised to stop by their home right away. Amelia talked with Rina briefly on the phone, and they arranged to meet at her office in an hour so Rina could resume her analysis of the budget law. They said goodbye with a kiss and made plans to meet that night. She watched him leave, and a vague and indefinable feeling clouded her spirit.

Emiliano's colonial mansion was in Coyoacán on a cobblestone street with tall birch trees. Isabel was an unusual Chilean, dark-skinned and with curly hair, easier to imagine on a beach in the Caribbean than in the Andes. The four-year-old who met him in the doorway had his father's face and his mother's hair.

The deputy director of opinion was on the terrace facing the rectangular inner courtyard, idly watching the rhythmical dripping of a gurgling stone fountain. On the table was a still-unopened copy of *El Mundo*. Despite his clean pajamas, his two days' of beard growth and gaunt face revealed the terror he'd been through.

"They're animals, Tomás," he said.

"You're safe now, Emiliano. It was a bad dream. Now it's over."

"They kept me handcuffed in a van the whole time, they didn't even take them off for me to sleep. The worst thing is they never even told me what it was about."

"Did they hit you?"

"Twice, I think, when I was complaining a lot and then when I asked for help when I heard voices out on the street. Both times, this guy called the Turk came in and kicked the shit out of me until the other guys made him stop. If they didn't, I think he would have killed me."

Tomás looked over his friend. Though the pajamas covered his body, he could see a bright contusion around his wrist. He held his torso at an odd angle and kept his elbow close to his ribs.

"I'm really sorry, Emiliano. They need to look you over. Let my driver take you to the hospital, you might have broken something."

"Isabel's going to take me now. But first, I need to ask you why they kidnapped me: I need to know if I'm in danger, if my family's safe. I only saw the boss at first, when he called you from my phone—a real nasty piece of work. I heard something about Milena. What's that got to do with me?"

"Nothing," Tomás responded, and told the story of the Croatian in broad strokes. "So as you can see, you have nothing to fear. It's got nothing to do with you. Take a few days, go somewhere, forget this nightmare. When you come back, it'll seem like nothing, a story to impress people with after dinner."

"Just a bad dream, huh? A story to tell after dinner?" Emiliano looked at Tomás with fury. He stood up from the chair and took down his pajama pants: on the right buttock, he had a fresh tattoo, an enormous B. "They raped me before they branded me. They told me I was their property now."

Forty minutes later, having listened to Emiliano's story, Tomás showed up at Claudia's house, profoundly aggrieved. The whole way, he asked himself how the hell he was going to keep the promise he'd made to Emiliano and kill the Turk.

For now, he needed to warn Claudia and the rest of the Blues that they were in the middle of a war with different rules from the ones they'd known before. What they'd done to Emiliano didn't make any sense: the violence was as gratuitous as it was savage. He assumed glumly that once again, this terrain would be far more familiar to Jaime than to the rest of them.

Claudia had been up all night but slept long and deep after getting word of Emiliano's freedom.

"Well, that's one crisis off the list," she said once they were in her studio, each with a cup of coffee in hand. This time, her husband wasn't there. "Now we'll have to get everything ready for the lunch on Monday with the president. I suppose we should get an agenda ready, even if it's just things we're going to throw out in the course of the conversation, no?"

"I guess so. Aggressions toward journalists haven't ceased and the economic situation at the daily papers is dismal. In other countries, they're looking into fiscal exemptions to alleviate the crisis news companies are facing. We could bring some of that up in our talk."

Tomás found it odd that Claudia wasn't talking about Milena, who had become an obsession of hers since her father's death. He wondered whether it was better to keep silent about the torment Emilio had been through and stick to the subjects Claudia proposed. If they did manage to forget Milena, maybe they wouldn't hear of the matter again, and they could go on with the already-hazardous job of running a newspaper. If they were lucky, the story of the disturbing black book was nothing more than a senile exaggeration of Don Rosendo's.

But he couldn't count on it. Deep down, Tomás knew he was fooling himself. The violence Emiliano had gone through had been ruthless and unnecessary. The rape and the tattooing took place after their meeting with Víctor Salgado; it was a warning.

He asked for a beer and proceeded to tell her what he had talked about that morning with Emiliano.

"He didn't let me leave until he'd made me promise the Turk would die, but I can't consider that," he concluded.

"Why not?" she said. "A piece-of-shit delinquent can't do something like that to a director from *El Mundo* and get away with it. I don't care if he dies under arrest or in jail, after he's been caught. We owe it to Emiliano, and we owe it to the paper."

It was as if Tomás were seeing Claudia for the first time. Her implacable attitude was more like Rosendo Franco's than that of someone who had studied the Renaissance in Italy. Apparently she had learned more Sicilian culture than Florentine.

"I understand what you're saying and I guarantee you that bastard will pay for what he did. But killing him . . . I don't know."

"If you don't want to get wrapped up in it, don't, I'll understand. I'll take care of it on my own. And don't even think we're going to hand Milena over to them. If they want war, they've got it."

Tomás didn't dare remind her that they didn't have Milena either. Her red hair and flushed face were the very image of indignation.

"Do you want to talk to the president about this?"

"I don't think so. If we do, how will we explain it when the Turk dies on us?"

Tomás couldn't help but laugh.

"Well, you're more of a bitch than you look like with that pretty face, if you'll let me say so, boss. Are you sure Rosendo wasn't getting you ready behind the scenes?"

"It's not about me, Tomás. The truth is, I'm not a fighter: just look at me with my marriage. But *El Mundo* is different. I grew up in a house where it is almost a religion: life or death, you defend the newspaper, and no blow goes unanswered. It's as simple as that."

"Agreed," Tomás said, a little rueful that he'd laughed at Claudia. "For now, we need to beef up security. I'm talking to Jaime today to put together a strategy."

"You think he can help us with the other issue, too? The Turk, I mean. Can you trust him?"

"Oh, I can trust him. Whether he's willing to help us or not is another thing, but I can ask."

She got up from her chair and walked over to him, then mussed his hair.

"Thanks, Tomás. Help me if you can, and don't judge me. I don't want this to push us apart."

He raised an arm to wrap it around her waist, but she moved away, turned around, and offered him a tequila.

"It's already noon, right?"

45

Milena

JUNE 2012

HER FIRST MURDER was so antiseptic it struck her as inoffensive, even a letdown. The Flamingos had started meeting again a few months before, but now they did so more discreetly than in previous years: a long lunch in some rented villa, the girls at nightfall, and talking till dawn.

Vila-Rojas instructed Milena how to approach Cristóbal Puyol at their next reunion. They called him the Catalan even though he was from Córdoba. He looked like a gypsy through and through, not just because of his brown skin and oily, curly hair: his florid shirts and the gold chain around his neck made him a dissonant figure among his colleagues. Despite his appearance, he was the most sought-after tax lawyer for local businessmen. Puyol had a natural instinct for finding cracks in the fiscal codes and exploiting their weaknesses to the maximum.

In recent years, Vila-Rojas had begun consulting with him on delicate matters. Generally, in these kinds of consultancies, quantities and the names of companies and shareholders go unmentioned: you state the problem, you pay a fee, and that's that.

But on one occasion it was necessary to show him all the contracts and documents for the establishment of a philanthropic organization whose real purpose was to send money back to the Ukrainian mafia after it had been laundered through tourism. Vila-Rojas wanted to be sure of the legal status of a recently created front organization that channeled resources to fake humanitarian causes in North Africa. The money was sent to local charities in Morocco, Algeria, and Western Sahara, but only a small part went to digging wells or building houses in the country. The biggest piece of the pie returned to Europe through fake purchases of Russian grain. It was a financial virtuous circle: the Marbella businessmen got a tax break thanks to their donations, and the Ukrainian mafia got back the money it paid to the hotels for nonexistent room charges at inflated prices.

But after Operation White Whale and the arrest of various colleagues, Vila-Rojas felt less sure that the foundation would pass unnoticed among the Spanish treasury inspectors. For now, he had diminished the quantity of donations and started investing more in housing construction in the Sahara. Still, Cristóbal Puyol was a weak link. If the Catalan fell, he could negotiate with the authorities by giving them Vila-Rojas's head.

The night of the party, at a spacious country house in the hills bordering Marbella, Milena had no problems getting close to Puyol. He had a thing for blondes, and she made sure to be the first to sidle up to him. She observed with satisfaction that he was already drunk, but Puyol didn't seem to want to make it easy on her: he called over another blonde, a Bulgarian named Alexa, and she settled in on his right. They spent a few hours in the living room among the other guests while the girls organized a striptease contest. Puyol was the clown of the group: he got up on the table and challenged the professionals.

The Catalan never left the two blondes alone. Convinced Alexa wouldn't move, Vila-Rojas approached her, saying he admired her tailored dress, then took her by the waist and led her off to dance.

The strategy worked out poorly: Puyol called another blonde to fill the gap she'd left behind. There was no lack of replacements. There were fifteen women for seven men.

A little before two in the morning, Puyol stood up shakily, his mind clouded but his burning desires crystal clear. He stripped off his clothes, sat in an armchair in the bedroom, and told the two girls to have sex with each other. After a while Milena got tired, but Alexa wanted to keep going. The Croatian's pussy turned her on. Milena feigned an orgasm to get Puyol on his feet. She knew what voyeurs liked.

"Come here, my lord," she said to him. "I'd rather finish off with your dick than with her little tongue."

Puyol didn't answer, but the invitation excited him. He took his member in his hand and shook it without taking his eyes off the raised ass of Alexa, whose face was still buried between Milena's legs. He stood up with a swollen dick, got in the bed on his knees, and penetrated the Bulgarian from behind. Milena sat up, left the bed, took something from the pile of clothing on the floor, and got behind him. While he rammed Alexa, Milena caressed his balls and anus, and he reacted with delight. Then she pushed a finger inside him. Just before he came, she took out her finger and slipped in the suppository, pushing it in as deep as she could. She kept her finger inside him until he exploded in Alexa's body and fell back, exhausted. Puyol didn't notice the foreign object inside him, or he didn't care. Either way, he collapsed and fell asleep.

Vila-Rojas had assured her that it wouldn't provoke a sudden death or anything like it. He just said she should wash her hands as soon as possible afterward, and she did as instructed. She grabbed her bag and went to the bathroom, still naked, and scrubbed herself furiously with alcohol.

The next few days, she kept her eyes on the copies of *El Sur*, a local paper that the guards would bring home along with *Marca* to keep up with the sports and politics, but she never saw anything about Cristóbal Puyol. Four months later, by the time she had stopped looking for news, another of the girls remarked that one of her clients, the Catalan, had shot himself. One of the obituaries stated that Marbella was in mourning over the death of a local accountant with an unblemished reputation.

From what Milena could gather—and as Vila-Rojas himself would later corroborate, with little enthusiasm and fewer details—they found Puyol's body naked in his home office on a Monday morning. His family—a wife and two daughters—had spent the weekend in Seville picking out gifts for one of the girls' upcoming wedding. On his desk, next to his body, the authorities found two lab reports with the same result: Puyol was infected with HIV and Hepatitis C. Though potentially fatal, both were treatable.

The next time she saw Vila-Rojas, in the suite in the Hotel Bellamar after Puyol's suicide, was the first time they made love. She took it as a kind of reward. It was also the first time she had an orgasm. She was surprised by the intensity of his reaction: she didn't know if he had a wife or girlfriend, and as far as she could tell from what her coworkers said, he never slept with professionals either. More importantly, it was the first time he had caressed her gently and given in to what he must have felt for her.

With time, she understood that what she'd done hadn't killed the Catalan, but that the infection had been the perfect pretext for someone to stage his suicide without arousing suspicions.

For the next few months, she went on seeing Vila-Rojas two or three times a week, telling him about the clients who visited her and the conversations she overheard. They didn't make love again until he presented her with the next case, but sometimes their information sessions would devolve into long conversations, stretching on past midnight. For him, she got deeper into the mission he had assigned her, and probing the other girls about the clients they saw, and she took further risks, trying to wheedle useful information out of her own. She'd go through phones, pockets, and wallets when the men weren't around. Pleased with his protégée's initiative, he gave her a cell phone and showed her how to take photos of documents, but she rarely used it: where she lived, they were contraband.

46

Amelia and Rina

FRIDAY, NOVEMBER 14, 1:30 P.M.

"I'M PREGNANT, VIDAL," Rina said, and he felt his heart skip a beat, and not only because he'd just eaten *tortas de tamal* they'd bought from a stand in Colonía Juárez.

She uncovered her belly, markedly swollen between her two hip-bones. Only then did he understand the joke, and he smiled laggardly.

"I think I need an Alka-Seltzer to abort," she added, rubbing her belly.

"You can have a chamomile tea, that'll help," he said.

He always thought of something witty to say seconds later, but never when he needed it. He asked himself how Luis would have responded to her joke. It was a lost cause, he thought, especially because his friend had been so worried about Luis all morning. Though he had tried to cheer her up, talking about the importance of her work at Amelia's office, Rina was distracted and stared at her phone's screen every few seconds.

In the end, they ordered a coffee in a bookstore on the Avenida Álvaro Obregón, and while they waited to be served, she browsed through the economics section, finding nothing she wanted. As a gift, he bought her Ian McEwan's *Sweet Tooth*, a love story with a happy ending that he had read on Tomás's recommendation months before.

The gift made her strangely irritated. Now she'd have to read it because he'd ask her every few days if she'd liked it. Vidal's constant attention wore her out. He reacted so intensely to everything she said or did. She missed Luis; his self-esteem was difficult to wound.

As if she had conjured him, Rina's phone rang in her hand and showed an unknown number.

"Hey, hot stuff, I'm at a public phone, I can't talk long."

"Are you okay?" she said, rushing out to the street, afraid she might lose her signal inside the building.

"Great. You? Did you already leave Lemlock? Are you free?"

"Yeah, everything's back to normal. Vidal's with me. I talked to Amelia and I'll be working in her office all day. I'm worried about you . . . " she said in a barely audible tone, noticing that Vidal had crept up beside her.

"I'm worried about you, too, but don't let it get to you. I won't be traceable while I'm working on what I told you about before. Don't worry about our friend, either. Everything's going to be okay, you'll see."

"Promise me you won't take unnecessary risks."

"I promise. I'll call you tomorrow. And stay away from Lemlock, nothing good comes out of that place. You're better off with Amelia."

"Done," she said. "I promise. You want to talk to Vidal?"

"Not now. Bye."

She wanted to say something more, but he'd already hung up.

Vidal was disappointed, but also slightly relieved, that he hadn't talked to his friend. He knew Lemlock was recording the call and they would have evaluated his ability to extract useful information from Luis during their conversation. He didn't want to disappoint his uncle, but he also didn't want to betray his friend. Vidal was playing a complex game, trying to get Milena back but also to protect Luis from the absurd risks he was running.

He tried to explain his strategy to Rina.

"Maybe the opposite is true," she said, "maybe the only way out is the one he's proposing: to manipulate information on the Net and try and take down Bonso's gang."

"What? That's what he's up to? How's he thinking of doing that?"

She decided it was better to stay quiet. Maybe she'd already said too much: she trusted Vidal absolutely, but he was too good a person. He'd be incapable of betraying her or Luis or of doing anything to harm them, but Jaime could get information out of him without his even realizing it. Rina appreciated what Lemus did, but she had to respect Luis's instincts. If he didn't want to share his plans, then she wouldn't do so either.

"No fucking idea. Hey, our coffees are getting cold, and the way we look right now, they'll think we're trying to leave without paying," she said, and dragged him back to the table they had left.

When they arrived at the PRD offices, Amelia was already waiting for them.

"Rina! Look at all that's happened since we last saw each other," Amelia said, and hugged her.

She had ordered sandwiches, coffee, and soft drinks that both of them turned down. Rina touched her belly again and remarked that she'd just miscarried.

Amelia informed them that Emiliano was free and there was nothing else to fear there. Rina cheered and Vidal tried to show the same enthusiasm, though he'd already found out from Jaime that morning. He hadn't wanted to share the news with Rina, thinking it would be best if she didn't know he attended Lemlock's planning meetings.

Rina felt calmer. She took the news as a sign that the gang they were up against wasn't as savage as the killers the mafia had hired to slaughter her family the year before. Vidal used this to argue in favor of Jaime and his ability to handle the criminals.

Rina decided to spend the next few hours studying the budget proposal in Amelia's meeting room. Vidal used the time to visit Rina's aunt and uncle's house and ask her cousin, Violeta, for a change of clothes for her, but he didn't dare mention she'd also asked him to pick up some pads. He preferred blushing in the pharmacy while he asked for a box of Kotex. Rina was impassive in her tone when she asked for them, as if she was talking about a tube of toothpaste. He didn't know the codes of conduct of girls of his age: that was something that was never talked about at his house. Back at the office, Vidal put together a Spotify playlist for Rina, and she found it perfect background music for her work.

"Vidal, I'm going to stay here the rest of the afternoon. If you want, we can see each other tonight at my uncle's place. You must have stuff to do in the meantime, right?"

"You're what I have to do right now. As long as Milena and Luis are on the run, they might need us. It's better if we stay together. Besides, I'm making headway on a piece of software Luis and I have been working on. So don't worry about me."

Rina kept looking at him, thinking she'd been ungrateful those past few days. She walked to the other end of the long meeting table, hugged him like a sister, and gave him a kiss on the cheek.

"You're a doll."

He tried to get up and almost tripped and fell. By the time he was standing, she was already walking back to the other end of the table.

Vidal's excitement came in part from the physical contact, especially because she was the one who'd initiated it, and also because he'd had to rush to cover the screen so she wouldn't see the report he was writing for Jaime.

Slowly he calmed down. It seemed Rina hadn't seen anything. Still, the scene made him feel like a traitor once more, especially now.

Later that afternoon, Amelia returned to the meeting room and the two women talked about the budget documents. Vidal went out to the hallway to make a call to Lemlock.

"What do you think of Jaime?" Rina asked when she noticed Vidal was gone.

Amelia looked at her closely.

"In what sense? As a friend, consultant, best man at a wedding?"

"Gross! Best man!" Rina protested with a cackle. "I think I'd rather not get married. No, I'm asking you, in a way, for Milena. He seems very interested in rescuing her and protecting her. Vidal trusts him completely, and Luis doesn't trust him one bit. In fact, it's the opposite."

"Well, they're both right. There are moments when you can't turn down Jaime's help. Other times, it's better to think twice. His assistance always comes with a price tag, and sooner or later, he'll make you pay up."

"And when he supports you, is he trying to help you or use you?"

"That's a question that you could ask about everyone, isn't it?"

Amelia recognized that what she had said was closer to Jaime's cynicism than to the idealism she once had. Her time in the world of professional politics had made her vision of life more bitter.

"Even in the support you get from your family, there's a tacit agreement of reciprocity," she continued. "Maybe *using you* isn't the best way to describe what somebody expects when they do you a favor, but there's always a personal motivation. Every Samaritan has his reasons for getting off the road to help a stranger."

Rina wasn't convinced. She didn't think benevolence needed an explanation. She didn't know why she wanted to help Milena, but she didn't need to invent a justification. But there was one thing

Amelia was right about: Jaime was far from altruistic in the services he offered.

"It's something I'll have to resolve alone, no?" she said.

"Jaime? Yeah, but I think Luis and Milena have a place in that, too. Don't take that responsibility on yourself."

She was going to reply, but Vidal's return interrupted her.

47

Jaime

INSTEAD OF HEADING a team meeting he had called his staff to Saturday morning, Jaime was eating breakfast with Tomás in front of Parque México.

"I'm not saying we should do it, but *if* we want to fulfill Emiliano and Claudia's wishes, do you think it could be done?" Tomás asked.

"Wait, are you telling me to take charge of assassinating the Turk?" Jaime responded, unable to suppress a smile.

"It's just a hypothetical scenario," Tomás responded, his eyes not shifting from the tablecloth.

"Of course it can be done," Jaime said, restraining himself. "That's not the problem."

"What is it, then?"

"According to Bonso's code, and the code of those above him, revenge multiplies exponentially. You answer a broken finger with a broken arm; you kill one of their guys, they leave six of yours with their throats slit. The death of a valued enforcer they'll punish by wiping out their rival's family. What I mean is yeah, you can get rid of the Turk, but you have to be ready for the war that comes afterward."

Tomás fell silent. The ethical fine points were minor compared with the violent consequences.

"It's not worth it," he said.

"Wait, that doesn't mean that it can't be done. You just have to find a way for others to get the blame. It's complicated, but it's doable."

"Let me talk to Claudia again first. Then I'll get in touch."

"Sure. In the meantime, we'll set up a security protocol for the newspaper's offices. Now that I've been there, I see it has tons of holes in it."

"I'm worried about Rina, Luis, and Vidal. Bonso and the bastards he runs with know Milena was in Rina's house. Claudia's exposed as well."

"Claudia's security isn't bad, it's the same as her father had, though I can go over their procedures. I'm keeping an eye on Rina and Vida, even if they don't know it. There's nothing we can do about Luis, he's on his own. The one who worries me is you. You're the most vulnerable piece in the puzzle. That driver you've got is fucking worthless, not to mention he never shuts his damn mouth."

Tomás asked himself how the hell Jaime knew about Silvano's chattiness, but he let the comment slide. Anyway, his friend was right; if they wanted vengeance, he was the ideal victim. And yet surrounding himself with a security detail didn't seem a viable possibility at this point in his life. It would mean giving up freedoms and taking on the symbols of a status he had always struggled against. For now, he would have to convince his daughter, Jimena, to leave the city, and for that, he'd have to speak with his ex-wife.

They said goodbye as on so many other occasions. They both felt a vague mutual contempt mixed with a slightly sick fascination with one another.

At the Lemlock morning meeting, Jaime's team had a profile of Bonso's gang, the addresses of a number of his houses, the webpages he operated and the intermediaries he used to produce and distribute pornography. It was good information for an ambush, if it ever came to that, but none of it suggested where the Romanian might be. Apparently, he had abandoned his routines and wasn't showing up at the usual places.

There was one minor step forward with respect to Víctor Salgado. He was cozy with the coordinator of the PRI senators and had ties to three governors whose chiefs of security he might have procured in Tamaulipas, Michaocán, and Colima, territories infested with drug cartels. But there was little information related to the financial circuits and the money laundering the ex-director of prisons was wrapped up in.

Milena's location was still a mystery, and Jaime was furious. Luis had done a good job of disappearing somewhere in Mexico City, and he only hoped he was as hard to find for Salgado and his people, too. At least Jaime had the advantage of monitoring the umbilical cord Vidal and Rina represented for the two fugitives.

On the most important point, there had been no progress whatsoever. The Interpol dossier on Bonso they had gotten hold of through back channels showed innumerable run-ins with the Spanish authorities, but all minor, nothing that led to Milena or Alka Moritz. Jaime had the best team of hackers in the country, but they didn't know who else to look for, or where, in the European files. It was still impossible to know what made the Croatian so important for the criminals.

At 12:40, Patricia burst into the office.

"Thanks to Vidal, the knot's coming unraveled," she said.

Lemus had asked for a fifth line of investigation: tapping into Luis's work sessions. Though his friend used a great deal of security, Vidal showed them the methods he used to erase his tracks and some of the accounts he used to receive messages. A few times, Vidal had hit on his codes for accessing the inner circle of Anonymous, the international organization of hackers and cyberactivists. He wasn't an active member, but he had collaborated with them on attacks in the past.

With that information, Lemlock's team, led by Mauricio Romo, was able to find traces of Luis's steps on the Net those past few hours. They saw he'd posted a request on the Anonymous message board to investigate a certain Agustín Vila-Rojas, whom he accused of using the web to launder enormous quantities of money coming from the Ukrainian mafia in Spain. Anonymous was usually interested in anything that concerned online criminal activity, but for now, Luis was only asking for documentation in the case. Thanks to the passwords Vidal had provided them, they found that one of his aliases had been used to access various pages in the Darknet linked to human trafficking.

Lemlock's operatives perused the pages Luis had visited and were unsurprised to find they were the same ones employed by Bonso and his hangers-on.

Excited by these discoveries, Jaime gave his hackers new instructions. The best ones should concentrate on searching for any and everything related to Agustín Vila-Rojas and the Ukrainian mafia in Spain. From the little Víctor Salgado had said, it was obvious that Milena had been close to someone powerful in the money-laundering world. He assumed Luis had gotten Vila-Rojas's name directly from her. A few keystrokes confirmed they were on the right track: Vila-Rojas was a highly regarded finance lawyer in Marbella.

Lemus slowly examined the face on the screen. He liked it: a rival cut from the same cloth. The mystery of Milena finally had a face.

48

Luis and Milena

SUNDAY, NOVEMBER 16, 2:00 P.M.

MILENA'S MEMORY WAS REMARKABLE, Luis thought as he watched her transcribing information on her clients: physical traits, the use of some characteristic phrase, the layout of the room, the song she heard an afternoon two years before. Luis had asked her to make an effort to remember everything she could about the Flamingos. When he came back that Saturday night, she handed him a handful of pages torn from her notebook. After going over them, he realized very little of what was there would help him tracking the crime syndicate from the Costa del Sol. He consoled himself thinking that at least it had kept her busy during the hours when she was shut up.

But still he picked up on the names of people and businesses here and there and decided to underline a few promising bits. Absorbed in his reading, he began to see the parade of bodies, the nightlife and its ephemeral pleasures, the human race reduced to the single instant when it satisfied its longings. There were no adjectives, but no concessions either: just a redoubtable description starting with some pregnant detail, a revealing phrase. All together, it was a unique and ruthless portrait of the prostitution trade.

Luis realized that, in their own way, Milena's observations constituted a fresh insider's perspective of a sordid world to which, at times, she seemed not to belong. He assumed Milena had survived by disconnecting herself from that life, and maybe that was why it was hard for him to imagine her in a brothel or a bar. During their long conversation the previous night, before bed, Milena had spoken of her village as if she'd just left it yesterday. She told him of the scent of the chrysanthemums flanking the tombs in the cemeteries, the rough cloth of the school uniform, the basketball hoop that never got used. But he couldn't situate her in those stories as a teenage girl from the village either. For ten years, Milena had lived in the bubble of her readings, her vocabulary was extensive and literary, and she could transport herself more easily than he to a Siberian landscape, or understand the many different varieties of jealousy.

But at other points in the conversation, she showed that, far from being emotionally distant, as she sometimes seemed, she was devoured from within by a deep resentment against those responsible for her tragedy. A part of her wanted to escape and forget. Another was determined to get vengeance.

That Sunday morning, they went to a street market to buy fruit and some clothes for him, and they had breakfast at a long table with benches in an outdoor cantina. Milena had never been in one, and the explosion of colors and scents fascinated her. She asked the names of the unknown fruits and vegetables, dazzled to see them for the first time.

Then they walked two blocks to get her newspapers. As her interest in the press grew, she seemed to be searching for something. At first, he thought it had to do with Amelia, whom Milena had seen in one of the newspapers he brought her that first day. In an interview, the PRD leader had pushed for a stricter law against human trafficking. The Croatian had commented admiringly on Amelia's arguments.

But as the days passed, he realized Milena's interest wasn't confined to local news. Now she was asking him for newspapers he couldn't always get hold of in the working-class neighborhoods he was moving through. Once in a while, she asked him to do a Google search on what was going on in Ukraine and she would read on the screen for a while.

"What does Croatia have to do with Ukraine?" he had asked the night before. "Do you have relatives there?"

"None. But the Ukrainian mafia in Marbella is powerful and it's split into two groups I knew well."

"And what's going on in Ukraine affects them?"

"A lot. One of the two groups is close to the pro-Russian president who left the country in February. The other isn't. My guess is how this all turns out will change things in Marbella, at least among the mafias."

Luis remembered vaguely the news he'd read at the beginning of the year about the pharaonic luxury the former president had lived in. Apparently he was just a puppet of Putin's. He recalled the images from television of the people running through the palatial chambers and artificial lakes after the escape of the leader who was now taking refuge in Moscow.

He knew Milena was still hiding something about her former life, but he didn't want to pressure her. Especially not now, when she seemed newly reborn just forty-eight hours after wanting to throw herself in front of the metro.

Luis knew they were running an unnecessary risk by showing themselves at the market or walking down the street looking for newspapers, but Milena was content and calmer with their new life. When she saw that he was enjoying it, too, she couldn't help but feel a hint of confusion.

Again, they had slept back-to-back, but this time he'd stripped down to his underwear and T-shirt. Unlike the first night, it was hard for him to get to sleep. He couldn't relax with Milena's body inches away. When he woke up, she had an arm around his torso and her breath was tickling his neck.

But he had to recognize that after the incident in the forest, she had avoided any gesture that might be interpreted as an attempt at seduction. She went into the bathroom fully clothed, showered, and dressed again before coming back out.

In the morning, while she washed up and he tried to concentrate on something else besides the sound of the water and her body covered in soap, he thought about Rina and the only shower they had shared together. Then he let himself go, feeling the warm certainty that came whenever he thought of Rina. He remembered, more than anything, the sensation of being exactly in the right place when he was with her. But there wasn't much material to feed his memories; he'd spent more hours with Milena than with the girl he was in love with. He told himself that the situation shouldn't go on much longer.

When he made it to a café that afternoon, the long session at the computer helped him leave any emotional dalliance behind. He was so focused on his investigation that he barely heard the alarm that told him he'd spent ninety minutes on the same connection at Gloria Jean's Coffee. He'd made a map of twelve places that offered free public Wi-Fi, and he shifted among them every hour and a half. It was an additional security measure beyond the firewalls and passwords that already protected him.

Thanks to the information Milena had given him about Vila-Rojas's operations, Luis had many leads to follow up on. Maybe the lawyer himself wasn't even aware of all the Croatian had managed to figure out since she crossed his path. Clients tended to be gossipy and presumptuous in their postcoital conversations, and Marbella's businessmen and politicians were no exception, especially when they thought they had a personal relationship with a prostitute. Milena had gone to many parties where men in power had chatted with one another as if they were alone. The women of the night were objects that passed unnoticed while the men talked businesses or bragged about their accomplishments. The satisfaction they expressed at a major deal, a successful meeting, or the start of a new project were loose facts she started weaving together when she saw a relationship between them and one of the Flamingos.

In a few hours, Luis accumulated a great deal of data. Much of it turned out to be useless, but it was plain to see that the biggest transactions, the most delicate tasks, sooner or later led back to Russia or Ukraine. Vila-Rojas appeared to be involved at two ends: when the dirty money made its way in and when it came back out clean. Both tended to lead back to citizens of the former Soviet Republics.

Luis hoped that some influential members of Anonymous would be interested in the matter, even if there was so much crime on the web that the organization barely pierced the surface of the Darknet. He had more hope for the email he'd sent to Bad Girl from Madrid, who was legendary among European hackers. He had met her in person ten months before, during his long stay in Barcelona. Bad Girl was her professional alias, though everyone knew her as The Mass. She did honor to both her nicknames.

A year before, a common friend had put the two of them in touch when Bad Girl was looking for a trustworthy Mexican hacker to avenge herself on a hotel chain in Riviera Maya that had ripped her off during her vacation. Luis helped her access the property registry in Quintana Roo and the digital archives of the local office of urban development. Thanks to him, she could publish on social media their violations of environmental regulations and the damages the Spanish businessmen had caused during the hotel's construction. For two weeks, the authorities had to shut down the bungalows they had built over a mangrove swamp.

Now Luis needed a favor in return. She and her friends could sift through Vila-Rojas's money-laundering networks faster than he could. He still wasn't sure what he was going to do with the information once he got it. To his surprise, Milena forbade his investigations from negatively affecting Vila-Rojas or his businesses. Luis didn't know if her attitude came from fear or some perverse sense of indebtedness to her mentor, but it was clearer and clearer that Milena's freedom would ultimately have to pass through the lawyer from Granada.

The calls for help he'd sent to Anonymous and Bad Girl allowed him to set aside the Spanish part and concentrate on Bonso and his allies. Here, he had a very clear idea of what he was doing. He posted warnings meant to poison Bonso's relationships with rival gangs: rumors of an HIV epidemic among the high-class girls from the main supplier of table dancers and accusations of embezzlement and fraud against Gardel, a major player from Argentina who brought Latin American girls into the Mexican market. He posted them on fake IP addresses tied to Bonso's computers and then lightly erased the trail. He figured any decent hacker would be able to follow his steps until they led back to the Romanian himself. And he knew the gangsters made use of them.

Last of all, he spent a few hours on the most reckless matter yet. He used the same IPs to enter a part of the Darknet where anonymous hit men offered their services, and promised a tempting quantity of bitcoins in exchange for Gardel's head. The system was simple and impeccable: the broker kept the bitcoins and would free them to whoever offered substantive proof of having carried out the mission. This way, it was impossible to detect where the order came from, who passed it along, and who accepted it. He trusted Gardel would find out about the threat and attribute it to Bonso thanks to the messages he had already posted elsewhere on the Net.

Luis looked up from his computer, with a sudden awareness of his surroundings. Two women were talking at the neighboring table about when and where you should wear a hat; he had crossed eyes with one of them a few times. Two yards away was a young man who hadn't taken his eyes off his tablet for half an hour, and the café employee, faithful to his job description, was ignoring everyone there. But he couldn't shake the impression that the atmosphere in the room had changed, and that those around him must somehow have detected what he was up to. He hesitated before hitting "Send," thinking of Jaime and how surprised he'd be when he found out his strategy for getting rid of Bonso. But he didn't want to be a killer. His cursor moved from "Send" to "Delete."

49

Tomás and Claudia

MONDAY, NOVEMBER 17, 3:00 P.M.

THEY FOUND THE PRESIDENT in a very good mood: the day before, the OECD and the Bank of Mexico had projected 2.4 percent growth in GDP for the year now coming to a close. Modest, but twice as good as the year before. The experts knew the largest part of the improvement had been the result of a favorable international climate, but that didn't prevent the government from trumpeting its virtues and attributing it to the reforms it had passed. The claims might not be true, but in a way it was fair to make them: when the nation's economy was plummeting because of an international crisis, as president he had borne the brunt of the blame. "You win some, you lose some," Tomás thought.

"Claudia, I appreciate the opportunity your visit has given me to reiterate my deepest condolences. An immense loss for the country," Alfonso Prida said as he walked toward them with open arms.

He squeezed Franco's daughter as if she were a beloved family member. The president was a handsome man with a juvenile aspect despite recently turning fifty, the kind of man who finds it easier to court women than make deals with other men.

"You must be overwhelmed with your new responsibilities, but you still look good," their host added as they walked to a room with views of his extensive gardens.

"Thanks. The truth is Tomás has taken on a great deal of the responsibility."

"Well, indeed, it is an enormous responsibility. *El Mundo* is a key institution in the nation's life," the leader agreed.

Tomás didn't know if the comment was ironic. He imagined his appointment hadn't been well received at Los Pinos. The PRI people would have liked a more accessible director, a journalist closer to the circles of power.

After a tequila and a bit of frivolous chitchat, they moved to a table set for three. Prida begged pardon for the first lady's absence, saying she was traveling, and it struck Tomás that, for the meeting's success, once Claudia noticed the president's flirting, the conversation turned into a push and pull closer to a barroom seduction than a confrontation between the First and Fourth Estates.

"Shoot straight with me, Mr. President: Do you really like to drink tequila, or is it just a patriotic gesture?" she said.

"The truth is," he said, "I prefer mezcal, but I thought you two would be too fancy for that!"

"When it's hangover time, it hurts just the same," she said. "I guess I'm lacking in the constitutional resources."

"It's an inherited trait," he said. "My liver was born wrapped in the presidential sash."

Mid-meal, Prida noted that *El Mundo* was the only daily that hadn't given front-page exposure to the economic windfall. Tomás held back from saying that 2.4 percent growth was far from a windfall, and tried to explain that under normal circumstances he would have given it more prominence, but not on the day they were paying the president a visit.

Prida confided that his office of communications had been enraged by the newspaper's apparent disdain, and even took it as a radical switch in the editorial approach, though he accepted the reasoning Tomás put forward.

"See why it's important we have these meetings regularly? Besides the pleasure of dining with the most beautiful publisher on the continent, it helps clear up misunderstandings."

"Not just that, but it lets us put some of the issues that are bothering us on the table," Tomás said. He described the aggressions journalists had suffered and the financial crisis at the newspapers.

Prida took notes in his pocket journal and promised that someone would call him to work out a strategy on both issues in the coming days.

As they took their coffee, Claudia brought up her worries about human trafficking, particularly in relation to women brought in from overseas, thanks to the complicity or negligence of the national immigration services.

"Inefficiency in that area is an old story," Prida said, "and it's gotten worse with the rise of international traffickers. But now we have the chance to clean house. Marcelo Galván resigned today. He represented the old guard there . . . He's going to Houston because of a sudden emergency, something with his health, apparently he's been in some kind of an accident."

Tomás and Claudia avoided each other's eyes. Claudia praised the flatware from Puebla and the décor in the cozy dining room, and no one brought the subject up again.

In the car on the way back to their offices, Tomás and Claudia congratulated each other for the meeting's success. Both noticed the effect of the tequilas they'd drunk and had to admit that the president's liver really was heroic.

"One thing I have to give the guy," Tomás said, putting his hand on her thigh. "The son of a bitch has good taste. You look especially good today."

Claudia turned her face to him, her nose almost grazing his, and asked in a scarcely audible murmur: "You really think so, babe?"

Tomás brought his lips near hers. They didn't touch. Claudia's driver interrupted them.

"A message from your secretary. They say it's urgent, Don Tomás," the driver said, looking at the cell phone.

Both realized they had left their cell phones off throughout the meal. Tomás turned his on.

Emiliano was killed five minutes ago. Two shots to the head.

50

Milena

FEBRUARY 2013

UNLIKE THE FIRST, the second killing she took part in had nothing subtle about it. Javi Rosado was different from her first victim, the Catalan, in every way. He was very image of his profession: a tidy, discreet, and meticulous accountant, short, prematurely bald, always dressed with a tie regardless of the merciless coastal heat. Moreover, he was the only honest member of the Flamingos, even if his job was laundering money: Rosado didn't run side businesses with his clients' money, skim additional commissions, or gouge them for operating costs. His life was officious and discreet, even austere. He was a confirmed bachelor, but with a single suffocating passion, literally: he liked to be choked when he came.

His discretion and honesty made him the only member of the Flamingos Vila-Rojas would do business with. They never shared an office, but they called each other constantly, knowing that they made a good pair: Vila-Rojas specialized in international finance and its legal aspects, and Rosado in the day-to-day accounting. The accountant's image, like a medieval scribe, inspired confidence among the mafiosos.

But the threats coming from the authorities turned Javi Rosado into a treacherous loose thread for Vila-Rojas. He knew if his friend disappeared, that would bring even more risks, because he was the only one of his colleagues he had known business ties with. A violent death would draw investigators looking into his dealings and his character. Then there was the fact that many clients wouldn't appreciate the elimination of a worker as useful and efficient as Rosado.

Fortunately, Vila-Rojas knew his secret and decided to take advantage of it. Once, two years back, in the middle of one of the group's parties, a hooker started screaming for help from one of the bedrooms. It was four in the morning, and Vila-Rojas was alone in the shadows, drinking his last whiskey before heading home. When he went to the room, he saw Rosado collapsed on the bed, faceup, with a scarf around his neck and one end of it tied to the bedstead. His face was red, and the veins in his scalp and forehead were ready to burst. Vila-Rojas loosened the knot compressing his throat, dumped the water from an ice bucket on his face and chest, and watched Rosado come back from the dead, retching. He pulled a thousand euros from his own wallet, passed it to the girl, and told her if she blabbed, she would pay with her life. Vila-Rojas closed the door and waited for his friend to recover. Twenty minutes later, Rosado swore he'd never do it again, and Vila-Rojas promised no one would find out about his deadly fetish. But that was before Rosado became a threat. At the beginning of 2013, the lawyer decided the moment had come to reward his colleague with one of those dangerous orgasms.

Two weeks before the Flamingos' next party, he invited him to lunch, saying he needed to consult with him on some technical details. For caution's sake, they'd stopped doing business together, but they still sought one another out for their respective expertise. Once his digestif was ordered, Vila-Rojas told him a secret: after he'd heard about his friend's weakness, curiosity had led him to try it out, though naturally taking the necessary precautions. That had led him to a professional who was an expert in a safe technique for choking a client and bringing him to orgasm without putting him at risk. He assured him he'd done it a half-dozen times, and the results were incredible. Her name was Milena, and he would bring her to their next party as a gift to him.

At first, Vila-Rojas had thought he'd make a deal with his pupil in exchange for her freedom: convince the Croatian to take the rap for involuntary manslaughter, which would carry a sentence of five to six years, only three of which she'd actually serve, and after that, she'd get a premature retirement with a nice sum of cash under her belt. He had already found the hooker Rosado had his little incident with two years before. If she got called to trial, she could confirm the accountant's dangerous predilection.

But that would mean losing Milena for the last and most danger- ous assignment. He decided that the deal he'd come up with for his accomplice might also be attractive for another woman from the same house, so Milena spent the next few days observing her colleagues and chose Velvet, a despondent Hungarian who had shown suicidal tendencies. Milena thought that deep down, the offer was a way of saving her life. Velvet accepted on the condition that she not have to participate personally in the execution.

Milena spent the next two weeks practicing in the scant hours she had alone. Vila-Rojas gave her a belt with a buckle similar to those on airplane seatbelts, though thinner. Two rings on the ends made it possible to tie on additional ropes that could be attached to some fixed point: pull on them, and the belt would close in inexorably on its prey.

The Catalan's death four months before hadn't left any special mark on Milena, nothing that would keep her from getting to sleep at night, or in the morning, as was usually her case. Besides being a criminal, he was known to abuse the prostitutes, and all she'd had to do was put a suppository up his ass. At least that's what she told herself to ease her spirit. From the first, it was clear to her that Rosado was going to be different. This time, she'd be killing him the same way her grandmother killed the chickens or her father the sheep, slitting their throats, which she'd never been able to watch without horror. During her last session with Vila-Rojas, he noticed her nervousness and stressed to her that Rosado was a criminal, too, that he didn't have a wife or kids, that his life was lonely and miserable. The same thing could be said of him, Milena thought.

On the night of the execution, things went as Vila-Rojas had planned, at least at first. The house that served as the setting, a holiday villa on the outskirts of the city belonging to the businessman Jesús Nadal, offered impeccable conditions. Vila-Rojas knew the place, because they'd thrown other parties there in the past. The main rooms on the second floor had a back door that led to a shared balcony, allowing movement from one room to the other unbeknownst to the other guests. He told Milena which room to choose and assured her he would take the one next door.

Until eleven, there were no hitches. But the arrival of various security guards alarmed the attendees. They inspected the place briefly and then stepped back to make way for Yasha Boyko, the Ukrainian head of the Russian mob in Marbella. He nodded to Vila-Rojas and gestured for the others to be calm. A bodyguard stayed beside the main door. The party atmosphere froze.

"Keep celebrating, my friends. I'm just passing through to say hello and have a drink with you. Don't you know I'm your host? I bought this property two months ago, but no worries, my house is your house."

Some of the partygoers turned their eyes to Jesús Vidal, the one who had thrown the party, and he lowered his eyes, embarrassed. More than one of the Flamingos wanted to leave, because no one wanted to be associated publicly with Yasha, even if in private they all wanted his business. But they couldn't insult the formidable capo, either. Getting on his bad side was more dangerous than attracting unwanted attention from officials from the ministry of finance. Everyone decided to stay at the event, but nobody approached the Ukrainian.

Yasha seemed surprised by the vacuum around him. He'd known about the Flamingos' reunions and the group's influence, and he had wanted to look like a big fish, popping in at one of their private meetings and showing this was his territory as well.

Yasha stopped a waiter, grabbed a glass of whiskey, and eyed up the guests. He noticed Milena standing by the enormous window, slightly separated from the group, and walked toward her.

"You're the only one who's not dressed like a tramp. The prettiest, too," he said.

Milena asked herself if the mafioso's presence meant they would have to abort the mission. She felt an enormous weight lifted off her back. The relief, and the many hours she'd spent at similar parties, made her respond automatically.

"And you're the only one in the room who's not shaking," she said. "You've got their hair standing on end."

Yasha laughed.

"Except for you. Not a single one of your hairs is out of place," he commented, and softly stroked the tips of her long blonde mane.

"Yours either," she said, looking at his bald scalp.

Both of them cracked up.

Even after they'd made physical contact, Yasha didn't give the sense that he was flirting. It was rather as if he was fulfilling a role that was expected of him. She looked at him closer, and seeing his tall, slender, somewhat-awkward body, she thought it must not be easy for him to play the part of mafia capo. At least, not among his countrymen, who tended to be immense, robust, ruddy-cheeked.

Yasha's build didn't project power or any capacity to intimidate. His advantages lay elsewhere, Milena assumed, and this made her sympathize with him.

From the other corner of the room, Vila-Rojas saw what was happening and was filled with jealousy. He watched Yasha conversing with Milena in her long, tailored satin dress, and she looked like a beautiful, untouchable goddess.

They went on chatting, isolated from the group but always observed, askance, by the rest of the participants, until Yasha decided his visit had served its purpose.

"Find me if any of these guys gives you any problems, dear," he said as he left.

"More likely it's you one of these guys is going to give problems, dear," she responded with a smile.

He turned around, still laughing, and headed toward the door to leave, saying goodbye to no one.

It was a while before the meeting recovered the cheerful atmosphere Yasha had interrupted. But the alcohol and the company of the women made the Flamingos relax again. Milena looked around several times for Vila-Rojas. When she caught sight of him, he squeezed his throat in a choking gesture, pretending to adjust the collar of his shirt.

When the night began, Vila-Rojas pointed Milena out to Rosado, and at a certain point, he approached her to ask if she would join him later. He spent the next few hours away from her. Milena liked it that way: the less she knew him, the easier her assignment would be. And yet she couldn't avoid seeking her victim out and watching his timid and diffident behavior throughout the course of the party. He settled down on a three-person sofa in the corner, resting a cushion on his knees, and hardly participated in the conversations around him. If a woman sat down beside him, he put a hand on her thigh, but barely addressed a word to her. If someone offered him a drink, he took the glass, drank a few sips, and left it on the table beside him.

Milena took him to be an observer, like herself, which made her feel a jab of regret. She saw later that he was a double risk to Vila-Rojas: he looked vulnerable and inoffensive, but probably knew more secrets than all his other colleagues combined. She also noted with worry that his fragile exterior might conceal a fibrous and stout body. When he finally took off his tie, she saw his back was firm, despite his thin frame and unimpressive height. At one point he moved his neck in slight circles, as if to hear the noises in his bones. She'd seen some of her gym-rat clients do the same. The fact that he wasn't getting drunk was also a bad omen for their plans.

Luckily the accountant was the first one to head for the bedrooms. That allowed them to choose the room and kept any guests from picking Velvet, who had stayed as far as possible away from the action.

Rosado walked over to Milena and again requested "the honor of her company."

"People say you can leave a man breathless," he said.

Milena smiled conspiratorially and said that for that kind of thing, she'd need Velvet's help, which made the man suspicious. She assured him the girl would be a spectator, just there in case of emergency. She explained that in the heat of passion, people sometimes lost track of their limits, but a trained assistant never did. He looked at Velvet, and the look of her convinced him.

When the trio moved toward the stairs, Vila-Rojas yelled from the other side of the room: "Velvet, put the squeeze on that accountant, you'll get five hundred euros if you get the lead out of him." A few colleagues looked over with him. Five minutes later, Vila-Rojas stomped up to the second floor, acting dead drunk.

When Javi Rosado took off his clothes, Milena lost whatever empathy she might have felt. His languid way of removing his pants and shirt and painstakingly folding them on the chair, and the way he ignored the girls' presence made her lose any sense of compassion. When she saw that he left on his socks and shoes, she knew he was the most brutal and insensitive kind of client. She took consolation in the idea that what she was about to do would be compensation for the insults she'd received from men like him.

Without compunction, he ordered her to kneel and suck his cock. Milena responded that she should set the scene before getting started. She trussed the two ends of the belt to the bedframe and left it in the center of the mattress. Once he slid his neck inside, all he'd have to do is lean forward, and the tension would be transferred to his throat. It was also just as easy to set him free by popping the buckle on one side of his Adam's apple.

The accountant examined the contraption, closing it and opening it several times, and seemed satisfied. Milena told him they should only do it in the missionary position so she could unfasten the buckle as well, if needed.

Once the preparations were over, he repeated his command for a blowjob. It was more difficult than she expected. After ten minutes, he still wasn't hard, and Milena asked him to get in the bed so she could put the belt around his neck. Afterward, she started over. Only then did he get the excitement he was looking for.

Velvet watched the action from a corner of the large room, leaning against the door that led to the balcony. When the man finally penetrated Milena, Velvet crept out, walked a few yards along the balcony, and knocked at the next door over. Vila-Rojas told her to come in, and they had a couple of glasses of gin and waited. Then he went to the neighboring room and watched in silence while the man wheezed and rammed, bent over Milena. Rosado would need only turn to notice his presence, but Vila-Rojas did nothing. He had told Milena he would act immediately, but now he decided he owed his old friend from the University of Seville the release he'd been promised.

Milena looked at Vila-Rojas standing behind Rosado's back and grew impatient. While the belt closed around the man's neck, his body came closer and his face grazed against hers. Milena started to panic. The noises coming from his throat were like nothing she'd heard before, agonized sounds that made her think of decomposing flesh and viscera. His eyes were bloodshot and his veins hard, like cables, and his face went from flaming red to purple. A thread of spit fell onto her cheek. Without thinking, she struggled to escape from beneath him, but couldn't.

Desperate, she moved her hand toward the buckle to set the monster free, and Rosado bent his arm to do the same. Vila-Rojas was faster than both of them: he leapt onto the accountant with all his weight in an almost amorous-looking embrace. Milena's face was an inch from Vila-Rojas's: his expression was excited, euphoric. Squeezed between the two bodies, Rosado gave a last, fierce jerk, but the two accomplices held him until the spasms came to an end. Only then did Milena feel Vila-Rojas's erection against her thigh.

Slowly, the three bodies broke apart. Vila-Rojas helped Milena out of the bed. He told her to pick up her things, go to the neighboring room, and bring Velvet back. When the Hungarian came in, the lawyer made sure she stank of liquor, helped her take off her clothes, and placed her where Milena had been seconds before. He ordered her not to move from that position and wait a few minutes before screaming.

Vila-Rojas met Milena in the next room over, stripped, and got in bed with her. They would wait for the others to respond to Velvet's screams. Only then would they come out, half-naked, and join the other guests, gawking at the spectacle of the accountant and the Hungarian. Vila-Rojas penetrated Milena as soon as their bodies touched. Three minutes later, she had the second orgasm of her life. He came inside her right afterward. The contact had been brief but intense. After the final tremor, he took her face in his hands and looked at her as he never had before. For a second, Milena thought she saw in his pupils a desolate, timid adolescent who had been stumbling through life since he was sixteen, like her. He seemed about to tell her something when Velvet's scream shook every room in the house.

She got three years for involuntary manslaughter, but she was only in prison eleven months. Following instructions from higher-ups, Bonso hired one of the best law firms in the port. No one in Marbella was surprised he wanted to protect his investment. Vila-Rojas kept his promise and gave Velvet a generous severance package. They never heard from her again.

The night of the murder, the lawyer took a ring of keys he found in the accountant's pocket, and in the early hours of the morning, as soon as the police were gone, he went to the victim's home and dug through his office. He didn't find any compromising documents: the accountant had likely prepared himself for the authorities' arrival. Still, Vila-Rojas told himself that what was dangerous about Rosado wasn't in any file, but in his head, and now that was no longer a risk.

Milena had nightmares for months, with demonic figures pressing down on her body and cutting off her breathing. Sometimes the monsters had Rosado's twisted face, other times the rueful face of Vila-Rojas. When she awoke, she'd be tense and sweating and, occasionally, strangely aroused.

51

The Blues

TOMÁS AND CLAUDIA SAID GOODBYE to the Mexico City chief of police and returned to the meeting room, where they saw Amelia and Jaime. Minutes before, they had gotten a call from a federal prosecutor who had assured the owner of *El Mundo*, on behalf of President Prida, that the government wouldn't rest until it had found the person responsible for the deputy director's death.

The four of them had a lot to talk about, but no one wanted to speak first. Claudia was profoundly depressed, Tomás overwhelmed, Jaime enraged, and Amelia confused. After they got the call on their way back from Los Pinos, Tomás and Claudia went to Emiliano's house to see Isabel, his widow. When they reached the mansion in Coyoacán, they found Jaime, who had gotten there first, as his offices were close by. Lemus, using his profile as ex-director of the intelligence services, had already talked with the head of the police squad in charge of the case and told him to go easy on the widow and pay extra attention to the crime scene.

It hadn't been pretty, Claudia trying to console Isabel. As soon as she saw Tomás, she tried to strike him.

"You son of a bitch," she yelled. "You said it didn't have anything to do with us, that we were out of danger."

When they finally calmed her down, she told them a man had come to the door and said Tomás had sent him and he had an envelope for her husband. Before going down, the deputy director smiled at his wife and said he was sure it was a bonus or something so they'd be more comfortable during their vacation. When he got to the door, he was shot twice in the head.

Two hours later, back at the newspaper's offices, Claudia still hadn't gotten herself together. Tomás either. They couldn't understand where they'd erred, what they could have done differently to save Emiliano's life, what the logic was in the criminals' behavior. Why let him go if they were going to kill him two days later?

"Marcelo Galván resigning," Jaime said, as though talking to himself. "It's their revenge."

"What the hell did you do to make that revenge an act of murder?" Amelia said, disgusted.

"Nothing serious, but the fact that Galván exposed Víctor Salgado as Bonso's protector meant a death sentence for him, that's why he fled to the United States. It'll take them a while to find him, but sooner or later, they will."

"What does that have to do with us?" Claudia asked.

"We pushed him out," Jaime responded. "It's not just them throwing a tantrum: with Galván gone, they've lost someone in immigration who will be impossible to replace, at least for now."

"Yeah, that's the key office for human-trafficking issues," Amelia added. "They're making us pay for their loss."

"And I guess in passing they're also sending us a message that they won't stop until they get Milena back," Tomás said.

"Well, this is fucked up, because I can't guarantee the safety of six hundred employees at *El Mundo*."

"You're right, Claudia, there's no defending against that. We're absolutely vulnerable."

"And they're not?" Claudia said. "The prosecutor can threaten Salgado, no? Arrest Bonso? We can't give in to extortion and we can't let them keep killing people, either. We have to put the pressure on Prida. *El Mundo* needs to start a campaign to expose Salgado."

The three of them looked at her respectfully. She was a fighter. Far from taking refuge in self-pity, she was ready to face up to whatever was coming, even if she wasn't sure of the ground she was walking on.

"If Salgado's right, there are powerful interests behind Milena, and the president will just put you off," Jaime said. "The attorney general's office might find a sacrificial lamb, or in the best case, turn in the body of whoever pulled the trigger on Emiliano, but never the person who gave the order."

"The police in the capital are running the investigation, but that doesn't matter for the case itself," Amelia added. "Most likely, the federal government will take over, since it's a crime against the press."

"And then, there's no proof that ties Salgado to all this, so there's nothing we can air out in the media besides the sins in his past," Tomás said.

"So we're fucked," Claudia concluded.

The four of them paused again, lost in their own worries.

"I've got other news," Jaime said. "We've figured out what Luis is doing on the Net. He covers his footsteps well, but we think he's trying to turn the human-trafficking mafias against Bonso."

"Is that good or bad news?" Claudia asked.

"It's irresponsible, and the consequences are impossible to predict. It depends on how good Luis is at making his bluff look realistic and whether there's already tension between Bonso and his rivals."

"But it may be they could finish Bonso off without us getting blamed for his disappearance, no?" she said, more excited.

"Or they discover the bluff and their vengeance is way nastier than killing a deputy director," Jaime responded. "They could blame the cyberharassment on the newspaper and assume the kid's working for us."

"And even if Bonso disappears, there's still Salgado, and he's the one pulling the strings," Amelia said.

"So what?" Claudia exploded. "Nobody can get rid of Salgado?"

Jaime looked at her again and thought that he liked the owner of *El Mundo* less and less every day. She didn't hold her tongue when it came to saying what she wanted.

"No one in this country is invulnerable," Amelia said. "But you don't solve problems by killing everyone who threatens us. As you told me, Salgado himself said that taking one link out of the chain only means having to go higher up."

"And I already know who the next link in that chain is," Jaime said. He would have preferred to keep his information to himself and stayed one step ahead. But he couldn't bear the feeling of powerlessness there. Somehow, it made him feel responsible.

Jaime informed them of Agustín Vila-Rojas and certain details of his activities. He didn't know much, but he was convinced that the Spanish lawyer was the source of the orders Salgado had received.

"Is there a way to get to him and apply pressure?" Claudia asked. "The Mexican ambassador to Spain is a family friend."

"Everything suggests he's one of the main finance guys for the Russian mafias in Europe, and that isn't small potatoes. These syndicates make the Mexican cartels look like kid's stuff. Vila-Rojas is one of the point men between the surface and the underground, where these groups' cash flows go. We're not talking about someone it would be easy to pressure."

Despite herself, Amelia admired Lemus. As if sensing that, Tomás burst out.

"I know the gringos have put their weight behind a unit tracking money laundering in recent years, with the Wall Street scandals and all. Your DEA contacts can't help you? It's worth knowing if the Spanish guy's on their radar, if we can step on his tail somehow."

"I looked into it and I may be getting some information soon, but I don't expect much. As far as money-laundering investigations go, the gringos are hypocrites: they know it's the key to stopping drug and arms trafficking, but they don't want to cut off the cash flows that make America the world's bank. China's showing up their economy on all fronts except the capital markets. Investors everywhere, even in China, keep on going to Wall Street. The authorities know as soon as they step up, the cash will go elsewhere. So my bet is they've got something on Vila-Rojas, but they won't want to share it."

He knew in the information market he was tapped into, everything could be shared in exchange for data, but he wasn't sure he wanted to pay the price.

Amelia's presence had kept Claudia from uttering what was tormenting her, but she finally took the plunge.

"The real question here is who killed one of our people. *El Mundo* can't just stand here with its arms folded. How are we going to answer this?"

The three of them weighed her words.

"Well, we need a plan of action for the next few hours," Tomás said. "All eyes will be on tomorrow's edition, including those of our enemy. It's important to get what we think out there."

"I suggest you take advantage of the solidarity of public opinion and the media to launch an attack against the mafias engaged in human trafficking, and if possible, the groups laundering money for organized crime. That way, at least they'll think twice before hitting you again," Amelia proposed.

"And how are you going to tie Emiliano to those mafias? You can't let out that it was payback for Milena," Jaime objected.

"There's no need to," Tomás responded. "We can say *El Mundo* was preparing an investigation into the subject and we received pressure from the mafias that made us call it off. Without accusing them directly, we could say we had a profile of Bonso and Salgado as representative parties in those networks."

"It's not bad, but you're talking all-out war," Jaime warned. "You think you can handle the backlash?"

"Do it," Claudia said to Tomás.

"Plus, this will make it harder for Prida's government to pass the buck," Amelia said. "With the eyes of the international media on Mexico, a second attack against a paper as important as *El Mundo* won't slide."

"I hope you're right," Jaime said doubtfully. He didn't like the frontal approach. They'd be at the mercy of their rivals' reactions, and those were impossible to predict. Further, their plan would render him unnecessary. "In the meantime, I'll keep investigating Vila-Rojas. That might get us a permanent solution," he said, getting up to go.

Impatient, Tomás got up as well and announced he would call a reunion of the editorial team to work nonstop on a cover.

Suddenly, Amelia and Claudia found themselves alone for the first time. They looked at each other warily: Claudia with a timid smile, Amelia with feigned camaraderie. Neither dared to speak of what was really going through their heads. Amelia would have liked to say that she knew about her and Tomás's little games, and add that she didn't own anyone and that Tomás was old enough to decide what he wanted, but she didn't. In the old days, she would have: anything was better than passing for a typical spurned girlfriend, the last one to find out about her man's infidelities. She said nothing because she understood the truth, that the issue was between Tomás and her, and was no cause for conflict between women. If he left her or cheated on her, it wasn't Claudia's fault.

Claudia would have liked to say that she and the journalist had become a professional duo, that they liked each other and that was all. She could have taken Amelia's hand and asked her not to confuse their companionship with something else. That would have made her feel generous, and also terrible about herself. Before, she would have done it, but not now. She'd decided she wouldn't be dishonest. The life she'd led until a few weeks ago was shattered, and she couldn't close the door to the new life Tomás might offer her.

The two women stood in silence, gave each other a kiss on the cheek, and separated. Amelia walked a few feet and then retraced her steps, deciding to say what she should have said before.

"I know you think you have a right to the black book and you've said no one can open it before you. You also want to be the first and only one to talk to Milena. I want to believe it's out of respect for your father, but people are dead, and it seems obvious the cause isn't her, but whatever's in her notebook. Otherwise, they wouldn't be knocking down walls everywhere they go. That's why I'm saying we have to find her and figure out what the notebook contains. I don't work for you and I'm not here to follow your orders."

Claudia was stunned by Amelia's bluntness. After a moment, she managed to recover.

"They're neither rules nor orders, Amelia. And I'm sorry you've taken it like that. It was just a courtesy on Tomás's and Jaime's part. Let's do what we have to do to keep this from leading to more deaths. I'm not your enemy."

No, but you are my rival, Amelia thought.

"So it is, then. If I find out what's in the notebook, you'll be the first person I call."

"My infinite thanks."

The women separated again. This time, there was no kiss on the cheek.

THEM VII

There's no woman as grateful as a reformed hooker. I know, because I married one. That life raked Augusta over the coals so bad, all I had to do was show her a little care and sincerity.

At first, she didn't believe me, even though I took flowers to every date and wrote her love poems. I even refused to keep making love to her at the brothel: all I needed was to rest my head on her chest and let her play with my hair. The truth is, it's not the sex that attracts me to whores, it's the romance. What's the charm in falling in love with a woman in an office or a café? Zero. They're all on the prowl for a husband, or at least a man that'll put them up.

With a hooker, things are more honest. It's a transaction, it doesn't aspire to being anything else, just the satisfaction of a need: pleasure in exchange for cash. The challenge is to find true love there where it's for sale.

I understood Augusta's objections from the beginning. Some guys go to them to mend a broken heart, guys with no balls that end up falling for a whore because she offers them words of consolation. These are dupes mistreated by some impossible love, still stinging from past rejections, and they mistake a caress for real passion. All the pros have been through that. They know behind the bouquets of flowers and the devoted lamb eyes there's a sad son of a bitch who will eventually throw their past in their face or ditch them when he finally comes across a "pure" woman.

But I overcame her resistance and after a year of courting her, I was able to convince her my love was real. I paid what she owed Fulgencio, the owner of the place, and we got married on December 29, the anniversary of my mother's death. She was a saint.

Since then, she's been devoted to me. She learned to cook the way I like, she changed how she dressed, she waited for me to come home like a faithful hound posted at the front door. No husband's ever gotten the kind of loyalty Augusta gave me.

But something broke. I started asking myself if behind that affection there wasn't some kind of desperate effort to suppress nostalgia for her past. When she was silent, it was like I could hear her humming the music in those dives where she used to work. How could she treat me that way, after all I'd done for her?

As you can imagine, I had to stop making love to her. I didn't want her comparing me to the thousands of clients who'd been between her legs. And when she told me one time she'd like it if I'd take her dancing somewhere, I understood the gutter has a stronger pull than love. Next week I have a meeting with Don Fulgencio.

J.I. OWNER OF SIERRA MORENA
CONSTRUCTION, THE SECOND MOST
IMPORTANT BUILDER IN ANDALUSIA

52

Rina, Vidal, Luis, and Milena

MONDAY, NOVEMBER 17, 8:20 P.M.

LUIS WAS CHANTING "Love Me Two Times" by the Doors, walking back to the hotel he and Milena had started to see as their temporary home. He had a baguette under his arm and a bag with cheese and wine for dinner, and on his back, his satchel with his laptop. But more importantly, his laptop contained the help he'd solicited from his friend Bad Girl in Spain. The little he'd been able to glance at was more than promising. She'd broken through all of Vila-Rojas's security features and figured out some of the avatars he used to connect with Russian-speaking contacts. Maybe Milena could understand some of their transactions. Judging by the few amounts he could decipher, the lawyer was moving an impressive amount of cash. That afternoon, he would send Bad Girl's report to Anonymous.

But for now, he was only thinking of the evening ahead of him. As on previous nights, they would eat from the wide window ledge that faced what would have been a depressing view in other circumstances: an anodyne street flanked with old buildings with flaking walls. But on those cold nights in the shadows, they shared memories, dreams, and frustrations in a way that is only possible under extraordinary circumstances.

It seemed to him that Milena had become another person. She would recite some story from her village or an anecdote about Bonso's brothel as if they had nothing to do with her. Luis felt there was more of her in the novels she talked about than in the years she had spent in Marbella, even in Jastrebarsko.

The night before, they had made love for the first time. They went to bed without touching, as before, but after those long confessions at the windowsill, something seemed to have changed. Lying faceup, they listened to each other's breathing in the darkness, and they guessed, more than felt, the heat and the weight of the other's body on the mattress they shared. Intimacy had grown over the previous days, and Luis's excitement mounted. Before realizing it, he turned over and laid his hand on her stomach. He felt her stiffen in the darkness, like an animal hearing a sound in the distance and waiting motionless for the next one to come.

"We're just passing through each other's lives, Milena. Let's live in the moment."

"Rina . . . "

"Rina's still with us, and in a way, she and I are just passing through as well."

She said nothing, then turned and kissed him. They lost themselves in a long embrace and her hands began to slide over his body. There was something virginal in the way she explored him, as if it was the first time she cared to know what a man's body was made of.

When he touched her firm breasts, Luis realized there wasn't a condom in sight, but when he penetrated her, any considerations beyond that total, savage frenzy were pushed aside.

Over and over that next day, the memory of her jumping out of the bed naked that morning came back to him. The embrace the night before had been all flesh, heat, torpor, but in the light of day, the innate elegance of her movements was hard to forget. She exuded sexuality, but also aesthetic refinement.

Luis told himself that today, they would do what they had done almost anonymously, and sometimes clumsily, the night before, but unhurried and in the daylight. If intimacy with Milena was going to be unique, without any follow-up chapters, he wanted at least to remember it fully.

The excitement Luis felt at the evening before him vanished when he saw the headline on the newspaper at the kiosk: "Deputy Director of *El Mundo* Executed." He bought a copy and read that Emiliano Reyna had been shot twice in the face when he opened the door to his home. He wondered if the unexpected reprisal had something to do with his digital harassment of Bonso or his investigations into Vila-Rojas's businesses. Whatever the case, the news hinted that all of them were in much greater danger than he had thought. If, from fear or prudence, Claudia and the Blues gave up the fight, they would also give Milena up.

He decided to call Rina, even though she was just six blocks from their hotel. He would have preferred to go further and call her from a public phone, but the matter was urgent.

"Hey, babe. I just found out about the murdered journalist. Are you okay?" he asked.

"I'm about to leave Amelia's office. Vidal's here now, he's insisting I not go to my uncle's to sleep, he wants me to stay at Lemlock, like on the first day. What do you think?"

"You know what I think of Lemlock, but this time it's probably for the best. It's just a precaution, I think you'll be safe there. But what worries me is the travel in between."

"Jaime assigned Vidal a couple of bodyguards, so I'll be okay. How are you? How's Milena? Is she feeling hemmed in?"

Luis swallowed.

"She stays shut up inside while I work all day. She's fine."

"Tell her she better not think I've forgotten about those Croatian recipes, and that one day we'll laugh about all this while she teaches us to cook them, all right?"

"Yep. Be safe and stay out of sight. I hope this is all over soon. Bye."

For the next few blocks, the warmth of Rina's voice enveloped him like a cloud, along with the memory of the intimacy and trust he'd felt with her from the beginning. There was something real there, and nothing could change that. The thought calmed him.

Before he went to the room, he stopped to reflect for a few seconds. He was afraid Milena would take Emiliano as another death that was her fault, one more reason to disappear or, even worse, to end her own life. But he decided to tell her anyway: he couldn't treat his companion in flight like a teenager, and he didn't want to hide information the way Jaime did, using it to play with others' lives.

Milena had an agenda that evening as well. Knowing each night could be her last, she wanted this one to be like no other. She had already told Luis about her crimes. Now she wanted to share her hopes for *Tales of the XY Chromosome*. It was the only project she'd ever undertaken with an eye to the future, the only trace her passage through the world would leave behind once she was gone. She had told Claudia and Rina of the stories' existence, but as if they were nothing special, a mere diversion. She was afraid they might think she was naïve or ignorant, but with Luis she didn't want to keep secrets.

She wanted to unveil to him the true purpose of those notes: to leave a testimony of what the men who paid for prostitutes were really like. If it wasn't for them, her name would still be Alka. She had seen how many fellow sex workers had been ground up by the inexorable machinery of the pimps and their clients. Bringing attention to *Tales of the XY Chromosome* would give a meaning to the awful trap life had set for her, and she hoped it would harm those who had abused her as well. She would have preferred to give their complete names rather than initials, but she was afraid it could keep her work from getting published.

When they finally met again in the hotel room, Milena read a cooling of Luis's feelings for her in his change of mood, but he dispelled those doubts when he told her about Emiliano Reyna's execution.

Milena seemed neither surprised nor disheartened by the news. She knew perfectly well what her pursuers were capable of. Time with Luis and the long conversations they'd shared had convinced her that she wasn't responsible for the deaths her escape brought about. Emiliano and whoever else fell were victims of the same force of destiny that had upturned her own existence.

Anyway, the journalist's execution confirmed what she already knew: that there was no way out, that she was living her last days, and that she should make sure they were as intense as possible. She agreed with Luis that they should stay hidden at all costs. She asked him to uncork the bottle of wine, then took her notebook out and started reading. That night, Milena had the first orgasm of her life that a man hadn't had to die for.

Seven miles away, Rina and Vidal were also spending a night together, but with little romance and no sex at all. She was too worried about the danger Luis was in to pay attention to Vidal's efforts to distract her.

"Now, when people talk in the bars, it's not 'Are you working or studying?' It's 'Apple or Android? Facebook or Twitter? Spotify or Blind?'"

"In New York it was 'cat person or dog person,'" she said, just to keep him from feeling let down.

"So are you a cat or dog person?"

"I'm someone dying to get some sleep," she said, bored, and took off the jacket Vidal had offered her an hour before, when they left Amelia's office. But when she saw his needy face, she felt bad. "Thanks a million. I've got a sweater in my suitcase you brought over from my uncle's," she said and handed the jacket back to him. "Thanks a million for everything, Vidal," she repeated, and gave him a goodnight kiss on the cheek.

"You don't have to say thanks for anything, Rina. You know I'm your best friend."

"I know."

Idiot, he said to himself when he was alone, his cheek still burning from the kiss. You don't want to be her best friend, you want to be her boyfriend, he thought.

"Vidal, can you come to my office?" Jaime said through the speaker of the cell phone in his shirt pocket.

He jumped up, and wondered what other tricks were built into the phone his uncle had given him.

"We've found Luis," Jaime said as soon as Vidal set foot in his office.

53

Jaime

THE LAST CALL RINA HAD RECEIVED, three hours before, was the key to triangulating Luis's position. Presumably Milena was with him.

They had run the various payphone calls through their geolocation program and found that all had been made near a certain underground station. The software, a program devised to optimize online deliveries for products throughout the city, identified Tasqueña as the likely epicenter for his travels.

The previous calls had been made from the phone booths around different metro stops, and once or twice from inside the station, but the last time he'd used a public phone five blocks away from Tasqueña. Lemlock's team took this as confirmation that he was going to the different stops with the sole purpose of calling her, but this time he hadn't bothered to catch public transport to look for a phone far from where he was staying.

When Jaime read the transcript of Luis's dialogue with Rina from that night, he saw why he'd been incautious. He'd just found out about Emiliano's murder and was more worried about getting in touch with his girlfriend.

Patricia had left two hours before with six detectives with fake badges and portraits of Luis and Milena, the Croatian's photo altered so her hair appeared black. Starting from the last phone he'd used, they dispersed through the area and interrogated the staff at the small restaurants and taverns. Patricia and a colleague checked out the eight hotels in the search perimeter.

Jaime was explaining to Vidal the procedure they'd followed to localize Luis when the call came in from Patricia: they were in room 312 of the Hotel Michoacán. Milena apparently almost never left the room, the person on duty said, but the boy who was with her came and went all day.

Patricia told her boss she had reserved two rooms: 311, which was next door, and another on the ground floor. She'd quietly put two agents in the first one, and the rest of them would be in the one at street level. Two of Lemlock's detectives would post guard fifteen yards from the entrance.

"Getting the girl out of there won't be any problem," said Ezequiel Carrasco, head of tactical operations at Lemlock. "We just have to make sure the kid doesn't get hurt trying to protect her, or that she doesn't do something desperate."

"It might be better to wait till the morning when Luis leaves," added Esteban Porter, an ex-Interpol official. "Two agents will intercept him in the hallway and another two will take the room key and go straight to Milena."

"So what if we take advantage of Luis and Milena's presence to trap Bonso or the Turk?" Jaime asked.

"You'd use Luis as bait?" Vidal protested.

"Don't worry," Jaime replied. "We'll take them both somewhere safe."

"That's not the problem," Porter said. "It's the carnage that could take place afterward. If they came with three agents before, imagine how many they'll bring this time."

"Don't tell me you're not used to getting shot at, my friend," ex-commandant Carrasco joked.

"It's not a matter of balls, it's a matter of strategy."

"Maybe you're right," Jaime interrupted. "Now that we know Víctor Salgado is behind this, we can assume they'll use cops again. Lemlock would have to do a lot of explaining for a shootout with so-called 'lawmen.'"

"Still, it's not a bad idea to use Milena to draw Bonso out of whatever hole he's crawled into," Porter said. "We could take him out with a sniper then and there, and if he doesn't show, we could track his men and figure out where he's staying."

"Good point," said Mauricio Romo, the chief hacker. "Even if none of the bosses come, we'll use the new scanner to sweep the vicinity for phones. Sooner or later, the agents he sends will have to report back for instructions, and when they do, we'll know the number he's using."

"It won't be necessary," Porter said. "I think one of them will be there: Bonso and the Turk are the only ones who can identify Milena. They must know about Rina and her similarity to the Croatian, and they won't want to run the risk of making a mistake. They're pros." For months, the head of overseas missions had been upset at Patricia's newly acquired status at Lemlock and couldn't help the jab at her spoiled operation in Marquesa.

"Fine," Jaime concluded. "We'll leak the information that Milena is in a hotel in Michoacán. We don't want them to think it's an ambush. Do it through the Net or maybe through one of the cops working for them. Give me options," he said, pointing to Romo.

"You want to go with a sniper or just a recon team to follow them from the hotel?" Carrasco asked.

"I prefer to track them, intercept their communications, and hit them when we know where the big fish are. There's no sense in going to war on the sidewalk in front of a hotel. Still, the sniper's not a bad Plan B," Jaime said, remembering Claudia wanted the Turk dead.

"Let's put a guy on the roof, someone we can trust, and keep him on an open line, so we can decide when the time comes."

When the assistants left the meeting room, Jaime held his nephew back.

"Don't worry, Vidal. It's going to work. Once we get their calls registered, they'll be sitting ducks."

"It's weird you use that term. I was thinking to myself Luis and Milena were the sitting ducks. I don't like it. Why don't we rescue them, get them out of those assholes' reach, and then confront Bonso?"

"Because this way, we can find them and we can choose the time and place when we eliminate them. Your friends aren't in any danger, we'll move them to another floor, but they can't leave the hotel. On the street, it will be impossible to protect them."

"Luis is never going to let you use him as bait."

"He will if you sell him on it."

54

Milena

AUGUST 2013

MILENA'S THIRD MURDER was the bloodiest. So many months had passed since Vila-Rojas mentioned the issue that she assumed he'd given up on his kill list. Often, he canceled her weekly meetings with the German, and even when he called her, she frequently found the suite empty. But Vila-Rojas still appreciated her intelligence and her powers of observation and was overjoyed at the depth of her reports. Their sessions, now further apart, had become like marathons analyzing the political and business alliances in Marbella. He started sharing information and hunches about his colleagues with Milena. The trust and complicity between them grew until it became a kind of intimacy, even without physicality.

One day, Vila-Rojas brought up Boris, Yasha Boyko's nephew. Boris was the son of Alexander Kattel, one of the first Russian mafia chiefs to set up shop on the Costa del Sol at the end of the eighties. His kid had practically grown up on the Iberian coast and had all his father's new-money defects and none of his virtues. Violent, out of control, slow-witted, and extravagant, he was hated and feared by his men, but never respected.

Alexander had died two years before in a Jacuzzi under murky circumstances, and his sister's husband had taken over as leader of the group. Yasha Boyko was far more cerebral than his brother-in-law.

He kept one foot in the criminal activities that united the Russians' interests and those of Alexander's brothers in Kiev, but he also looked westward, moving part of the group's operations into legal or quasi-legal businesses in the area, thanks to his relations with businessmen in Mediterranean countries. Vila-Rojas was his close counselor and his financial adviser.

Yasha wasn't a threat, regardless of what he knew. Even if he was arrested, he'd never breathe a word. His financial consultant's help was what would make it possible to keep his hands on his fortune—or part of it—through his incarceration. But Boris was a different story.

The kid was going mad because his uncle kept him on the sidelines, and his uncle seemed tired of his nephew's screwups and scandals. It was getting harder and harder for Boris to maintain his lifestyle. In recent months, he had gone to Vila-Rojas twice to ask for money, knowing the lawyer was in charge of the gang's finances, and both times, he had gotten an envelope of cash and Yasha had heard nothing about it. But it was clear that Boris was a ticking time bomb: there was a veiled threat in his requests, and moreover, his lack of discipline was turning him into a weak link. If he was arrested, he could give Vila-Rojas up, whether as a bargaining chip to save his skin or just because he was too stupid to know better.

There were many reasons to take Boris out, but it wouldn't be easy. Alexander's brothers in Ukraine resented Yasha, riled up by the comments made by Boris and his mother Olena, the widow of the former boss. Though the boy's outbursts troubled all his relatives, his uncles would never accept being ordered around by someone who wasn't their blood.

Vila-Rojas decided to do his boss—and himself—a favor, even knowing that Yasha would have to kill him if he ever found out about it. There wasn't a lack of options for doing Boris in, the problem was figuring out how to do it without dying in the process.

The Ukrainian was obsessed with the Hell's Angels and had done everything possible to turn himself into a character from *Mad Max*: he drove a Harley-Davidson with straight pipes, wore high boots and a leather jacket, even in summer, covered his chest and arms with neo-Nazi tattoos, and became an assiduous follower of the small circles of bikers that congregated on the Costa del Sol.

For three months, the lawyer prepared Milena so Boris would find her irresistible: hair buzzed almost to the skin, eyebrow piercing, leather outfits, a taste for heavy punk rock and powerful motorcycles. Some of the garments she wore came from Vila-Rojas himself, and he made her try them on in front of him in the suite they occasionally shared. In those private exhibitions, Milena thought she saw pride and even excitement in him.

Covered in black leather that gripped her flesh like a second skin, with unbelievably high heels, she started drawing people's attention in the seedy bars the Russian frequented. At Vila-Rojas's instructions—and with the prior agreement of Bonso, she assumed—she would show up with the Turk, though he kept his distance, as if he were her bodyguard. Mastering the huge motorcycle Vila-Rojas gave her was the hardest part of her training, but after practice every afternoon for a month, she started to like it. In the end, even the Turk had to admit that she had become a daredevil on her Streetfighter. And when she finally tamed the metallic beast, he gave her a leather vest.

"You earned it, Checkers," he said to her when he handed her the gift, and turned away before she could say thanks. A faithful follower of all televised sports, the Turk had started calling her that after the white and red checked flag the Croatian athletes used.

With the jacket as the last piece, Milena was an Amazon of the asphalt, the queen of the underground. The Russian picked up on her immediately in the tiny world of metal bars in the port. After a few weeks, he was obsessed with her.

Milena hardly even had to change her story. She just said a sheik had fallen in love with her and given her a small fortune to pay Bonso for her freedom, but instead of looking for another life, she opted for a promotion. Now she worked as a madam in charge of the Romanian's whores and spent her free nights pursuing a passion she'd never been able to cultivate before: biker culture. Boris felt he'd met his soul mate. Little by little, he developed a taste for Milena's company and shared his true dream with her: to bump off his uncle Yasha and become successor to his father, the great Alexander Kattels. Time and again, he boasted of the strategy he, his mother, and his relatives in Kiev were devising, the details of his enemies and allies, and his hated uncle's weak points.

Vila-Rojas knew the next phase would be much more complicated: turning Boris on to heroin. Again they were mistaken: Boris had been an addict three months back. Milena, too, though not nearly as bad. Saying she had a sure supplier, she was the one who brought drugs for the couple. She would shoot herself up with plain water without his knowing it, but did have to take the drug once or twice. Before Boris Kattel died of an overdose, Vila-Rojas had to spread the rumor about the Russian's new taste for the needle among his family and friends. When the time came, his body would be covered in track marks.

One night, Boris cut short their date at the One Percent, a bar where they often met, and asked Milena to go somewhere else with him. She hesitated because the Turk wasn't with her, but she figured Boris was just taking her to another dive. Milena followed him on her bike from Puerto Banús into the hills. When they crossed into a residential area and she saw the huge mansion with its byzantine cupolas, it was too late: she was going to meet Boris's mother.

If she's not an opera singer, that's a hell of a waste of a ribcage, Milena said to herself, remembering one of her grandfather's phrases, the first time she saw Olena, Kattel's widow. The voice the woman greeted her with didn't let her down.

"So you're the whore that stole my son from me?" she said in dreadful Spanish when they were greeting each other. "He doesn't come see me anymore now, he just goes to those nasty dumps with all the hoodlums and druggies. Is that where he met you?"

Milena didn't want to get on the woman's bad side, but she also didn't want to fold in front of Boris. She just needed to watch them for a moment to see that the son's submission to his mother's will was absolute. She caressed him like he was a month-old baby. She pinched his cheeks, adjusted his shirt collar, even cupped his balls when she asked Milena whether she was with him for his wallet or the good sex.

The worst was the painstaking examination the woman subjected Milena to: she regretted her eyebrow piercing and exaggerated makeup. Milena lost the aplomb she'd shown till then in front of the Ukrainian. She could barely hold his stare and spoke in a barely audible voice.

Ultimately, she didn't pass Ms. Kattel's examination—far from it. Not because she considered Milena a bad influence on her son, but because she detected something fake about her: clearly her femme-fatale persona concealed something else. The assessment was reciprocal, and Milena could tell that behind the expansive, blathering woman was an alert and calculating mind. She sensed that Boris's mother was the one pulling the strings, and if he was successful with the power grab, she would become the real leader. When she shared this perception with Vila-Rojas, he was surprised: he'd found her a woman of bad taste and limited intelligence, though he admitted she was a force of nature. From the moment of Milena's report, he began to see her with new eyes, and tried to find out all he could about her and her activities.

After that visit, Boris stopped seeing Milena. Vila-Rojas feared Olena was investigating her, and told her to keep her front up even at Bonso's house, to go on driving the motorcycle and continue showing up at One Percent. Boris appeared two weeks later as if nothing had happened, though he occasionally made jokes about his mother's impression of Milena. The absence seemed only to have caused his desire for Milena to grow. Now he insisted they spend all their time together, and she wound up ending most of her nights in his luxurious apartment a few blocks from where his mother lived. From that moment on, the Turk stopped accompanying her, and was only around once in a while, when the couple passed through One Percent.

One time they received a visit from a group of Russians, clearly different from their compatriots living in Marbella. Their dress, accent, and gestures suggested they were more likely government workers than mafiosos. That made Milena pay attention. When Boris told his guards to leave the apartment and Milena to go to the bedroom so he could speak to his guests, she stepped on the balcony with the excuse of a smoke. From there, she could hear the conversation a little better. Neither Boris nor the other two men took any precautions because she had always concealed her knowledge of Russian. She could only hear Boris and one of the guys, because the other spoke too softly. She understood there was an operation afoot, coming from the Kremlin, to recruit the Russians in Marbella to help with its international initiatives. Boris insisted that he and his mother, with help from his uncles in Kiev, were the right people for the job on the

Costa del Sol. Yasha might be Ukrainian, but he was no friend to the Russians, Boris told the operatives.

They met several more times over the following weeks, at the apartment and at various restaurants. She tried to memorize the names of go-betweens, agents, and front businesses, the Russian and Ukrainian middlemen who would be in contact with the people in Marbella. At night, she would write everything down in the hidden pages of her notebook. In the end, it turned out to be unnecessary. On one of the last nights she spent with Boris, he passed out from his substantial intake of alcohol and meth and she took snapshots of the papers he'd put in his safe. Days before, she had found the combination inside the guitar he never played but also never let out of his sight. She was impressed by the number of bank accounts, their balances, and the names of some of those Russians who never went to the whorehouses and wouldn't be associated with the mafia, even if they did reside in Marbella. She wrote everything down in tiny letters in her black book.

Something inside her made her hold back sharing what she'd found out with Vila-Rojas. The crude, manipulative attitude Vila-Rojas sometimes showed with her made her anxious and distrustful. Plagued by these feelings, she decided to go on accumulating evidence before making a decision.

Boris always traveled with an entourage. Milena suspected that at least two of them, a little older than the rest, were following orders from his uncle Yasha, probably to keep him from getting in trouble. The lovers normally shut themselves up in the bedroom in Boris's apartment when they wanted to get high, but his guards were never far away. Milena wouldn't let the execution take place in the building because then she would be at the mercy of his vengeful mother. She would have preferred somewhere public where the police and the paramedics could get involved after the overdose. Vila-Rojas accepted her conditions begrudgingly.

Boris's obsession with Black Zero, a Belgian heavy-metal group that played now and then at One Percent, gave her and Vila-Rojas the opportunity they were waiting for. The Croatian convinced Boris that shooting up at the beginning of the show would make it a night to remember, as long as they did it right: a little bit of the new meth that was coming in from Morocco, and then heroin afterward. She promised him she'd take care of all the details.

If everything worked out right that night, she would have her freedom once and for all. Vila-Rojas had assured her that as soon as the scandal subsided, she could go where she wanted with a hundred thousand euros in her pocket. But Milena wasn't sure she could make it: the pill she was going to feed the Ukrainian would put him out, but she would still have to give him the deadly injection. Not that she cared for the guy—on the contrary, she thought he was cruel and despicable—but still, she was preparing to kill someone with her own hands.

When she went to the bar with the Turk in tow that second Saturday in January, she found Boris at his regular table surrounded by his friends. During the hour they had to wait for the group to go onstage, Milena drank more than usual. The Russian's gesticulations, the veins pulsing in his neck, his unmistakable voice, his favorite drink in his hand—all those things gave evidence of the explosive vitality in the boy's body she was about to snuff out forever. In no time, that universe of throbbing organs, febrile globules, neuronal circuits, and shuddering hormones would be nothing more than an inert lump, with no possibility of coming back.

Vila-Rojas had told her that the drug cocktail would be foolproof if she administered it in the right order: she should give him the pill when the group started up with the first song, and then take him to the women's bathroom fifteen minutes later and give him the heroin. She would take the same stuff, but in smaller doses, and the medical examinations would show that she was drugged up, too. The lawyer handed her two packages marked "Death Kit" and "Dream Kit."

When Black Zero finally started playing their thunderous tracks, she was feeling woozy from the four martinis. Nervously, she fingered the two plastic packages in the pockets of her leather jacket: Boris's kit on the right, hers on the left. But when the time came to give the Russian his pill, she wasn't sure which was the right one, and she didn't take her pill: she was afraid the combination of alcohol and meth would make her lose control and she would screw up when the time came to deliver the lethal dose. Boris swallowed his pill, and not long afterward, she saw his eyes become lost and his voice confused by an unmanageable tongue.

Ten minutes later, Milena whispered for him to accompany her to the bathroom. The bodyguards tried to follow them, but the Turk cut them off. She had offered him a fat tip if he would help her fulfill Boris's fantasy of having sex in a women's restroom. The bodyguards reluctantly agreed to stay outside after making sure there was no one else in the bathroom.

The Russian was in a hurry. He rushed into a stall, lowered the toilet seat, sat down, and uncovered his right arm. She let Boris's haste pull her along and pulled the syringe from her jacket and prepared the mixture while he tied off his biceps with a rubber tube. Unable to wait, he tried to take the needle from her, but she slapped him away. She was afraid that he would screw up the injection. Later, it occurred to her that if she'd let Boris shoot up, she wouldn't technically be his murderer, but at the time, all she wanted was to finish what she'd started.

She injected him and watched the drug flow through his body. He stretched his neck out inhumanly, as if trying to see something on his scalp. His legs shook, and he gave off a strange high-pitched scream.

The bodyguards shoved the Turk aside and entered the bathroom. They found Milena leaning over Boris's body, the syringe still poking from his right arm, like a sword buried in a dying bull. One grabbed her by the collar of her jacket and slammed her against the wall, and the other unholstered his pistol to take out the Turk. The Turk already had his pistol in hand, and floored his aggressor with two quick shots to the chest and the other with two to the back. It seemed impossible that a heavy-metal group could make more noise than a Beretta, but nobody rushed into the room. The Turk grabbed Milena by the wrist and jerked her onto her feet. A thread of blood ran from her head and onto her jacket. They left the bathroom and headed toward the exit, and Boris's friends, still sitting at a table in front of the stage, noticed nothing.

They left Milena's motorcycle in the parking lot and took the Turk's car. As soon as they were away from the bar, the Turk called Bonso and explained what had happened.

The Romanian was watching an episode of *Game of Thrones* with Mercedes, a Moroccan girl. Indignant, he was complaining to her of the perversity of Cersei Lannister, the incestuous queen, when he received the call. What the Turk had just done meant a death sentence for them both: everyone in Marbella knew Boris was untouchable, that his mother was more powerful than him, and that the Russian mafia was implacable when it came to blood. Everyone also knew the Turk was his right-hand man.

He threw the telephone against the wall. The solution, if there was one, was way out of his hands: Vila-Rojas, he thought. He picked the phone back up, called the Turk, and gave him his orders.

55

Vidal, Milena, and Luis

TUESDAY, NOVEMBER 18, 8:20 P.M.

IT DIDN'T GO DOWN the way Jaime had planned. Just after eight in the morning, Vidal called at the door of the bedroom where Milena and Luis were staying in the Hotel Michoacán. Luis opened cautiously. Fingers of sunlight came through the cracks and pointed accusingly at the scene. Milena had a sheet pulled over her chest, and his friend wore nothing but a pair of pants he seemed to have thrown on before opening the door. The disordered bed, their clothes thrown haphazardly over a chair, and the bottle of wine on the nightstand were the very image, almost the cliché, of a secret fling. Luis's first feeling was of irritation, his second of indignation, and then both were pushed aside by a more selfish thought: Rina would have to find out what had happened there.

Luis looked at the ground and invited Vidal in.

Vidal explained Jaime's plan.

"With a little luck, Bonso and the Turk could be taken out today. All you two have to do is go down to the lobby so the lookouts they send in will confirm that you're both here. After that, everything will be finished and you can do whatever you want."

"There's nothing I'd like more than to see Bonso and the Turk fall. But it's way more complicated than that," Milena objected.

"You don't understand, the whole country is up in arms after the death of the *El Mundo* editor; even the president wants to get involved.

Claudia and Tomás ate with him yesterday. It's over, Milena, there are much bigger forces than any threat you're running away from. And those forces are working in your favor. Take advantage of them and get free for once from whatever it is they have over you."

"You're the ones who don't understand!" Milena insisted, and looked to Luis. "Can you leave for a moment, Vidal? I need to talk to Luis alone."

Vidal looked at the two of them, utterly confused. He thought he was bringing good news and that his only task would be overcoming Luis's natural resistance to collaborating with Lemlock. The advantages of the plan were so evident that he assumed his friend's pragmatism would keep him from giving in to his prejudices.

"Luis, convince her. If we wipe out that gang, we'll have to negotiate with Vila-Rojas. Yeah, that's right: we know about Vila-Rojas." Then he left the room.

Milena leapt from the bed and started talking while she buttoned up her shirt.

"There's something I can't tell you. If Bonso dies in these circumstances, it will cause a video to get leaked that will lead to Vila-Rojas falling, and probably Yasha, the leader of the Ukrainian mafia in Marbella, along with him. That could cost me my life. I can't tell you more because I don't want to put you in danger. The less you know, the better."

Luis reflected briefly.

"Bonso shouldn't fall into the trap Jaime's set for him," he said.

"Exactly, but your friend Vidal won't understand that."

"I think we already lost Vidal some time back."

"You think?"

"He's not a bad guy, but he's like clay in Jaime's hands. If they knew about Vila-Rojas, they've intercepted my encrypted messages, and they could only have done so because he revealed one of my passwords."

"So how are we going to keep Bonso from falling into the trap?"

"I already have the email addresses his organization uses. The problem is, Lemlock does, too, or they will soon, so they'll find out I'm the one spilling the beans. If they didn't care for me before, now they'll see me as an enemy."

"They'll like you less, and I'll like you a little more. Thank you, Luis," she said, looking in his eyes. He didn't know how to answer.

56

Tomás and Claudia

TUESDAY, NOVEMBER 18, 11:00 A.M.

HE WOKE UP AT 5:20 in the morning, as if he were a computer terminal hooked up to the Net. That was the hour when *El Mundo*'s digital edition went online, long before the deliveryman would leave the print version at his apartment. The journalist knew the headline he read on the screen: he had written it himself. It wasn't the lead story that attracted his attention, lurid as it was: "Deputy Director of *El Mundo* Assassinated by the Mafia." What he was looking for was the second story: "Salgado, Godfather of the Human Traffickers." He read it, knowing that from then on, there was no turning back. It was an ultimatum, a declaration of war that wouldn't end until one of the parties was eliminated.

The night before, he'd given instructions to a half-dozen of his best investigative reporters to give all their time to documenting the trafficking rings, especially the ones selling women, and the protection they received from the authorities. Two of them focused exclusively on the criminal careers of Víctor Salgado and his affiliates, with the plan of publishing additional pieces in the upcoming weeks. Tomás knew that if they managed to convert the ex-public official into an exemplar of corruption and the story took off on the social networks, no one would dare to protect him. Governors, ministers, and senators who owed him favors and even their jobs would suffer sudden attacks of amnesia: in politics, loyalty only prevails when betrayal doesn't offer dividends. They would have to make Salgado a hot potato, a pariah no one could help without paying a high political price.

Tomás told himself he'd have to consult with Vidal to see what steps should be taken to make the ex-prison director's story go viral. The headline wasn't enough, not now, when no one but the political and cultural elites read the daily papers and watched the news. *El Mundo*'s accusation of Salgado would be like a bomb going off among the political class, and everyone would have to take cover. But Tomás needed more. The system had to leave the capo high and dry, even put the squeeze on him, and—why not?—lock him up. There were more than enough reasons to do so. But for that to happen, he'd need public opinion to question authority so intensely that inaction would come with a political cost. Only the social networks could have that kind of effect: memes and hashtags that could make the former jailer into a figure as well known as he was contemptible.

The night before, he had called various foreign correspondents to alert them of the attack on the deputy director. He made no mention of Milena and stuck to explaining the newspaper's investigations into Víctor Salgado, offering human trafficking and money laundering as the most probable motives for the aggression. His friend Peter Dell, a correspondent with the *New York Times*, assured him he would place a story on the paper's front page.

Four hours later, at *El Mundo*'s offices, Tomás was waiting on Vidal to start a meeting with those responsible for the online edition. He knew the newspaper's tech guys were good, but he preferred to have someone he could trust on his side before crucifying Salgado on the social networks. While he waited on his nephew, he went into Claudia's office.

"Any reaction from Salgado?" she asked.

"None. But as they said in the old days, no news is good news."

"Prida talked to me half an hour ago. Very restrained. He put all the federal government's resources at our disposal to find those responsible for the crime. I told him they wouldn't have to look hard, everyone knows Víctor Salgado."

"And what did he say?"

"He went off on a tangent. He assured me that he'd told the attorney general not to spare any resources in the investigation."

"Well, he's going to seize up when he sees the article in the *New York Times*."

"Hopefully the authorities will do something before Salgado takes his revenge. Where do you think he's going to come from?"

"It's impossible to know, but we've beefed up security everywhere. The Mexico City chief of police has sent out extra patrols. Did your mother finally get out of the city?"

"She's on a plane right now, I convinced her to go to Miami for a few days. And you? And your daughter?"

"I'm going to have lunch with her, I didn't want to say anything over the phone. I want her out of town. Maybe she can go to a friend's house in Cuernavaca where she spends a lot of time. It's not easy to persuade her. She's hardheaded, you know? You'll meet her eventually."

Claudia nodded, concealing the warmth that flooded through her breast. "You'll meet her eventually": a phrase that foretold paradise.

"I don't want anything to happen to us," she said. "Not to us, not to any of our people. Not now, when we've begun something that could be so important for you and me."

Whether she meant *El Mundo* and the news cycle, or the closeness between them, his life was finally beginning to make sense. In a little less than a year, he had gone from being an insignificant columnist with just a handful of readers to the head of the most important journalism resource in the country. And the hopeless, fleeting affairs he'd carried on for years were over, making room for a real relationship with one of the two women who had come into his life. He knew the ambiguity with Claudia and Amelia couldn't go on forever. One way or another, he'd have to take a decision soon.

An attack of nostalgia struck him when he imagined either of them gone. The desolation was just as intense whether he imagined losing the absolute intimacy he shared with Amelia on the weekends or the joyous life he could lead by Claudia's side.

For years, he'd wanted Amelia's love, and now that he had it, he couldn't just let it go. But there was something that didn't click in his relationship with his old friend: he had the feeling he wasn't always on her level, that sooner or later she would notice his weak points. He always felt pushed when he was with her: to be more intelligent, more vivacious, a better person than he was. For his lover, the universe was imperfect and their voyage through it brought along the responsibility of making it better. It was a notion Tomás could agree with in theory, but he knew he lacked the spirit or the disposition to make the sacrifices it implied.

Claudia, on the other hand, belonged to that species that came into the world to enjoy it, and would do so as long as she didn't leave it worse off or impose on the happiness of those around her, and Tomás could embrace that philosophy more readily than Amelia's messianic tendencies.

Vidal interrupted Tomás and Claudia as he always did, knocking lightly and discreetly on the iron door to Claudia's office.

"They told me to come in, that you were waiting on me."

Tomás greeted his nephew with a relieved smile. He led him to the meeting room in his offices, where the teams who ran *El Mundo*'s website were waiting for them, and explained their mission: skewering

Salgado on the social networks. Vidal listened to the newspaper's community manager talk a long time about Kohl's, hubs, and spheres of influence, tried to imagine what Luis would do in his shoes, and took the floor. It turned out that when Rina was gone, he could do an acceptable impersonation of his friend's talent, and when the meeting was over, everyone looked at him with respect.

That hadn't been the case with Luis that morning, when he visited the hotel. When they said their goodbyes, he saw a gleam of contempt in his eyes.

57

Milena

JANUARY 2014

IT WAS AN AREA CLOSE to the Málaga airport that Milena had never been through before, and if she had, she wouldn't have known anyway, because the night was dark and lighting almost inexistent on that street. At last, the Turk stopped the car on a corner lined with warehouses. She heard the screeching of a rolling gate being raised up: an obese man tugged at the chain and squinted to confirm the driver's identity. The Turk pulled inside and the gate went back down.

It was a huge, rectangular space, around half the size of a football field. As Milena walked to the stairway leading to the lone office inside, she thought she saw the outlines of figures in the dim light. The Turk ordered the fat guy to wait at the gate to let Bonso's car through. He would be showing up any minute.

"Now, Checkers, while we're waiting on the boss, tell me what shit you've gotten us into."

There was no apparent rancor: just the voice of a person wanting to take advantage of the time he has left. She understood that he'd just killed two thugs and her fate depended on what she said next.

She considered keeping up the story of the accidental overdose but didn't think Bonso or the Turk would buy it. For months, they had seen her weave her web around the Ukrainian, and she imagined that Bonso's approval of her nocturnal outings with the Turk was part of his agreement with Vila-Rojas, so she left out the details of the murders of his other associates but didn't hide the details of the plan she'd tried to carry out that night.

The Turk listened to her without reacting. The deep bags under his eyes and his long face made her think of an old Saint Bernard that's seen everything.

"I knew you were up to something like that, but I never thought you'd fuck it up so bad. That's the problem with amateurs, you think you're clever," he said with contempt.

Milena nodded, not inclined to argue. Boris's spasmodic body rose up in her memory, and again she felt the wound burning on her forehead. A tone still thundered in one ear from the bullets fired in the cramped women's bathroom.

"So who are those guys?" Milena asked, pointing toward the figures shifting in the back of the warehouse.

"They want to be Europeans."

"So what are they? Africans?"

"What the fuck do you care?"

Milena didn't answer. In reality, she didn't care. She just wanted to stop thinking about the tiles in the bathroom and forget the greenish foam she'd seen bubble from Boris's mouth. She remembered she still had a syringe in her jacket, the dream kit, and she thanked the gods for the opportunity to evade the difficult moment before her with drugs. The foretaste of relief suffused her body: she slipped her hand into her left pocket and found it empty. First, frustration struck her, then confusion: she pawed her right pocket and found the syringe she was looking for. Only then did she realize she had given Boris the wrong dose.

"Agustín wanted to kill me," she said to herself in a barely audible voice.

"What?" the Turk asked.

"Both doses were lethal," she answered, and opened her fist to show the syringe in her hand.

She looked at the dream kit and the force of her addiction pushed her with febrile intensity. Dream or death, whatever that precious liquid inside would bring her—she didn't care at that point.

The arrival of Bonso's car distracted her for long enough that the Turk could pull the plastic bag out of her hand and put it in his pocket.

The Romanian ran up the metal staircase with thundering and frenetic steps. He tripped on the last one and walked into the make-shift office with a movement that made Milena think of someone swimming the butterfly.

But Bonso wasn't a man with much sense for the ridiculous. Stumbling only increased his fury, and Milena was resigned to being the victim of his wrath.

But the Romanian's survival instinct was far more powerful than his tantrums. He might be prone to fits, but he was the kind of guy who squeezed his toothpaste from the bottom of the tube. He rinsed off his sweaty face, sat in the chair the Turk had left for him, and asked for the details about what had happened at One Percent.

Milena started to describe the events, but the Turk interrupted her, and rightly: her need for drugs and her raw emotions were making her babble nonsensically. The Turk took over and told him everything from the time they entered the club to when they arrived at the warehouse and about Vila-Rojas's plans to eliminate Boris.

"That son-of-a-bitch lawyer," the Romanian spat when he heard the end of the tale. "And you? What are you doing sticking your nose in where you don't belong?"

"It's the life, boss," the Turk responded, holding his stare.

Bonso stood up to get a closer look—still not that close—at his underling. It was the first time he'd seen the Turk show something other than absolute submission. The Romanian paced in a circle around him, arms akimbo, without taking his eyes off of him.

Milena couldn't help but admire the midget's steely resolve. The Turk didn't flinch, either, he just watched his boss with the cold calm of a cobra waiting to strike. Bonso finally returned to his seat.

"Luckily for you, I have our safe-conduct on me," he said, taking a few DVDs in slipcases from his coat pocket. "Let's hope Vila-Rojas is better at making deals with the Ukrainians than planning murders. We've got him by the balls."

The Turk took the DVDs and looked at his boss, intrigued.

"Remember two years ago when Vila-Rojas came into my office and bought that whore and gave me instructions for her to work under his orders, but to stay in my house? I got all that on tape," the Romanian said with a smile, gesturing toward the envelopes the Turk held.

Milena remembered that the Romanian had come up filming hardcore pornography and distributing videos of bestiality, pederasty, and S&M. He'd given it up after an official investigation into snuff films, but his ability to manipulate video files remained intact.

"Well, if Vila-Rojas wants to save us in exchange for this, he'll have to hurry, because they must be combing Marbella for us already."

"He's almost here. Now I need you to lend me the fat guy who opened the gate so he can go spread these discs around: there are two houses where he should drop them off, and the other two he'll mail. They're going to old friends, guys I trust, who know to get them around if they don't hear from me. That'll protect us from that goddamn lawyer."

"Yeah, he's the type to hold a grudge," the Turk admitted.

"And you—what do we do with you?" Bonso said, turning to Milena. "I always said there's something not right about a whore who reads books. You got a second life after you ran off to Madrid, and look how you pay me back for it. You've fucked us all."

Melina nodded reluctantly. Bonso was right.

"Kill her," he ordered the Turk. "Put the body in the trunk of the car and dump it somewhere when we get out of here. But send the DVDs first, in case that fucker shows up early."

Milena had been waiting for this death sentence, and only hoped it would be quick and painless.

She told herself to choose carefully what she thought about in her last minutes of life. She tried to remember her childhood in Jastrebarsko, but all that came into her mind were vignettes from the biography of a person who was no longer her. In the same way, she rejected the images of recent years that pounded against her closed eyelids: the whorehouses she'd lived in or the scenarios with her clients, repeated a thousand times. The time she really wished to say goodbye to had been spent in front of an open book. She would miss the people she had taken refuge in to make her existence easier: now she invoked them to better bear her passage into death. She said goodbye to Anna Karenina, to La Maga, to all the heroines whose skin she'd lived in throughout the course of those years. All were dead, and now she would join them.

The Turk's steps on the metal stairway resounded in her brain like bells counting down: fourteen steps, and Milena's breathing in time with them. When he entered the office, she was hyperventilating.

"I don't know if that's the best thing for us, boss," the Turk said, jerking his head toward Milena.

"What? Getting rid of the bitch?"

"Yeah. Vila-Rojas wanted to kill her, too. She saved herself because she didn't take the shot. No one thought Boris would start screaming like a madman. It clearly never occurred to him that she might have a way out. The best thing for him was if she croaked from an OD, because if the Russians got hold of her, they could make her talk."

"So?" Bonso replied.

"We're going to negotiate with Vila-Rojas and he wanted to get rid of her, so having her in our possession gives us an advantage, doesn't it?"

Bonso hesitated a few moments and then nodded.

"I'll be goddamned. You're right. Beyond the video, she's the proof that Vila-Rojas killed him. And if everything goes to shit and the Russians come down on us, they'll be wanting to get hold of whoever killed Boris. She could save our skin either way."

They spoke of Milena as if she weren't present. She thought they would have been more nervous about ditching a car than deciding what to do with her life. She wondered if the Turk might have some ulterior motive in rescuing her beyond mere canniness. "Checkers" was almost a kindness compared with the other nicknames in whorehouses: Fleabag, Hairy, Darky, Hick. In the past three months, while he accompanied her during her conversion into a biker chick, they'd only talked a few times, but she thought she could sense the Turk's pleasure on those motorcycle jaunts. She remembered the vest she had gotten when her training was over, which she hadn't thought much of at the time.

Milena came back down to earth as quickly as she had left: a part of her was sad at leaving Anna Karenina & Co. behind. She wasn't even sure what she'd heard was good news. If she fell into the Russians' hands, she'd end up yearning for Bonso's dogs.

"Take her in the back with the others, I don't want Vila-Rojas to see her. We'll figure out where we put her later," Bonso said, looking at a message coming through on his phone. "Here comes the asshole now."

Milena and the Turk rushed down the metal stairway.

"Thanks," she said when they were alone.

"Don't get your panties moist, Checkers," he answered.

She spent the next hour in the shadows, occasionally observing the three men arguing around the desk in the office. The light that shone over them, the height of the platform, and the darkness in the rest of the building made it look like a theater scene.

Sick with uncertainty, the twenty or so Arabs surrounding her followed the movements of the three actors beneath the spotlight, convinced the men were deciding their future. There was never a play so keenly observed. In shaky Spanish, one of them asked Milena what was going on. "Don't bother me," she responded in Serbian. Another Arab leapt toward her, his face suddenly lit up, and begged her in that same language: "Please, we've been here a week without knowing anything."

Goddamned globalization, Milena said to herself. The night had exhausted her, and she would have rather let them fuck her than give them explanations. But as she swept her eyes over the group, she saw the silhouettes of women and children, and remembered those first days after her capture. She spent the next half-hour trying to calm them down, once she'd made sure they were nothing more than run-of-the-mill illegal immigrants. Bonso kept them till their families sent money to cover their expenses, real and imagined. In the end, Milena was happy for the distraction of speaking Serbian again, even if the process of translating her words into Arabic was laborious, because it allowed her to forget Boris and Vila-Rojas for a while. After all, it was her future, not theirs, that the men were arguing about up there.

58

Jaime

WEDNESDAY, NOVEMBER 19, 1:00 P.M.

CLAUDIA AND TOMÁS had beaten Víctor Salgado. The political apparatus abandoned one of its own.

Jaime had figured out Salgado's name was mud in the highest spheres of power. The chiefs at *El Mundo* had managed to make the ex-warden the villain of the day on social media. The article in the *New York Times*, with its withering emphasis on corruption in Mexico, was the last straw. The reporters, conveniently tipped off by *El Mundo*, used the attorney general's press conference to announce the capture of a leader of the Zeta cartel and to pepper the official with questions about Salgado.

Lemus's team intercepted the instructions sent from the attorney general's office to the public ministries and the police departments to look into any accusations against Salgado and dust off any investigations that might be pending in the far-flung corners of the Mexican judiciary. He still hadn't issued an arrest warrant, but now it was just a matter of time.

Jaime figured that at some point that morning, President Prida had weighed the powers pitted against each other and decided to cede to the pressure of public opinion. That didn't mean that the delicate ties between politics and money laundering were broken: they'd just need to have a talk with Salgado's bosses and get someone else into his place. In the end, they'd have to give something for the ex-official's head: the hardcore money guys never took a loss.

Jaime figured that he was the one who had come up short. Tomás and Claudia would feel satisfied that their strategy had been a success even though he'd advised them against it. Tomás hadn't rescued Milena or even come close, but he'd managed to do away with the immediate threat looming over them. That meant Jaime had lost. The possibility of solidifying his influence at El Mundo was almost gone now, and Claudia would continue looking at him with mistrust.

He hadn't managed to strike a decisive blow against Bonso either, let alone bring the Turk's head to the newspaper chief. Once more, Luis had frustrated his plans by alerting the pimp's gang, apparently through email. If the boy had followed the Croatian's instructions, her relationship with Bonso must have been more complicated than hunter and prey.

The situation had changed with Víctor Salgado out of the picture, though how still wasn't clear, Jaime thought. The old Mexican was Bonso and Milena's protector in the country and the one responsible to people back in Spain for assuring that local conditions were ripe so the two of them could make good on whatever deal they had set up back in Marbella. Even with Salgado gone, probably on the lam at that very moment, the deal remained in force. The description Emiliano Reyna's maid gave of his killer matched the Turk's profile in the file Interpol had passed along. It seemed neither his gang nor his bosses back in Spain would give up in their search for Milena, even if they'd avoid another public scandal after what had happened with Salgado. Claudia and Tomás didn't know about how far the matter was from resolved, or if they did, they preferred to ignore it.

Jaime called a team meeting.

"We've found three houses belonging to the gang and we're track-ing all the inbound and outbound calls," said Patricia. "Any minute now, we'll localize the phone Bonso is using."

"Anything new in Spain?" Jaime asked.

"Yes," Esteban Porter responded. "My contact in Interpol in Madrid hit me up for ten thousand euros, but it was worth it. According to him, half that cash is going to an official from the Marbella police who swears to him that just before Bonso and Milena disappeared almost a year ago, some guy named Boris Kattel and two of his bodyguards were murdered in a dive bar in the port. He OD'd, they were shot. Boris was the son of the former head of the Ukrainian mafia in the south of Spain. Apparently he'd been going out with Milena a few months, and she was the one who turned him onto heroin."

"Then the question is: why is she still alive?" Commandant Ezequiel Carrasco interrupted.

The group fell silent.

"Is there anything else on Vila-Rojas?" Jaime asked.

"They don't have much at Interpol. He's kept clear of the ongoing investigation into corruption and money laundering in Marbella. Dozens of big shots have taken a fall, but his file is clean, even though he's always been on a list of suspects."

"Any luck hacking into his email or any other accounts?"

"His tech stuff is state-of-the-art, we need a little more time to crack it," Mauricio Romo responded. "He's clearly been shifting his operations from local to international circuits. Most of the trans-actions take place in London and New York, and a lot in Gibraltar, which is like the Cayman Islands of the Mediterranean. Almost all we can find is money that's already been laundered, which his trusted brokers shift back and forth for him between funds and other types of speculative investments. He sits on the boards of more than twenty companies, all of them top-tier. Incidentally, three or four of them have operations in Mexico: one of the biggest construction firms is on the list, and a Spanish hotel chain with a heavy presence on the Riviera Maya. He must be one of the main financial advisers for organized criminals in Europe, maybe the most important one in Spain."

"Too big a player to be dabbling in hookers," the commandant said.

"No, I don't think that's it," Jaime said, "but clearly there's some kind of relationship with Milena, that's what we've gathered from Luis's searches, and she's got to be the one feeding him clues. The question is, what ties them together?"

"Everything points to some link to what happened to Boris and Milena. If he's handling that kind of money in Marbella, it has to be coming from deals with the Russian mafia."

"More than deals, I'd say he's their money man," Porter concluded.

"Then that's it," Patricia said. "The link between Milena and Vila-Rojas is Boris. They knew each other, they had business together, and she was mixed up with him when he died."

"Which brings us back to the commandant's question," said Jaime. "Why are Milena, Bonso, and the Turk still alive if they were caught up in the murder of a big-time mafioso?" Jaime asked like a teacher waiting for the obvious answer.

"Vila-Rojas is protecting them," Patricia said.

"And he's protecting them because . . . "

"Because he's in love with Milena," Mauricio Romo, the young hacker, said.

"Don't be silly," Jaime said. "If it was that, he wouldn't have her working as a hooker in Mexico."

"Because he's involved," Porter said.

"And because the people we're trying to track down have proof of it," Patricia continued.

"That's the only thing that could explain why Milena would try and keep them alive even when she's doing everything she can to get away from them. She doesn't want them to be her pimps anymore, but she knows that if one of them dies, whatever is keeping the Russians from avenging themselves on her disappears," Jaime finished with a smile.

"Knowing what we know now, our hands are tied," Patricia said.

They all sat there without speaking, taking in her words. All of them except Jaime.

"Not necessarily. This could be the opportunity of our lives," he said after a pause, his smile now broader. Then, he rattled off a series of commands: "Get a bead on Bonso and the Turk for once and make a plan to bring them in alive. Tell me when it's ready: you're in charge, Commandant. Don't let me down. Now that they don't have Salgado's support, they're vulnerable, at least for a while. Patricia, set up a security cordon around Milena: protect her, but also keep her from getting away." He pressed the button on the intercom and told his secretary to get in touch with the Mexican ambassador in Spain and get him a plane ticket for Madrid the following night.

59

Amelia

WEDNESDAY, NOVEMBER 19, 6:00 P.M.

IT WASN'T A GOOD DAY for Amelia, either: for some time now, she'd gotten nothing from politics but intrigue and backstabbing, and from love, nothing but lovelessness. After a week buried under budget projections, she felt like an expert in public finances. That very night, she was headed to a meeting with the congressmen from the party to define their strategy before the upcoming vote, but already she was feeling discouraged. The president's party controlled just over 50 percent of the votes, which meant debate would be rhetorical and, ultimately, useless. Her colleagues at the head of the PRD argued for the importance of the legislative tribune to help the people understand that the party was defending the interests of the working classes, but Amelia thought that was ridiculous. Voting to fulfill an obligation, with no chance of influencing the outcome, wasn't only pointless, it was an act of complicity. She had agreed to take part in politics to intervene in the country's public life, not to give excuses to those in power.

Her relationship with Tomás was still at an impasse. They'd barely seen each other over the weekend; for the few hours they were together, they took refuge in routines that had once been an oasis of relaxation but were now automatic, a reflex that kept them from that warmth that separated love from merely living together. Or at least that was how it seemed to Amelia.

Beyond all that, she thought she'd found a new spot on the back of her hand. She'd never been a hypochondriac, but she couldn't help asking herself if those new spots were a sign of cell death, a manifestation of some invisible cancer gestating deep inside one of her vital organs. She knew Tomás would laugh at her worries and push aside her fears with an ode to her firm breasts or satiny thighs, but she couldn't help feeling sadness, provoked by reasons of the heart, and discouragement brought on by politics. Maybe it was depression, an affliction that had always seemed as alien as malaria, a terrible thing that happened to other people, but not to her.

She told herself it wasn't Tomás who was making her sad, no matter how much the possibility of losing him tormented her. She had never depended on a man to make herself feel alive or useful. She decided to sketch out a plan, as she'd done so many times in her life. She could do more than stand there like a spectator watching the tragedy Milena was living through. For more than a decade, she had been one of the main activists in the country combating human trafficking and prostitution. The Croatian's case offered the chance to put a halt to the infiltration of European mafias into Mexico's sex-trafficking networks. She wouldn't let Milena end up the victim of Jaime's dark machinations or Claudia's blitheness. She decided for the first time to make use of her political influence to aid one of her own causes. But first, she would have to get her hands dirty.

An hour later, Rina and Vidal showed up. It wasn't easy to convince him to disobey Lemlock's instructions and come to her office. He said they shouldn't move, for security reasons. Amelia had to leave a message with Jaime's secretary telling him that she needed Rina, and when she received a courteous no, she asked whether the girl had been kidnapped. Apparently, Jaime decided it wasn't worth it to go to war with Amelia, and he allowed Rina to go, telling Vidal not to let her out of his sight. Now that Lemlock had Luis and Milena under their power, Rina had lost strategic value.

Once they were in front of her, Amelia noticed how impatient Rina was with Vidal's attentions and remembered the closeness between her and Luis.

In less than half an hour, Vidal and Rina brought the president of the PRD up to date on all that had occurred in the past few days. The contrast between the fine points in each of their versions led Amelia to think that the distance between them was due less to matters of the heart than to Rina taking Luis's side, Vidal working for Jaime, and Rina seeing this as a kind of betrayal. Their stories gave Amelia some sense of the situation: Claudia wanted the Turk dead and Jaime hoped to offer her his head as a trophy; for reasons that were hard to understand, Milena was opposed to seeing her pursuers dead; Víctor Salgado had bolted, and a certain Vila-Rojas was the new puppet master. Jaime had Luis and Milena holed up in some hotel in Tasqueña.

Amelia remembered a position called zugzwang in chess—the only one of her father's pastimes she had shared with him. Zugzwang was a situation in which one of the players is obliged to move, but any move he makes can only worsen his situation. Striking out against the gang hunting Milena would work to the Croatian's disadvantage, but not doing so could hasten her death or capture by the traffickers and a descent back into prostitution. A Gordian knot without a clear solution.

But for an activist like Amelia, any strategy to help had to start with the victim: she was the thread that could cause the whole web to unravel. Consequently, the first step was to rescue Milena from Jaime's clutches, and the second to work out a safe and definitive escape plan. A half-dozen times, Amelia had successfully orchestrated the relocation of victims to other countries with new identities. The Mexico City chief of police, her friend and tireless suitor, could offer the muscle she needed.

She could also use an ally inside Lemlock, and for that reason, she'd need to win Vidal back. She seized the moment when he went to the restroom—maybe just as a pretext to speak with Jaime—and revealed her plan to Rina. The girl was enthusiastic: patching things up with Vidal and freeing Luis and Milena were her primary objectives as well, though not necessarily in that order. It took two hours of convincing, but finally Vidal agreed to become their informant. A long, warm embrace from Rina sealed their accord, at least for the moment.

Afterward, Rina let herself out. She wanted to dive into an analysis of the budgets. She knew that at this point, there was little useful in whatever she might bring to the table, but she felt she had failed Amelia by being gone so many days during this crisis with Milena. She hoped to show her value as a consultant for future assignments.

"In a way, Jaime is right," Vidal said when they were alone.

"How so?"

"People aren't what they say they are, and sometimes they don't even know what they are," he responded. That argument had sounded so irrefutable coming from his uncle but nonsense now that he was uttering it. "What I mean is, what Lemlock does is very important for discovering people's true intentions, what they do and don't do when they think nobody's watching. You'd be surprised by the technology Jaime has to find things out." When he heard his own words, the young man turned white and glanced at Amelia's cell phone on her desk and touched his own in his pants pocket.

"Including us, right?" Amelia asked.

Vidal nodded his head slowly, and went on to detail the vast operation Lemlock had set in motion to keep all of them under their control, including his own spying on Rina and Luis. When he finished, he cried like a baby and Amelia took him in her arms. Then she asked him to go keep Rina company.

When she was alone, she called Jaime, and he arrived twenty minutes later.

"What's the emergency?" he asked in her office. "We've got a leak and we're about to figure out where Bonso's hiding out. You pulled me out of a meeting for a potential mission." In reality, Jaime was thankful for the opportunity to see Amelia one-on-one.

"I want you to tell me what you're up to with Vidal. He hasn't got the stuff to become a KGB apprentice. And while you're at it, you can tell me what right you have to tap our cell phones."

"I'm not your enemy, Amelia," he said, and Amelia had the wry recollection of hearing the same words from Claudia a few days before. "None of us has got a grip on Vidal. He's disoriented and insecure. I'm just offering him an alternative. But maybe I'm giving him a glimpse of shit he's not ready for. Let's talk about this another time."

"And let's not forget, we're not his parents," Amelia responded.

"No, unfortunately neither of us is," he said, and put a hand on her shoulder.

Amelia pulled away with a soft shrug.

"Espionage is unacceptable . . . " she started to say, but Jaime interrupted.

"You should know that people like you, me, and Tomás are already being watched and listened to by more than one office. It's not a bad thing that someone on our side is doing it, too, but for our own good. I can intercept the people stalking us. More than once, I've blocked parts of a sensitive conversation of yours so that it wouldn't be captured electronically. If I stop listening in, do you think the others will, too?"

She recalled intimate conversations with Tomás and some delicate topics that had come up with her political colleagues. The better part of her relationships, both personal and professional, were carried out by telephone and email. If what Jaime was saying was true and he was listening in on all her conversations, he knew her better now than anyone else in the world.

"Don't worry," Jaime said. "I've seen to it that all the files and recordings related to you are treated with absolute discretion. I'm the only person who can access them. And believe me, none of it will ever be used against you. No one will take care of you the way I do. You know that, right?"

She said nothing, and he grasped her shoulders again, this time with both hands.

"Amelia, just accept it. You and me being together was always in the cards. When you were twenty, you were already more of an adult than the rest of us, and I understand that my father was more mature, more imposing, than I was. But I'm convinced that deep down, I was the one you were looking for in that relationship. Now we can try. I never stopped loving you."

Jaime brought his face close and kissed Amelia on the lips. She didn't move, surprised and overwhelmed by the feelings that rose within her. She would have liked to push him away, indignant, but she didn't want to hurt him. And a part of her explored that kiss, looking for traces of the father's passion. Maybe that was what she found, or maybe it was just knowing that someone desired her when her lover might be about to abandon her for another woman. Regardless, she felt a pleasant gust of air traveling over her body.

A message arrived over Telegram and interrupted their embrace. Jaime's professional habits got the better of him, and he looked at the text: "We've found Bonso."

THEM VIII

I admit it: in an ideal world, prostitution wouldn't exist. Or lies, envy, or guilty pleasures. But none of that's going to disappear, first of all, because of our biological makeup. It's only in textbooks that grand causes and noble principles triumph; in real history, and not in that golden-age bullshit they teach us in school, it's the lower passions and unsatisfied obsessions that are the real motor of world events.

It's not that we act like pigs, but we'll never get anywhere denying our place in the animal kingdom. We're designed for satisfying the basic conditions of survival and reproduction. Look at the Norwegians: they try and ban sex for cash, they think they've gotten past racial discrimination, too. And that works till one of those modern-day Vikings comes along and takes out a hundred of them to remind them they still belong to the human race.

So it doesn't matter how much deodorant we lather on; we're still armpits, fluids, and cracks. It's better to live with it than against it. Those moral codes built up to go against hormonal tendencies are nothing more than self-justifications for cowards.

For thirty-nine years, I've lived faithful to the requirements of my orifices. I don't have anything to regret, and I bear it all with same dignity of a blighted old oak. It's only some days that the Hepatitis C and the latent syphilis get to me. It doesn't matter. One way or another, I don't have many years left.

C.B. EX-MAGISTRATE
OF THE SUPREME COURT
SPAIN

348

60

Tomás

"YOU'RE OUT EARLY TODAY, BOSS."

"Today I could manage it," Tomás responded, not especially in the mood to chat with his garrulous chauffeur. They rounded the Avenida Insurgentes on the way to his apartment in the Colonía Condesa. He thought the journey would be a brief one; midweek, at that hour, there was barely any traffic.

"The one in the middle's not bad," said the driver appreciatively, and pointed at three women posted on the corner. "But the other two should find something else to do. Children, drunks, and panty hose always tell the truth."

Tomás followed his gaze. They were three hookers braving the cold night anxiously at the intersection of Insurgentes and Álvaro Obregón. The spectacle brought to mind Milena, and with her, the murder of Emiliano Reyna. For the past few hours, Tomás had been able to evade the subject thanks to his routines at the paper, which he'd had to turn to as soon as the threat of Salgado had disappeared. Tomás saw little difference between his own duties and those of a factory foreman or insurance exec: marketing, personnel management, and budgets. As he opened the door to his apartment, he was convinced that all that would have to change, and he would need to hire a right-hand man for those administrative tasks.

And yet it was his left arm that caught him when he fell to the floor after receiving a blow to the back of his neck. He was struggling to get up when someone behind him turned on the light and he was able to make out the figure in the living room.

"So, dickhead, who told you men solved their problems by running and squealing to the papers?"

Salgado had settled into the easy chair with a glass of whiskey. On his lap was an open album of family photos Jimena had given her father the Christmas before.

"What are you doing here? The police are after you," Tomás said, more confused than afraid.

"You fucked up my life, but I'm not the type to go down alone."

"You son of a bitch. What did you expect? You killed Emiliano for no reason."

"For no reason? Who the fuck told you to get mixed up in things that didn't concern you? You're in over your heads. How else was I going to let you know?"

Tomás noticed the closed curtains and figured he had few chances to save himself: Salgado wasn't there to negotiate. Salgado raised two fingers of the hand resting on the arm of the chair, and Tomás felt a kick in his ribs. He got on all fours, trying to catch his breath, and received a kick to the opposite flank from another man.

"I just came here to say no one fucks with me. I'm going to put two bullets in your skull and from here, we'll go to Vicente Suárez Forty-Six. We won't play kickball with your wife and daughter, though. We'll come up with something better, you sack of shit."

"What's in it for you? You'll be the first one they suspect."

"I'm a dead man, if that's any consolation to you. The cops aren't the ones I'm worried about."

"Then you need to run. Why are you here wasting time on us?"

"Run? At my age? How undignified. I'd rather have a little fun before I meet my maker."

"Go have fun with your whore of a mother," Tomás finally said.

"Nah," Salgado replied. "For this party, you're providing the women. Anyway, you're out of whiskey. Hopefully Teresa's cellar is better stocked." Turning to one of his gorillas, he added, "Kill him, but grab a pillow first. I don't want you waking up the whole building."

Tomás decided to end his life with a bit of dignity as well. He raised his hands to show he wasn't going to try anything crazy and nodded toward the sofa that rounded out the scanty furnishings in his living room. He preferred to sit rather than kneel while he waited for the coup de grâce from the thug who was returning from the bed just then with the requisite pillow. As he stood, Tomás asked himself when the last time he'd changed the sheets was, and was glad to recall that the cleaning woman had done it the day before.

That was the last thing he thought. Then came a noise at the door, two quick hisses, the sound of a body hitting the floor, then another two hisses. When his hands landed on the chair and he turned around to see what was happening, he saw a black mass pointing a long pistol at Salgado. The silencer looked like the ones in the movies, but the noise was different. He saw the two bodies lying on the floor, one of them starting to bleed, and thought of his maid again, a woman with a very nasty attitude. The other man lay faceup, hugging the pillow he had pulled into himself for protection.

Two more hisses cut short the movement Salgado was attempting, and a pistol hung from the hand that had just given the signal for Tomás to be punished. The other, resting on the chair, still held onto the glass of whiskey. That seemed like the only thing that hadn't changed in the last minute.

Tony Soprano ignored him as he approached the three bodies and made sure each of them was on its way out. One of them, the guy with the pillow, got a bullet to the forehead for good measure. Tomás would have preferred otherwise: the first six shots had been in a confrontation of three against one, which had taken guts, but the last was a summary execution.

Jaime's gunman didn't seem too worried about these ethical considerations. After a quick glance to make sure the journalist was unharmed, he ignored him, and he didn't seem to care about preserving the crime scene: he dragged the three corpses across the floor and leaned them against the wall to one side of the door. Then he went through their pockets, taking their wallets, cell phones, a couple of knives, keys, a pack of Marlboros, two condoms, a lighter, and coins. He went to the kitchen and rifled through the drawers until he found a plastic bag, and he put each item inside, except the wallets and phones, which he slipped into his pockets.

The fat guy stopped worrying over his victims' bodies for a moment to type something into his phone and returned to his labors. Two minutes later, Jaime burst into the room, followed by three other men.

"Are you okay, Tomás?"

"Me, yes. Them, no," he answered, unable to take his eyes off Salgado's body.

Jaime nodded, and his men looked for blankets to wrap the three corpses up in. He walked to the cabinet where his friend kept his liquor and poured out two shots of tequila. He gave one to Tomás and sat down where Salgado had been resting moments before.

"They were about to execute me," Tomás said, almost to himself.

"I know. And now it's all over. Drink your tequila."

Tomás downed it in a long swig and then looked at Jaime, as if noticing his presence for the first time.

"How did you know? How did you get here so fast?"

"Well, you asked me for help guarding the newspaper, so I put someone there to watch your building. If they'd already offed a deputy director, it wasn't crazy to think they'd go after the director next, right? I was told some suspicious guys had gone inside, so I decided to come around after I left my office, and I sent my best man ahead of me."

Jaime wasn't lying, not completely, though he thought it best to omit that he'd tapped his friend's phone and installed microphones throughout his house a few days before. A locksmith had gotten him the key to the front door.

"Where are we now, with Salgado out of the picture? Will there be revenge?" Tomás asked.

"I doubt it. He was cornered. I don't even think his organization knew he was coming to pay you a visit. We'll dump the bodies and that'll be that."

"Well, I owe you one, brother. This was close," Tomás said, moved.

"No sweat. It's my specialty," Jaime responded, waving his friend off.

"I guess while Bonso and the rest of them are on the loose, we're still not out of danger, are we?"

"No," Jaime said. "But we've already got a bead on them. Tomorrow morning, we're moving in."

"Are you going with Lemlock, or are the authorities getting involved? It's dangerous, no? Last time, you lost three men."

"Now they're alone. The police who protected Bonso were Salgado's men. I want to take them out before the new guy in charge assigns them another police escort."

"And what will you do with Bonso?"

"First, I'm going to find out what his real relationship with Milena is. After that, we'll know what to do." They both thought of Claudia's order to execute the Turk, but neither of them mentioned it.

Jaime left after promising to call first thing in the morning, once he had the mafiosos under control. He told the journalist he'd leave a guard posted in a car outside his house, and made a few other security recommendations. Tomás realized his friend was squeezing all he could out of the fact that he'd saved his life. What had just happened would mark a definitive change in the strange, sometimes fierce balance of power that had existed between the two of them since their boyhood.

On his way back to the office, Jaime was ecstatic. He had Milena in his power, and soon he'd have Bonso, too. He was confident that in a matter of days, when he sat down with Vila-Rojas, he'd have several aces up his sleeve, and he'd be able to negotiate with the Spaniard for more than just Milena's freedom. And then there was the kiss between him and Amelia. It gave him a feeling of completion.

He fantasized about financing huge projects with the help of laundered and gray-market money from the European mafias. As a protector of the investments and business dealings of Mexico's organized criminals, Salgado had been primitive. Jaime told himself he could bring a new dimension to the relationships between shady financial operations and profit-yielding businesses in a society as flexible as Mexico's. A proper broker between Prida's government and the capital chomping at the bit to break free from the new restrictions imposed by Wall Street. He smiled to himself: all the pieces fit together perfectly.

61

Luis and Milena

WEDNESDAY, NOVEMBER 19, 11:50 P.M.

A FULL DAY BEHIND CLOSED DOORS had done little to calm Luis down, and it didn't help that they'd taken his computer and cell phones. Milena joked about his withdrawal: a smoker without cigarettes or a drunk without alcohol wouldn't have paced back and forth as much as he did in Room 312, where they were confined. During the first few hours they were in custody, Patricia had tried to converse with them, but Luis assumed she was only after information. Finally she stopped dropping in on them.

They knew the warnings they had sent to Bonso to keep him from falling into Jaime's trap had worked, not only because Lemlock took his electronics, but also because their guards seemed so much less tense.

"We have to get out of here. There won't be any attack. Now they can't even say they're protecting us. This is kidnapping, pure and simple."

Milena smiled. In fact, she'd started to enjoy every minute of this forced custody. She felt that within those four walls, for that unusual period of time, there were no rules or loyalties, and she gave herself over completely to love for her cellmate. She had never cultivated tenderness, and now she was moved by the barely perceptible groans Luis let out as he fell asleep or the sight of the shaved nape of his long neck. She hadn't had a single romantic relationship: with Rosendo

Franco, she had been more a refugee than a lover, and though it was hard to get a grip on the nature of her own feelings for Vila-Rojas, she knew his attachment to her had been mixed with rational calculation and unconfessed passion.

Far from his friend's romantic reveries, Luis stretched his torso out the window for the umpteenth time, looking for a way out. He thought just how far he'd have to jump to grab a tree branch and keep from plunging to the pavement.

"If we try at four a.m., there's a good chance we'll make it. They have a car on every corner, but I doubt they're awake all night. If worse comes to worst, they'll just take us back to the room."

"If worse comes to worst, we'll crack our heads open on the sidewalk," she said, laughing. "I'm not worried about it, it can't be any harder than pole dancing, and we did that for years to stay in shape. I'm worried more about you," she added, her eyes looking down at Luis's left leg.

"Four doors down from this hotel is that covered walkway where we had that orange juice you like so much; from there we can exit out onto a cross street," he said, ignoring her look.

"And your things, your phone and computer?"

"Everything important is on the Net. Besides, sooner or later I'll get them back, from Vidal, I suppose."

"Then I'll put my notebook and the passports in my bag and we'll go," she said.

"Passports?"

"I didn't tell you I was from Veracruz?" she said with a coquettish smile. "But I could be from Yucatan as well. Bonso has my original passport, so Rosendo got me a Mexican one so I could travel. Later it turned out he did it twice, with two different people, and both passports worked. They're authentic documents, they haven't been falsified, just like the birth certificates I got in Perote, in Veracruz, and in Valladolid, Yucatan. Look, let me introduce you to Margarita Valdivia. Or do you prefer Margarita Salazar?" she said, and passed him the documents from her pocket.

Luis scanned them and then looked her in the face.

"I like Alka," he said, and grabbed her by the waist and kissed her. Then he made love to her ardently, thinking it would be the last time.

They nodded off for the next few hours wrapped around one another. His sleep was fitful, interrupted by dreams in which he careened into the abyss. He could no longer sleep once three in the morning struck. He listened to Milena's breathing and felt the weight of her thigh on his leg. The position had become uncomfortable, but he tried to tell himself her powerful muscles were transmitting some sort of vigor into his irreparably torn ligaments. The memory of Jaime made him think any risk was worth it to keep from being the prisoner of that man who had ruined his life: they would escape, he would call Rina, and with Amelia's help, they would get her far from her pursuers' reach.

Twenty minutes later, they were examining the tree branch. She was calm, but he was nervous, knowing how weak his left leg was. One of the two cars had disappeared, but in the other, parked twenty yards farther away, the outline of a man was visible.

"I'll go first," she said, seeing Luis's hesitation.

She passed her belt through the loops on her backpack to pull it tight into her lower back, crouched on the windowsill where they had told each other so much in the course of those nights, leapt, and landed astride the branch. Luis considered that his testicles wouldn't resist an impact of that kind. Assuming, that is, that he managed to do what Milena just had.

She descended a few yards, sat on a thicker branch further down, and waited for her friend with a smile—mocking or inviting, he wasn't sure, but it worked, because he stopped wavering. He imitated the position he had seen her take, and when he threw himself toward the tree, his fears came true: his left leg lacked the strength, and he fell more than flew. What saved him were his stature and his long appendages: he managed to grab the branch with both hands, but he felt dread as the weight of his body overcame the strength of his knuckles one inch at a time. He looked down at the concrete twenty-five feet below, and wondered whether he'd survive the fall.

Suddenly he felt her thigh slide between his and push him upward. Milena, who had been behind him up to then, was holding onto the branch as if it were a beam resting on her shoulder, and she had bent a leg to hold up her friend for a moment. He blessed his lover's powerful thighs, got a better grip on the branch, and bent his waist until he managed to get his legs wrapped around the tree. Exhausted, he held his position for a few moments. Finally, he heaved, pressed his torso tight to the branch, and sat up.

They stopped to look at the street through the foliage. The man's shadow hadn't moved and there wasn't a trace of other people or of vehicles circulating. They descended on the side of the trunk opposite the car and ran alongside the wall until they reached the entrance of the walkway lined with shops. Then they walked for hours through side streets toward the city center. They knew no one would miss them until nine in the morning, when they usually ordered their breakfast, but they wanted to get as far away as possible from Lemlock and its men. At one point, in a crosswalk, she took his hand, but he let hers go a few feet later. To him, it seemed like an act of loyalty to Rina, the least he could do.

At seven, they drank a juice at the first post they found open and then hailed a taxi. It took them almost an hour to reach the PRD offices in the Colonía Roma. They didn't talk much during the trip, and when they did, it was about trivialities: the cold weather, Milena's athleticism, the awful state of Luis's jeans. Nothing pertaining to the intimacy they'd shared over those days or their imminent meeting with Rina.

When they got out of the taxi in front of the PRD, they met Alicia, Amelia's secretary, who was walking into the building just then. She led them to the president's meeting room, where she called her boss to let her know about the unexpected visitors.

62

Jaime

IT WAS HARD TO BELIEVE the little man swinging his legs in the chair had brought such worry to the world, or at least to *El Mundo*. Jaime stared at Bonso with absolute fascination before entering the room with the two-way mirror to interrogate him. A short guy, tubby, fifty-six years old, if his passport was to be trusted, tan skin crusted with acne, hair dyed light brown. Not the kind of physique you win with in life. One more reason not to underestimate him.

Bonso, the Turk, and two underlings had been captured in an apartment in Villa Olímpica. The four of them were asleep when Jaime's people rushed in. They'd found them thanks to their surveillance of the guards who took care of the gang's brothels. At last, one of them had gone to the hideout where the Romanian and his right-hand man were holed up.

"What kind of cops are you? I have a right to speak to my lawyer and to make a call to the embassy," Bonso demanded when Jaime entered the interrogation room.

Again, the director of Lemlock admired his aplomb.

"The type of cops that don't show up on any organizational chart. The kind that can do what they like with scum like you."

"I'm a foreign citizen, I have rights."

"Salgado had them, too, I guess. Now he's got nothing," Jaime said, and showed him the photo of his body on the screen of his mobile phone.

Bonso looked at it, and Jaime could see he was finally afraid.

"And you know what? I had less reason to kill the colonel than you and the Turk, so let's cut the bullshit. My job is to give a picture like this one, but of you, to the people who hired me. Think you'll leave a photogenic corpse?"

"Why am I alive then?"

"Because I'm trying to figure out if you're more useful that way than dead. That'll depend on you."

"I've got money, all the women you could want." Now the Romanian's voice was like a ringmaster's. His face lit up with a smile that aimed to enthrall.

"All I'm interested in is what you've got on Vila-Rojas and what you're trying to find among Milena's things."

Bonso's face contracted, and a burst of terror clouded his eyes.

"Vila who? I don't know what you're talking about," he said, trying to look composed once more.

"I'm not going to waste time playing cat and mouse, and you shouldn't either, since you only have an hour left before you're dead. Look at the clock on the wall: in sixty minutes, someone will be here to torture you. Not to get information out of you, but just to be sure you die painfully. You have fifty-nine minutes to make a decision."

"Wait. If you kill me, you won't get anything!"

"If I kill you, it'll be because you decided not to give me anything. At worst, I'll be doing the job my client asked for and turning in your bloody body. Besides, it's always possible that your pal is more attached to his life than you." Jaime turned around and headed out the door without waiting for a response.

When he reached the other side of the mirror, Patricia and Commandant Carrasco were waiting for him with a coffee in hand.

"Think he's going to talk?" Patricia asked. She had less training than the other two in high-pressure interrogation techniques.

"We'll know for certain by the way he looks at the clock these next few minutes. I'd say yes, though," Jaime replied. "This guy's a survivor."

"Well, you didn't give him much reason to think you were bluffing."

"I'm not bluffing," Jaime said, taking the first sip of his coffee.

The three of them concentrated on Bonso.

Aware they were observing him from behind the mirror, the Romanian stared down at his fingernails, and after a thorough inspection, he began to clean them, slowly and meticulously.

"The son of a bitch is good."

"He only has ten fingers," the commandant responded.

Once the thumbnail on his right hand had been freed of any grime it might have harbored, Bonso looked up, tugged at his hair, and glanced furtively at the clock. Fourteen minutes had passed. When the first half-hour was over, he started glancing over every two or three minutes, and after a quarter till, he never took his eyes off the second hand. With five minutes remaining, he knocked on the glass, first with resignation, then desperately. Jaime let the clock run down until there was a minute left, then walked back into the room. By then, the prisoner was frenetic.

"I've been calling you for ten minutes," he said anxiously, turning to the mirror, as though to recruit witnesses to his behalf. He wasn't sure whether Jaime had come in as a negotiator or executioner.

"Then convince me that what you've got is enough to make me disobey my clients' orders," Jaime said, and sat down casually at one of the chairs placed around the long table.

"The only thing that's kept me alive is a stash of documents. If I turn them over to you, I'm a dead man."

"If you don't turn them in, you'll be dead sooner. You've already lived a minute longer than you deserve. Your move."

Bonso took a deep breath.

"What I know is they're trying to get hold of some papers of Milena's, but I'm not clear on the details. Until five weeks ago, all they wanted was for us to keep a close eye on her, because she needed to be available to consult with someone in Marbella about information she had. I never knew what it was about. When she split with the guy from the newspaper, I tried to get her back for the colonel . . . "

"Salgado?" Jaime interrupted.

"Yeah, him. He said that as long as the line of communication with Spain wasn't broken, everything was okay, and that fucking with Franco could cause a big stir."

"So what happened five weeks ago?"

"No idea, they just said we needed to get rid of the whore and all the documents she had, no matter the price."

"Who gave the order? Vila-Rojas?"

"Probably I should tell you what happened that last night in Marbella."

63

Milena

JANUARY 2014

"WHAT THE FUCK HAPPENED at One Percent?" Vila-Rojas asked Bonso, enraged, after he'd charged up the fourteen metal steps to the brightly lit office in the old warehouse on the docks in Marbella.

"What happened was that Boris's execution, the one you ordered, got out of hand, and you've got us in the middle of some serious shit," Bonso responded.

Vila-Rojas scanned the room for cameras and microphones before answering.

"I don't know what you're talking about."

Bonso waved him off.

"Boris died of an overdose administered by Milena, according to your instructions. Your whore already confessed to us."

"Who is this Milena and what does she have to do with me? It's pathetic to try to incriminate me with what one of your hookers says," Vila-Rojas responded loudly, continuing to look for some surveillance device.

"What does Milena have to do with me? Don't be an ingrate, Agustín, she's been working for you for two years. I have the video at my house from the night you bought her from me. I asked you for a hundred thousand euros, and you offered two with the condition that she would only obey your orders from that day forward. I have ten copies of that video planted in places I can trust." In fact, there were only four, but the lawyer had no way of knowing that.

Vila-Rojas motioned for them to follow him and led them downstairs to his car, parked close to the entrance in a barely lit corner of the warehouse.

"I'd rather talk here," Vila-Rojas said, leaning against the car. "What are you planning on doing with these videos?"

"Nothing, as long as I stay alive. If not, my friends have instructions to send them to Boris's mother and uncles, in Marbella and in Ukraine as well."

"There's no saving the Turk. It was supposed to be a thing between two junkies, but he turned it into a gun battle. No way the Ukrainians will let him live: he killed two of them and shot one in the back. Same goes for Milena. But I can save you. It's just a matter of convincing them that this was a lover's quarrel gone wrong. The Turk got jealous and wanted Boris off the scene."

Boris shook his head.

"A jealous lover who plans an overdose and then shoots the place up? You think these Russians are morons? No, the doomed romance story ain't going to fly. You won't save me that way."

"Then what's your recommendation?"

"I don't know, lawyer, you're the one who's in Yasha's good graces. You'll come up with something, right? And if not, then we're both fucked."

"Where's Milena?" Vila-Rojas asked.

"I've got her. Don't worry."

The lawyer took a long time to reflect. Bonso kept his eye on him throughout.

"There's no reason Yasha has to find out," he said finally. "You two get out of the country, tonight if possible. The best thing would be somewhere in South America, Colombia or Mexico, that's where my best contacts are. Yasha will have no choice but to go after you with everything he's got, but I'll make sure he keeps his hands off if you guarantee me those videos never appear." Vila-Rojas could never trust Bonso, but at least he had bought some time to deal with the incriminating videos. What was important was that Yasha's men, or even worse, Olena Kattel's, didn't catch the Turk, Bonso, or Milena. "She stays with me," he added, realizing the girl was a loose end.

"What good is she to you? She's a hot potato here in Marbella," Bonso said, remembering what the Turk had said about keeping her in their possession.

"That's my business, not yours."

"You're going to kill her, and then there goes my only proof that I had nothing to do with what happened to Boris."

"Don't be ridiculous. Milena's my property. I wouldn't destroy what's mine, right?"

"Well, I don't believe you," Milena said, emerging from the shadows from behind Vila-Rojas, where she had heard these last words. "I don't trust you."

"You stay out of this, you dumb slut," Bonso said. It's your fault we're in the middle of this. This is men's business."

Vila-Rojas looked at her, surprised.

"I had a deal with you, and I'm still planning on keeping it, honey," he said to her.

"A deal? You motherfucking pig. You gave me two death kits. You wanted to kill me." She looked toward the Turk, who removed the packet with the syringe from his pocket.

"That dose isn't fatal!" Vila-Rojas shouted, rolling up his arm and exposing the inside of his forearm. "Shoot me up!"

Milena looked at him with curiosity. After what she'd been through at Vila-Rojas's side, everything was confusing. She wanted to hug him and take refuge in him, but she also wanted to respond to his dare. In the end, she did neither.

"Let's call Yasha," she said.

"What? Are you crazy?"

"He's the only one who can guarantee my life. I have exact information about what's being planned against him. He wouldn't want me dead, I can promise that."

"I've got that same information," Vila-Rojas objected, furious. "You're the one who gave it to me. You're completely expendable."

"You're wrong. I have a lot more than what I told you. What they're planning will wipe you and Yasha off the map. Believe me." She wasn't very sure of what she was saying, but her categorical delivery had its effect on the lawyer.

"Call Yasha," Bonso interrupted menacingly.

The Romanian figured if what Milena said was true, the Russian boss was a better life insurance policy than Vila-Rojas. Deep down, he knew there was no hideaway that could keep him safe from the mob. The only possibility of survival was for Yasha to let them escape while pretending he was on the hunt for them.

Vila-Rojas looked doubtfully from one to the other. Dealing with Yasha was a risk, but it might well be the safest bet. If the mafia captured Bonso, which was far from improbable, he would fess up and Vila-Rojas would end up rotting in the sea. It was better to bring Yasha in and let him hear it from the horse's mouth. Anyway, eliminating Boris benefited him, and if the videos became public, it would hurt Yasha, too. Olena would think Vila-Rojas was working under his orders, no matter how much the boss denied it.

"You better have something good," he said before filling his lungs with air and typing a number into a phone Milena had never seen.

Then he walked away a few feet and spoke for several minutes. He returned to Milena's side and passed her the phone.

"Your turn."

They listened to her speaking Russian. Bonso followed her words like dogs chasing birds flying by overhead in the vain hope that one might fall into their teeth. By Bonso's face, it was clear he understood Milena's mentions, in Russian, of Boris and other members of the Kattel family, but little else apart from the occasional word.

When she hung up, they pelted her with questions, but all she said was that Yasha was interested in what she'd told him. She'd gone for broke in her conversation with Yasha. She'd revealed to him two key things: the plot Boris and his mother were hatching to overthrow him, which caught his attention, and the attempts of the visiting agents from Moscow to set up relations with the Russo-Ukrainians in Marbella, which he blew off.

Five minutes later, the four of them twitched when Vila-Rojas's cell phone made a strange noise that echoed through the domed ceiling of the warehouse. The screen briefly lit their expectant faces.

"It looks like we're free," Vila-Rojas said with relief after a brief conversation. "He wants to see me in an hour to set up the details of your escape. For now, you need to leave the country. He wants more information from Milena, but he thinks it's too dangerous to have her around. It's enough for him if she ends up somewhere the Kattels can't see her and he can get in touch with her by phone. You get to keep your lives and he'll set you up in business on the condition that you become her protectors: that means taking care of her but also not letting her out of your sight. He needs her alive, in a safe place, and far away. If we comply with those conditions, we'll all survive. When things die down, he wants Milena back here. He wants to know the details of everything Milena heard when she was with Boris. He had no idea the Kattels were plotting against him, not the ones here and not the ones from Ukraine."

"We're going to be fucking babysitters," Bonso complained.

"Or cadavers. You pick."

"They're going to put us in business? Because I only know one."

"Then that'll be it. That way, it's easier for her to go unnoticed. Besides, I don't think Milena has another trade, either," Vila-Rojas said. "Yasha didn't say to treat her like a queen, you can put her to work, but no risks."

Looking at Vila-Rojas's eyes, hearing the hard words that sealed her fate, Milena wondered again if the dream kit had been lethal. Maybe she had never meant anything to him. Maybe she had been a mere tool, and was now nothing but a burden he needed off his hands.

She thought of the Arabs there in the back of the warehouse and wished she were one of them. She had seen their anguished faces, furrowed from uncertainty, but also from the hope of finding a different destiny. Besides, they had each other. While Vila-Rojas and the others conferred about their escape, she looked down and saw a fissure in the warehouse's cracked and crumbling cement floor that ran all the way to the wall. She walked over it, as though she could fall inside and disappear once and for all.

She was awakened from her stupor by a kiss on the forehead and the steps of Vila-Rojas moving away and getting into his car. She saw how the night swallowed the taillights of the Mercedes before the other men hurried to close the gate.

64

Amelia and Milena

WHEN AMELIA ARRIVED, the four young people were already in the meeting room. After telling her boss about Luis and Milena's sudden appearance, Alicia must have alerted Rina and Vidal, too.

Luis and Rina were standing up next to the window, murmuring sweetly to one another while he stroked her cheek tenderly. Vidal and Milena seemed to have given their blessing to their friends' affections, because, though their arms were still around each other, they had interrupted the embrace they'd greeted each other with to turn their heads ninety degrees to watch them. Amelia didn't know which image was more moving to her.

She was seeing Milena for the first time, and what she saw helped her understand the uproar the girl provoked. It was hard to stop staring at her face, not to mention her slender body with its statuesque balance. Amelia told herself that if ordinary humans had been stamped out by a machine, Milena would have been hand-finished and detailed.

"Milena," Amelia said simply, then walked over and embraced her.

Amelia was a good hugger, the Croatian thought. She gave off a powerful, calming force, and for the first time in years, Milena recalled lying in her mother's lap.

When they pulled apart, the others came over to greet her, and they all brought each other up to date. Luis described what he and

Milena had done from the moment they went into the forest. Amelia noted that his story didn't flow as naturally as when he'd spoken to her before and that he chose his words carefully, omitting any mention of what he might have felt: cold, hunger, sadness, fear, desperation. His curtness must have been meant to conceal what had actually happened between those two fugitives while they were on the run.

She looked at Rina askance, but saw nothing beyond her absorption in her boyfriend's story. Either her faith in him was blind, or she had decided that whatever had happened was irrelevant compared to the joy of having him back. Both possibilities struck Amelia as admirable.

Vidal's attitude was different. While Luis spoke, he stared at the tray of cookies next to the coffee, as if he couldn't decide between one and the other. He listened to the story with either the impatience of a person who already knows what he's hearing or the incredulity of someone doubting it. He would have liked to come right out and accuse his friend, make him confess what had really happened in that hotel room. But he avoided confrontation, telling himself that this was the wrong time to put on a spectacle.

Luis looked worriedly at his friend's face as he finished his story, but he was convinced that Vidal wouldn't bring him any trouble.

"So what happened with Jaime?" Amelia asked. "Any advances?"

It took a second for Vidal to realize the question was for him, but he was happy for the opportunity to go over Lemlock's achievements, even if he felt less responsible for them after his confession to Amelia. He told them about the capture of Bonso and the Turk and the interrogation taking place at Lemlock's offices. This information stunned the others, and they didn't speak as they tried to weigh the implications.

"In the end, this doesn't change anything that I wanted to propose to you, Milena," Amelia finally said. "You can't live running from what happened in Marbella, no matter what it was. Everyone has a right to a second chance, and you'd be surprised how many times we've found that second chance for women who thought they'd lost everything."

Milena wriggled nervously but held back.

"We can get you a new identity and send you somewhere in Canada, Australia, or New Zealand, where your appearance won't attract so much attention. There are international networks to support women who have been victims of trafficking, and they have very strict, professional protocols," Amelia went on.

Everyone looked at the Croatian's face, expecting some kind of reaction. The PRD leader pressed on.

"You don't owe anything to the people pulling the strings in Spain, and even less to Bonso and the Turk. They took ten years from you, exploited you horribly, took away your youth. But you have another forty or fifty years ahead of you. What happens to those bastards after you're gone isn't your responsibility. It's the price they pay for their crimes. You were a victim, nothing more."

Milena imagined herself in some village in the north of Canada, working as a cashier in a supermarket in the middle of nowhere with an apron with "Mary" embroidered on it. She didn't have the energy to take the countless little decisions a life of her own would require. So many years subject to other people's whims had caused the muscle of her will to atrophy. It would be so nice to stay with Luis and let him handle everything important. Even the months she'd spent under Rosendo's protection seemed like paradise compared to what might await her in some backwater surrounded by pine trees. A blonde downing a bottle of whiskey in the solitude of her kitchen. Once again, the metro tracks looked like a good option.

"Milena," Luis said. "The future can be whatever you want it to be. We'll visit you, we'll publish your *Tales of the XY Chromosome*, and maybe you'll go on writing. Or maybe you'll decide to open a restaurant in Montreal. We're still waiting to try your cooking, right?"

Milena thought it over. Perhaps he was right. A depressed cashier in a logging town wasn't the only possible future. But whatever happened, she'd always be looking over her shoulder.

Amelia had wanted to offer a plan for Milena first, to show she was on her side, but she couldn't go on ignoring the delicate matter of the black book.

"It's not just you they're looking for, right? The people on your trail have torn up furniture and walls wherever they've gone. You need to trust us now: your secret has cost people their lives, and it could continue to do so. It affects everyone involved, and it's obvious there's more to all this than a couple of lowlifes trying to get back a runaway prostitute."

Milena looked down.

"You don't have to bear this alone," Amelia added, and stretched out her arm to stroke Milena's cheek with her palm.

The girl began to sob, crossed her arms over her chest, and collapsed into Amelia's arms. Amelia held her. She'd never been to the Adriatic, but it seemed to her that Milena smelled of the salt of cold, remote seas. Despite her physique, the girl emanated a fragility that Amelia found moving.

After a while, Milena pulled away, grabbed her bag, took out the notebook, and gave it to Amelia. Then she crumpled into one of the chairs surrounding the long meeting table.

The others walked over, but Amelia fended them off.

"Give me a few minutes," she said, then took her place at the head of the table and began to read.

Luis, who already knew the story of *Them*, rushed to the computer on the other end of the table and began to type vigorously. He was impatient to see his email after so many hours, but he hadn't wanted to interrupt his reunion with Rina or the meeting with Amelia.

When he saw a long email in code from Anonymous, he smiled at Milena, but she didn't react. The Croatian followed Amelia's eyes while she flipped through page after page of narrow writing.

While Luis and Amelia read in silence, Vidal looked at his phone. Rina stood up and walked behind Luis's back, trying to see what he had on the screen.

Amelia started flipping through the pages faster. The stories were affecting, and she could imagine the devastating consequences they would have for the people mentioned. She admired Milena's powers of observation and her sensitivity as she recorded the pretexts these men offered to justify their actions. Was it really enough to whip the mafia into such a rage? Maybe one of the celebrities in those pages had found out what they contained and had paid the criminals to make sure the information disappeared. Probably no one but Milena really knew what secrets the black book held, but many were afraid of its potential revelations.

Luis's interruption showed her hypothesis was incorrect.

"Vila-Rojas is a hell of a customer," he said. "Between Anonymous and Bad Girl we almost have a complete account of what he's been up to in recent months. You know he spent a few months in Moscow when he was twenty-two?"

"How old is he?" Amelia inquired. "When was that?"

"He's fifty-three," Milena responded, her eyes still pinned on Amelia.

"It was in 1983," Luis said, quickly scanning the text.

"In the Soviet days," Amelia said pensively.

"So he speaks Russian?" Milena said.

"He writes it, too," Luis confirmed. "Anonymous translated some of the messages into English, but they said the ones in Russian were addressed to pages used by Kremlin intermediaries."

"What are we looking at here, Milena?" Amelia asked, holding up the black book.

Milena got up from her chair, took the notebook from Amelia's hands, carefully pulled away the endpapers and laid it on the table. All could see, in very small letters, a list of banks, account numbers, Russian names, and import-export businesses with transfer receipts.

"What is this?" Amelia asked. "Is this what the people hunting you have been looking for?"

"Yeah, I guess," Milena said. "It's stuff that fell into my hands by chance and I held onto it because I thought it could be important, but I wasn't completely sure. What I've been hearing about the crisis in Ukraine has made me think that yeah, maybe it is. The way they've been chasing after me proves it, no?"

Luis thought they had confessed everything to each other during those long conversations in the half-light. He thought he had, at least. He shoved aside his growing resentment and concentrated on the monitor.

"The report I have here might be related to what you're saying. It has more than twenty pages, with all the emails transcribed in it. From what I see so far, it shows an intense exchange of information between collaborators between Moscow and Marbella, between Vila-Rojas and someone named Olena. I'll have to read it closely to confirm."

"What do you mean, Vila-Rojas?" Milena asked. "Olena would have ties to Moscow, but not Vila-Rojas."

"Well, the past few months, they've had a serious exchange going on. Olena Kattel, right?" Luis asked, reading directly from the screen.

"Look," Milena said, incredulous. "Vila-Rojas worked for Olena's rival. Besides that, he's responsible for the death of her son. How could he be her ally all of a sudden?"

"The information is cut and dry . . . " Luis insisted, going back over the screen. "It's about Moscow and money to support Ukraine."

"I can't believe they would just talk openly about this stuff over email," said Amelia.

"It's not so strange. Even lots of specialists think using the Darknet and digital cryptography make their communications impenetrable. But for a dozen or so hackers, there's no firewall that can't be breached," Luis said proudly. "They didn't even use any kind of code apart from initials. They thought their software guaranteed their security."

Now that Milena knew Vila-Rojas spoke Russian, it was clear he had understood the conversation she had with Yasha ten months before in the warehouse. The Russian boss hadn't cared that the men from Moscow had visited Boris; all that mattered to him was the plot the Kattels were cooking up against him. But Vila-Rojas was a different story. During her time in Mexico, Yasha had called her about infiltrators his rivals had planted in his ranks and other things related to Boris's uncles in Kiev. He had never asked her anything else about the information concealed in her notebook, though she had told him it existed. Vila-Rojas obviously hadn't been so uninterested.

Milena said nothing while the others went on speculating about her notebook and the Russian mafia. She couldn't make Agustín and Olena fit together. And it distressed her to think of the consequences that alliance could give rise to. With mounting angst, she recollected the threats, the shattered walls, the bodies mowed down in the course of her flight. She thought of Vila-Rojas again and felt the air resist entering her lungs.

Amelia's phone rang. It was Jaime.

"We need to meet. Vidal told me the girl was with you. We also have the info on Luis's screen. My team's decoded it, and I need to let you know what it's really about. I suggest you all come to Lemlock, we've got the people you've been looking for."

"Let's go," Amelia told them. "Jaime's got Bonso and the Turk."

In the car, she called Tomás and told him they needed to see each other at Lemlock. She wanted him at her side. Then she made another call, and this one filled her with well-being.

"Claudia," Amelia said. "Your father's not in the black book. You can rest easy." She hung up before the other managed to react.

65

The Blues

THEY MET IN JAIME'S OFFICE, though it made Amelia uncomfortable knowing that everything that took place there was being recorded. After what she'd found out, she was certain nowhere was private. At least she managed to convince Vidal and Rina to leave them alone. She had the feeling the Blues' reunion would get rough, and she didn't want more witnesses than necessary.

As always, Jaime surprised them with the overwhelming amount of information he'd managed to bring together on the mafia and money laundering on the Costa del Sol. Tomás, Milena, Luis, and Amelia listened to him raptly.

"This is the Americans' file on Vila-Rojas," he said, showing them a thick sheaf of documents in front of his chair. They were sitting around an enormous glass table that served as the Lemlock director's occasional desk.

Luis was uncomfortable as he observed the information flickering on the enormous screens around them, but he was still impressed with the technology in the large office. Tomás was uneasy, being the least informed of those assembled there, and the authority Jaime got from sitting at the head of the table irritated him. Milena looked at the extensive garden behind the sliding door on the rooftop terrace, terra-cotta colored and full of plants, an agreeable contrast to the

378

cold, efficient feel of the industrial cement and glass elsewhere in the building.

"The file brings together reports from numerous American investigative units on Vila-Rojas and the Russo-Ukrainian mafia in Spain, and includes data from the FBI, the CIA, the Department of the Treasury, and the NSA," Jaime added proudly.

He had reason to be proud: it wasn't easy convincing Robert Cansino, the coordinator of US intelligence services in Mexico, but they'd been friends for twenty years, since they'd studied together in the interrogation seminars run by the CIA. It also helped that he'd passed off to Cansino a list of crooked Mexican judges that Lemlock had found on the drug cartels' payrolls.

"The death of Alexander Kattel, the former leader of the Russian mafia in Marbella, three years ago, led to a kind of split," Jaime explained. "Yasha Boyko, his brother-in-law, inherited his position but had a shaky grasp on power. The widow, Olena Kattel, and her son, Boris, never fully recognized his authority. Almost from the beginning, they tried to boycott Yasha and sided with Alexander's brothers, who ran the group's affairs in Ukraine. Yasha's response was to expand operations in the Mediterranean and the Americas to break away from his pro-Russian colleagues. If a definitive split took place, he would already have his own economic base."

"And that's where Vila-Rojas comes in," Luis said, annoyed at Jaime's authoritative tone.

"Right," Jaime agreed. "That's where Vila-Rojas comes in. The lawyer became the go-to guy for virtually all of Yasha's new enterprises and, to a large degree, his face in the businesses where he deposited his laundered money. In the Americans' reports, he shows up as a member of the board of twenty or so important European firms. Three of them move huge sums in public works in Mexico."

"And what about his relations with Moscow?" Milena asked.

"This is where Luis's work was important," he responded, taking a brief bow toward the younger man. "Not even the Americans knew that Vila-Rojas had switched sides. Thanks to the report from Anonymous, we could see that Vila-Rojas had entered into communication with Olena and Boris's people in Moscow."

"Since when?" Milena asked again.

"Two or three months back," Jaime responded.

"Two or three months back . . . this past summer, then," Tomás noted. "Just when the West decided to impose sanctions on Putin for supporting the rebels in Ukraine. I wrote an article about how the Kremlin wouldn't refuse support to the pro-Russian militias in the war, but would have to use more subtle means. They tried to mask it as humanitarian aid, but Brussels threatened them with even-harsher sanctions. I suppose it was then that they looked for other ways to get the transfers through."

"Like the Russo-Ukrainian community in Marbella," Amelia added.

"But is Marbella really that important?" Luis asked. All he remembered of it from a brief visit was a marina and yachts.

"Marbella is the Babel of the Mediterranean," Tomás responded.

"Babel, Las Vegas, the Cayman Islands, all wrapped in one," Jaime said. "The society Gil y Gil ushered in is still unscathed. Arab sheiks, white-collar ex-cons from Northern Europe, Latin American cartels, mafias from the former Soviet Republics, elite global tourists looking for pleasure: all of them converge there. Millions of euros in real estate and tourist developments are visible, but there's far more living and breathing underneath the surface."

"And how important is the Russian community in Marbella?" Amelia asked.

"It's huge," Jaime responded. "There are thousands of Russian homes in the area, and they have extraordinary buying power. There's a lot of millionaires, and among them you've got representatives of different branches of the Russian mafia. The biggest is the Ukrainian, and that's why Moscow is interested in turning the area into a beachhead for infiltrating Western Europe."

"And the old guard, like the Kattel family, would have been the perfect link, but they needed someone like Vila-Rojas," Amelia said.

"Precisely," said Jaime. "It's not clear whether Olena sought out Vila-Rojas or Vila-Rojas went after Olena, but he must have looked at the matchup and decided it was time to change outfits."

"But Yasha?" Milena said. "He's not the kind you can trick that easily."

"I guess Yasha was happy last February when the pro-Russian government his rivals supported fell. Maybe he got sloppy and thought his triumph was in the bag."

"If it's like you say, and Vila-Rojas has changed sides, Yasha's days are probably numbered," Milena said. She imagined a long crane with a broken neck plunging toward the ground.

"So what does all that have to do with Milena?" Luis butted in, putting his hand on top of hers.

"Bonso confessed that five weeks ago, he got an order to get rid of her and any information she might have."

"Vila-Rojas," Milena mused in a somber tone.

"What's important is what we're going to do now," Luis said.

Tomás and Jaime looked at the Croatian. Her sunken chest and bent back showed what was happening in her mind: scenes of the nightmares that she had lived through in that closet ten years ago, plastic unrolled at her feet and Bonso's two dogs, the conversation with Vila-Rojas on a yacht rocked by the tide the night they met, the iron complicity that she'd thought unbreakable after three murders, the orgasms they'd shared. And finally, the betrayal. The order Agustín had to have given to kill her.

"And why the need to have her dead?" Tomás asked.

"The black book," Amelia responded. "I don't know how or why, but it has the information on the operation Moscow was running out of Marbella."

"In the hands of the EU authorities, that would be enough to bring the whole thing down," Jaime said.

"Which means Milena is still in danger," Tomás said. "It's not just destroying the book, but her, too. Neutralizing Bonso or the Turk solves nothing. Salgado was right, there's someone higher up on the chain that takes over."

"And?" Amelia asked. "We can't just sit here with our arms crossed. We can hide her, change her identity. I know how to do it."

"Better yet, we can publish the information," Tomás said with sudden enthusiasm. "When it's public, she won't be relevant anymore."

"And it will bring an end to a clearly illegal operation that is sustaining a ridiculous war," Amelia added.

"I've got a better idea," Jaime said with a smile, and turned to Luis. "Why don't you take Milena out onto the terrace? I think a little air would do her good."

Luis understood that whatever Jaime was going to propose, he wouldn't do it in his presence. And Milena was dejected. She got up when she heard Jaime's request.

"I need to see Bonso," she said. She had to hear from the Romanian himself that the plan to kill her had come from Vila-Rojas.

"Later," Jaime said. "When the meeting's over, I'll take you to see him. He's downstairs in a locked room."

"I'm not moving from here till I do," she responded.

Jaime considered the circumstances, picked up the phone, and ordered them to bring the pimp upstairs.

When he arrived, the Romanian was flanked by two enormous men, or at least they looked enormous, given the prisoner's diminutive stature. He seemed to have shrunk even more since Milena had last seen him. But nothing about him inspired tender feelings or compassion: too many years of abuse kept her from seeing him as anything but her implacable punisher. The others examined him, and felt a kind of disappointment after all those days of uttering his name with fear. Tomás had to remind himself that this insignificant-looking gnome was responsible for Emiliano's death.

Jaime dismissed the guards after looking over the table on the terrace where they sat their prisoner to make sure there was nothing he could use as a weapon. He assumed Luis was big enough to ward off any attack the man might try in the presence of his former slave. The kid stood three yards from Milena and Bonso, halfway to the now-closed sliding door that led from the terrace to Jaime's office. He wanted to eavesdrop on the people inside, but he was also interested in the exchange between Milena and her pursuer.

Once the Blues were alone, Jaime spelled out his plan.

"Bonso will hand over the copies of the video to me, we have the DEA files on Vila-Rojas, and the black book will bring down Moscow's operation in Marbella. That's a mountain of reasons to get Vila-Rojas in here to negotiate. We give him everything in return for Milena's absolute freedom. He acts up, and we publish everything."

"That's a twisted way of helping her, don't you think?" Amelia said. "Keep a war going on her behalf?"

"You haven't heard the second part of the plan. This is the really important thing. We now have the opportunity to use those laundered funds to help make our country prosper." Jaime stood up and used his whole body to emphasize his words. "With his help, it's possible to bring those flows of laundered money into Mexico in unprecedented proportions. If you think about it, it's compensation for a country that's been bled dry by the First World's drug markets. I've got the necessary relations with leaders in the Mexican government who can divert that income into massive projects that will bring wealth and jobs to huge swathes of the country."

"Jaime, are you fucking nuts?" Tomás burst out.

"Think out of the box, put your prejudices aside. Just imagine, for example, a continental alternative to the Panama Canal, an ultra-modern high-speed railway network over the Isthmus of Tehuantepec—a system that could move shipping containers at a low cost between the Pacific and the Gulf of Mexico. Fine, so some people in the Ukraine die," he said, raising his hand to keep Amelia from cutting him off, "but remember the misery that lies between Puebla and Nicaragua and the economic boon a project like this could represent. Every day, Central Americans and Mexicans in the southwest die from violence and poverty. This could help change that. And it would only be the beginning." Jaime examined Amelia's face, hoping the arguments on behalf of the poor would have an effect on her.

"Got it," Tomás said. "So you want to turn Mexico into a criminal state tied to organized crime."

"Don't be so hypocritical. Las Vegas is a city built on mob money; Switzerland's prosperity comes in large part from money laundering; same with Gibraltar, Monte Carlo, and the Caymans—and the gringos let it all slide. In Mexico, we could go one better: it could be a landing zone for gray-market capital looking for flexible but responsible governance."

"And you think you can trust a person like Vila-Rojas, someone who just turned his back on his boss? That's who you want to build up Mexico's future prosperity with?"

"Fine, maybe he's not the guy for the job, but he's a foot in the door."

"Enough," Tomás said. "We're publishing, and that's that."

"Wait. Give me four days. Anyway, tomorrow's Friday, that's a bad day for world-shattering news. The weekend will take away the impact. Publish on Tuesday."

"What do you think you're going to make happen in four days?"

"Tonight Esteban Porter is flying from Mexico City to Málaga for a chat with Vila-Rojas. He'll give him a preview of the DEA file we have. That should be enough to get him for a meeting in London the Sunday after. I'll go there and we'll have a little chat about international capital flows and setting up an operation in Mexico. With a little luck, he'll hook me up with some of his acquaintances."

"Sounds a little rushed, no?" said Tomás.

"It's not like you give me more options if you're planning on publishing. I'll try my luck."

In fact, Jaime still hoped to talk to Claudia when he was back from London. She was much more realistic than her two friends. With the help of some cabinet minister, he might have a chance of convincing her not to publish for reasons of state security.

Amelia was about to say something when a terrifying scream from the terrace brought them to their feet.

We're the cockroaches of the human race: disgraceful, bearers of all that is bad, objects of disgust. And like the cockroaches, we've been here since the beginning of time and we'll still be here if humanity finally manages to snuff itself out. Deep down, a pimp is as indispensable as any other organism in the great chain of life.

Every blessed day, millions of men go see some tramp to get serviced, and they want her to be healthy and clean and treat them right in exchange for their cash. They want to blow off a little steam and not end up in jail or called out or beaten up. Us, the pimps, the procurers, flesh-peddlers, what have you—we're the ones responsible for making sure they get that service. We're the true pros in the skin trade, even more than the whores, most of whom think they're just in it for a time, even if they end up dying in it. We're here to stay: misunderstood and hated, but always sought out.

It makes me laugh when they call me cruel. Come on, that's like criticizing a dog for wagging its tail. A kindhearted pimp would do more harm than good to a whore. There's no room for heart here, it's all hard and fast rules, and any transgression comes with a nasty punishment. That's the only thing that keeps disobedience at bay.

And let me tell you: being a pimp requires Spartan discipline in body and mind. You think it's easy to hold back when one of the girls takes a liking to you? It happens a lot, you know, with the Stockholm syndrome and all that. You live around vice, but you can't pick up vices. You have to be absolutely cold to keep your girls in line.

Any pimp worth his salt is a master at mixing the right dose of terror with the occasional consolation. You need the gift of gab and real intuition to make a bitch understand that she has no place in the world besides whoring *herself out for my benefit, even if other guys, ten or twenty a week, try and convince her otherwise. It requires restraint and special abilities to kill the hope in their soul without destroying their body.*

To sum it up, my friend, the next time you go to a hooker, take a minute to reflect and thank the pimp that made it all possible.

BONSO

66

Milena

"THINGS AREN'T LOOKING GOOD for you, Bonso," she said once they'd sat down at the table on the terrace.

"I've made it through worse," he responded. But the rings under his eyes and his haggard face showed the trials he'd been through in the past few hours, maybe even days.

"Well, the game's up," she said. "I don't know what will happen with you, but you won't see me again. The agreement from that night's been revoked."

"Revoked? Why?"

Milena thought he knew what the word "revoked" meant, but she wasn't completely sure.

"To start with, because Vila-Rojas ordered you to kill me, didn't he?" She asked as if it were obvious, but she held her breath while she waited for the answer, her heart pounding against her chest.

"Seems like a lot of people want you dead."

"That's not going to happen. The people in there have enough ammunition to negotiate with Marbella. After that, we'll all be free."

Bonso turned to look at Jaime, considered his strength and poise, and thought Milena could be right. The implications threw him off. As if he could no longer conceive a life apart from the one he'd been living in recent days.

"I'll have to talk to Vila-Rojas," he said. "I don't take orders from whores."

"Talk to whoever you want. You won't see me again."

"Don't get clever. If what you're saying is true, all that means is you'll be mine again. You belong to me. When your contract with Vila-Rojas is up, you'll be back on the team. No more privileges, princess. You'll have to shake your ass again." Bonso seemed revived from listening to his own voice.

Milena realized that according to the pimp's code, nothing had changed. She'd never be out from under the yoke of exploitation. In fact, things had gotten worse. The stories of some of her clients in the black book reverberated in her mind. Fury did the rest.

She leapt up, grabbed Bonso by the armpits, and raised him up to her chin. His body was light, much more fragile than she'd thought. Luis had gotten distracted, trying to hear something Jaime was saying. Everything took place in an instant. She marched the two yards to the balcony's edge, legs spread like someone toting a large pot of boiling water, took a breath, and threw him over the edge. Kicking and thrashing, Bonso fell backward, shrieking like an angry baby in its crib, until his head struck the pavement sixty feet below. Luis made it to Milena's side in time to see the red blot diffusing over the gray of the sidewalk.

Milena looked up into the midday sun, closed her eyes, and took a deep breath. After a few seconds, she looked at Jaime, who'd rushed out.

"Where is the Turk?"

Something has changed in Milena. I don't know if it's the black hair beneath her blonde wig or the way she moves. Her gestures and words aren't the same as before, when she was there without being there, when she used to sit in those rooms trying to make her body undetectable. Or maybe it's her slight Mexican accent that makes her different. Tropical words, sweet, musical, even if her face still looks steely. "Let's go chat in my room," she whispered after we met in the bar. "I have something that will interest you. About Yasha Boyko."

I didn't want to see her. When Jaime Lemus told me she was also staying at the London Park Majestic and that she wanted to tell me something about the Ukrainians, my first reaction was to make an excuse and keep my distance. The last thing I wanted was a bunch of whining and recrimination. But my meeting with the Mexican put me in a good mood. If half of what he says is true, those investments on North America's doorstep could be a golden opportunity. And Lemus seems like a straight shooter, according to all we've found out. The file he handed off to me shows it. The goddamn Yankees know more than I thought. In the end, curiosity about the Kattel family got the best of me. Yasha never told me what his phone calls with Milena were about, but they must have been important if he kept saying that she had to be under strict watch. Lemus is asking for Milena's freedom in exchange for keeping a lid on the information from Moscow. If we're in business, I need to look her in the face and make sure she'll keep mum.

We went up in the elevator and didn't utter a word. I just took a step back and looked at her. I wanted to find the keys to unlock that unknown person. Even her clothing now has nothing to do with what she used to wear in Marbella. A wide-brimmed hat, big sunglasses, and a short gray designer dress, tailored—completely vulgar.

I don't like this Milena. She doesn't drink in my words, she doesn't follow my gestures like before. Her face doesn't change with the inflection of my voice. But I can barely contain the excitement she provokes. The feeling is unexpected, uncomfortable. I follow her into the room and rush to sit down in the only chair so she knows I'm not there to take off her clothes. I try and take a harsh tone with her, but my erection works against me. She looks at my crotch, and her face shows no reaction. But she sits on the bed, stretches out her arm until she reaches the open bottle of champagne chilling on the nightstand, and her fingers wrap around the neck and caress the gilded paper before folding it down. She fills a glass, walks over, and hands it to me. I'm surprised by the savage urgency of my hands longing to grasp her waist. The memory of possessing her in the past is no consolation for the desperate craving blinding me now. I empty the glass and am thankful for the tickle of bubbles on my dry throat.

She goes back to the bed and serves herself one. She starts speaking before she drinks.

"The only thing I wanted was for my femur not to be used as a sword."

I see how the long muscles in her thighs tense when she crosses her legs, and think, that must be the most beautiful femur in the world. She starts telling some story about a Germanophile grandfather and a restaurant in Berlin. I can barely hear her with the bubbles now bursting in my head. I try to remember what I drank with the Mexican, and how much. From where I sit, I can see she hasn't drunk a drop. Something isn't right.

Milena keeps talking, but now she's started unbuttoning her dress down the front. I know I should do something to rouse myself, get off the chair that's imprisoning me, but I can only watch, hypnotized, while her dress slips slowly off her, gliding past her hips.

I try to get up, not knowing if I want to touch her flesh or escape the room and leave behind this feeling of danger. My muscles fail, I try to say something, but my tongue is like a wooden spatula. Milena towers over me in her stiletto heels and underwear. She bends over to pull down my pants; my hard-on hasn't gone away. I look at my swollen dick for a minute before she straddles me and I see it disappear inside her. We come together easily. The brief feeling of intimacy is interrupted when she utters what she's really come to tell me.

"I helped you eliminate the ones who threatened you, who threatened your comfort. Today, you'll do the same for me. You're the only one who keeps me in the past. Today, I'm here to free myself. I'm doing it the way you taught me. I'm fucking you so I can kill you, Agustín."

She says it gently, her warm breath on my ear sending waves of pleasure down my spine, even if her words are horrible. I understand what she's saying, and for some reason, it doesn't alarm me. Maybe it's the tranquilizer that's paralyzing me, or maybe the sensations in my groin. I concentrate what's left of my strength on penetrating her, a last act of resistance that ends in surrender when I come inside her.

Milena pulls away from my embrace, and that's when I see the tears in her eyes and the syringe in her hand. She places her other hand at the base of my dick and squeezes until she finds a thick vein, makes the injection, and walks away.

Moments later, my breathing grows labored and the room starts to go blurry. Even so, I can make her out, now fully dressed, walking toward the door. She turns and contemplates me. It's impossible to speak. I try to project the depth of my hatred with my eyes, but weariness overcomes me, and the feeling of ridicule when I imagine myself in a shirt, cufflinks, and a tie, but nude from the waist down, legs splayed and a syringe hanging out of my limp cock. She smiles and a look I've never seen before crosses her face. It's not the Milena from before. Then she turns and disappears from my life. Along with everything else.

AGUSTÍN VILA-ROJAS,
LAWYER, GRANADA

EPILOGUE

Everyone

TUESDAY, NOVEMBER 25

IT WAS MILENA HERSELF who told Jaime, sitting beside him on the return flight from London to Mexico, about Agustín Vila-Rojas dying of cardiac arrest a few hours before. The news hit the Lemlock director with the force of a hammer. When he left the Spanish lawyer, still alive, at the London Park Majestic, he thought he'd built an alliance that would put his ambitious plans for Mexico into motion. Full of regret, he figured that possibility was now gone forever. Could Milena have had something to do with his death?

But then she pulled him out of his nightmare. It took her a few hours on that long flight, but in the end, she convinced him that her proposal was even better than an alliance with Vila-Rojas.

On Monday night, at Lemlock's offices in Mexico City, Milena called Yasha and told him about his money man's betrayal. There was more than enough proof. Esteban Porter, who was still in Marbella, sent an email with fragments of Anonymous's report on Vila-Rojas and Olena's dealings with each other, and she passed these along as well. More important still, she sent him the news that would come out the next day in *El Mundo*, and afterward in the international press, about the conspiracy between Moscow and members of the Russo-Ukrainian community in Marbella. Milena exaggerated Jaime's merits in the discovery of the plot and then passed the phone over to Lemus.

Yasha was stunned by the revelations, but thought he could make a clean escape if he took advantage of the time difference between the continents. He had Tuesday morning to make his moves in Spain before the news was published in Mexico and New York. Through his trusted contacts, he could claim credit for informing the authorities of what the Kremlin had up its sleeve. Jaime was ecstatic. In the end, it looked like doing business in Mexico with the head of the mafia on the Costa del Sol was a far better prospect than with the deceitful Vila-Rojas. They agreed to meet in Europe as soon as things calmed down.

"Take care of Milena," Yasha told Jaime before hanging up. "That woman's worth her weight in gold."

So that Tuesday morning, Jaime had reasons to smile. And the meeting he'd just had with his team confirmed it. For now, his business had done adequate damage control after Bonso's death. The authorities had accepted their version: he came to Lemlock looking for a job, got turned down, and committed suicide. Thanks to solid PR work, the news barely made a ripple that weekend.

With the Turk, things turned out worse. Jaime had thought of offering Claudia his head as a sign of his ability and, above all, his loyalty. He even thought of giving her or Tomás the opportunity to execute the bastard with their own hands. It would have been a blood secret to bind them together for the rest of their days and assure his continued influence at *El Mundo*. But Milena's attitude toward the Turk put an end to that possibility.

Still, she'd been highly efficient where it really counted. She managed to talk her way onto the flight to London to "say goodbye to Vila-Rojas," which he'd found strange, even if he wasn't able to prevent it. That was the condition she'd laid down to get the Turk to admit to where they kept the videos, and he needed those videos to get in the good graces of the man he thought would be his future business partner. He wasn't sure of her motives for wanting to talk with the person most likely to have initiated the chase against her, but he figured they shared a history more complicated that just the overdose that had killed the Russian kid. Anyway, things had ended in the best possible way. With his new relationship with Yasha, he could build a solid alliance between the immense assets of the underground economy and the flexible stability of the Mexican state.

With the additional resources, he would even be able to get a foothold at *El Mundo*. The paper would go on losing money, and, with time, he could intervene to bail it out, and not only to keep it from shuttering. With the right support and the right people pulling strings, he could place it in a media conglomerate, with TV and telecommunications branches. Remembering the paper, he thought of Tomás, and smiled smugly: his friend literally owed him his life. He hoped that from then forward, the Blues would ease off with their harsh judgments of his methods.

Now more than ever, he felt he was a better companion for Amelia than Tomás was. His friend's idealism was an obstacle, but he trusted the endless waves of reality that politics brought would erode her naïve idealism. Amelia had lost her innocence some time ago, and eventually she'd lose much more than that. Sooner or later, things would turn romantic between the journalist and Claudia. Tomás's heart was volatile and his dick had a mind of its own. When he betrayed her, Jaime would be there for Amelia. He'd soon have her in those Egyptian earrings he'd hoped she'd put on twenty years before, but for now, he'd tell her his passion was real and let that information settle in.

He thought the deaths of Bonso and Vila-Rojas would please Claudia, or at least help her get over her deputy director's death. He hadn't been able to present her with the image of the Turk's dead body the way he would have liked, but she had to understand he was a mere trigger man carrying out his bosses' orders: Bonso's, Salgado's, and, further up the ladder, Vila-Rojas's. And now they were all dead. After Vila-Rojas perished in London, Jaime called Tomás so that he could give Claudia the news in person. He preferred to let the journalist get the credit, and hopefully much more than that, from *El Mundo*'s owner.

Jaime wasn't wrong: Claudia was overjoyed. Tomás told her as tactfully as possible to avoid wounding her sensibilities, but she had a strong stomach when it came to revenge. She thanked him effusively, as if Tomás himself had shot Salgado, stopped Vila-Rojas's heart, and pushed Bonso over the ledge.

Claudia was pleased: the threat against the newspaper was neutralized, and the enemies who had dared to defy it were dead. That same morning, she read through the black-covered journal, which Milena had given her the night before after returning from London. In total, there were fifty-eight stories about *Them* with the title *Tales of the XY Chromosome*. All together, a long list of reasons men give themselves to justify prostitution. Though the signatures at the end of each story were only initials, and most of them were from Spain, she recognized a half-dozen Mexicans. In fact, everyone could identify them, and even if the material had no legal value, it would be enough to destroy the reputations of the men it mentioned. She could understand her father's suspicion: he'd probably found out about the book, maybe even read a story or two. The old man must have feared she'd get spiteful or he'd say the wrong thing and wind up in there.

It gave Claudia a strange but agreeable feeling to become the benefactor of her father's former lover. In front of her lay the package she had picked up under the domed ceiling of the bank twenty days before: a half-million dollars, a handwritten note, and a sheet of paper with his letterhead. Her fingers traced out Rosendo Franco's familiar signature and her eyes were trapped by his posthumous words.

Dear Claudia:

I beg you, don't judge me, just help me carry out this last wish. I wanted to save the family the discomfort of reading this last part of my will.

Alka Moritz has made me infinitely happy in the final part of my life. That doesn't affect the love I feel for you and your mother. I hope you can understand that.

With what's in this bag, I hope to give her the opportunities life has denied her. Don't take that satisfaction from me. This is nothing more than a thank-you from an old man to a friend who transformed his winter into spring.

I trust you.

PS: AlkaMilena lives in Cópernico 26–201, Colonía Anzures.

Reading the text slowly, Claudia was moved by how her father called his lover AlkaMilena, fusing her real and assumed name in a clumsy attempt to hide her profession. She was proud, almost like a child, that he had trusted her to carry out this task, which might have seemed unnatural earlier. Even if it meant giving the Croatian a sum that could have gone toward the newspaper's struggling budget, she was happy contributing to Milena's new life. It made her feel generous, mature. She consoled herself with the thought that there was almost certainly no trace of the money on the business's balance sheet, and depositing it would have been complicated. Most likely it had come from the safe where they kept the income from the classifieds, not all of which was reported to the revenue service: customers didn't ask for a receipt when they posted an ad to get rid of a secondhand fridge or put a puppy up for sale.

She was roused from her meditations when Tomás entered her office, proud to show her references from newspapers and websites all over the world to the article *El Mundo* had published. One of them, from the Associated Press, caught her attention.

THE RUSSIAN MAFIA GOES TO WAR IN UKRAINE

MEXICO CITY/MADRID/AP

In recent months, the Kremlin has employed the Russo-Ukrainian mafia in Marbella to establish a network for the distribution of financial resources and materiel to the rebel militias in Eastern Ukraine in an attempt to evade sanctions imposed on Moscow by the European Union.

An exclusive investigation at the Mexican newspaper *El Mundo* reveals contacts between Russian agents and Olena Kattel, an alleged head of a mafia faction on the Costa del Sol, concerning the establishment of a series of shell companies in Spain for the purpose of funneling money to the insurgent groups. The article gives bank account numbers, startling deposit amounts, and the names of the businesses created. Atlantic Import-Export, Baltic and Mediterranean, and Wood, Aluminum, and Steel Inc. are just a few from among a dozen titles employed. On the board of these companies are numerous prominent members of the Russian community in Marbella.

After Brussels levied sanctions on Moscow this past summer in retribution for the pro-Russian militias' insurrection against the new Ukrainian government, Putin's regime attempted to disguise its support as humanitarian aid. Nonetheless, European governments denounced these donations as a subterfuge to keep the uprising alive and threatened Moscow with a new round of sanctions.

Presumably, it was then that the Kremlin decided to draw on its relations with leaders of the Russian community in Spain to find an alternative route for its aid.

The press office of the Brussels government gave assurances that an investigation will be carried out. It has not discarded the possibility of additional sanctions if there is confirmation of Moscow's involvement in the construction of a financing network to support the war in Ukraine from Western Europe.

The news has shaken the Russo-Ukrainian community in Marbella. Authorities are currently seeking out Olena Kattel, widow of the alleged former head of the Russian mafia in the region, but she has not yet been apprehended.

Yasha Boyko, a distinguished leader of the Ukrainian immigrant community in the south of Spain, has declared in the name of his compatriots that the vast majority of Eastern European residents of Marbella are peaceful neighbors who uphold the law, and that their presence has been one of the factors in the region's prosperity.

When she finished reading, her eyes were damp. Finally, the newspaper her father founded had caused the world to shake. She looked
at Tomás, moved by what she'd read but also by his enthusiasm as
director, his loyalty, his generosity. She told herself that now that the
crisis was over, she'd have to face up to the collapse of her marriage.
She didn't want to spend another day feigning a relationship with
someone she had begun to scorn.

"Let's go to New York for four or five days and soak up the journalism culture," she told Tomás. "We'll see people from Columbia, from
the *New York Times*, from the weeklies. We'll recharge our batteries
and get out from under the pressure of the daily grind. What do you
say? In two or three weeks, maybe?"

It might not have been professional, striking up a romance with
the director of her newspaper, but she didn't want to let the chance
slip. Life had put enough responsibilities on her shoulders without
her imposing sacrifices on herself. She decided to let things follow
their course, even to give them a little nudge.

"It would be worth it," Tomás said, recalling the pale skin and
red hair atop the sheets in a room at the Plaza Hotel facing Central
Park. But he thought of Amelia and something clenched in his
stomach. He supposed it was a foretaste of the sense of loss he would
feel if he broke with her, and he couldn't bear it. He preferred to
concentrate on the difficult task at hand: turning *El Mundo* into a
paper of reference for public opinion. It would be a tough job when
the blogosphere was pushing paper aside. He needed to find a business model where the digital edition could hold onto the current
editorial staff: he'd need all the help he could get, no matter where
it came from.

He thought of the Blues and the possibility of them making a mission out of *El Mundo*'s retrenchment. Maybe he could bring Mario

onboard when he came back from Puerto Rico. For a long time, he'd had a sense that the university job was a disappointment. He could give him a hand with the opinion page, which had been vacant since Emiliano's death.

The murder of his collaborator made him recall Jaime, a vicious guy but loyal in his own way, and always with a trick up his sleeve. With his support, the newspaper could find shortcuts and powerful backers. Jaime never ceased to amaze him, sometimes in the worst way, but in the end, he knew he could always count on him, especially when it came to life or death. A shiver ran over his body as he remembered Salgado's corpse on the chair in his living room.

It struck him that for two nights now, he'd been looking for excuses to stay with Amelia and not go back to his apartment. It was time to move, but they couldn't live together yet. Perhaps he could find a place closer to her home in Colonía Roma, or halfway between the newspaper and Amelia. But perhaps that wish was a projection of an inability to choose between two women's love. He put the thought out of his mind. That night, and the rest of the week, he would sleep with Amelia, and that would be enough to stave off the demons lingering around his heart and his groin.

The demons pestering Amelia, on the other hand, had little to do with her heart and a lot to do with her guts. That morning, she'd found out that the coordinator of her party's representatives in Congress had already negotiated the necessary votes with President Prida's envoys to pass through the next year's budget with an ample majority. There had been no point in revealing to her colleague those lines on the budget, masked as social services, that were only there to push the vote in the government's favor. Her colleagues had given in to the executive because, *thanks to their negotiations*, pensions for the handicapped had gone up. To Amelia, the sudden acquiescence of the left's leader had more to do with his own career than with the well-being of the disabled population.

Again, she considered renouncing her party's presidency and exposing the shady accords the leadership carried out behind the public's back. But just as before, she thought this would do more harm to the left's already scant chances of influencing policy in the Prida government, and he and his successors could easily be in office for decades. She swallowed the bad taste in her mouth and tried to comfort herself with the unexpected and inspiring end of Milena's story.

With Jaime involved, it was natural that many questions remained unanswered about Vila-Rojas's strange death in London and the Turk's sudden disappearance. Jaime was like that: he always took care of business, but he never got into details. And to prove what Tomás had already said, Jaime had literally saved him from certain death. Her partner's commentaries were vague, but she assumed that with time she would find out the details of the story in the darkness of their bed, where Tomás liked to share his secrets.

For the first time in her life, she asked herself if Jaime might not be right when he stressed that you needed harsh methods and a strong stomach to fight the rot in the system. She remembered again how the coordinator of her representatives had betrayed her, and asked what Jaime would have done in her shoes. She was shocked by the depths of her resentment: not even Lemlock, she imagined, would be willing to do what she had imagined doing to the representative's testicles in an attempt to dissuade him from his plan.

Maybe she was unfair with Jaime: her friend was capable of going into the shadows time and again, but he never got lost there. His recent declarations of love had made her uncomfortable. She'd known of his feelings since her adolescence, and they had been a source of tension running through the strange family of the Blues for decades. She briefly imagined the possibility of becoming his lover, but it made her shudder. She remembered the thick hair on his muscular forearms and her own hair stood on end as she thought of Carlos Lemus, Jaime's father, whom she'd idolized twenty years before with the intense fervor of first love. To Jaime's sorrow, she'd never stop seeing him as a weaker version of his powerful father.

Those juvenile flings recalled to her, with a healthy tinge of jealousy, the spontaneous commitment that Luis and Rina seemed to feel for each other: a pure attraction that was safe for now from the complaints, small and large, that life tended to impose. Or maybe she was being unfair, because an attraction like that was so foreign and unbelievable to her. After all, Luis and Milena's escapade had been a first test for whatever was brewing between them. It must have been a torment to Rina, knowing they were shut up in some ratty hotel room, but her attitude with Milena was absolutely selfless. Once more, she admired her collaborator, though in the end she didn't know whether for the generosity of her heart or her unbelievable capacity to ignore whatever bothered her. Maybe she was interpreting as maturity what was nothing more than the girl's practical approach to a fleeting winter romance.

Vidal could have used something like that, and he didn't hide the sadness Luis and Rina's affection produced in him. Friday night had been humiliating: excited by what seemed to be the end of the story, the three of them dragged Milena to a cantina and ended the evening at midnight in the Plaza Garibaldi, world capital of mariachi music. The whole time, Vidal kept glancing at Rina, trying to focus on her vulgar gestures and hollow words, anything that might break the spell and relieve his longing. But what he observed only fed his passion.

Urged on by Luis and Milena, to the delight of the tourists, Rina did the Mexican Hat Dance on one of the tabletops around midnight, and no one mocked her, not even when she slipped and fell facedown onto a chair. She stood back up, not without a certain gracefulness, to take in the applause. It was fascinating, even incomprehensible to Vidal, who could never shake off the feeling that those around him were judging him, that Rina's body could keep moving, totally indifferent to others' opinions.

Luis seemed to appreciate that as well, and Rina's vitality drew him like a magnet, with the advantage that he didn't have to forget about her, at least not for now. After the partying was over, the four of them went back to Rina's apartment. The bedroom arrangements brought joy to some and sadness to others. Milena settled into the armchair in the living room, and Vidal stretched the rug out into a makeshift bed, lying down there and trying to ignore the tormenting sounds coming from Luis and Rina in the bedroom.

Vidal took consolation in the thought that now, his life had a direction. He would become Jaime's model pupil, and later, a successful executive. He saw himself at twenty-nine, emanating the same authority and aplomb as his instructor, and that image helped soften the effects of being there, fifteen steps from his beloved, who was lying in bed with someone else. He recalled Jaime's advice and convinced himself that Rina would be his, sooner or later. He would just have to wait until Luis decided to disappear, and he would have to figure out how he could help make that happen.

But disappearing was the last thing on Luis's mind that night. He had made love to the apple of his eye slowly, attentively, stopping to caress parts of her body as though wishing to substitute for Rina the memory of the skin, the scent, the contours of Milena, which were still present in his hands and on his lips, to stoke his passion for the one with the ardor the other had inflamed. Over and over, images of Milena's flesh leapt into his mind, and he kept pushing them aside, telling himself his relationship with the Croatian had been irreplaceable, but also unrepeatable.

For the first time in years, Luis didn't have a plan. He had come to Mexico City for a doctor's visit, and his return ticket to Barcelona was for the following weekend, but Rina—and then Milena—had come into his life. He decided to cancel his flight and stay on in Mexico for the next few weeks while he finished designing a program he had agreed to write for a shopping center. They had paid him a fortune to come up with highly efficient, rather devious marketing software. It offered free Wi-Fi to anyone who set foot in a mall in Houston, and once users accepted, it registered their every step: which stores they went to, which windows they stopped to look at; an enormous mirror tied to mobile geolocation technology allowed them to know the user's sex, approximate age, and ethnicity. With that information, it could bombard them with personalized ads for special offers as they passed through the different businesses. It was like Big Brother, but commercial rather than political.

Though he got a kick out of designing such programs, Luis was increasingly uncomfortable with their profit-seeking manipulation. After crossing paths with Milena and getting to know Amelia and the causes she fought for, he found his old work childish, frivolous, and dispiriting. Maybe his newly explored ability to combat human-trafficking networks could help rescue other victims of the mafia. Once the dust settled, he would approach Amelia and—why not?—Milena herself, to talk about putting an operation together. But he had no idea what Milena wanted to do with her life.

Nor did Milena. She couldn't identify with the name Alka anymore, even if she had woken up that Tuesday murmuring it like a mantra. She had slept in the suite Jaime used when he spent the night at Lemlock's offices, but Claudia would be passing through later. At night, back from London, she had spoken on the phone to Rosendo Franco's daughter, and was surprised by her warmth and generosity. She implied that she had a big surprise coming and offered to let her spend a few days in her apartment in Cuernavaca while she decided what to do with herself.

But all she wanted was to be rid of Milena once and for all. That same morning, she thought she would settle her accounts with the Turk and everything would be over. Letting him go was one of her conditions in the exchange for the videos. Lemus had been more curious than frustrated by her decision, and she didn't really know why she'd come to that conclusion, either. There was nothing she wanted less than to ever see the Turk again, but she tried to explain her actions to herself by saying it was something she owed him. After all, he'd saved her twice: once in the women's bathroom, when Boris's thugs had come after her, and again on the docks in Málaga, when Bonso wanted her dead. She insisted on accompanying the Turk out to the street to be sure Jaime was actually letting him go. And once they were on the sidewalk and saying goodbye, they looked at each other in silence. Then, with a pleading look in his eyes she had never seen before, the Turk asked her to come with him, so they could run away together. After Bonso's disappearance, her old watchdog's life was as wrecked as her own, or maybe more so. She refused and watched him walk away, overwhelmed and confused, eroding into a silhouette less substantial than the trail of cigarette smoke he left in his path. To her surprise, something dark inside her pushed her, for a fleeting instant, to follow him, to lose herself with him, to lose herself in him.

It was only then that she took stock of what had happened in those past few days. Without Bonso and the Turk, she was free.

Without Vila-Rojas, she was unfathomably empty. She tried to erase the last ten years of her life from her mind and to go back to age sixteen, when the future was an open field full of endless paths. But she couldn't identify with that teenager who had existed in a previous life. Someday she would visit her family in Croatia, but she would have to be ready for it, and even more, they would have to be ready for her. She had less desire to go back to Marbella, even if Yasha had promised her a life of ease there. The mere notion of setting foot in the city where she'd been exploited day after day made her ill. Plus, there was Olena Kattel: she wasn't sure what Yasha had said to Boris's mother to keep her from seeking vengeance. Probably he had told her that her son's killer was already dead. All the same, the Costa del Sol was off-limits as long as Olena was alive.

She wondered whether she should move to Madrid or Barcelona. That made her think of Luis. She shook her head, looked at the outline of the purse sitting on the coffee table, and remembered the little black book she had loaned to Claudia. She shivered with satisfaction, and immediately, she knew what would happen next.

She still had a bit of unfinished business from her past: publishing a book with the stories she'd gathered through the years. That was the only way she could close the circle and say goodbye to Milena forever. Tomás had offered to print them in *El Mundo* in installments, promising the effect would be explosive. He even said he would talk to his colleagues about getting them into the daily papers in Madrid, Barcelona, and Seville. Milena saw that finally, her life could have a direction, even if she didn't know where she'd end up. She decided she would just navigate, like the seafarers of old, from one horizon to the other. She opened the new black book Luis had just given her and reread the text she had written in it the night before: *Tales of the XY Chromosome. Them: Agustín Vila-Rojas.* It felt good. Before she knew it, her mind was cooking up another story, but now, for the first time, the passages would be drawing on a life that was no longer hers.

AUTHOR'S NOTE

The links between fiction and reality are close throughout the book. The author has taken a few liberties for the sake of the novel's plot. One of them has been a slight transformation of the composition of the community of citizens of former Soviet Republics residing in Marbella. Gangs originating in Russia and Ukraine are not necessarily the predominate ones in the port city, though they are important. A journalistic report from 2004 designated the Ukrainians as dominant in Murcia, Alicante, Huelva, Cuenca, Badajoz, and the south of Valencia. In Marbella, apart from Ukrainians, Lithuanian, Armenian, Georgian, and Romanian gangs are active. Naturally, their composition changes over time. It goes without saying, in the words of Yasha Boyko, that the vast majority of Eastern European residents of Marbella are peaceful neighbors who uphold the law.

In the description of the merciless organizations in charge of sexual slavery, no literary license has been taken. The phenomenon has worsened in recent years as a result of the globalization of human-trafficking networks. The typology of customers described in *Them* draws on an ample bibliography. For general interest, I would highlight three works in particular: *The Industrial Vagina: The Political Economy of the Global Sex Trade* by Sheila Jeffreys (Routledge), and two extraordinary investigations by Victor Malarek—*The Natashas: The*

Horrific Inside Story of Slavery, Rape, and Murder in the Global Sex Trade (Arcade Publishing) and *The Johns: Sex for Sale and the Men Who Buy It* (Arcade Publishing).

Lydia Cacho drew my attention to the theme, Guillermo Zepeda Patterson helped me with editing, and Camila Zepeda was a stimulus and a constant sounding board. Alejandro Páez took a great deal of work onto his own shoulders so I would have time to write. Alma Delia Murillo was an accomplice to whatever part of me is a writer, and most importantly, she made me happy throughout the process. I owe all of them my thanks.

ABOUT THE AUTHOR AND TRANSLATOR

Journalistically speaking, JORGE ZEPEDA PATTERSON has accomplished everything: newspaper's managing editor, magazine founder, television anchor, newspaper political columnist, and author of half a dozen books on current affairs. After spending decades researching and writing about political power, he found that only fiction could explain the way in which the brain of a politician works. *Los Corruptores* (2013), his first novel, was finalist for the Dashiell Hammett Award. His second novel, *Milena* (2014), won the $800,000 Premio Planeta. Born in Mazatlán, Mexico, in 1952, Zepeda received a master's degree from the Facultad Latinoamericana de Ciencias Sociales and a doctorate in political science from The Sorbonne. After his journalistic training at El País, he was the founding editor of the newspapers *Siglo 21* and *Público* in Guadalajara, and was later editor-in-chief of *El Universal.* He has authored numerous books on political analysis, and his weekly column appears in over twenty newspapers in Mexico. He currently edits the news website SinEmbargo.mx.

ADRIAN NATHAN WEST is the author of the novel *The Aesthetics of Degradation* and translator of numerous works of contemporary European literature. He lives between Spain and the United States with the cinema critic Beatriz Leal Riesco.